A WEDDING AT

Bella Osborne has been jotting d[...] can remember but decided that [...] year that she finished a full-length novel.

In 2022, *The Promise of Summer* was the joint winner of the RNA Jane Wenham-Jones Award for Romantic Comedy.

Bella's stories are about friendship, love and coping with what life throws at you. She likes to find the humour in the darker moments of life and weaves this into her stories. Bella believes that writing your own story really is the best fun ever, closely followed by talking, eating chocolate, drinking fizz and planning holidays.

She lives in the Midlands, UK with her lovely husband and wonderful daughter, who, thankfully, both accept her as she is (with mad morning hair and a penchant for skipping).

Also by Bella Osborne:

It Started at Sunset Cottage
A Family Holiday
Escape to Willow Cottage
Coming Home to Ottercombe Bay
A Walk in Wildflower Park
Meet Me at Pebble Beach
One Family Christmas
The Promise of Summer

Bella Osborne

A Wedding at Sandy Cove

avon.

Published by AVON
A division of HarperCollins*Publishers* Ltd
1 London Bridge Street
London SE1 9GF

www.harpercollins.co.uk

HarperCollins*Publishers*
1st Floor, Watermarque Building, Ringsend Road
Dublin 4, Ireland

A Paperback Original 2022
1
First published in Great Britain by HarperCollins*Publishers* 2022

A catalogue copy of this book is
available from the British Library.

ISBN: 978-0-00-846493-6

Typeset in Minion by Palimpsest Book Production Limited, Falkirk, Stirlingshire
Printed and Bound in the UK using 100% Renewable Electricity at CPI Group (UK) Ltd

MIX
Paper from
responsible sources
FSC C007454

This book is produced from independently certified FSC™ paper to ensure
responsible forest management.

For more information visit: **www.harpercollins.co.uk/green**

For Louise

PART ONE

CHAPTER ONE

It is a truth universally acknowledged that a bride in search of the perfect dress must be a total pain in the bum.

'I want to be a princess,' screamed the diminutive blonde. Ella had seen similar meltdowns many times before at Frills, Frocks and Fairy Tales but usually the culprits were bigger. This one was seven years old and accompanying her stressed-out mother to her first wedding dress appointment.

'But you are a princess, Angel,' said her mother as she snatched dresses off the rails and the child ran around the shop like a Tasmanian devil on Red Bull, trampling Ella's toes and almost knocking over a vase. Ella caught it just in time. Her heart thumped away with the stress of it all. Angel – was that her name or an ironic term of endearment? Ella didn't like to ask.

'I want a tiara.' The little girl was on tiptoes and reaching for the sparkly headgear which was thankfully out of reach.

'Can she have one?' asked the mother. She leant in conspiratorially and whispered, 'To play with.'

'They start at a hundred and twenty pounds and if she were to break it then—'

'Okay. I get it. Come here, Angel, and help Mummy choose a pretty dress.'

The child gave Ella a parting glare and she disappeared between two dresses. Ella hoped her hands were clean. Wanda would have a fit if she found sticky marks on any of the gowns. Wanda owned Frills, Frocks and Fairy Tales; but she was late in this morning because her grandmother was unwell. This happened quite regularly and Ella was certain that Wanda had forgotten telling her that all her grandparents were dead. Clearly this ailing grandma was fictional. But then it was Wanda's shop so it wasn't for Ella to scrutinise her excuses. Wanda paid Ella to be the dedicated seamstress for the store and it was a job that Ella loved. Sales was Wanda's territory; finding the right gown for a bride really wasn't her forte – she was far better suited to being behind the scenes. She also had a lot of work to be getting on with, she needed to hurry Flora, the bride-to-be, along.

'What sort of dress did you have in mind?' she asked.

Flora did something akin to jazz hands before pulling a tatty-looking notebook from her bag. 'I started this when I was a kid. And I've cut out articles and pictures over the years and popped them in. It's my wedding scrapbook.'

She opened it up and handed it to Ella. 'I like this neckline and this skirt style or that one, or this look but with that sort of bodice but more sparkly.' She pointed at so many different things it almost sent Ella cross-eyed. 'Although not exactly the same as that one because it's a bit tacky. I also like this, and this and that if it were less shiny. Oh, and a puddle train.' She looked very pleased with her requirements. To Ella it was like Frankenstein was creating a wedding dress. Ella wasn't sure how to tell her that she'd not seen anything quite like that and there was probably a good reason why. 'I guess everyone has one of these. Don't they?' said Flora proudly thumbing the scruffy book.

'Er. I've not seen one quite like this,' said Ella diplomatically. 'Do you have a budget in mind?' She knew Wanda would be appalled that she'd asked this question as her aim was to sell the most expensive dress possible.

Flora turned a few pages in the scrap book. Ella caught sight of some peephole bras. 'Wedding night lingerie,' Flora explained, hastily turning the page. She tapped her finger near some workings out. Her budget was at the lower end of the store's stock but they did have some beautiful dresses she could afford.

'Let me choose a few styles for you to try on and then you'll start to get a feel for how they look on your shape.'

'I want to try on a dress too!' said the little girl, her face appearing between two dresses not unlike Jack Nicholson in *The Shining*, only scarier.

'Are you a bridesmaid or a flower girl perhaps?' asked Ella.

The mother's expression hardened. 'She's an attendant. We don't like gender stereotypes.'

'Right. Sorry,' said Ella, feeling chastened. The bride gave a tight smile. 'Does she need an outfit?' asked Ella deliberately avoiding the word 'dress'.

'She wants a suit like her daddy.'

'That's cool,' said Ella, selecting a couple of dresses for Flora to try

'No! Now I want a dress,' yelled the child. 'This dress.' She grabbed hold of the one Ella had just selected and clung on.

Ella handed the gowns to the bride with the child still attached. 'If you'd like to go into the fitting room.' She pointed the way. 'I'll be back in a moment.'

Ella escaped to her little workroom. It was barely more than a cupboard but it suited her. She opened a drawer and pulled out a tin that she kept for these sorts of occasions. She returned to the fitting room. 'How are you getting on?' she asked.

Flora pulled back the curtain to show that she had a dress half on and her child was hugging her legs stopping it going any higher.

'Would you like to play with these?' Ella put the open tin on the floor. It was full of cotton reels. The little girl looked at them and then at Ella with a pitying expression.

'Why?'

'Because you can build things and roll them?' They usually kept toddlers amused, perhaps at seven she was too old. Ella didn't know. She didn't have children and as an only child she had no nieces or nephews either.

'It's okay,' said Flora, sporting the same pitying expression. She addressed the child. 'You can be good, can't you Angel?'

'What do I get for being good?'

Flora tilted her head and couldn't have looked more yummy mummy if she tried. 'My love and affection,' she said.

Angel started to cry. 'But I don't want that!'

'Okay, okay. If you're very good. I'll get you a new phone,' she said. Ella couldn't help the jump her eyebrows made.

The little girl seemed to consider this for a moment before skulking out of the fitting room and sitting on the floor nearby. Peace reigned for a few minutes and Ella was able to help Flora try on a few dresses until the woman's mobile pinged and she felt compelled to check it. She gasped. 'Ohmylife! I don't believe it.'

'Is something wrong?' asked Ella, although the bride was dragging her palm over her face which didn't bode well.

'My chief bridesmaid has just posted that she's having her head shaved for charity.'

'That's brave,' said Ella. 'Well done her.' The icy glare from the bride told her she'd said the wrong thing.

'The date is a week before my wedding. I will have a bald bridesmaid! How selfish is that?' She was turning a strange colour as rage crept into her words.

'Maybe she can postpone the head shaving,' suggested Ella, scrunching up her shoulders in preparation for a backlash.

'She's got a big event with press planned, a donation page and her insta post has been liked by Davina McCall!'

Ella found she was blinking at the ferocity of the words. She wasn't sure what she was meant to say in this situation. Generally she worried about saying the wrong thing. About upsetting people. But this was her worst nightmare. She was so far outside her comfort zone she could send it a postcard. *Did people still send postcards*, she wondered. It had been so long since she'd been on holiday she didn't know.

'What do I do?' demanded the bride, her eyes alarmingly wide.

Ella didn't get to answer because the child was whooping with delight and both Ella and Flora realised at the same time that she was no longer near the fitting room. They dashed out into the shop to see the little girl flinging fistfuls of sequins into the air like sparkly confetti.

Of course Wanda chose that precise moment to show up. 'What on earth?' She glared at Ella as if it were her decorating the shop carpet in sequins. As usual Ella's stomach muscles tensed – something she struggled to do in yoga class but could achieve without thinking thanks to one look from Wanda. 'Stop!' she bellowed. The child halted mid hurl and stared at Wanda. Angel's bottom lip started to wobble. 'You can clean this up right away.'

'It's okay. I'll sort it out,' said Ella, instantly feeling bad.

'I meant you, Ella,' said Wanda, with a dismissive shake of her head. She turned to the bride. 'I am so sorry, let me find you the perfect dress.'

'Darling, leave those now,' said Flora to her daughter. Wanda escorted Flora back into the fitting room and Ella watched as the child defiantly tipped up the bag and emptied the remaining sequins onto the carpet before following her mother.

'Mummy, what happens if you put a phone in the toilet?'

'Why?'

'No reason,' replied Angel, giving Ella a look any Bond villain would have been proud of.

CHAPTER TWO

It wasn't every day you had a unicorn dancing in your kitchen. Ella was quite enjoying the elaborate dance moves which included the running man and something crossed between 'Staying Alive' and 'Gangnam Style'.

'Please tell me you're not planning on wearing that to Brittany's wedding,' said Ella.

After a brief but intense tugging match Lucy removed the unicorn head and plonked it on the kitchen table. 'I thought it might be fun for the hen night but now you mention it who wouldn't want a unicorn as a bridesmaid?'

'Brittany?' suggested Ella, flicking the switch on the kettle. It was May and Brittany was due to get married in a little under eight weeks at a particularly special venue – Sandy Cove. Not only did the Sandy Cove Hotel have a top reputation, the setting was picture perfect. As they were her two best friends both Ella and Lucy were bridesmaids. 'Coffee?'

'Good idea. But we'll probably need alcohol once we've seen these blooming bridesmaids' dresses.' Lucy flopped down on a nearby kitchen chair. 'Has she given you any clue as to what they look like?' Lucy looked concerned.

'No, but this is Brittany. Reliable, traditional, conservative Brittany. I'm sure we don't need to worry.'

Lucy's expression said different. 'Ten pounds says they're hideous.'

'I'm sure they'll be lovely.'

'Ella, you're too nice. I bet if the Gruffalo turned up in the bridal shop you'd still tell them they looked like Angelina Jolie.'

'Everyone looks fabulous in a bridal gown,' said Ella, making the coffees. 'And personally, I think the Gruffalo would look magnificent in a tiara.'

'Everybody looks good in a tiara,' conceded Lucy. They both nodded earnestly. 'But not everyone looks good as a bridesmaid. I can't believe I agreed to this.' Lucy took her drink. 'Is this your *fifth* time as a bridesmaid?'

'Eighth,' said Ella with a small wince.

'Bloody hell,' said Lucy. 'Don't you get some sort of prize for that? I'll get Guinness World Records on the line.' Lucy pretended to get her phone out.

'I did quite a few when I was little,' said Ella, trying desperately to justify the record number of times she'd been called upon to undertake the task.

'It's because you're gorgeous,' said Lucy, giving Ella a once-over. 'You'd look amazing in a sack. Which might actually be what Brittany wants us to wear. Tall, gorgeous, chestnut-haired people like you can pull off anything. Me on the other hand who is not blessed in the height department and has—'

'Beautiful raven hair and porcelain skin,' cut in Ella, who had always envied Lucy's complexion.

Lucy twisted her lips. 'Lank goth hair and skin like a ghost with the exception of the army of freckles which I actually think are breeding.' Lucy leant forward so Ella could get a better look.

'Classic Irish colouring,' stated Ella.

'Whatever you call it I will most likely look like Morticia

Addams has been shrunk in the wash. And I'll be wearing a sack. I'm not looking forward to it.'

'You're really worried, aren't you?' Ella was surprised. Lucy was feisty and fearless and, in all the years she'd known her, had never shied away from a challenge. And yet here she was clearly bothered about being a bridesmaid.

'Not *worried* exactly.' Lucy nibbled at the edge of a fingernail. 'More apprehensive.'

'There's nothing to it,' said Ella. 'It's primarily about making sure the bride's day is perfect.'

'Yep. That's precisely what's worrying me.'

The doorbell chimed and Ella went to answer it. A harassed-looking Brittany barged past her holding aloft two long dress carriers. 'I'm sorry I'm late. Roadworks coming out of Norwich were hellish. Then I realised I had nothing in for tea so I had to divert to Sainsbury's. There I bumped into my heinous cousin who still pronounces my name Britney as in Spears rather than Brittany as in ferries. And I swear she was pitching to be a bridesmaid.' They were in the kitchen before Brittany took a breath.

'It's fine. We have plenty of time to do the dress fittings,' said Ella.

Brittany looked questioningly at the unicorn mask. 'Do I want to know why there's the severed head of a mythical creature on the table or not?' asked Brittany.

'I thought *The Godfather* needed updating,' said Lucy.

Ella hung the dress carriers over the living room door and resisted the temptation to have a sneak peek inside. She remembered her mum taking her to a haberdashery as a small child and feeling like she'd entered wonderland. She'd been wowed by the different colours, patterns and fabrics and from then on she'd been hooked.

'Does Wanda know you're moonlighting?' asked Lucy when Ella returned.

'I think she's guessed. She made a few pointed remarks after Brittany picked up her wedding dress.'

'Is Wanda still a cow?' asked Lucy. Ella had worked there for four years and while Wanda was sometimes a difficult character, she loved everything else about her job.

'She's not that bad,' said Ella. Although Wanda's rant, after discovering the shop phone handset stuck in the U-bend, was still ringing in her ears which was ironic because the phone wouldn't be doing that any more.

'She was rude to you the day I bought my wedding gown,' said Brittany.

'You should leave,' said Lucy.

'Yeah there's a million job vacancies for seamstresses in the Norwich area.' Ella rolled her eyes.

'Then at least stand up for yourself occasionally. Bullies like Wanda get a kick out of putting others down and she'll keep doing it until you stand up for yourself,' said Lucy.

'She's not a bully,' said Ella a little perplexed.

Lucy and Brittany looked at each other and then back at Ella. 'She kinda is,' said Brittany.

'She's a one hundred per cent certified bully,' said Lucy. 'I'm sorry, Ella, but . . . no it's okay. Forget I said anything.' Lucy sipped her coffee as if trying to stop herself from blurting something out.

'Come on. But what?' asked Ella, intrigued. It wasn't like Lucy to hold back.

Lucy put down her mug. 'Okay. Here it is. People bully you, Ella. And you don't fight back. I wish you did stick up for yourself more but it's not something you do. You trust people to be decent and they crap all over you.'

Ella was surprised by Lucy's statement. 'No, they don't.' Although images from her past were flashing through her mind.

Lucy held out her hand and began counting off. 'Kids at school—'

'Everyone gets that,' said Ella dismissively.

'No, they don't,' Lucy continued. 'That girl at university who kept hiding your things and calling you mousy.'

'That was just uni banter.' Ella could feel her shoulders tightening.

'No, it's bullying.' Lucy tapped another finger. 'The guy who owned the ice cream shop, he bullied all three of us. Wanda we've already covered. Toad—'

At the mention of Lucy's name for her ex-boyfriend Ella held up her palm. 'Todd was a lot of things but he never bullied me.'

Lucy pushed her lips out in an exaggerated pout. 'All the sly comments about your job; calling it dolly dress-up, never acknowledging the talent and skill it takes – that's a form of bullying. Always choosing where you went and what you did because he was paying. Talking over you, dismissing your point of view and making jokes at your expense.' Lucy sat back in her chair. 'Bottom line, call it what you like, it's all bullying.'

'I don't know. I like to help people and sometimes I guess they take me for granted.'

'You're too nice, Ella. You need to stand up to people,' said Lucy.

'Easier said than done,' she replied.

'Fake it till you make it,' said Lucy. 'Pretend you're the sort of person who doesn't take any crap and you'll become that person.'

Ella swallowed hard. She felt like she'd been slapped. All that Lucy had said was true but she'd never thought of it that way and it was an unhappy revelation. Deep down she knew Lucy was right but hearing it all grouped together was a bit of a shocker. Calling it bullying put a whole different slant on things and there was far too much for her to unpack at once. Ella did what she usually did and shoved it to the back of her mind and mentally roped it off with warning tape.

'Shall we get to work then?' suggested Ella, clapping her hands together.

She had everything ready in the living room. Dressmaking was her passion and she had all the essentials at home: numerous sewing boxes, two sewing machines and she even had a step for Brittany to stand on making it easier for her to work around the bottom of the dress.

'This is soooo exciting,' squealed Brittany. Ella mimicked her giddiness and Lucy made a half-hearted attempt at jazz hands before Brittany virtually skipped into the living room. It was hard not to feel happy around brides, maybe that was what had drawn Ella to her job. She loved the role she played in making people's dreams a reality. She saw so many brides – all shapes, sizes, colours, temperaments and characters. They had all found the person of their dreams and yet she was still very much alone.

Ella and Lucy waited outside while Brittany put her dress on.

'Are you still seeing . . .' It took Ella a moment to recall the name of Lucy's latest man. 'Cory?'

'That's just sex on a mutual demand basis. We're not exclusive. Otherwise they get all clingy and before you know it you're choosing hideous bridesmaids dresses for your best friends.' Lucy shivered at the thought.

'Having a boyfriend or even a husband wouldn't be the worst thing that could happen.'

'No, I agree,' said Lucy. This time looking serious. 'Death is the worst thing that can happen. But, in my book, marriage comes in a close second.'

Ella didn't agree. Ella's parents were the perfect couple and had a wonderful marriage. They had set the bar exceptionally high when it came to relationships. The way her parents doted on each other was exactly what she wanted from a partner. 'You're cynical even for a cynic,' said Ella.

'Unencumbered sex is the way to go. You should try it. It's freeing.' Lucy swirled her hands in the air.

'I'm fine as I am,' said Ella emphatically.

'Sure you are. But there's a guy at my gym who would be fun

for you,' said Lucy. 'I can hook you up if you like? Or are you still getting over Toad the shitweasel?'

Ella was affronted. Not by her turn of phrase – she was used to Lucy's colourful descriptions. She'd tried to impart some on Lucy but she couldn't seem to get them right. 'I am completely and utterly over Todd the um . . . turd-panda. Thank you very much.'

'No, you're not,' called Brittany from inside the living room, she had obviously been listening to their conversation.

'Are you ready?' asked Ella, keen to end the discussion about her ex.

There was the brief sound of shuffling before the door opened and Brittany gave them a shy smile. 'How do I look?'

Ella's eyes darted over the gown, quickly assessing what needed to be taken in, let out and taken up. 'Completely beautiful,' she said.

'Like you've been eaten by a giant cloud,' said Lucy. Ella nudged her. 'But a nice cloud. An obviously quite enormous . . . marshmallowy mass. But huge and super fluffy and . . .'

'Shut up,' said Brittany, although she was smiling. 'I know it's big but so am I and I love it.'

'Then that's all that matters,' said Lucy.

'Right. Let's get it to fit you perfectly,' said Ella.

Lucy got out the champagne and they all chatted while Ella worked at pinning and unpinning until she was happy the dress would look like it had been made solely for Brittany's body – something she prided herself on.

'I'll unzip you and you can slip the dress off, be careful not to catch yourself on any pins,' said Ella.

'Oh no. I don't want to take it off yet.' Brittany pouted. 'And I want you both to try your dresses on so I can see how we look together.' Brittany grinned, enthusiasm radiating off her. Lucy failed to hide a grimace.

'Sure. Are you going to do the unveiling?' asked Ella, nodding at the other dress carrier still hanging on the door.

Brittany got down from the little podium. 'Close your eyes.' She was grinning broadly. Ella had a good feeling about this. Lucy was shaking her head. Ella closed her eyes and waited. She heard Brittany undo the long zip, there was the sound of rustling as the dresses were removed and then at last Brittany spoke, almost bubbling over with excitement. 'You can look now.'

Ella was the first to open her eyes. A quick glance at Lucy revealed she was squinting through one eye. Ella doubted that would make the sight look any better.

'They're . . . um . . .' Ella was desperately trying to find positive words. Brittany's phone rang and Ella was glad of the interruption.

'It's the videographer,' said Brittany, by way of explanation. 'Try them on,' she added with a wide smile and she left the room.

'This is a wind-up, right?' Lucy's voice was low and desperate.

'I'm afraid I don't think it is.' Ella had most likely seen thousands of dresses over the years but none quite like the ones in front of her. They had something similar to a high polo neck collar, puffball shoulders attached to long sleeves, and a long skirt all in some sort of ruched shiny fabric.

'What colour is that?' asked Lucy, her mouth actually falling open.

Brittany popped her head around the door. Her grin still in place. 'It's latte. Isn't it divine?' She nodded at them before returning to her phone call and stepping back into the hallway.

Lucy deftly kicked the door closed. 'Latte? It's sodding brown,' she said in a frantic low whisper. 'And it's not even a nice shade of brown it's . . .' There was a moment where Lucy looked like she was going to spontaneously combust as she fought to find the right words. 'Dog diarrhoea brown!' Lucy shook her head. 'Put a bonnet with it and I'll be Little Poo Peep.'

Ella was sucking her teeth. 'Maybe if there was less of it.' She ran a finger over the ruffles.

'Long sleeves in July? There won't be an ounce of our flesh on

15

show. We'll look like we've been rolled in poo. I'm definitely wearing the unicorn head to the wedding now – at least nobody will recognise me.'

It was hard to disagree. Ella struggled to find anything positive to say. 'On the plus side,' she began. 'You've won a tenner.'

CHAPTER THREE

Ella was still thinking about Brittany's bridesmaids' dresses when she walked into Frills, Frocks and Fairy Tales the next morning. Lucy had begged her to find a way to improve them and she'd been awake half the night pondering the different options. She had dismissed Lucy's suggestion which was to burn the dresses and start again. Whatever she did she needed to be mindful of Brittany's feelings because she seemed to like them although she had said it was the colour she liked above the style of the dress and also the fact her mum had got them for a bargain price on eBay. At least they were the right sizes and didn't need much alteration. Lucy was seriously considering putting on a few stone before the wedding in an attempt to get out of wearing hers.

Ella opened up the little shop. She quite liked being there on her own for the first half an hour or so. She wasn't entirely sure how it had happened but soon after Ella got the job Wanda had given her a set of keys, in case she was ever off sick, and then gradually opening up had been left to Ella more and more. But, as the owner, there had to be some benefits for Wanda – or owner and proprietor as Wanda liked to style herself. Ella quite liked the idea of being her own boss one day. She wasn't sure she'd be able to do what Wanda did, owning a shop required a big investment and a certain level of self-assuredness, neither of which she had but it was good to have dreams.

They only had a couple of brides booked in which was handy because it meant Ella could get on with alterations and this time of year it was always super busy. Despite Ella's continued reminders Wanda was forever squeezing in more even though Ella told her she was maxed out. But then who ever wanted to tell a bride they couldn't help them?

'You will not believe what happened last night after you left early,' said Wanda, walking into the shop.

'I didn't leave early, I just couldn't stay late because—'

'We had a browser who wanted to try on. Normally I'd book them in for another time but I could tell she had already fallen for the Rue de Seine and didn't want her finding it cheaper on the blessed internet. Then a bride turned up to collect a dress and I couldn't find it which threw her into a huge flap.'

'You should have called me,' said Ella. She was certain there was nobody due to collect yesterday but she still hated the thought of a bride being distressed.

'I did manage to find it *eventually*. But not before the bride had sobbed her heart out. Your system is shocking.' Wanda waved towards the back room where Ella kept the dresses in strict sections depending on where they were in the fitting and alteration process and within those sections they were hung in alphabetical order – which all made absolute sense to her.

'Sorry. What was the name of the bride?'

'Jennings. I was so stressed I've booked myself a massage for this afternoon.'

Ella was listening while she scanned her client book. 'Jennings is down for collection on Friday. Why did she come early?'

'I don't know,' said Wanda, looking affronted. 'Something about her mother having a chemo appointment.' Wanda puffed out a breath. 'So you're fine to cover this afternoon, yes?'

Wanda employed Ella as in-house alteration service enabling her to sell the dress and alterations as a package rather than the bride having to take the dress elsewhere. It also meant she could charge more for the convenience. Wanda was talented at sales. She had an eye for matching dresses to brides and was especially good at pushing the limits of their budget. She also had part-time staff who covered Saturdays and busy periods but Ella was the only seamstress.

'To be honest I'm stacked out,' said Ella. Wanda froze like she'd stepped in a cow pat. 'I've got two first fittings and four dresses I have to finish today and one of those has quite extensive changes,' added Ella. The extensive changes had been thanks to some suggestions from Wanda because she didn't stock exactly what the bride wanted but was determined to close the sale, however, Ella wasn't brave enough to say that.

'Oh, but you work fast. You'll simply whizz through those.' Wanda pouted. 'Pwitty pwease.' She fluttered her false eyelashes which made Ella want to poke her own eyes out with a rusty pin.

What choice did she have? 'Fine. But I'd best get on.' It was going to be a long day.

Ella had only completed one dress when Wanda popped her head around the door. 'Very close to a sale but the bride is wavering. Can you reassure her you can make this perfect?' Wanda was gone before Ella could reply. She stopped working and followed Wanda through to the fitting rooms. A woman in her mid-thirties was standing on a podium in a dress two sizes too big. It was easy to see why she was sceptical.

'Hi, I'm Ella, I'm the seamstress here. That dress is stunning on you.'

'Thanks.' The bride looked doubtful.

'I'm sure Wanda explained we can't stock each dress in every size but I promise you when we get the size twelve on you and take up the hem and remove an inch from here.' Ella indicated the shoulders. 'And adjust the top of the bodice to fit your bust. It will look and feel perfect.' Ella smiled and the shy bride smiled back but didn't look totally convinced.

Ella applied some strategically placed bulldog clips and folded over the excess material on the shoulders. 'See?' she asked the bride-to-be's reflection in the mirror but she already knew the answer from the woman's expression.

'Yes. I can see it now. It's beautiful. Thank you.'

'No problem.' Ella had to stay holding on for a few minutes because the bride was captivated like a budgie when it sees its reflection.

The bride turned to face Wanda. 'What sort of discount can you do?' This was probably the worst question anyone could ask Wanda aside from, 'Has anyone ever told you you're the spitting image of Angela Merkel?' Tension gripped Ella's shoulders as she saw the colour rise up Wanda's neck. It was like watching a volcano about to erupt.

'I'll leave you to . . . umm . . .' Ella let go of the dress and ran for cover.

Ella was shattered by the time she got home. She pulled one of her premade batch meals of Bolognese from the freezer and while she set some spaghetti to boil, she rang her mum and dad. There was no answer. Since her father had taken early retirement they were hardly ever in.

Her kitchen door swung open, making her jump – her cat, Pirate, meowed a welcome. A few months ago Brittany had turned up in tears with a sorry tale of a stray black cat who'd had an argument with a moped and come off decidedly worse. In an attempt to calm Brittany down Ella had somehow agreed to adopt the animal sight unseen. As it turned out that was likely the only way he would have found a home because, although she now loved him very much, he really was the ugliest cat she'd ever seen. In the accident he had suffered terrible injuries. The vets had worked wonders and he'd pulled through but on his left side he'd lost an eye, part of his lip and a back leg.

She had just sat down to her meal when her phone rang. It was her parents.

'Hi Ella,' said her mother.

'Hi, where were you when I rang?'

'Your mother was on the other line and I was in the loo, Pumpkin,' said her dad. They were both on the call – they did this a lot.

'Ew, too much information, Dad. How are you both?'

'I've been checking that my new clubs work,' said her father, which was code for he'd been out golfing a lot.

'Busy with the show,' said her mum. She worked part time at the dance school she used to own and every summer they put on a big display to showcase what the children had learnt that year as well as presentations of all those who had passed grades. 'Have you just got in from work?'

Ella had to stifle a yawn. 'I'm afraid so.'

'That Wanda is working you too hard.' Her dad always said that.

'It's always busy this time of year.' Ella tried forking up some of her dinner but it all refused to stay on the fork.

'And that Wanda is too mean to take on someone else. It's not right. There're children in sweat shops in the Third World who don't work as hard as you. Aren't I right, David?'

'That's possibly an exaggeration, Sandy,' said her dad. 'But your mum's right, you do work hard and I'm not sure you're as valued as you should be. You have a real talent, Ella.'

'Thanks. But you guys have to say that.' She smothered another yawn. 'I'm thinking of coming over next Saturday.' It was best to check otherwise she'd rock up and they'd be out. They both had a better social life than she did, which was a little depressing.

'I'm free all day,' said her mum.

There was a pause on the other end before her dad spoke. 'Busy in the morning but afternoon is good. What sort of time?'

'Come for lunch,' said Sandy. 'I'll make us something nice and we can have a girly natter until you dad gets in.'

That sounded like bliss. 'Great. I'll see you both then. Love you. Bye.'

She didn't go home as much as she'd like. They lived in Norfolk too, around the coast in Heacham, so in theory they weren't too far away. But thanks to no motorways and mainly single lane roads, with more than their fair share of tractors, it took her an hour and a half to get there on a good run. Meaning she couldn't just pop in but she spoke to them a lot on the phone.

Ella finished her meal and was running a bath when a text arrived. It was from Lucy.

Have warmed up the guy at the gym for you. His name is Stuart and he's an estate agent but don't hold that against him lol. He's single, above average looking and works in Norwich. Shall I give him your number? L x

Ella sighed. What did she have to lose?

***

Lucy found herself in a chain coffee shop waiting to meet Brittany for lunch. She was on her guard because although Brittany had said she wanted to talk about Ella, Lucy was still half expecting her to turn up with some animal reject. Brittany came dashing into the coffee shop and almost knocked a coffee out of someone's hand.

'Oops, sorry!' she called over her shoulder as she darted across to her friend.

'I bought you a cheese toastie and a coconut flat white,' said Lucy, pulling out a chair.

'I think I should be marrying you,' said Brittany, plonking herself on the seat.

'Don't even joke about marriage. You know it brings me out in hives,' said Lucy with a shudder. 'Are you alone?' she asked, giving Brittany the once-over. Her bag looked overstuffed which was a worry but it wasn't moving or making a noise which was a relief.

'Yes, I'm alone.' Brittany let out a nervous giggle. 'You sound like a spy.'

'Just checking you've not brought along any gimpy guinea pigs, traumatised tortoises or radioactive rabbits?'

Brittany held up her palms. 'No, but there is the cutest—'

'La, la, la, not listening,' said Lucy, putting her fingers in her ears.

'Fine,' said Brittany, twisting her lips. 'Anyway, I wanted to talk to you about Ella.' She looked at her plate. 'After I've eaten this. I'm famished.'

Lucy sipped her espresso while Brittany munched on her toastie. 'I don't think you need to worry too much about Ella. She's got a date on Thursday night.' Brittany looked amazed. Lucy was quite proud of herself for having set Ella up on a date. Ella was still getting over Todd. Even a sceptic like Lucy had to admit they had looked like they were together for the long haul. Lucy wasn't a big fan of Todd's, he was a bit too showy for her liking and he overpowered Ella. He was an internet entrepreneur who liked to brag about being a millionaire, manage and control everything and surround himself with pretty things that made him look good. Lucy was pretty sure Ella had ticked a couple of boxes as she'd been a pretty thing he could control. Everything seemed to be going well until Todd had announced he didn't want a long-term relationship so for Ella's sake he had packed up his things and left for the foreign legion. Actually, the last bit Lucy had made up, but the truth was he did seem to have disappeared. He had deleted his personal social media accounts and had his mail redirected to his parents' place. It was all very strange, but then he was from Suffolk.

'But she's not over Todd,' said Brittany, her eyes going round. 'She was devastated.'

'I think she was more blindsided. She thought she'd found a like-minded person to spend forever with, but Toad didn't feel the same. A date is part of her moving on and doing something for herself.' In true Ella style she had blamed herself for the whole sorry affair, put on a smile and carried on putting everyone else's needs before her own.

'If you think that's what she needs,' said Brittany, not looking convinced.

'I do,' said Lucy. She felt she had to look out for Ella. It had been that way since year five when Adam Burston had asked Ella to check if his pudding smelt okay and when she'd had a sniff he'd pushed her face in it, covering her in custard. Ella had simply walked away, still dripping custard, whereas Lucy had been so cross she'd tipped the bowl over Adam's head and missed the bus home thanks to a lengthy detention. Lucy couldn't stand injustice and while she had learnt that tipping sponge pudding and custard over someone's head wasn't the answer, she had realised she could make a difference to people like Ella who were pre-programmed not to stick up for themselves. Hence, she had studied law and was now a well-established family lawyer.

Brittany licked her fingers and leant forward. 'Who is Ella going on a date with?'

'A guy from my gym.'

Brittany looked instantly disappointed. 'Just some random hook-up? Ella's not like you.' Lucy gave her a questioning look. 'You're different that's all. Ella is looking for what me and Grant have.' Brittany seemed to glow at the mention of Grant's name – it was that or the grease from the cheese toastie.

The more Lucy witnessed the more she was certain humans weren't meant to mate for life. It was a rare thing in the animal world – swans, puffins and seahorses were all she could think of. With the possible exception of captive giant pandas who didn't have a lot of choice – a lot like the Norfolk dating pool – pretty much all other species went with the flow, mating with whoever was handy and that made sense to her. Hook up for a bit of fun as and when and then when it gets a bit dull say farewell and move on. It avoided all the angst, tears and heartache and suited her perfectly.

'Grant and I . . .' began Brittany.

'Are pandas,' said Lucy, without thinking. Brittany looked confused. 'Or swans. Together for life.'

Brittany paused for a second. 'That's made me well up. Swans. Aww.'

Lucy smiled, she'd recovered that quite well. 'Swans but without the hissing, flapping and biting.' Maybe she should have kept her mouth shut.

***

Against her better judgement Ella found herself on Thursday evening sitting at the bar in an olde worlde pub waiting for Stuart the estate agent to show up. He'd texted to say he was running late which wasn't a great start. She'd told him not to worry and that she was happy to wait. Her phone was keeping her entertained because Lucy was messaging every couple of minutes either for an update or to share top tips on hooking up. Ella knew she was out of practice but at twenty-nine she wasn't exactly past it.

She sipped her tonic water and took in her surroundings. Lucy had recommended the pub – Ella had never been but its thriving restaurant had a good reputation. If the happy faces of the diners were anything to go by it was probably worth a return visit to try the food.

There was a beam and brick open wall separating the restaurant and bar from her seat allowing her to comfortably do a little unobtrusive people watching. There were a couple of groups but the tables were mainly occupied by couples. They spanned the age spectrum from the barely out of their teens couple who only stopped holding hands long enough to feed each other, to the grey-haired couple who chatted non-stop and laughed a lot. It was the older couple who fascinated Ella more; she wondered how long they'd been together. The man had his back to Ella but she could see the woman's every reaction. She had fabulous cheekbones and more than an air of Meg Ryan about her. Her eyes sparkled as she and the man Ella assumed was her partner talked and ate.

Time passed and Ella checked her watch. Stuart was now twenty minutes late and there'd been no messages for a while. She tried hard not to sigh. She'd not been hanging too many expectations on this blind date but watching the couples in the restaurant had made her realise that it was simple things like a shared meal out she'd been missing since she and Todd had split. She missed a lot of other things about him: the reassurance he'd given her, the help with decision making and that feeling of being cossetted and kept safe. It was like her armour had been stripped from her and underneath she was naked, vulnerable and self-conscious.

She was half watching the restaurant now but as the older couple stood to leave she caught a glimpse of the man and although it was only a moment there was something extremely familiar. It couldn't be. Could it? She finished her drink and leant to see around the pillar which had been partially obscuring her view. As the male diner helped the woman put on her coat they laughed and for the first time that evening his voice was audible and Ella felt sick to her stomach. The man was her father.

CHAPTER FOUR

Lucy checked her phone – still no word from Ella which had to be good. They had a sign for 'Come and rescue me now' and she hadn't been expecting that as Stuart had seemed quite sane. She'd briefed Ella not to talk too much about weddings, which she appreciated was difficult in her line of work, but bride chat was a sure-fire way to set alarm bells ringing in most men's ears.

Ella and Lucy had always supported each other and since custard-gate they had been inseparable. They'd grown up in Heacham which was Hunstanton's quieter neighbour and a popular place for people to retire to. Lucy's grandparents had been one of those couples who had always dreamed of retiring to the seaside although when they'd pictured that idyllic scene she doubted they had planned to have their daughter move in to their tiny bungalow too.

Despite her mother's laissez-faire attitude to most things including herself, Lucy loved her mum but now she was an adult she could appreciate how frustrating the situation must have been for the whole family. Her mum, Terri, had never managed to carve out a career; instead she had had a series of low paid jobs meaning money had always been an issue. Coupled with Terri's love of fighting for a cause and an inexplicable ability to fall in love with useless men it meant she was frequently on her own wondering how she was going to pay the rent. And while moving in with Nan and Grandad had solved their money issues, five people in a two-bedroom bungalow was always going to be a pot waiting to boil over.

Lucy had been more than happy to escape to Ella's house on a regular basis. David and Sandy Briggs were the parents Lucy had always wished she'd had. Sandy was a great cook and there were always snacks when they got in from school or hot chocolate in the winter. And when Sandy made hot chocolate it came with whipped cream, mini marshmallows and chocolate shavings on top. At home if she wanted hot chocolate she had to make it herself by chipping away at out of date cocoa powder only to end up speed stirring the lumpy mass around some warm milk – it wasn't the same.

Ella had been surrounded by love and happiness which in some respects was wonderful, but Lucy could see that their opposing upbringings had given them very different perspectives on relationships. Lucy had learnt that she needed to look out for herself and that self-preservation was the key to avoid being continually let down. Whereas Ella was still trying to find someone to look at her the way her father looked at her mother. Lucy could definitely see the appeal but was it really worth the effort and the risk?

With over forty per cent of marriages ending in divorce the odds were decidedly dodgy. But then on the bright side it kept her in a job. Lucy tried to concentrate on the 'Without Prejudice' offer letter she had drafted for a client who was in the early, and currently amicable, stage of their divorce. She tidied up the paperwork, she'd finish it in the office when she was firing on all cylinders.

She checked her phone. No update from Ella – she'd grill her tomorrow. Nothing from Cory, her current hook-up. It wasn't that late, definitely still time for a booty call. She fired off a cheeky text and went for a quick shower.

Lucy was towel drying her hair when she saw she had a missed call from Cory, so she called him back.

'Hey, you,' she said, starting to feel quite seductive. 'Are you on your way over?'

'Lucy, sorry, I can't make it tonight.'

Her shoulders slumped. The downside of spontaneous was that other people sometimes had plans. 'That's a shame but hey it was just a thought.' Did she hear him sigh?

'Look this is a bit awkward but I'm kind of seeing someone.'

She hadn't been expecting that. 'We never were exclusive. That doesn't have to be the end of our arrangement. Does it?'

'Yeah. It kinda does.'

'Not an open relationship then?' She liked to check where she stood.

'Nah, it's pretty serious to be honest with you.'

Lucy sniggered. Cory wasn't serious about anything and certainly not about relationships. Which was why they were perfect for each other. 'Serious? Yeah right.'

'I'm sorry, Lucy. I mean it. This woman has completely stolen my heart.'

'Okay, well. I hope it works out for you and if it doesn't at least you know a good divorce lawyer.'

'Cheers, Lucy. I knew you'd be cool. Take care.'

Another one bites the dust, she thought. Maybe she would finish that 'Without Prejudice' offer letter after all.

***

Ella wasn't going to make a scene, that wasn't her way, but she had to find out what was going on. Why was her dad out with another woman and who was she? Her pulse started to race as all manner of horrors sped through her mind. *There had to be an innocent explanation,* she told herself. Her parents were rock solid and had been for almost thirty years. They were the foundations on which everything she held dear had been built – there couldn't possibly be anything wrong. She watched the back of her father as he courteously stood back to let the woman exit the restaurant first. Now was her chance. She had to follow them and challenge him in the car park. She had no idea what she was going to say. Her father opened the door, his palm on the small of the woman's back – it was such an intimate and proprietorial gesture that it shook Ella. She was glued to the scene. Her father was oblivious and with a cheery wave to the waitress, they left.

For a moment Ella was stunned and stayed staring at the now closed door. She needed to do something. Ella grabbed her handbag and marched through the bar. She was reaching for the door when a hand landed on her shoulder making her jump. She spun around and came face to face with a dark-haired man a few inches taller than her, with dark stubble and a worried expression.

'I'm sorry. I didn't mean to make you jump.' He held his hands up as if surrendering.

Brilliant, she thought, *what great timing Stuart has*. For a moment she was filled with indecision. She didn't want to be rude to Stuart, but he had kept her waiting for almost half an hour. He was strikingly good-looking in a rough and ready sort of way with wavy black hair and eyelashes any woman would kill for. Not what she'd been expecting of an estate agent at all. The sight of him had distracted her from her mission. She was running out of time. A quick decision was needed.

'I'm sorry. I just need to—' She pointed to the door because she didn't know where to start when it came to explaining this.

'Actually, could we sit down and have a chat?' he asked. His eyes were wrinkling at the edges as he smiled awkwardly. He was seriously sexy, maybe there was something in this casual relationship thing Lucy raved about. Although his manners weren't great – he hadn't yet apologised for being late. 'Let me buy you a drink,' he said, stepping towards the bar.

'Er, okay. A tonic water please.' Ella waited for a moment and the seconds thudded by in her head. 'Look, sorry, I'll be back in two secs, I have to do something.' With that she dashed out of the door and into the car park. She scanned it quickly and caught the sight of the rear of her father's car heading up the road. Something akin to a medicine ball descended into her stomach. She was tempted to jump in her car and follow them but that was far too stalkerish and now poor Stuart was buying her a drink she could hardly run off without any explanation. She huffed out a breath, composed herself and strolled back inside as calmly as she could. She'd push this nightmare to the back of her mind, have one drink with Stuart and then go home and most likely be awake all night worrying about what the hell was going on with her father.

Back in the bar Stuart was paying for their drinks. He turned in her direction, a deep frown across his forehead but his expression lightened when he saw her return.

'Sorry about that,' said Ella.

'Did you catch them?' he asked.

The question surprised her. Obviously he'd realised exactly what she was doing. Now she'd have to explain or look like some weirdo who chased strangers out of pubs. 'No, I missed them. But it's fine. It was just my dad. But he didn't see me. I'll catch him another time.'

He looked surprised. 'Your dad?' He passed her the tonic water.

He picked up his glass and they went to sit where she'd been before, but he sat down opposite, blocking her view of the restaurant. The sight of her father and the other woman would be forever etched on her brain.

Ella gave herself a mental shake and tried to switch into casual chat mode. 'Were the roads bad?' she asked. He frowned at her. 'On your way here. Was it busy? The roadworks out of Norwich are a nightmare, aren't they?'

31

'Um, yeah. They can be. Look, what made you come here tonight?' he asked.

Wow that was blunt and her surprise at the direct question was probably scrawled all over her face. 'I'll be honest. I wasn't sure because although it's been six months since I split up with my boyfriend it was a serious relationship that I thought was going to go the distance. It's taken me a while to get my head around it all. I've not wanted to meet anyone else. And—'

Her mobile rang and she scrabbled in her bag to answer it. 'I'm sorry,' she said.

'It's fine. It might be someone important.'

She looked at the screen display and then back at the man in front of her. It clearly said, *Stuart calling*. 'It's . . . um . . . you,' she said.

'What's me?' he said, looking as confused as she felt.

She hit the green button and cautiously answered the call, half expecting the man in front of her to pull a phone out of his pocket. 'Hello?'

'Hi Ella. It's Stuart. I thought for a moment it was going to go to voicemail. I'm so sorry. On top of the traffic jams I've had a tyre blow out on me. I've put the spare on but it's one of those space saver things and I daren't go too far on it. What I'm trying to say, really badly, is can we postpone tonight and meet up another time.'

Ella blinked. The man opposite was watching her intently. 'Okay, Stuart. Let's rearrange.'

'Great. I'll text you. Bye.'

The call ended and Ella put her phone away without taking her eyes off the man in front of her. 'You're not Stuart,' she said at last.

He narrowed his eyes. 'No, I'm Kit O'Leary.'

She took a sip of her drink and wished it had a couple of gins in it. She had absolutely no idea what was going on.

Ella put down her tonic water. 'I thought you were Stuart,' she said, partly by way of explanation but mainly because she was trying to uncoil the mix-up in her mind.

'Who's Stuart?' asked Kit.

'He's this blind date my friend . . . actually I think it's irrelevant who Stuart is. What is relevant is who the hell you are.' She'd just given this stranger a potted history of her love life and he'd stopped her going after her father. Which she was now certain would have provided clarification and resolved all the worries that were currently invading her brain.

'I told you, I'm Kit. But you've not bothered to tell me who you are.'

How had she become the bad guy in this surreal episode? 'I'm Ella.' Her good manners made her offer him a hand to shake, which he did, cautiously.

'And that charmer was your father, right?' He gave a nod towards the door.

She didn't like his tone and she certainly didn't like her father being called a charmer. 'Yes, that was my father. What exactly is going on?'

'That's precisely what I was hoping you were going to tell me. You were watching them on the sly exactly the same as I was. Let's find out what we each know. You can go first.' Kit stared at her unblinking as he took a swig of his beer.

Ella held her palms up. 'Let's start again. I was meeting a man here—'

'Stuart,' added Kit with a smile playing at the edge of his lips.

'Yes, Stuart. But he was late.'

'Stood you up,' offered Kit.

'No, there were roadworks and he had a puncture.' She felt she needed to defend Stuart in his absence.

'If you say so,' said Kit. His cheek twitched dismissively and it irked her.

'Anyway, I was waiting for Stuart and I was watching the people in the restaurant and I realised one of them was my dad. But I only knew for sure when they were leaving and I was about to speak to him when you stopped me.'

Kit's expression changed. 'You didn't know he was going to be here?'

'Obviously not. But clearly you did. So why were you here spying on my father?' She straightened her back and stared him down.

Kit met her gaze with hard, dark eyes. 'Because he's having an affair with my mother.'

CHAPTER FIVE

Ella held up both her palms in an attempt to stop his words slapping her. What was he talking about? Her head was spinning.

'That woman is your mother?'

'Hey, you can back off with the *that woman* inferences. She's very respectable.'

'So's my father! He's happily married and has been for almost thirty years.' Ha, she felt she'd played her trump card.

'Looks like *almost* is the key word in that sentence.'

He was infuriating. 'As in they have been married for almost thirty years. But hang on. Aren't we leaping to a huge conclusion here? It could be completely innocent. We don't know that they are romantically connected.' She banished the images of the woman touching her father's arm as they laughed together. 'They might just be friends, or business associates.' She felt she'd hit on something there and she pointed at Kit to pick up the baton and run with her theory.

Kit was slumped back in his seat regarding her. 'My mother is a retired coroner so unless your father has a body and he'd like to know the cause of death I'm not sure it's a business meeting. And she works in a charity shop on Wednesdays. What does your father do for a living?'

'Retired general manager for a large shoe company . . . large company, not large shoes.' She felt she had to clarify.

'Then I think we can rule out business,' said Kit.

'Maybe they're old friends.' Ella was aware she was starting to clutch at very flimsy straws.

'What's his name?'

'David Briggs.' She didn't like the way Kit was watching her. 'What's your mother's name?' she countered.

'Jane O'Leary.'

The name didn't ring any bells with Ella. She was beginning to feel despondent. All roads were pointing in the worst possible direction. 'I don't understand it. My parents are devoted to each other. Always have been. There must be some other reason.'

Kit shrugged. 'Is he some sort of con man?'

'What the hell?' She was riled now. 'No, he is a family man who plays golf, dabbles in the garden and is terrible at DIY. He never forgets a birthday or anniversary. He leaves messages on my mum's pillow when he's away golfing. And he is always on the end of a phone when I need him.' Her lip wobbled so she stopped talking.

Kit shrugged. 'I'm just saying. My mum is a wealthy widow, maybe that's the attraction.'

'I'm not sure why you seem to think my father is the guilty party here. She was all over him tonight.' The images were still vivid in her mind. 'Maybe it's a honey trap. Perhaps it's a black-mail set-up. Your mother could be a blackmailer.'

Kit shook his head and calmly finished his drink. 'Now, you're being ridiculous.'

'Fine. I'm seeing my parents on Saturday when I will be able to sort all this out.' She stood up to leave, she couldn't wait to get away from Kit O'Leary and his unpleasant accusations.

'Hang on, don't go getting all offended.' Kit waved his hand in an offer for her to sit down but she stayed standing. 'Let's see if we can work out the best way to approach this. Please.' She wavered and he spotted it. 'I'm sorry if I've upset you.'

'Apology accepted.' She sat down. Ella drew in a breath to calm herself. 'I'm sure there's a simple explanation.'

'There might be but there has to be a more subtle way to find out than putting either of them on the spot. I'm not sure challenging your dad is the best thing to do. Most people would deny it and act defensive. That won't get us anywhere.'

He had a point. She was also keen not to upset her mum unnecessarily. 'Okay what about your mum? Is this out of character for her?'

'Since my dad died and . . . well, it's been a tough couple of years to be honest with you. She started seeing this guy and . . . long story short he was some lowlife trying to con her out of money. I challenged him and he vanished. I thought we were muddling along all right and then a few months ago she started going out again.'

'A few months ago?' Ella couldn't hide her shock.

'Yeah. Sorry. I think they've been seeing each other for a while. If that is what's happening,' he added pre-empting Ella's challenge. 'She was getting more phone calls and meeting up with a friend she called Davine. And after last time it made me suspicious but my spider sense was triggered when she started looking at holidays abroad but shutting her laptop down as soon as I approached and generally being evasive about stuff. That's not like her. She's open. Honest. I thought I'd follow her tonight and see this Davine for myself. Check the con man wasn't back in town and well, you know the rest. At least it's just an affair, assuming your dad's not a crook.'

'He's definitely not.' Ella felt thoroughly deflated but she wasn't ready to accept that her father was cheating on the word of a complete stranger. 'We can't be judge and jury based on your hunch that they're seeing each other. There might be a simple answer to all the questions we have.'

'There might be . . .' He paused and his lips pouted slightly. 'Perhaps the simple answer is that your dad and my mum are in a relationship.'

'This is all too much for me to take in.' The foundations her life was built on were no longer rock solid and it scared her.

Kit's expression softened. 'Let's swap numbers and maybe we can discuss what, if anything, we should do?'

Ella didn't sleep well that night. Even Pirate gave up and went to snooze in his basket rather than deal with her tossing and turning. It felt like everything she held true was beginning to unravel. She had always seen her parents as having the perfect relationship – full of love, trust and devotion. Now she was questioning everything. Her mum and dad had the sort of bond she wanted. Or so she had thought until a few hours ago. In fact she had a feeling she'd been unknowingly searching for it most of her adult life.

They had set the standard and had set it incredibly high and she had never wanted to settle for anything less. Now it appeared the whole thing was in tatters. Her heart broke a little for her mother. She dreaded to think how she would feel when she found out, assuming she didn't already have her suspicions. The wife was always the last to know, that was what they said. She didn't deserve this. If this was an affair, was it her father's first or had there been others? Or was it a one-off fling? All the questions whirled around Ella's mind.

Eventually she got up and got ready for work. Pirate was particularly attentive and followed her around the house as if sensing her distress. That or he was angling for a treat. He sat at her feet while she had some toast and gazed at her adoringly. At least someone loved her unconditionally and the feeling was mutual. His huge ears with the little tufts on the end twitched as her mobile sprang into life.

'How'd it go? Did he stay over? Are you seeing him again?'

'Good morning, Lucy,' said Ella. 'Stuart got a puncture.'

'Do you mean in a condom or is that a euphemism for erectile dysfunction?'

Despite everything Ella snorted a laugh. 'No, his car broke down. But that's not the half of it.' She proceeded to bring Lucy up to speed on her evening from hell.

She heard Lucy puff out a breath. 'Blimey that's a lot to take in. How are you feeling?'

'Honestly? Awful. And I've arranged to go over to theirs tomorrow. And now I've agreed with this Kit guy that I won't say anything and already I'm getting hot sweats just thinking about it because I'm worried I'll blurt it out. And in the back of my mind I'm still hoping it's something and nothing. That Dad will be able to explain it all away and everything can go back to normal.' She waited but there was no response from Lucy. 'You've gone very quiet.'

'It's just that in my experience, and I'm speaking professionally here, married men don't meet other women for cosy meals alone for any other reason than they're having extra-marital sex with them.'

'Thanks for sugar-coating that one.'

'You're welcome. Maybe you should look at it from a different perspective. They had a good run, your mum and dad. Way longer than most marriages and they were happy.'

'I'm not sure I've got to that stage yet, but thanks. And thanks for not volunteering your services as a divorce lawyer.'

'Again, you're welcome. Do you fancy a drink tonight? I can see if Brittany can tear herself away from seating plans.'

'Thanks, that'd be great.'

'What are friends for, if it's not to encourage you to get off your face on wine?'

Ella's mood wasn't exactly brighter when she went to work but she had managed to package up the situation with her parents and stuff it to the back of her mind. It was getting more crowded than a Primark sale back there. She made herself a coffee and left Wanda's ready so she only had to add hot water to it. She leant against the worktop in the tiny kitchen and sipped her drink. They had a rule that drinks never left the kitchen to avoid any disastrous accidents with the dresses.

The door opened and in strolled Wanda. 'Having a break already?' Ella wasn't in the mood for Wanda's snide and uncalled-for comments. What Lucy had said the other night about people bullying her was still festering in a corner of her mind like a forgotten yogurt at the back of the fridge.

'It's five to nine. Therefore, right now I'm not being paid, even though I have already opened up, sewn on eight additional pearl buttons to a dress and checked the diary for the day.'

Wanda looked at her askance. 'Someone got out of bed the wrong side.' She re-boiled the kettle and folded her arms.

Ella almost automatically apologised but she thought of Lucy's statement about her not sticking up for herself and she stopped her apology escaping by biting her lip. Wanda was watching her and Ella caved. 'I've just got a lot on that's all.'

Wanda didn't reply, but she stared at the clock until it clicked onto exactly nine o'clock. 'You'd best get on with it then because I'm paying you now.'

Ella had one last defiant sip of her coffee before ceremoniously tipping the rest down the plughole and leaving the room. She wasn't usually disobedient, but it felt good and today she definitely needed something to lift her spirits.

***

Lucy dealt with divorce on a daily basis but hearing about Ella's parents had made even her hardened heart feel blue. She didn't believe in happy ever after but she had to admit she had thought the Briggses' marriage was rock solid. It just went to show you that you never really knew what went on behind closed doors and that people only showed you what they wanted you to see. The Briggses house had always been a happy one, an oasis for her as a child, and the thought of that evaporating was most definitely a sad thing.

She had a busy day ahead but she liked that. Her first client was the one she'd drafted the 'Without Prejudice' offer letter for. Hopefully it would be a straightforward case – that was always best for everyone involved, including her.

Lucy had presented the document to her client, a Mrs Maxwell, a whole five minutes ago and the woman was still reading and rereading the document. Not that that was a bad thing – she would always encourage people to check any documentation – but this did seem excessive given the full explanation Lucy had provided, that they were laying out terms they felt would work for everyone.

At last Mrs Maxwell spoke. 'I don't think my husband should have any contact with Alabama and Finley.'

'I see.' Lucy did not see at all because at the previous meeting, where she had asked her what she wanted, Mrs Maxwell had been adamant their teenage children weren't to miss out on time with either parent. 'Has something changed?'

Mrs Maxwell pulled out a tissue and blew her nose although there was no sign of actual tears. 'I should have realised when my daughter stopped going swimming that there was an issue, but I dismissed it as her being a fickle teenager. But this morning I walked in on her getting dressed and she was covered in bruises.'

'I'm sorry,' said Lucy. 'That must be distressing for you. Did she say how she'd got the bruises?'

'My husband did it.' The poor woman seemed shocked by her own words.

Lucy pushed the box of tissues across the table and Mrs Maxwell helped herself.

The rest of the meeting had been interspersed with Mrs Maxwell's tears and reassurances from Lucy that she would do all she could to protect her daughter. She also offered advice on keeping them all safe and offered to help her report the assault to the police if she wanted to. Lucy gave her some leaflets on the

National Abuse Helpline and the local women's refuge, but it appeared Mrs Maxwell was planning on staying with a friend until she found somewhere to move herself and her children to. Mr Maxwell had been rumbled and that meant they would be taking a different approach with the divorce. Sometimes things just didn't go to plan.

CHAPTER SIX

Ella had a first fitting with someone. It was a beautiful sleeveless ivory gown with a high neckline and A-line skirt and Ella was looking forward to seeing who had bought it. She got the fitting room ready and hung up the dress. The bride arrived a few minutes before her appointment time carrying a very large bag and introduced herself as Lianne. Once the standard 'congratulations, when is the wedding, I bet you're excited' conversation had been dispensed with Ella got to work.

'If you want to take your clothes off apart from underwear and pop the dress on. Then give me a shout and we'll see what needs altering. Okay?'

Lianne agreed and Ella left her to it. When Lianne let her know she was ready, Ella pulled back the curtain. Usually what she saw on the other side was a bride standing demurely on the small podium rather than the sight of someone wearing large black headphones and brandishing a glowing blue lightsabre.

'Woah!' said Ella, stepping backwards. Lianne looked alarmed by Ella's reaction. Had she been expecting Darth Vader? 'Er . . .' Ella was truly lost for words.

'I'm Princess Leia,' said Lianne.

'Of course you are,' said Ella, remembering she'd read an article somewhere that when people were struggling with an alternate reality it was better not to contradict them.

'For my wedding. It's a theme wedding,' explained Lianne.

'Oh, I see.' That made slightly more sense. Ella was relieved. 'I'm sorry, I hadn't realised.'

'What?' said Lianne, lifting one side of the large headphones. 'I'll take these off as I can't hear properly with them on. They were just to give the effect. My hairdresser will do my hair in side buns on the day but I wanted to see what it would look like. Get the whole effect.'

Ella nodded and tried to give a reassuring smile, but Lianne was still wielding the lightsabre. 'Obviously the length needs fixing and a little off the waist.' Ella was keen to focus back on the dress.

'And sleeves,' said Lianne.

As there were no sleeves, Ella assumed she meant the shoulders. 'The shoulders look fine but I'll take a look,' said Ella.

'But it needs the big sleeves like Carrie Fisher's dress.' Lianne reached into her giant bag and pulled out a laminated A4 *Star Wars* poster and handed it to Ella.

Ella scanned the picture and then looked at what the bride in front of her was wearing. There was not a lot that was similar. The situation started to dawn on Ella. 'You want me to make this dress look like the one in the picture?'

'Yeah, the lady who served me said you were a whizz with a sewing machine.' Lianne grinned.

A whizz maybe but a miracle worker no, thought Ella. 'You see the thing is that the dress you have chosen was made in France and the chances of getting the exact same material are . . . well, they're not even very slim, there is no chance because this designer is particularly secretive about their designs and materials.'

Lianne looked crestfallen. 'But the woman said you could. And this is the closest dress I've found apart from those awful costume hire places and then you look like a cheap knock-off Princess Leia and not a bride.'

44

Ella hated letting anyone down, but this situation wasn't of her manufacturing. 'Hang on a sec,' she said, and she dashed out the back to where Wanda was thumbing through a bridal magazine.

'I think we should look at stocking more coloured gowns. It seems to be a growing trend,' said Wanda absent-mindedly.

Ella ignored the comment. 'I have a bride in the fitting room who seems to think I can magically turn her dress into this.' She brandished the *Star Wars* poster.

There was a flicker of confusion before Wanda cottoned on. 'She's a sweetheart isn't she? Utterly bonkers obviously. Is there a problem?'

'Yes, there's a problem. This dress has sleeves.' Ella tapped the laminated poster for effect. 'And the one she has bought does not.'

'It doesn't have to look exactly like that does it?'

'It's a theme wedding, so I'm going to say it absolutely does. And now she's expecting me to add sleeves.' Wanda looked at her blankly. Ella was feeling brave. She pulled back her shoulders, she could stand up to Wanda. 'Seeing as you sold her the dress would you like to speak to her?' Ella felt immediately proud of herself.

'No,' said Wanda, pushing out her chin.

Not the response Ella had been hoping for. 'Okay, let me rephrase that. I can't sew on sleeves, and you need to tell her that.' Standing up for herself was a whole new experience.

'But that's what I pay you to do. I pay you to alter dresses,' said Wanda. 'If you're not up to the job I'll have to find someone who is.'

Ouch, that wasn't where Ella had expected Wanda to take the conversation. 'I'd be interested to see anyone add sleeves and make a decent job of it. Matching to that material will be near impossible and I certainly don't have the time to source fabric along with everything else.'

Wanda did not look pleased. 'Then tell her you don't have the skills required.' Wanda went back to perusing her magazine.

'Okay but then she'll probably want a refund.'

The R word made Wanda's head snap back up. 'Fine. If you're incapable I suppose I'll have to sort this out.' Wanda stormed out tutting as she went but Ella had a little bit of satisfaction in that she had provoked a reaction. Even if it wasn't the one she'd been hoping for and it had come with a thinly veiled threat of dismissal.

After a lot of discussion and some frantic googling Ella offered Lianne a partial solution in that they would give the effect of sleeves with a tuille wrap which could be removed later enabling Lianne to focus on being a bride rather than Princess Leia. The end result was that no refund was required, Lianne was happier and Ella had even more work to do. Lianne came out of the changing room with her lightsabre stowed safely in her large bag.

'Thank you. It wouldn't look like a *Star Wars* wedding if the dress wasn't right,' she said.

'I'm sure with your accessories you'll be the perfect Carrie Fisher, and when you're standing next to your Han Solo everyone will know exactly who you are,' said Ella, with a smile.

Lianne frowned at her. 'But my fiancé is going to be Chewbacca.'

Ella was looking forward to sitting down that evening with pizza and a glass of wine with her best friends. Wanda left before five because, as usual, she had something vitally important to do, leaving Ella to lock up. It had gone six and she was pulling down the blinds when her phone rang. It was Kit, the guy from the pub. She felt a certain amount of trepidation as she answered.

'Hello, Ella Briggs.' Yes, she was being overly formal but the fact he was calling her had thrown her.

'Hi. It's Kit O'Leary. Your dad and my mum are—'

'Yes. I know who you are.' She didn't want reminding about the situation.

'Can you talk?'

'Only for a couple of minutes, I'm just leaving work.'

'It won't take long. I've been thinking about our parents and . . . can we meet up? I think this conversation would be better face to face.'

'I guess.' She had no idea where he worked or lived but had gleaned from his accent that he was local. 'I'm at work in Norwich right now.'

'Whereabouts?'

'Over the water. Off the Sprowston Road.'

'Perfect. Text me the details and I'll be there within thirty minutes.' Ella sighed into the phone. 'I'll be there sooner if I can, but you know what those roadworks are like. Ask Stuart.'

She smiled. 'Okay but if you're not here in thirty minutes I'm out of here.'

'Deal.' And the line went dead. She texted him the details and went to make herself a coffee. In fact it did give her a chance to get a few admin bits up straight and she was quite intrigued as to what needed a face-to-face chat as opposed to one over the phone. A tiny part of her was also looking forward to seeing Kit again because while he was quite annoying and more than a little brusque he was easy on the eye.

Twenty five minutes after their call there was a loud rap on the door.

'I made it,' said Kit, tapping his watch.

'You did. Come in.'

He seemed a little hesitant at first, his eyes darting around the shop's interior, which amused her but then how many men had ever set foot in a bridal shop? Probably not many. 'This is where you work?'

'No, I'm a very niche burglar,' said Ella with a smile.

'Touché.'

She showed him over to the purple chaise longue usually frequented by emotional mothers of the brides. They sat down and she realised he took up more space than she was expecting and now they were quite close together.

'It's, um, nice.' He was taking it all in. 'This your business, is it?'

'Goodness no, I just alter the dresses.' She was done with the small talk. 'What was it you wanted to discuss?'

'Two things. One – Mum left her phone unattended and I had a quick look.'

'That's sneaky.'

He gave a cheeky little smile. 'I know. I felt bad about it.'

A thought occurred to her. 'Do you still live with your mum?'

'Still? No. I left home years ago.' He gave a tinny laugh. 'But . . . I am currently living in the same house as her. Yes.' He fixed her with a defiant stare.

'O-kay.' In her book that was exactly the same as still living with your mum.

'You wouldn't be judging me, would you?' She'd clearly hit a nerve.

'Certainly not,' she said, trying not to snigger. So much for his rugged manly image.

'Anyway.' He ran his bottom lip through his teeth. 'I'm sorry but the things this Davine was texting my mum was stuff only people in a relationship would share. I mean you don't suggest someone wears a particular colour of underwear if—'

Ella held up her hand to stop him talking. These were details she didn't need. It was bad enough without conjuring up lurid pictures in her mind. 'Okay. And the second thing?'

'I've got a proposition for you.' He raised an eyebrow suggestively.

She felt panic rising in her stomach. 'I'm seeing Stuart next Thursday—'

'Not that sort of proposition.' Did he just smirk? 'I've been thinking over our situation and while maybe you and I didn't see eye to eye, I think we can both agree that we'd prefer our parents to not be in a relationship with each other. I don't want Mum getting mixed up with some chancer.'

'Hey. She could do worse than my dad.'

48

'And she has. Look he might not be a grade A con man, but he is a cheat because he's still married, and my mum deserves better than that.' Ella opened her mouth, but Kit kept talking. 'And you want your folks to reach their ruby wedding anniversary, right?'

'Obviously but there's not a lot we can do about it.'

'Actually, I think there is. If we put our heads together I'm sure we could come up with some ways to push them apart.' He made a firm separating gesture with his hands.

'And exactly how do you propose we do that?'

'For a start I was thinking maybe you could add something to this discussion rather than keep being negative.'

Ella pulled her chin back in surprise and then remembered how that gave her about six chins in photographs so she jutted it out instead. 'I am not being negative. I'm being practical. They are two very different things. This isn't *The Parent Trap* and neither of us are Lindsay Lohan.'

He furrowed his brow. 'Weren't those kids trying to get their parents together rather than apart?'

It was a good job he was pretty because he was incredibly annoying. 'Yes, but the point I'm making is we're not little children which means getting our parents to do what we want is not going to be easy.' Although as Mummy's boy still lived at home perhaps he might have more leverage, but she wasn't brave enough to say.

'Maybe not. But the alternative is to accept that your parents' marriage is about to implode and my mother is likely to get her heart broken. I think it's worth a shot. Don't you?'

'I don't have any other ideas,' she conceded.

He checked his watch. 'You need to go. I won't keep you any longer. I'll get in touch about us having a proper planning meeting – maybe you could bring some ideas along. But play it cool when you see your parents tomorrow. Don't say anything that could derail our plans before we've even hatched them. Okay?'

Ella was astounded by his manner. She already had a list of

people who had bullied her in her life and she wasn't about to let Kit O'Leary add his name to it. 'Gosh you're bossy.'

He had the look of someone who wasn't used to being called out. 'It's known as leadership skills.'

'Only because you're a man. If you were a woman people would call you bossy. How about I get in touch with you?'

The corner of Kit's mouth twitched. 'Okay. I look forward to hearing from you.'

CHAPTER SEVEN

Lucy wasn't in the mood to try on the bridesmaid's dress again but Ella seemed to need to keep busy so she indulged her by putting it on. She teamed it with the unicorn head for comic effect.

'You look ridiculous,' said Ella.

'Brittany chose it.'

'Not the dress, the unicorn.'

'I can't look any worse,' said Lucy, striking a pose. Ella was giving her a hard stare. She reluctantly took it off. 'Seriously, what can you do to improve the faeces frock?' Lucy flapped the skirt.

Ella narrowed her eyes. 'I want to offer Brittany a few suggestions, but I need to be careful because I don't want to upset her.'

'Upset Brittany? She wasn't worried about deeply offending us when she chose these.'

'Don't be mean,' said Ella. 'And get on the stool then I can at least mark the length.'

'Don't mention stools. I look like one. One giant festering—'

'Stool,' said Ella, pointing forcefully.

Lucy did as she was told which meant she could see her reflection in the TV screen. It did not look good. 'Do you think perhaps it's a joke? A sort of friendship test to see if we will do literally anything for her. Including wearing these monstrosities.'

Ella, who was on her knees pinning the bottom of the dress, looked up at her. 'And you think she's going to turn up tonight with two more dresses that are completely flattering, make us look amazing and suit both our colourings.'

'That would be nice but possibly a long shot.'

Lucy bit the inside of her mouth while Ella worked away. She stared off into the middle distance deep in thought. 'You're quiet. Is everything okay?' asked Ella.

Ella had always been perceptive. Lucy had a lot on her mind right now and she knew she'd have to update them on the Cory split when Brittany arrived so she'd wait rather than have to explain it twice. And if she was being truthful it wasn't the only thing bothering her. 'There's this case at work. I can't tell you any details because of confidentiality but I thought it was going to be a straightforward one and it's not.'

'Kids involved?'

'Yeah. It's not nice. Had the mum in tears in my office.'

'Can you help her?' Ella knelt back on her haunches.

'Yeah, I think so. I mean I can sort the divorce and make sure the kids are protected but it won't stop her having to go to court. Sometimes I wish I could wave a magic wand.'

'I know you'll do all you can and you might not realise it but I'm sure you'll make a huge difference to this family.'

'Thanks.' Sometimes you needed to hear that.

'I think we can make things look a bit better even if they haven't really changed.'

'I guess,' said Lucy.

'I meant the dress.' Ella hoiked up the puffball sleeves and pinned them down.

The doorbell rang and Ella went to answer it.

Brittany came in and on seeing Lucy both her hands shot to her face. 'What have you done?'

Uh oh, here we go, thought Lucy.

'I was having a play around with some options. If you don't like them, they're only pinned,' said Ella quickly.

'Like them. I love them!' Brittany gave Ella a hug.

'Great. I was thinking we could maybe be a bit more drastic with the neckline and also add a cream sash. To emphasise the dress shape and to highlight your coffee and cream theme.' Ella's words tumbled out at speed.

'Latte,' said Brittany.

'Yes, latte. And I could run us up a little shrug each in the same cream fabric as the sash but we'd need to lose the puffball sleeves. It's entirely up to you. These are just suggestions.' Ella held up her palms.

'But they're great suggestions that would really make these dresses unique,' cut in Lucy, nodding enthusiastically in the hope of swaying Brittany.

Brittany pouted. 'Difficult choice because I do think the sleeves are fun. Don't you?'

Lucy grimaced but Ella was giving her a death stare making her change it to what she hoped was a neutral expression. Brittany looked to Ella for an answer. Lucy held two pairs of crossed fingers behind her back.

'I think puffball is maybe a little . . . vintage, and I know you were going for a more modern look,' said Ella. Always the diplomat. 'And I could tack one dress first before you make any firm decisions.'

Lucy held her breath. 'Okay,' said Brittany at last. 'Let's bring them up to date.' Lucy punched the air. At least something was going her way.

***

Ella was pleased to be curled up on her sofa with a glass of red wine in one hand and a large slice of cheese pizza in the other.

'Kit sounds like a right arse,' said Lucy, after Ella had filled them in on recent events. 'Sounds like he's using you to control his mother's life.'

'I think that's a bit of a stretch,' said Ella, a little surprised that she was defending Kit of all people. 'He's concerned about a parent, same as I am.'

'It's probably more a tribal defensive thing,' said Brittany, licking tomato sauce off her fingers. 'You know. From when we lived in caves and hunted woolly mammoths. They still have the same urges as early man.'

'Neanderthal man has a lot to answer for,' said Lucy.

'You don't really think men are still like that, do you?' asked Ella, putting down her wine because her pizza needed two hands.

'Totally,' said Lucy.

Brittany nodded her agreement. 'I don't think they realise it or even mean it. It's stamped on their DNA. It's the need to protect. Anyone want the last piece?' Brittany pointed at the pizza box.

Lucy shook her head. 'I'd best not have any more. I won't be using sex to burn off calories for a while.'

'You've not dumped Cory?' Ella loved Lucy but as soon as anyone got close she ran for the hills.

'No. *He* dumped me.' Brittany gasped. 'I know right? And get this. The reason is because he thinks he's found a serious relationship. I mean, please. Cory will be bored and back under my White Company duvet cover before you can say Kama Sutra.'

'I'm sorry,' said Ella, reaching across and giving Lucy's arm a squeeze. Lucy always made out she was indestructible and nothing ever phased her but Ella had known her a long while and she wasn't as tough as she thought she was. Yes, there was an outer shell for protection, but underneath Lucy was equally as vulnerable as everyone else she just did a better job of hiding it.

'I'm fine. It's his loss.' Lucy took a large slug of wine. 'It's not like I wanted to marry him or anything.' She shuddered.

'Don't shoot me down,' said Brittany, waving the last piece of pizza. 'But maybe you shouldn't be blinkered. I wasn't looking for love when Grant ran his supermarket trolley into my ankle. But there it was in all its bruise-inducing glory in the middle aisle of Iceland.'

'Nor was I when Todd bought me a drink in that bar.'

'Er, yeah you were,' said Lucy. 'You both were. It's like you two constantly have a vibe. It's not a criticism, it's the way we're programmed. Women are expected to find a man and settle down. And that's fine if that's what you want. It's not for me.'

'You've not tried it so how do you know?' asked Brittany.

'Because I know I don't want to have to compromise on every little thing. To have to stop and think before I work late or accept an invitation out, or having to iron his stuff as well as my own to avoid looking petty, and watch stuff I don't like on the telly, or have to see his parents every Christmas and make space in my wardrobe for his stuff.' At last she took a breath. Brittany's eyes were wide. For a whole minute nobody spoke.

Ella decided it was probably best not to argue with her. She searched for a change of subject. 'Let's get back to my problem. What on earth do I say to my parents tomorrow?' She regarded the two solemn faces staring blankly at her.

'I hate to say it, but I think Kit is right,' said Brittany, leaning back and patting her middle which Pirate, appearing out of nowhere, took as an invitation and jumped onto her lap. He kneaded her leggings before curling up and going to sleep.

Lucy sucked her bottom lip. 'I think you need to ask a few key questions but they have to be uber subtle. Open questions that will get your dad talking. The more he talks the more likely he is to trip himself up.'

'But what if he does trip himself up and Mum notices and the whole thing detonates in front of me.' Ella felt sick thinking about it.

'Then you need to get him on his own,' said Lucy, topping up her wine.

Ella didn't like to admit exactly how uneasy she was about seeing her parents. Usually she was excited to catch up with them as she didn't get to see them as often as she'd like. And while her parents did annoying things that all parents do – like her mum trying to feed her up and her dad checking her car tyres on the quiet – there was also something reassuring about it. They only did those things because they cared.

She had a waft of nostalgia as she turned off by the lavender farm and pootled through Norfolk's windy roads, past brick-and-flint cottages and pretty gardens. She drove her car onto their gravel drive and her mum was out to greet her before she switched off the engine. She looked well and was smiling. Ella was already analysing things. *Act normal*, she told herself. *Pretend nothing has changed*. Although an annoying little Kit-sounding noise in the back of her mind told her everything had.

'Hi Mum,' said Ella, getting out of the car.

Her mother wrapped her in a tight hug. 'It's good to see you,' she said without letting go. 'It's a lovely day so I've done us a chicken Caesar salad but looking at you I should have done a hotpot. Have you lost weight?' asked her mum, looking concerned as she ushered her inside.

'My weight is fine. I'm fine,' said Ella, following her through to the kitchen.

'How's that awful boss of yours?' asked Sandy, giving the bowl of already prepared salad another hearty toss.

'I challenged her this week,' said Ella.

'Well done you. How did she respond?'

'Basically threatened to sack me.'

Sandy sucked in a breath. 'That woman is out of order. You should call her bluff. She won't be able to find someone with your skills as easily as she thinks.'

'I would be out of a job though, so maybe not the best way to prove a point.' Ella nicked a grape from the fruit bowl.

'You could set up on your own. You've got the talent. Look at that prom dress you made yourself. It was fabulous.' Sandy divided the salad between three plates.

'Nice idea but premises in town are expensive and I'm not sure I'm cut out to be a boss.'

'Don't put yourself down. You could do anything you put your mind to.'

'Thanks, Mum. Anyway, how are you?' It was hard not to watch for a reaction.

'Busy with the show. If I have to sew sequins on another leotard I might—'

'No, not the show. You. How are you?' Was that too forceful, Ella wondered, as her mother tilted her head.

'I'm fine. And Nan sends her love. Your dad and I popped over there last weekend. We were thinking of having a barbecue here for Nan's birthday next month. I've pencilled a few dates on the calendar, let me know what works for you. Grab the croutons and we'll eat outside,' said Sandy, picking up two plates.

It was bright and the garden looked a picture. 'Dad's been busy out here,' said Ella, sitting down.

'It's only a few new plants. Have you got any news?'

Kit flashed into Ella's head which gave her a bit of a shock. Her mother was waiting for a response. 'Er, me? No nothing newsworthy. But Brittany brought over the bridesmaids' dresses.'

'How exciting, what colour are they?'

'Latte,' said Ella.

Sandy wrinkled her nose. 'What colour is that?'

'It's basically brown.'

'Oh dear.' They heard the sound of tyres on gravel, followed by a car door. 'Here's your father. Fingers crossed he played well or we'll never hear the last of it,' she said with a chuckle. Her light attitude broke Ella's heart a little.

Her dad came straight through the house and into the garden and gave her a kiss on the cheek. She hadn't been prepared for the anger which washed through her at the sight of him. How could he be cheating on her mum? She tensed her jaw to stop her blurting something out. He walked around the table and kissed his wife. His hand lingered on her shoulder and Sandy patted it automatically. They were so in tune with each other. What the hell had changed?

'This looks good.' He stole a piece of bacon from Sandy's plate and she gave him a friendly swipe.

'Yours is on the counter and there's extra sauce in the fridge if you want it. How was your game?'

'We won by two shots,' he said, giving them a double thumbs up, before strolling back inside to get his lunch.

Everything was completely normal so how come everything felt like it had changed?

CHAPTER EIGHT

At lunch Ella kept fairly quiet and answered any direct questions but otherwise studied her parents. If her father was cheating, there was nothing here to give it away. She wasn't sure if that worried her more. Was he far better at deception than she'd ever thought possible? They went for a walk along the beach where a few families were enjoying the sunshine; some children playing rounders using upturned sandcastle buckets as bases; a toddler squealing with delight as the gentle lap of the water met his toes and others stretched out on towels catching some sun. Otherwise they virtually had it to themselves. It fascinated Ella because she knew a couple of miles along, the beaches at Hunstanton would be teeming with visitors on a sunny day like today. Heacham was the shy cardigan-wearing neighbour to Hunstanton's party girl – a bit like her and Lucy.

Ella and her parents walked together and chatted about old, shared memories which made them all laugh. It was lovely and yet somehow tinged with sadness like the yellowing pages of a much-loved paperback. Kit could have got this all wrong. Maybe her dad wasn't this mystery Davine his mum was sexting.

'I'm going to head back. You two can stay,' said Sandy.

'Yes,' said Ella, hoping she hadn't sounded too keen. 'If that's okay.'

'She's still daddy's girl.' Her father gave her a one-armed hug and then tickled her ribs, exactly like he'd always done.

'See you both back at home,' said Sandy. She pulled her sunglasses from her hair, put them on and strolled up the beach. Ella watched her go. Her mother was tall, elegant and stylish – she looked amazing. Ella hoped she'd look that good in her fifties.

David waved a hand in front of her face. 'Penny for them.'

'Mum is beautiful.'

Her father followed her gaze. 'Yes she is.'

She badly wanted to ask if he was cheating on her. But she couldn't. Part of her didn't want an argument and she also didn't want to have to explain to Kit that she'd messed things up. And what if it was all a fantasy? How much upset would that cause if she accused her own father of having an affair?

'Shall we walk up to the bench?' suggested Ella.

'You're a creature of habit, Ella Briggs.' He was right. There was a bench that she and her dad had always walked to, for as far back as she could remember. The bench was where they had sat her down as a child and brushed sand from her toes. Where they'd wrapped her in towels when she was cold from swimming in the sea. Where they would sit with hot drinks from the little café in the cooler months. It was an anchor she was keen to cling to right now.

They strolled along the beach and Ella composed her question in her mind. 'Tell me what you've been up to, apart from the garden and golf.'

'Not a lot. We saw Nan the other day.'

'Yes, Mum told me all about that. I'll mark on the calendar which weekends I'm free for the barbecue. What else?' She looked along the beach and counted the breakwaters until they became a blur to avoid staring at her father.

'Lounging in the garden when it's been sunny. Walks down here. Oh and badminton on a Tuesday night.'

'With Mum?' She shouldn't have queried that.

'Yes. Why?'

Sod it. Now what was she supposed to say? 'Only she sounded a bit bored with playing badminton when I spoke to her on the phone the other week.' She was the most awful liar.

'Really? Huh. I hope she's not playing just for me.' Those were the words of a kind and caring husband, not an adulterer. Ella was starting to think Kit had got this all wrong.

***

Lucy had assumed the hen night would be the fun part of being a bridesmaid – how wrong could she be? Brittany's sister, Lorraine, was chief bridesmaid and therefore had the responsibility of organising the hen night jollities. It was abundantly clear from the many emails that she was taking this particular part of her role seriously. Ella had already declared that she would go with whatever the majority wanted to do but Lucy couldn't relinquish her liberty so easily.

While she did appreciate it wasn't easy to plan an event which was suitable for a wide variety of women including aunts, colleagues and friends she didn't feel it needed the eight emails she had received thus far on the subject. Lucy wasn't looking forward to meeting Lorraine if she talked the way she typed – at great length and without ever getting to the point. Inevitably, on top of the eight original emails from Lorraine, there was now an untangleable train of replies from the circa fifteen people invited. Why, oh why, did people always hit reply all?

It was hard to keep her mind on fun and frivolity when her day job was taking up so much space. The Maxwell divorce case had turned nasty. The husband had been outside the office. He'd started out reasonable but had soon turned to shouting when he realised she wasn't about to tell him where his wife and children had moved to. If she was honest it had shaken her a little. She'd been challenged before, of course she had, most frequently in a court room but there was something about this man that was etched in her mind. His vehemence at being innocent mainly. Her focus had to be on doing the best she could for the wife and children and that was all she could do. It had also conjured up memories of one of her mother's unsavoury boyfriends who had shouted at her and blamed her for causing trouble. She returned her attention to the job in hand.

There were lots of gushing emails about them all wanting to make it extra special for Brittany closely followed by their own thinly veiled requirements. You'd have thought Brittany was a child princess rather than a thirty-year-old veterinary nurse who loved 80s disco. Of course Lucy wanted Brittany to have a good time, but she knew that could be achieved quite simply by her being surrounded by people she liked with a glass of something fizzy in her hand. Lorraine had dismissed this suggestion because *they could definitely do better than that for someone as special as Brittany.*

Lucy waded her way through threads about who else should be invited, preferred dates, duration, allergies and far too much detail regarding Auntie Rita's skin condition. But it was the many excited suggestions that almost tipped her over the edge. They ranged from Butler in the Buff to Inflatable Slip n Slide with optional jelly add-on, via Body Painting and Zombie Bride Escape Room.

By the seventh email trail it appeared they were honing things down and thankfully there was no more mention of the Dominatrix Masterclass although someone who signed themselves off as Midge was still up for this at another time if anyone fancied it – nobody had replied. Lorraine had summarised the key requirements for the hen night: a weekend event at least two weeks before the wedding and something that would be fun, cultured and mean-ingful. Lucy wasn't sure that any of the things she'd seen mentioned would fit this criteria and was almost looking forward to seeing what email eight would reveal as the header purported to divulge the proposed hen night extravaganza in detail.

'Crap on a cracker,' muttered Lucy as she read the eighth email. Lorraine had outdone herself. There was a timed itinerary and a quick scan told Lucy she was going to hate every minute of it.

While she was shaking her head at email number eight and its excited reply train, email number nine popped into her in box. Another wonderfully worded passive-aggressive tome from Lorraine reiterating her job title of Chief Bridesmaid and asking everyone to please deposit £224.94 each into her bank account ASAP and at the latest by the end of the next day. It was elaborately decorated with champagne bottles, pounding hearts and smiley face emojis. Lucy puffed out a breath. Nope she was never, ever getting married.

⁎

Ella wasn't sure that having a virtual stranger come to her house was the best idea, but they couldn't talk freely at Kit's because he lived with his mum. She'd suggested another pub but Kit felt they were noisy and it would be easier if they met at hers. If he was a murderer then this was a very convoluted way of identifying his prey – nevertheless she had Lucy on Alexa Drop In, meaning she could shout and help would be on its way. He'd said he couldn't stop long which was a relief. Ella hated it when people outstayed their welcome and she never felt she could say anything for fear of seeming rude.

He rang the doorbell exactly on time. She checked her hair in the mirror as she passed. Not that it mattered how she looked because she didn't care what Kit thought. She opened the door and got an instant waft of aftershave. 'I brought beer,' he said, holding up four bottles.

Her face probably gave away her thoughts on beer but Kit didn't seem to notice. 'I've got the non-alcoholic version for me because I'm driving.'

'Wild,' she said, beckoning him inside.

'A fan of drunk driving are you?'

Straight into the fight, thought Ella. 'No. That's very sensible of you. This way.' She was in for a fun evening. 'I'll stick to coffee if that's okay with you.'

She directed him into the small living room and went to sort things in the kitchen. When she walked into the room he was having a good look at the photographs she had on the wall. 'This your mum?' he asked.

'Yes, that's her.' Ella braced herself for a snide comment.

'She's a good-looking woman.'

What should she say to that? 'Thanks. Were you expecting her to look like Godzilla?'

He chuckled. 'I don't know really.' She handed him a glass and a bottle opener and he sat down in the chair Pirate favoured. 'How did it go on Saturday?'

She took a seat on the sofa. 'I didn't notice any cracks in my parents' relationship.'

He sucked in a breath. 'Are we still in denial?'

How could she not bristle at that? 'I'm simply pointing out that there is still a possibility that you could have got this all wrong.'

'Then why are we about to work out how to split them up?'

It was a good point. 'Okay maybe I am still a bit in denial. But we have no concrete proof.'

His expression softened a little. 'If this is all some crazy misunderstanding then we'd only be splitting up two people who aren't together in the first place, so no harm done.'

That made her feel better. 'Okay. I've been having a think like you suggested. And I propose we draw up a list of areas of attack and then whittle it down to our best options.' She held up a pad and pen.

Kit was concentrating on pouring his beer. 'And what options have you come up with?' He eyeballed her as the beer foamed up.

She'd not got that far. She was hoping the list idea was enough. Work had been super busy and this really wasn't something she wanted to spend too long thinking about because it instantly upset her. 'Well . . .' Why was it impossible to think straight when he was watching her like that? 'You see the thing is . . .'

'You have no ideas do you?'

'Yes I do.' She took a moment to think of something. 'Maybe we focus on my mum's good points and highlight to Dad how wonderful his wife is and then he won't . . . um . . . want to do anything with your mum.' Her cheeks flushed and Kit's mouth twitched at the corner.

'You're suggesting we big up your mum.' She nodded. Ella was quite pleased with the idea she'd conjured off the top of her head. 'To remind your father what a fabulous wife he has as well as having my wonderful mother as his mistress. He'll feel like a dog with two tails. And after we've boosted his ego to a stratospheric level tell me how will this split them up?'

And that was the problem with being put on the spot. She had another think. 'How about the other way around. We tell him everything that's wrong with your mum. All her bad habits. All the irritating little things she does that he may not have noticed but will drive him crackers.' She was on a roll. 'Ooh and all the skeletons in her closet.'

Kit did not look like he was keen on that idea. 'What exactly are you saying about my mum?'

Ella realised her mistake but before she could apologise Pirate came to her rescue. He jumped on the arm of the chair right next to Kit making him jump. When Kit turned to look straight at Pirate he recoiled. 'What the f—'

'Hey!'

'Sorry that is one ugly . . .' He dragged his eyes away from Pirate to look at Ella who was giving him a hard stare. 'What the hell happened to it?'

She was tempted to say 'he's the last person who called my dad a charmer' but instead she opted for the truth. 'He got hit by a moped.'

'Poor thing.' Kit looked momentarily concerned.

'He lost a leg, an eye, part of his lip and he's deaf in one ear,' explained Ella.

His concern had been replaced by a grin. 'Goes by the name of Lucky?'

'Yes, he does,' said Ella deadpan.

The grin fell from Kit's face. 'Really?'

She was pleased to have caught him out. 'No. His name is Pirate.'

'How appropriate. Although he is lucky to have landed a home like yours.'

Pirate eyed the stranger as best he could and then stuck his tongue out at him. He didn't exactly stick his tongue out, but he had this unfortunate habit of letting his tongue loll out of the gap in his lip and Ella liked the idea that he was blowing a raspberry at Kit on her behalf. Pirate walked over Kit's lap a few times, evidently trod on something he shouldn't have because she saw Kit wince. Pirate seemed to decide that if Kit was sitting on his chair then by rights he could sit on him.

'I take it you're not allergic?' she asked.

'No. I'm more of a dog person. But he's fine there.'

'Good because I wasn't going to move him,' said Ella. Something in Kit's manner brought out her defiant side.

Kit's eyebrow jumped at her comment. 'Right. Back to our parents. Any other ideas?'

'No. How about we hear what suggestions *you* have come up with?'

He scratched his head. 'I think we need to keep them apart. Maybe come up with reasons why they can't meet up.'

'Ground them you mean?' She tilted her head.

'What we need is to know when they're planning on meeting up and then spring something on them moments beforehand,' he suggested.

'Great idea with one tiny flaw. We have no way of knowing

when they are meeting. It's not like my dad will have put it on the kitchen calendar.'

'True. But Mum will have to let me know.'

'Why ever would she do that?'

He broke eye contact and became distracted by the cat, concentrating on giving him a head rub. Pirate gazed up at him adoringly – traitor. At last Kit spoke: 'We share childcare duties.'

'Oh, I see.' She hadn't been expecting that. 'I didn't realise you were a dad.'

'I'm not. Isaac is my nephew. My sister's son. She died in an accident at work . . . well anyway.' His head snapped up and he glared at Ella, as if somehow she had forced him to share something he now wished he hadn't.

'I'm sorry, that must have been hard on you all.' She instantly felt for Kit and his loss. Ella had sailed through life only losing a couple of grandparents when she was small. She'd not had someone close to her ripped from her life and she couldn't imagine how hard that had been for Kit. She was reminded that you never knew what other people were dealing with.

He nodded. 'Thanks. We share responsibility for Isaac.' He looked to the ceiling. 'Responsibility is the wrong word. That makes him sound like a burden and he's not. Mum and I let each other know when we're going to be out. Someone has to either be with him or, if he's at school, near enough to collect him if he gets sick.'

'How old is he?'

'He's four. He's into building stuff and digging holes.' Kit's face lit up as he spoke. He seemed to sense Ella studying him and he swallowed. 'You know what kids are like.'

Nope she had no idea. Kids weren't her thing at all. Why did people assume that all women knew what kids were like? They glared awkwardly at each other for a moment. Ella cracked first. 'The next time your mum is seeing Davine we need to come up with a way to stop one or both of them from going.'

He nodded. 'Do you know what, Ella Briggs? I think we have the makings of a plan.'

The next day Ella completed a final fitting with a bride and returned to her workstation to see she had five missed calls. Her heart sank when she saw they were all from Kit. She called him back.

'At last,' he said. 'I've messaged you but you didn't reply.'

'I am busy at work.'

'I'm guessing it's right up there with UN ambassador,' he said. She didn't respond. This was exactly the sort of thing Todd used to do. 'You know I'm joking, right?' he asked.

'Shall I belittle your job and see if you find it equally amusing?'

'I'm sorry, Ella. I honestly wasn't trying to do that. You're absolutely right and I apologise. Please feel free to belittle my job.'

In the silence that followed Ella realised she didn't know what he did for a living. 'And what is it that you do?'

'I run my own building company.'

She hated being put on the spot. 'Then unless you are building a reimagined Taj Mahal I doubt what you do is earth-shattering either.'

'We're currently building a community centre for under-privileged kids.'

Ella rolled her eyes. She couldn't catch a break with this guy. 'Well done, Mother Teresa. Why was it you were desperate to speak to me anyway?'

'Mum has a date with Davine.' Something squeezed at her gut. 'I suggest—'

'Ella, is that a work call?' Wanda was glaring from the doorway.

'Er, no.' Why didn't she just lie? She was rubbish. 'Was there something urgent?'

'This is urgent,' said Kit into her ear.

'Bog off,' she replied. Wanda's eyes pinged wide.

'Not you, Wanda. The person on the phone.' She waved her mobile for emphasis.

'Wanda? What sort of name is that?' asked Kit with a chuckle. She ignored him.

'I wanted to talk to you about the garment steamer,' said Wanda. Ella waited but Wanda was still looking at her. 'Okay.'

'Perhaps you could take that call in your own time?'

'She sounds like a bundle of fun,' muttered Kit.

'I'll call you back this evening,' Ella told Kit.

'No, we need to—' She ended the call. She'd deal with him later.

'What is urgent about the garment steamer?' asked Ella, now that it had been pointed out to her Ella was increasingly irritated by Wanda's attitude towards her.

'It needs a service arranging,' said Wanda and she walked away. Ella was tempted to throw something at the door but the only thing to hand was a bag of sequins and she knew how long they would take to pick up, instead she settled for a silent scream.

Wanda's face reappeared and she baulked at the sight of Ella with her mouth open wide and vibrating with pent-up rage. Ella stopped her scream, sat bolt upright and felt colour bloom on her cheeks. Wanda shook her head like a disappointed teacher. 'And we're out of coffee,' she added.

CHAPTER NINE

Ella's day didn't improve much. She had a bride in tears because she'd put weight on and not just a couple of pounds. It was the difference between a gliding zip and two sides of a fastening that were as likely to join up again as Liam and Noel Gallagher. She had reassured the bride that she would let it out as much as she could and the bride had pledged to stop stress eating doughnuts so hopefully between them they would find a solution. Each time Ella encountered her Wanda shook her head and it was driving her crackers. For once she was glad when Wanda sloped off early.

Ella had run herself a bath with Pirate watching her from the safe distance of the toilet cistern. He was fascinated by the bubbles but knew not to get too close after one unfortunate encounter a few months prior where he'd discovered exiting a bath with one back leg was virtually impossible to do unaided. Although his thrashing about had fluffed the bubbles up a treat.

Ella lay there and, as she often did, she overanalysed her day. She was getting more and more fed up with Wanda. She knew there were worse jobs and worse bosses but it was starting to get her down. She felt like the junior, not someone who was skilled at her job. She never received any praise, just criticism. She wondered if Wanda only employed her to have someone to lord it over. There were plenty of freelance seamstresses whom the shop could direct brides to, she didn't have to employ Ella. But then Wanda would miss the extra cash that the packaged service generated. And the brides liked the convenience of it too.

Ella dried off and put on her Minnie Mouse pyjamas – her parents had bought them as a joke Christmas present but they were actually very comfortable. She put her long hair into a towel turban and settled herself on the sofa while a pasta bake, which she had hastily thrown together, cooked in the oven.

Pirate joined her and was pummelling her legs to make them extra comfy when the doorbell rang. She went to the door but given her outfit she wasn't opening it unless it was either a close friend or an emergency on the level of *we need to evacuate your house because marauding zombies are heading this way.*

'Who is it?' she called.

'Kit.'

Ella had a minor paddy and stamped her bare feet on the cold tiles. 'Now's not a good time, Kit.'

'You didn't call me back.'

Bugger it, she'd got caught up with work and forgotten. 'Sorry. I'll call—'

'Could you open the door?' She scratched an eyebrow. Decision time. 'Are you still there?' he asked.

She was being daft. She could wear what she liked in her own house, and she had no need to be on ceremony for him. Ella opened the door. She saw him take in her pyjamas and a smile instantly appeared on Kit's face quickly spreading into a broad grin. 'What?' she said, tilting her chin in challenge.

He shook his head as he came inside. 'Nothing at all. I like what you've done with your hair.'

'Anything else? I mean do please get the comedy lines off your chest.'

His grin diminished. 'I can see this isn't a good time.' Ella reached for the door in the hope he was leaving. 'I won't keep you long,' he added, walking through to the living room.

She followed him. He confidently picked up Pirate, sat down in the chair and placed the cat on his lap. Ella curled up on the sofa and couldn't stop a giant yawn escaping.

'That boss of yours is a bundle of laughs,' he said.

'I don't suppose you have that problem, running your own business.'

'I have other problems, but no, the boss isn't one of them. He's a great guy.' He flashed her a toothpaste commercial smile to show he was joking.

She was tempted to say his boss was also annoying, infuriating and highly aggravating but she didn't have the energy to antagonise him. 'I'd like to be my own boss one day.' She wasn't sure why she'd said it out loud.

'Why not now?' He watched her closely.

'Premises are too expensive.'

'Why do you need premises. Couldn't you work from home?'

'Not really. It wouldn't look very professional having brides in here.' She indicated her tiny living room.

'You could easily convert your garage.'

'Probably not that easy. It'd all cost money. I'd likely need to get planning permission and plans drawn up and stuff. I don't know if it would be possible.'

'I do. We do that sort of work all the time. You don't need planning permission. You just need to get agreement from the council to run a business from here. You might also want to check with your mortgage provider to be on the safe side. It's an integral garage on a newish property – converting the space would be straightforward. I noticed you've already got access from the garage into the house. All it needs is to replace the garage door with a front door and a window. Line, insulate and plaster the walls, fit the electrics, put in a proper ceiling and relevel the floor – job done.'

How could he have solved her problem so easily? 'I'm not sure I could afford it.'

'I'll take a quick look before I leave and I'll send you a quote. I'll do you a good deal.' Kit gave her a close-the-deal smile which she suspected he flashed quite often. Although he did have a sexy smile which matched the rest of him.

She could see no harm in a quote. 'Er, okay. Thanks.'

'My pleasure. Right. Project Split. What's the plan to disrupt the rendezvous?'

Ella stretched out on the sofa and patted her lap to encourage Pirate to move off Kit. He barely opened his eye. If he kept this up she was going to downgrade him to the cheap tuna. Kit was looking expectantly at her. 'Right. Could you say that Isaac is sick?' she suggested.

Kit tensed. 'You don't cry wolf over a child's health. And I wouldn't want to teach him to lie.'

Ella was taken aback by the force of his reply. 'A no would have done.'

'Sorry. You're right. I'm a bit protective of him.'

'Understood. Apology accepted.'

They nodded at each other like Victorians about to dance. 'I could say I didn't feel well,' said Kit.

'There you go then.' She stifled another yawn. At this rate she'd fall asleep in her pasta bake.

'But I never get ill. Mum would think there was something seriously wrong with me.'

'You could have picked up a bug. Twenty-four-hour tummy trouble. Lock yourself in the loo and spray a lot of deodorant before you come out. I'd believe that.'

'We'll call that Plan B.' He didn't look convinced. 'How could we derail your dad?'

'Anything that needs him to come all the way over here will make him super suspicious or, worse still, very worried.'

'Urgent phone call then?'

'About what?'

'I don't know, Ella. What causes you trouble in life?'

She gave him her best 'Are you serious?' face. 'Nothing much,' she said, while she ignored the long list accumulating in her mind like someone was speed typing.

Kit fixed her with an intent gaze. 'Go on. I'm interested.'

Ella paused. He was still waiting. 'I hate having a mortgage and owing money. I can't handle it when people don't like me. Like Wanda. I have tried many times to connect with her but it's impossible. I worry what people think of me. I'm a woman who doesn't feel maternal.' She watched for the usual surprise she saw on everyone's face when she said that, but it didn't show on Kit's. 'I fear that's impacting my parents because I'm an only child which means I'm potentially taking away their chance to be grand-parents.' She concentrated on a pyjama button. She looked up and immediately felt self-conscious for opening up like that. 'Sorry. I'm waffling.'

Kit wore a kind smile. 'For what it's worth. I think you're worrying about what other people think rather than what you want. If it feels like it's the right decision for you then that's all you can go with. You shouldn't have to compromise to please others.'

She nodded. 'Thanks.' She felt vulnerable and yet at the same time it felt safe to open up to Kit. Maybe it was because he'd previously shared with her about his sister's death. She wasn't sure. But now she needed to get them back on subject. 'But there's nothing there that's going to have Dad dashing over.'

'Could you make something up about Stuart? How is Stuart by the way?' A smile played on his lips.

She'd almost forgotten about her blind date. There had been a couple of text exchanges but nothing for a few days. 'He's fine as far as I know.'

Kit arched an eyebrow. 'Not had that date yet then?'

'No, but we will. Assuming his car is fixed.'

She could almost see the light bulb go on above Kit's head.

'How about your car breaks down and you call your dad. I could loosen something under the engine.'

Was he for real? 'Firstly my dad knows nothing about car engines, second I'm a member of a breakdown service and third why would I drive a car anywhere with a loose thingy under my bonnet?'

Kit rolled his lips together. 'Fair point. Where does that leave us?'

'I think we're back to you and your gippy tummy.'

Kit looked resigned. 'Great. Okay we'll go with that. I'd best leave you in peace. I'll keep you posted.' He lifted Pirate into his arms and stood up. She swore he could have taken the cat home with him, he seemed quite happy with Kit. The two-faced feline. He put him down on the chair and Pirate curled up again. 'I'll check out your garage and send that quote across.'

She was interested to see how much it would cost but she wasn't going to start making plans any time soon. People like her didn't become their own boss just like that and certainly not on a whim of some random builder.

Wedding season was starting to pick up and Ella's work diary was busy. She was doing final fittings for a number of brides every day. But Wanda had managed to squeeze in a first fitting. Ella really didn't know how she was going to manage even one more gown. Her schedule was maxed out already.

'Wanda, why have you booked this in?' asked Ella.

'Because we sold her the dress.'

Ella resisted the temptation to roll her eyes. 'I figured that part but why are we not explaining that we have no more capacity for alterations this side of October?' There were other seamstresses who the brides could go to. It wasn't as convenient but there were other options. Although Ella had to concede that anyone worth their salt would likely already be booked up.

'She bought it from us last year,' said Wanda, looking disinterested.

'Then why wasn't she already on the list?'

Wanda sighed heavily. 'Because that wedding didn't go ahead. I had sold her the full package and I wasn't about to give a refund. She held onto the dress and now she's going ahead this year. Recycling at its best.'

Ella was interested now. 'Same groom?'

'No idea.' Wanda returned to her computer screen where she was studying toenail fungus cream.

Ella would have liked an apology or at least some admission from Wanda that another dress on her already maxed out list was unacceptable. She waited but Wanda said nothing. 'This has to be the last one. I literally can't fit in any more. I will be working all hours as it is.' Ella got no response, so she walked away before she said something she'd regret. She'd made it across the shop before Wanda called after her.

'That is what I pay you for.'

Ella froze. She turned on her heel and was heading back to give Wanda a piece of her mind when the door opened and the bride-to-be with the recycled dress came in. Ella halted. Standing up to Wanda would have to wait. Ella fixed on a professional smile and went to greet the customer.

Ashley, the bride, had brought her mum with her which was always nice. Ella checked all the key details, gave the women a glass of cheap fizz each and moved the gown into the cubicle. 'Okay, Ashley. If you want to pop your clothes off apart from your pants and shoes. Let me know if you need a hand putting the dress on,' said Ella, pulling the curtain across. 'And stand on the podium when you're ready. Be careful not to tread on the dress.' The mother of the bride waited on the chaise longue and got out a fresh packet of tissues.

Ella hovered around checking the clock on the quiet. She really needed to get on. She couldn't hear much happening inside the cubicle. A dress as extravagant as this one made a noise when you put it on. 'Is everything okay, Ashley?' asked Ella.

'Fine.' Came back the clipped response.

'She was out last night,' whispered her mum. 'I think she's got a bit of a headache.'

Great, thought Ella, a bride with a raging hangover. Eventually she heard movement. 'Ready,' said Ashley and Ella joined her behind the heavy curtain.

Ella did a quick assessment. The dress was a good fit. She was relieved there wasn't a great deal to do. She set about pinning up the bottom of the dress. Ashley was quiet and didn't engage in any conversation. She was looking quite pale. Ella hurried along and at last pushed the final pin in to place.

'There, let's show your mum.'

Ella pulled back the curtain, Ashley stepped out and on cue her mum burst into tears. Ashley walked out to view herself in the overly large mirrors of the shop.

'You look beautiful,' said her mother with a sniff.

'Ashley, more fizz?' asked Ella, waving the bottle in front of her to distract her from her reflection.

Ashley and Ella made eye contact through the mirror. Something passed between them. Whether it was the change in shade of Ashley's cheeks to white with a hint of mould green or the slight retch, Ella wasn't sure but as fast as she could she put down the bottle and in one swift motion she unzipped the dress and got it off Ashley as quickly as she could. 'Toilet's in the back,' said Ella, pointing.

'What's the matter?' asked her mother. But before she had finished the sentence Ashley was already running through the shop in just a tiny thong and high heels.

There was a slam of the toilet door followed immediately by the sound of vomiting at very high volume. It was even enough to drag Wanda out of her office.

'Is everything all right?' she asked as the retching continued.

'Might be something she ate,' said her mum, looking embarrassed.

There was a moment where nobody spoke but the noises coming from the loo were too much for Ella. It sounded like a sea lion attempting to sing opera.

'How many bridesmaids?' she asked, trying to ignore the horrors reverberating from the small toilet.

The woman looked hugely relieved to have something to discuss. 'Four. All adults. She's not bought the dresses yet. There's a difference of opinion on them. Sorry.' She directed the apology at Wanda who was now staring in the direction of their small loo and cringing.

'That's lovely,' said Ella as Ashley made a noise like Pirate when he had a furball stuck.

Eventually the toilet door opened and a pallid-looking Ashley crept out with her hands covering her breasts.

'You've got . . .' Ella indicated something unpleasant on Ashley's chin. Automatically her hand shot to her face uncovering her right boob. A cheer went up from outside the shop. She looked past Ella and screamed. Two teenage boys were staring wide-eyed through the glass and holding up their mobile phones.

CHAPTER TEN

Lucy had had one of those days. The sort where even the things that did go right were wrong. She'd had a new client who wanted to file for divorce because he thought his wife was about to start proceedings and he wanted to get in first. A wife who had proactively devolved the shedload of dodgy stuff her husband was involved in to his boss and when he was fired had been dismayed that he couldn't afford to pay more child support because he'd lost his job. And the couple who had shouted at each other for half an hour straight over who should have their collection of ornamental camels.

On top of all that she had also been bombarded by frantic calls from the father in the Maxwell case where the daughter had confessed that the marks on her body were from his abuse. Mr Maxwell was trying to find out where his family had moved to. Lucy was obviously not going to tell him or pass on any messages, something he struggled to comprehend. Each of his calls became more desperate until it ended with Lucy threatening to involve the police if he harassed her further. It was never a nice situation to be in and thankfully was quite rare.

She was glad to leave the office. It was a weeknight but there was a cheeky little Pinot Grigio chilling in her fridge. She had been saving it for the weekend but she was going to treat herself to a couple of glasses as compensation for the day from hell. As she walked to her car the light was fading but there were still people about. Some looked like they were going out rather than heading home like she was. She zapped her car to unlock it and as she got in, someone swiftly entered through the passenger door and shut the door.

It was a man in his late forties. Well dressed but unshaven and red around the eyes. 'I know what you said about the police but—' It was Mr Maxwell.

'Get out!' said Lucy forcefully.

'Don't panic. I'm not going to hurt you,' he said. His wild eyes didn't fill her with confidence on that score.

'I know you're not, Mr Maxwell, because if you did you would obtain a criminal record, likely end up in prison and may find it even trickier to gain access to your children. Now please get out of my car.' Her words were confident but she was shaking.

He looked alarmed by her response. And then in an instant he burst into tears. Proper gut-wrenching sobs. 'I can't go on. I don't know what I've done wrong. Nobody is telling me anything.'

Lucy had a list of things but knew it wasn't wise to detail them while he was sitting a few centimetres from her and in an unstable state.

'I am sorry but I cannot help you, Mr Maxwell. You need to speak to your own solicitor. Now will you *please* get out of my car before I call the police.'

He looked pleadingly at her. 'But you know where my wife and kids are. You can fix all this.'

'There's a process and we're following it. Last chance,' she said, pointing at the door.

His jaw twitched. 'I'm not leaving until you tell—'

He didn't get to finish the sentence because Lucy leant on the car horn which blasted out making them both jump. She kept the pressure on and within moments people were approaching the car to see what was wrong.

Mr Maxwell held his hands up, nodded and left the car.

Lucy let out a breath and removed her hand from the horn. She needed a moment to compose herself.

A rap on the window made her jump and she let out a small squeal of alarm. There was a concerned-looking elderly woman peering at her. 'Are yer orrite?'

Lucy took a steadying breath and buzzed her window down. 'Yes, thank you, I'm fine,' she replied with a smile. Thankful for the woman's kindness.

'Was with the blessed hootin' then?' She walked off shaking her head and muttering, 'Thas a rummun.'

**

Ella's phone pinged as she was getting dressed. It was Kit. It said: *Here's the quote that could change your garage and your life.* ☺

She shook her head and opened the attachment. It was all professionally detailed but she scrolled impatiently to the bottom. The figure there surprised her. It was far more affordable than she'd thought. She took a moment to look at what was included – everything she needed to convert her garage into a workable business space. He'd even detailed bespoke carpentry for shelving, hanging and a workstation – this guy was thorough. She sent it to her printer so she could jot some notes on it while a bubble of excitement fizzed in her gut. She'd always been a saver but had been able to amass quite a bit while she'd been with Todd because, despite her best efforts, he liked to pay for everything. She knew how much she had in her savings account and while the garage conversion would clean it out, what else was she saving it for?

She had a lot to think about and she wasn't someone who made hasty decisions. She pulled the quote from the printer and for the first time noticed the header. O'Leary Builders. Of course she'd heard of them, their vans were everywhere. It would seem Kit was underplaying his position as the owner of a local business empire.

81

Ella had a productive morning adding extra beading to an already stunning bodice. These jobs took time but were therapeutic and very satisfying. In her mind she was picturing her transformed garage, all painted white and fitted out. She'd even pictured a chaise longue – maybe she could find a nice one for a good price. Perhaps even a chandelier to add a little sparkle for when brides came for fittings and some powerful lighting around her work-station. 'Ouch!' She'd pricked herself with the needle because she'd not been concentrating. She sucked her finger quickly – blood was the last thing she wanted to get on an expensive dress. She shook her head – she was getting carried away with herself. After all her own business was just a pipe dream because she wasn't brave enough to quit a steady job.

She could hear raised voices coming from Wanda's office but she ignored them and finished off the last bead before studying her handiwork. It was an excellent job even if she did say so herself. It was impossible to tell which beading was original and which she had added. She smiled because the bride this was for had been particularly lovely and she knew how pleased it would make her to see the end result.

Her phone buzzed into life. It was Kit. Obviously he was keen to get an answer on the quote. Well, she wasn't going to be bullied into anything. She answered it in between sucking her finger.

'Hi Kit. Thanks for the quote. I'll obviously need time to consider it.'

'Of course. The work schedule is pretty busy right now, we'd not be able to start for at least twelve weeks.' The thought of that both disappointed and excited her.

'Okay. Like I said. It will need a lot of consideration before I make any decisions.'

'Sure. Anyway, we have a huge problem,' said Kit.

Ella removed her finger which inadvertently made a loud sucky noise down the phone. 'What?' she asked.

'Mum messaged to ask if I can pick Isaac up from school because she's gone out unexpectedly with a friend for lunch. And that friend is Davine.'

'Bugger it,' said Ella, her mind racing to try and think of what they could do. 'Your diarrhoea needs to happen now!'

Kit spluttered a laugh on the other end of the phone.

'Ella.' Wanda's tone was brusque. 'Is that another personal call?' Ella looked up. How long had she been standing there?

'It is but it's quite important.'

Wanda's expression conveyed that she didn't agree for one second. 'Not as important as what I need to discuss with you right now.'

'Stand your ground,' came Kit's voice in her ear. 'She needs you more than you need her.' His words made her straighten out her spine.

'I'll be a couple of minutes, Wanda, and then I'll be right with you.'

'Excellent,' said Kit encouragingly. 'Polite but firm.'

'Now, or you can leave my employ right this second.' Wanda's stare was cold and unwavering. She'd not seen her look quite this cross before.

Ella swallowed hard. 'Don't let her intim—' started Kit but she ended the call.

'What's wrong?' In her mind Ella immediately sifted through all the dresses she had recently altered trying to think of what she could possibly have done wrong.

'The vomiting bride from yesterday is all over the internet semi-naked thanks to you. Now she's threatening to sue the shop. I want to know what you're going to do about it.'

Ella blinked. 'Erm, well.' Kit's words echoed around her brain – stand your ground. 'Actually, I don't think it was my fault. She came here with a hangover. It was her who puked all over our toilet facilities. And seeing as it was me who cleared it all up, I emphasise again *all over* them. I'm sorry to disagree with you but none of what happened was because of anything I did.' She folded her arms as if punctuating her little speech with a full stop.

Wanda's face turned an unhealthy colour and she thought she saw a muscle twitch near her eye. This wasn't good. 'It was *you* who removed her dress in the middle of the store.'

'Because she was about to vomit all over it!'

'But you did it in front of members of the public.'

'It's not like I was selling tickets! Those kids just happened to be there.' The exchange was making her heart race.

'It was definitely nothing to do with me. I'm not being hauled through the courts for something that was your mistake. As owner and proprietor I wash my hands of you. You're fired!' Ella felt like she'd been physically winded. Was this what standing your ground got you. She couldn't lose her job. Panic gripped her. Ella opened her mouth to protest. 'Don't beg. I mean it. You no longer work here so get out.' Wanda lifted her chin and oddly it cheered Ella to notice some stray hairs on it. Which was good because concentrating on them was stopping her bursting into tears.

'Fine,' she said, her heart pounding as she began grabbing personal items from her workstation and thrusting them into her bag.

The shop door opened and Ella's midday appointment came in. She and Wanda turned to look and realisation dawned on them both.

'You have to work your notice or you're in breach of contract,' said Wanda hastily. Ella was immediately torn. How could she walk out and leave all these brides in the lurch?

PART TWO

CHAPTER ELEVEN

Ella's heart was thudding in her chest. What was she meant to do? Ella went over what had happened in her mind. She'd thought she was helping by getting the bride out of the dress before it got covered in sick but now that bride was all over the internet she felt awful for the part she'd played.

'Hi,' said the woman who had walked in for a scheduled final fitting. She gave an awkward wave as if sensing all was not well.

Despite what had just happened Ella wasn't the sort to let people down. She made a split-second decision to deal with this customer and then she would call Lucy. She'd know what to do – or at least Ella hoped she would.

'Your customer I believe,' said Wanda pointedly. She turned on her sensible heel, stalked to her office and closed the door. That woman was unbelievable. How could you sack someone one moment and then tell them they had to work their notice the next?

Ella was hopping mad but she pushed it to one side. 'Hello,' she said to the customer. 'Your dress is already in the cubicle if you want to go through. You know the routine.' The woman went into the fitting room and Ella pulled the curtain across.

Ella marched over to Wanda's office and opened the door. 'After

I have dealt with this customer I am seeking legal advice.' She shut the door again so Wanda didn't have time to reply. She fired off a quick text with lots of exclamation marks to Lucy. This was a nightmare.

Thankfully the fitting went well. There were a few tears but they were all happy ones. The bride was pleased with how Ella had added a series of hidden buttons and loops under the train so it could be lifted off the ground to create a bustle effect. Ella slipped the gown out of the cubicle while the bride was getting dressed and packaged it up in the carrier ready for her to take home.

Wanda appeared as if from nowhere. Ella flinched and saw the glee in Wanda's eyes. Had she learnt how to teleport? 'I've taken legal advice too. You are in breach of contract if you do not work your full notice period which I believe is three months.' Ella knew her face must have dropped because it felt like a bowling ball had been attached to her chin. Wanda couldn't hide her self-satisfied smirk.

'Three months?' That couldn't be right.

'I believe so,' said Wanda. Ella didn't trust her at all. And the wording she was using sounded like she wasn't sure.

'I will check my contract this evening, when I go through it with my legal adviser.' Wanda's smug expression faltered. *Ha*, thought Ella, *gotcha*.

They both slapped smiles on as the bride came out of the fitting room. Ella wished her well and sent her off with her precious dress. She skirted past Wanda and back to her workstation. She didn't breathe out until she heard Wanda's office door slam shut.

Ella pulled out her mobile phone and ignoring the many text messages from Kit she dialled Lucy's number.

'You all right?' asked Lucy.

'No. Wanda has sacked me because a bride flashed her boobs at some kids who filmed it and put it on the internet and now the bride wants to sue Wanda and Wanda says I've got to work for her for another three months.' Ella realised she'd not taken a breath.

'Slow down,' said Lucy. 'Right. Point number one. Not your fault if a bride flashes someone. It's her issue if there is video footage and she needs to take action to get it removed from the internet.'

'But I took her dress off her in the middle of the shop because she was about to barf on it.'

'Again. Not your fault. Assuming you didn't hold her down and forcefully remove said dress then she was complicit in the action.' Ella puffed out a huge sigh of utter relief. 'Point three: if that is all Wanda is using as evidence for termination under gross misconduct then you can sue her for unfair dismissal. Point four: it isn't usual for an employer to enforce a notice period after dismissal but they can. Anything else?'

'Just that you're blooming brilliant, slightly scary and I'm hugely grateful that you're my friend.' Ella felt much better after speaking to Lucy.

'My pleasure. Three months' notice feels like a lot for your line of work.'

'I thought that. I'm sure it's less but I'll have to dig out my contract to check.'

'Are you owed any holiday? You could use what you're owed to cut down any notice period.'

'Goodness. Probably loads. I'll work that out this evening too. Are you okay?'

There was a pause before Lucy replied. 'I'm fine.' Ella got the feeling that was a lie.

The rest of the afternoon Ella and Wanda stayed in their respective domains. Ella checked through her drawers and put a few things in her bag so if she had to exit at short notice, she wouldn't have too much to gather up. The thought of leaving triggered polarised emotions. Could this be the shove she needed to start her own business? That seemed like such a huge life decision to make. She wasn't sure she was ready to walk away from a regular income and job security although the latter was obviously now in question. Her phone pinged with another text from Kit. An image of him shot into her mind. A particularly sexy version of him. She shook it away. That wasn't helpful. She'd abandoned his call after Wanda-gate and hadn't replied to his many messages. She hoped he'd been able to put project diarrhoea into action without her.

When the clock hit five Ella was out of the shop door without a backward glance. Wanda was still there, she could lock up for a change. Ella pulled out her phone and scanned Kit's messages as she walked to her car. They were a mixture of support for her situation with Wanda and dismay at their plot to scupper their parents lunch plans being foiled. The last message made her smile.

Hope you didn't get too much flak from your boss. Feel partly responsible. Instead of waiting for my workforce to come free I can start your garage conversion at the weekend if that helps ☺

What did the smiley face mean? Was that a joke? She dialled his number and he answered it immediately.

'Hi Kit. Do you mean it about starting the building work this weekend?'

'Yes, if you don't mind me bringing along a helper.'

'Of course not.'

'So you're doing this?' he asked.

She took a deep breath. 'Yes. I'd like to accept your quote.' Inwardly she squealed.

'Great. But maybe I should point out that my helper is four years old and his experience is limited to Play-Doh.'

'Ah, Isaac.'

'I've got him on Saturday as Mum is visiting her sister.'

'Are you sure? Not Davinc?'

He laughed. 'No definitely not Davine this time but they did meet up today. I'm sorry I couldn't stop them. She'd already asked where I was working before she dropped it on me and I was stuffing my face with a doughnut at the time so I could hardly feign an upset stomach.'

'Never mind. We'll have to come up with something else.'

'What happened with your job?' he asked.

'I've been fired although I don't think she can lawfully dismiss me because I've not done anything wrong.' She gave him an update on the vomiting bride and he went quiet. 'Kit? You still there?'

'Yes,' he said, followed by a snort. 'Blimey, hashtag naked bride – she's gone viral. No wonder she was after Wanda. But she looks good in a thong. The bride, not Wanda. I'm guessing Wanda's not a thong kinda gal.'

It made Ella chuckle. 'Poor bride though. I do feel sorry for her.'

'There's a lesson in not overdoing alcohol. What are your plans for the evening?'

'Alcohol with friends,' said Ella with a giggle.

'Then I expect to see you in a thong and heels all over Twitter tomorrow.'

Was he flirting with her? 'I'll do my best.'

'I'll be over by about ten o'clock Saturday morning, okay?'

'Brilliant. See you then.' She felt excited. But that was only because of the garage conversion. This was it. She was doing it. She'd started the ball rolling. The first step to being her own boss. What the hell had she done?

***

Lucy was glad to have something to take her mind off the Maxwell case. Despite her best efforts it had been playing on her mind and she was extra cautious when leaving the office. And while there had been no repeat of the car invading incident she did keep getting the feeling she was being watched. More than once when she'd checked over her shoulder she had seen the same tall hooded figure somewhere nearby, but that could just have been her imagination in overdrive. The three friends had gathered at Ella's for their usual evening of catching up over wine and food.

'Auntie Rita has a fungal infection,' said Brittany. 'I hope we're not doing a spa.'

'For the umpteenth time. It's more than my life's worth to disclose what we are or aren't doing on your hen night,' said Lucy.

'What *are* we doing?' asked Ella. Lucy scowled at her. 'Oh, okay. Tell me later.'

'Anyway,' said Lucy, raising a glass. 'Congratulations on starting your own business.'

Lucy was chuffed that Ella was striking out on her own. She'd been telling her for years that she was undervalued and despite how it had come about she was pleased to see her friend taking back control.

'Thanks,' said Ella but the way she retreated into the sofa told Lucy a lot.

'Are you excited about it?' asked Brittany.

'Terrified,' replied Ella, tugging at a hangnail with her teeth. 'I don't know the first thing about setting up and running my own company. Converting the garage is going to be an upheaval and that's the easiest part of all because I'm paying Kit to do it for me. I've got to work everything else out myself.' Her eyes were getting wider. 'All the things that Wanda did at Frills, Frocks and Fairy Tales I'll have to do. On my own.'

'What did she do exactly?' asked Lucy. From what she'd picked up from Ella over the years Ella was pretty much running the day-to-day business.

'Well, all the payments in and out, managing the accounts, dealing with complaints and . . . um . . .' Ella put a finger to her lips, she seemed to have run out of things.

'For payments in you need to set up a business account at the bank and they'll advise on easy ways to receive money. There's loads of apps for bookkeeping and you are amazing at what you do so there won't be any complaints. I think you'll be fine.' Lucy gave Ella a little nudge. 'Cheer up. This is the best thing that's ever happened to you. With the possible exception of the day the ice cream van came to our school playground.' It was nice to see a smile return to Ella's face even if it was only briefly.

'And I'll need a website.' Ella bit her lip.

'That's simple, you can set one up yourself. You need to get the URL for the company name and you're away,' said Lucy.

'What's your new business called?' asked Brittany.

Ella bit down hard on her lip and winced. 'You see I've not even thought about that. I literally have no idea what I'm doing.' Ella ran her fingers through her long hair. 'What am I doing? This was a bad idea, wasn't it?' Her eyes darted agitatedly between her friends.

'No, it's a good thing,' said Brittany.

'We'll come up with a name now,' said Lucy, putting down her glass so she could concentrate on being creative. It wasn't her strong suit. She much preferred facts and figures. 'I'm guessing we can think of something better than Frills, Frocks and Fairy Tales,' said Lucy with a derisory sniff.

'Aww I always liked that name,' said Brittany. 'At least it's memorable. Puns are funny too.'

She did have a point. 'How about Thread Needle Street?' suggested Lucy, quite pleased with her offering.

'Isn't that a place in London?' asked Ella. 'That might confuse people.'

'Pins and Needles!' blurted out Brittany.

'Sounds like a Botox clinic,' said Lucy. 'In fact, I've a feeling we had a case against them last year.' Brittany pouted. 'You could try something factual like Wedding Dress Alterations.'

Ella yawned. 'Sorry, I wasn't being rude. But that is a bit bland.'

'It's a Stitch Up!' said Brittany excitedly. The others laughed. 'Is that a no then?' She looked disappointed. 'What if you use the word sew – S.E.W. and play with it like . . . um . . . Crafty Sew N Sew.'

'I like it, but it sounds more like a hobby shop,' said Ella.

'Or a dodgy divorce lawyer.' Lucy laughed. 'How about Sew Lovely?' she suggested, running with the theme.

'I like it, but what about Oh Sew Special?' asked Ella, her eyebrows arched.

'Bloody brilliant!' said Lucy and they all drank to that.

CHAPTER TWELVE

After a good chat with Lucy and Brittany Ella felt a lot happier about the huge change she was embarking on. They were enormously supportive and had both helped to allay some of the many fears she had about branching out on her own. Friday at work had been busy for both Ella and Wanda which thankfully had kept them out of each other's hair. Most brides started looking for dresses about a year in advance. Any new sales Wanda made were for brides who would have someone else making their dress alterations which did feel kind of weird because she'd worked there so long.

As it inched towards five o'clock Ella could feel trepidation squirming in her gut. She had rummaged through her important papers file the night before and uncovered her contract. She wasn't looking forward to challenging Wanda about it, but the deed had to be done. Her plan was to hit her with the facts and then run away for the weekend.

Ella tapped on Wanda's office door. She could see her sitting inside ignoring her. It didn't help her stress levels. At last Wanda turned to glare at her through the glass. 'Come,' she said like a Victorian school ma'am.

'Wanda. I found my contract. My notice period is two weeks.'

Wanda pursed her lips. Ella wasn't expecting an apology, but some admission of error would have been nice. Although she suspected Wanda knew all along that her notice period wasn't three months, she had been trying it on. Taking her for the fool she'd been for the last four years to work for someone who didn't appreciate her and treated her badly.

'Any decent person wouldn't leave countless dresses incomplete. The very least you could do would be to ensure this summer's gowns are ready,' said Wanda without even looking at Ella.

Wanda was unbelievable. 'My schedule is maxed out until October based on the number of brides *you* have booked in. You should have thought of that when you sacked me. I have calculated that I am owed eleven days holiday which means my last day was yesterday.' She turned to leave.

'Maybe I was hasty,' said Wanda. Ella waited, still facing the door. 'If I have your assurance that you'll not act irresponsibly again then perhaps you can keep your job.'

There had been a number of times over the last twenty-four hours when she would have happily accepted Wanda's retraction, but things had changed. Thanks to Kit's suggestion to convert her garage and the support of her friends, Wanda was dealing with the makings of a distinctly different Ella. She was still unsure as to whether she could pull off setting up a company and being her own boss, but she now knew she wanted to try. She spun around to face her boss. Wanda wore a nonplussed expression and was clearly expecting Ella to beg for her job back.

'Are you reinstating me?'

'I'm saying I'll consider it. If I have an apology and confirmation that you take full responsibility for the naked bride incident.'

Ella laughed and Wanda looked cross. 'They sue me instead of you? Are you seriously expecting me to rid you of all accountability?'

'It was your fault.'

'No. It wasn't. How about this as a compromise.' Wanda's cheek twitched at the word. 'I admit to nothing because none of it was my fault. Instead of being sacked, I resign. I will give you more than three weeks' notice of which I will work two and take some of the holiday owed to me for the third week. And we'll make it effective from Monday because I know we have a bumper lot of brides booked in and I'm kind like that. Therefore, my last day in work will be two weeks on Monday.' With that she slammed the door, returned to her desk where she hastily drafted a letter of resignation which she handed to Wanda.

'Ella, you will regret this.'

'Possibly,' said Ella, 'but at least it's my decision.' And with a spring in her step she left for the weekend.

Saturday felt like a big day, as if it marked the start of a whole new chapter for her. Ella was up bright and early. She tied her hair up in a scarf and set to sorting out the things currently stored in the garage. She appeared to have a tendency to collect tins, and lots of boxes of fabric, wool and offcuts that she was loath to throw away but were taking up room that she now needed. There was a box of childhood keepsakes including gymnastic trophies, some books and a sad-looking teddy bear. She took him inside; he didn't deserve to go to the tip or be relegated to the shed which was where a lot of the stuff was going to go.

She was dragging a large box of junk out when a truck with the O'Leary Builder's logo emblazoned on the side pulled up and reversed onto the drive. Kit jumped out.

'Have you started without me?' he called as he walked around to the passenger door.

'I'm clearing out the rubbish.'

'I can work around that for now. But if you've got anything for the recycling centre, I can take it for you.'

'Thanks.' He seemed to be a lot more helpful now she was paying him.

Kit opened the cab door and helped down a small dark-haired boy who was clutching a woman's bag to his chest like it was a life raft. Ella brushed her hands together to rid the worst of the dust and went to greet them.

'You must be Isaac. I'm Ella,' she said. Isaac stared at the ground. She looked at Kit. He mouthed, 'He's a bit shy at first.' She nodded her understanding. 'Would you like something to drink?'

Isaac nodded. 'I'll have one too please,' said Kit. 'First rule of building: never start without a cuppa.'

'Builder's tea with umpteen sugars by any chance?'

'Wow. I'm shocked. You're assuming I conform to the stereotype,' said Kit, with a frown.

She was suitably chastened. 'Sorry. What would you like?'

Kit grinned. 'Extra strong builder's tea with milk and two and a half sugars, please.'

She shook her head at him. 'Come on, Isaac. Let's leave Uncle Kit to get on with the work while we get the drinks.' He frowned hard and in that moment looked very much like a mini Kit with his dark eyelashes and full lips. He held on tight to his bag.

'This way then.' She walked through the garage and a quick glance over her shoulder let her know Isaac was following her.

Ella's experience with children was limited to bridesmaids and page boys. She'd even fitted a dress for a five-month-old who was to be wheeled down the aisle in a flower-decorated pushchair. Thankfully they'd not been able to find a matching dress for their spaniel. She wondered how they'd keep Isaac amused all day; she wasn't sure how old cotton reels would fare for a prolonged period.

'Orange juice okay?' Isaac nodded. 'Is it fun having a day out at work with your uncle?' Isaac didn't reply. Ella put the kettle on which filled the silence for a while. 'Do you like building things?' she asked as she made the drinks. No reply. 'Being a builder sounds like a lot of fun to me.' Isaac clutched his bag and stared hard at the kitchen floor tiles. 'What's your favourite thing, Isaac?'

'Farts,' he replied. Thankfully Pirate interrupted the conversation by hopping into the kitchen to inspect the new arrival and made a beeline for the little boy.

Isaac gasped and reversed away from the cat.

'It's okay. I know he might look a little scary but he's a softy. You can stroke him if you like.' Isaac screamed as Pirate hopped after him. 'Or not, that's fine too.' Isaac screamed again. Pirate spun around. Thanks to being deaf in one ear he often misjudged where noise was coming from. It gave Isaac a few moments to scurry around the table and to take shelter behind Ella.

The garage door flew open and in two strides Kit was in the kitchen. 'What happened?' he asked. Isaac ran to him and Kit protectively scooped him up while glaring at Ella. She picked up a confused-looking Pirate. Kit and Ella faced each other with their charges held securely in their arms.

'He's just a bit scared of Pirate,' said Ella, giving the poor cat a rub around his ears.

'I'm not scared,' snapped Isaac, jutting out his chin.

'See he's fine,' said Kit. Looking at Ella as if it had been her screaming.

'Good. Here's your drinks.' She nodded at the mugs on the counter.

'Come on, Isaac. Let's get to work.' He put the boy down, picked up the drinks and went through to the garage. Isaac glared at Ella before disappearing after his uncle. When she heard the door to the garage thud closed, she relaxed a fraction. Pirate's tongue lolled out of his damaged lip. He wasn't the prettiest feline, she knew that, but she adored him and couldn't help feeling Isaac had overreacted.

'It's okay boy. I love you,' said Ella, kissing the top of Pirate's head. The cat purred his response.

Pirate went off to have a staring contest with next door's Persian, who was of a nervy disposition, and Ella went back to sorting out the many things she had stored in the garage. When she'd moved out of Todd's, and back into her little semi she'd been letting out, she'd dumped quite a bit in the garage and now she realised if she hadn't needed it in over six months it was likely she never would. She hadn't a clue why she'd insisted on taking the framed caricatures they'd had done on holiday in Spain. They reminded her of the many trips they'd been on and made her overly conscious of her teeth. She popped them back in the box for the shed.

Kit was removing screws from the garage door at speed and Isaac was sitting on an old paint tin peering into his bag. When she approached he quickly closed it.

'You can sell this, you know?' said Kit, tapping the garage door.

'Good idea.'

'Saves you or me getting rid of it too. I'll put it in your back garden for now.'

'Okay.' There was an awkward moment where they looked at each other, realised, and both appeared to panic slightly.

'Screw,' blurted Kit. Ella knew she was pulling a confused face. 'Screws, plural. If you've got a plastic bag, you can keep all the screws for the door together.'

'Great.'

He held up his screwdriver. 'Back to work.'

She pointed to a box. 'I'd best crack on with the sorting.' *Crack on?* Great, now she sounded like a radio announcer from the 1940s.

They worked side by side for a bit. When he asked, she helped him move the garage door, which was far lighter than she'd imagined it would be, into the back garden and they propped it against the shed. Kit dropped the back of the truck to reveal a number of grey blocks. She suddenly had visions of the front of her house looking like a bus shelter.

He clocked her expression. 'It's okay. They're for the inside. You won't see them when I've added the wall lining and plastered it. And one of the brickies who works for me will pop by to match the bricks to the rest of the house and build up the front wall.'

She was relieved. 'What about the window and door?' She had visions of him bricking the whole thing up.

'I've ordered the same to match what you've got but you can have something different if you like.'

'I meant for tonight. There will be holes in my house.'

'I'll board it up. It'll be fine.'

She wasn't sure she liked the idea of part of her house looking like a squat, but it was only temporary. A gust of wind blew through the garage and Ella saw Isaac flinch. That was the thing with the Norfolk coast – even in summer the wind was chilly. 'He's welcome to watch TV,' she said. Isaac's head spun around and for the first time he smiled.

'I'd rather he was where I can watch him.' Isaac's smile flipped upside down.

'There's no damage he can do in there. I need to get some lunch anyway, so I'll keep an eye on him.'

'Okay,' said Kit and Isaac jumped to his feet.

'Come on, Isaac, let's see what's on the TV.'

'Have you got Disney Plus?' he asked.

'Sorry, no.'

'Sky?' She shook her head. 'Netflix?' His voice had a more desperate edge with each question.

'No but I'm sure we can find something you'll like.' She really hoped that would be the case.

They entered the living room and Pirate yawned and stretched. Given the earlier incident she was quick to reassure Isaac.

'He won't hurt you, Isaac. He's very friendly.'

'Rufus doesn't like cats,' whispered Isaac.

Ella felt a memory stir somewhere in the back of her mind. She'd had an imaginary friend at that age too. As an only child it was a comfort to have someone to play with and also to blame when things went wrong. And in this instance they were handy for expressing your emotions through. 'It's okay. Pirate will love Rufus.' Isaac looked unsure. 'I promise. Pirate loves everyone.' She nodded and Isaac looked relieved. He put his bag on the sofa next to him, took over the remote control and scrolled through the channels like a pro. He was quite the connoisseur. Ella left him to it and went to fix herself some lunch.

She was cutting her sandwich in two when Kit came in. He had that glow about him that men get when they've been doing manual work. He held up an aluminium foil package and a Paw Patrol lunchbox.

'I can guess which is yours,' she said, nodding to the lunchbox.

'I never miss an episode.'

'Have a seat,' she said.

'I'm a bit dusty.'

'You look fine to me.' As she said it, she felt her cheeks flush. Thankfully Kit seemed oblivious.

'I used to eat lunch in the cab if I was working on a job but I haven't got my hands dirty for quite a while.'

'What do you fancy?' Her cheeks began to burn. 'I mean I've got Diet Coke that's cold or there's always a non-stereotypical cup of tea?' she offered.

He smiled and it reached his eyes. 'Coke would be great, thanks.'

She was getting the can from the fridge when all hell broke loose in the living room. The sound of things crashing to the ground was mixed with Isaac squealing. Ella and Kit dashed from the kitchen. Unfortunately, they both tried to go through the doorway at the same time and then lost valuable moments as their manners got the better of them and they each offered for the other to go first before Kit dashed through and into the living room.

Ella wasn't sure what she was expecting to find and given the scream she had feared the worst. The crash had been a row of books coming off the bookshelf and taking her money plant and pot down with them. It now lay in pieces with earth strewn across the floor. Isaac was standing on the sofa – he looked unharmed, which was a relief. The cause of the clatter was the cat on the bookshelf. Pirate was frantically sniffing up and down but on closer inspection it appeared he wasn't alone.

'Arghhhhhh!' shouted Ella, pointing to the next shelf up where a pale grey rat was peering over the edge at the cat.

Kit strode over and scooped up the vermin. Ella let out an involuntary squeal. This guy was hardcore. She'd have wanted a full hazmat suit and a baseball bat before she would have gone within ten feet of the rodent. He cupped it in his hands. She was about to suggest they put it in the wheelie bin or over next door's fence when Isaac opened up his handbag and Kit dropped the rat inside. Ella blinked. Pirate was still stalking up and down the shelf. His good eye having missed the rat above his head.

'What the—?' She looked from Isaac and back to Kit who gave her a cheery shrug.

Isaac pouted hard in Ella's direction. 'You *promised* he'd like Rufus,' he said accusatorily. She had no idea what to say.

CHAPTER THIRTEEN

Lucy hadn't heard any more from the father in the Maxwell case and based on conversations with the mother, she and the children seemed to be coping fine in their temporary home. The daughter refused to share her injuries with anyone, not even her doctor, so there was a lack of evidence and she was insisting that the police weren't brought into it. Lucy could still use the situation to argue that the father shouldn't have shared custody but instances where there was proof of abuse or admission of guilt were simpler. Lucy hadn't signed up for this career because she was looking for something simple. She enjoyed the trickier cases. It made her feel like a detective piecing everything together. Although this time the outcome she was after wasn't a conviction but an opportunity for her client to move on.

And all because they fell in love and got married. At least her own mother had never married, that was a blessing given all the losers she had dated. Random men had swanned in and out of Lucy's life – some were indifferent to her, others thought they had the right to order her about and a couple even gave her the occasional slap when it suited them. It made her cross to think of it. Although it wasn't the men she blamed, it was her mother.

Thankfully most clients were straightforward and no violence was involved, they simply got bored with their spouse and that was what caused them to have affairs or start to hate each other. Oddly she did see the same people returning. Usually a few years later but here they were again in the same situation although second divorces could be even more complicated as there were often children from previous marriages to consider. Messy didn't even cover it.

Her approach to relationships was infinitely better. Why buy the whole pig when you only wanted the sausage? It was still a mystery to Lucy why people seemed to abandon all common sense when they fell in love. Maybe the fact she had never felt that strongly for anyone explained her lack of understanding. Or, perhaps, as she frequently wondered, was love entirely a myth? Something conjured up by Hollywood to make money. Convention still dictated that you were meant to find a mate and settle down, there was also the animal instinct to have offspring – Lucy mused that it was simply a combination of those factors that led usually sane people to declare they were in love and abandon all sense.

Whatever it was it kept her in business. She finished a client meeting and returned to her office to find a large box on her desk. For a moment she was cautious – had Mr Maxwell sent her something threatening? She didn't own a horse or a rabbit but she now feared for her garden gnome. Then she remembered the hen party items she'd ordered. Lucy was keen to get into the spirit of things and if Lorraine wanted them all to dress up in cowgirl-themed clothes then she wasn't going to be like the kid who wore their school uniform on mufti day. Although she had frequently been the kid who had no uniform on any day. She opened up the box, pulled out the invoice and quickly checked everything was in order. Whip – check. Cowgirl hats and crop tops times two – she'd also ordered for Ella because she had enough on her plate right now without having to worry about hen night shenanigans. She ticked them off as she put them on her desk. Neckerchiefs in green, two packs of willie straws and a penis-shaped whistle. There was a cough from her doorway where her boss was surveying the scene.

He went a similar shade of pink to the straws. 'Actually. I can see you're busy. I'll come back later.' Lucy resolved to keep a pack of willie straws in her drawer if that was all it took to fend off additional work coming her way. She smiled to herself as she returned everything to the box.

After a good day she walked to her car carrying her large box of hen night novelties. Even though it was a warm June evening, and still light at nine o'clock, she now parked in a well-lit car park in direct view of a security camera. If she was going to be assaulted or kidnapped she at least wanted there to be unequivocal evidence when it came to prosecution. She scanned the area as she neared her car. There was nobody else about. She noticed something under the windscreen wiper. Most likely a flyer for a DJ she'd never want to see or a car washing service she didn't need. She rested the box on the bonnet and unfolded the note. She froze. It was a note from Mr Maxwell. It was polite and requested that she meet up to allow him to tell his side of the story and once again he professed his innocence. Panic shot through her. She could hardly defend herself with the willie straws this time. Lucy automatically spun around but quickly realised she was alone and the note had likely been left hours earlier. She wanted to screw it up and throw it on the ground but this was evidence of his continued harassment, so she folded it up and put it in the side pocket of her bag. She flung the box in the boot and hurriedly got in the car. She gave a quick glance in the back to check she was alone and locked the doors. She'd be glad when this case was over.

***

Ella was desperately busy at work. There was no way she could complete everything in the remaining two weeks – it was impossible. But it didn't stop her wanting to. She hated the idea of letting anyone down. She didn't know if Wanda had found a replacement yet because she wasn't talking to her unless strictly necessary. Wanda called her through to confirm a dress could be altered. She felt a pang of disappointment that she wouldn't see the finished article.

The woman was in her thirties with a classic hourglass figure and the dress looked stunning on her. Ella made some adjustments around the bodice and then jotted down some additional notes for whoever took over.

'If it's tightened here, it won't gape at the front like it is now,' explained Ella, holding the dress.

The bride put her hand to her mouth as happy tears welled in her eyes. 'I'm sorry for getting emotional. You are clever. I wouldn't know where to start,' said the bride.

'Thanks, but I'm afraid it won't be me who is altering your dress.'

The woman looked confused but Ella felt she had to be honest. 'I'm leaving in two weeks to set up my own business but whoever takes over will make the alterations and I'm sure they will do a good job.'

'I'm guessing the new business is still dressmaking.'

'Alterations.' Ella smiled at the thought. The fear and the excitement were more evenly weighted now work was coming on in the garage. As Kit had had to slot her conversion into an already busy schedule, they'd agreed that it would be done in between other jobs. It seemed that if it rained he sent men to her house to work which was fine with her.

The bride sighed. 'That's a relief. I'd rather you did the adjustments.'

'Sorry but I can't. You're paying the shop for the package.'

'Shame.' The bride looked disappointed. 'Can't I just buy the dress and then ask you to alter it?' She beamed a smile at Ella.

This was extremely awkward. Ella poked her head out of the curtain to check they weren't being overheard. Wanda was on the phone in her office which was a relief. 'I'm sorry but it wouldn't be ethical of me to suggest that you did that.'

'I understand,' said the bride. 'What's the name of your business?'

'Oh Sew Special,' said Ella, quite proudly as she unzipped the dress and helped the bride out of it.

'Great name.'

'Thank you.' Ella left the bride and indicated through the glass panel in Wanda's door that the bride was ready to pay before getting back to her sewing machine.

She was finishing off a hem when Wanda marched in. 'What's going on?'

Ella found she could deal with Wanda's bad attitude a lot better now she was counting down the days. A little glance at her calendar and its series of big red crosses buoyed her resolve.

'I don't know, Wanda. What is going on?'

'What did you tell that bride?'

'That taking up the hem was standard and that the bodice could be altered to stop it gaping at the front.'

'Then why has she not purchased the package to get those alterations completed?'

Ella frowned. 'I don't know.' Then realisation dawned. She'd given her the name of her new company. Was she going to wait until she'd left and get in touch? It was a definite possibility. That was what Ella would have done if she'd been in the bride's situation. Her guilt probably showed on her face.

Wanda leant closer. 'If you are poaching my customers for another shop . . .' she began.

'How would I do that when I don't currently have another job to go to?'

It stopped Wanda instantly. She gave herself a little shake. 'I'm not in the least bit surprised nobody else will employ you.' She walked off and slammed her office door. However stressful being self-employed was it couldn't be as bad as working for Wanda.

Ella took her red pen and put a big cross through the date. Another day closer to working for herself rather than warped Wanda.

When Ella pulled up at home there was an O'Leary's van on her drive. It was a surprise because it hadn't been a rainy day but she was pleased to see it. She parked on the road and walked back to the house. When she got there she did a little leap of joy. She now had a window and a door and under the window the grey blocks had been replaced by bricks that matched the rest of her house. It looked like it had always been like that. She peered in the new window, cupping her hands around her face to block out the sunshine to help her see better. There was nobody there.

All of a sudden, Kit stood up right in front of her, making them both jump.

'Argh!' she yelped.

Kit grinned back at her. 'You can come in,' he said, opening the new door. She could have skipped through it she was so excited. 'Welcome to Ella's Alterations,' he said.

'Ooh, that's a good name but I'm calling it Oh Sew Special,' she said, stepping inside and marvelling at how very different her garage looked.

'Probably too many Ls in my suggestion anyway. Don't want to get tongue-tied on the phone. Do you like it so far?'

'It's incredible.' The builders had already put in the floor, wall insulation and drywall a few days earlier, making the inside already look more like an actual room. But now it had a good-sized window and a half-glass door to let in lots of natural light.

'I was just checking a few things. I'm thinking a wall here,' said Kit, standing two-thirds of the way down the room and splaying his arms out. 'That way you can have this space for customers and the other side for your work area and storage.'

'That'd be great. Feels weird that I'll soon be working here.' The sensation inside her was similar to aeroplane turbulence, but she had no seat belt to cling to.

Kit checked his watch. 'I'm finished but if you've got a couple of minutes maybe we could have a chat.'

'Of course. Come through,' said Ella, heading for the hallway.

'Actually, I was thinking maybe a walk on the beach?' He shrugged one shoulder. 'I've been in the office all day sorting out VAT. This is the first time I've been out.'

'Beach it is then.'

They locked up the garage. Although, she thought to herself, she would have to stop thinking of it as her garage. As if interrupting her thoughts, Kit pointed above the new window. 'A big sign would look good there,' he said.

'I don't think I want to be that bold. I was thinking just a plaque on the door.'

'Fair enough.'

They took the short walk down a couple of lanes, past chocolate-box cottages and flint-studded walls until they popped out on the seafront. Trimley-next-the-Sea neighboured Happisburgh and was quite similar but differed in that, thanks to some concrete sea defences installed after the 1953 storms, it didn't suffer the same devastating level of cliff erosion. Trimley somehow managed to escape the tourist invasion each year. Like a forgotten enclave it had no need for arcades or caravan sites and therefore wasn't besieged at the first ray of summer sunshine, like many of the other towns along the Norfolk coast. The promenade, such as it was, remained deserted.

'I'm sorry about Rufus,' said Kit.

'That's okay.' Kit had apologised profusely on the day and explained that he had no idea that Isaac had smuggled the rat out in the handbag.

'Is he okay?'

'Currently serving a life sentence in a new giant cage with wheel, house and fun climbing area.'

'That doesn't sound too bad. And has Isaac forgiven me?' she asked.

'I think you're okay. Has Pirate?'

'He's stopped searching the bookshelf.'

They went down onto the sand. The light breeze coming across the North Sea made Ella wrap her jacket around her, as her thin top wasn't enough to keep her warm.

'You okay? We can go back,' offered Kit.

'I'm fine. I'm not really cold and I like the smell of the sea on the wind, it's refreshing.'

As the plan to derail the lunch date between David and Jane had failed they had resorted to highlighting their parents' flaws, although all they had come up with was that David played a lot of golf and Jane occasionally smoked.

'How's it going with drip-feeding subliminal messages to your mum?'

Kit nodded. 'I've been trying to bore her with golf. I figured if I went on and on about it she'd be so bored that David mentioning it might tip her over the edge.'

'Excellent.' Ella was pleased. 'I made something up about someone smoking near me and how horrible it was, but I don't think Dad picked up on it. It was a bit too obscure.'

'Yeah, thing is, the golf chat might have backfired. This morning Mum told me she's thinking about having golf lessons.'

'Nooooo!' It surprised even Ella how vehement her response was. A nearby group of gulls took flight.

'I know.' Kit winced. 'We need another plan.'

Ella still wasn't sure that her father was having an affair but she liked the chats she had with Kit. They'd brokered an odd sort of friendship over their shared cause. 'Jane wouldn't be as keen on golf or my dad if it messed up things she wanted to do. I could buy Dad some tickets for a golf event that clashes with something important in your mum's diary. She'd think he was selfish which might work.'

Kit pouted. 'And by golf event you mean what exactly?'

'No idea. Bugger it.' Ella was amazed by how hard it was to

split people up. 'How come when I go out with someone, I do everything I can to make sure they're happy – I worry about all the many little things that could put them off or spoil things and do all I can to ensure we stay together and we split up anyway – but when I'm actively trying to find a way to separate these two, there's nothing?'

When she looked across Kit was giving her a strange look. She'd said too much. The words had all come tumbling out like fish out of a trawler net. His wavy hair was ruffled by the wind, his dark eyes narrowed. 'Do you think maybe you try a bit too hard?'

Ella stopped dead. 'What do you mean?'

'Exactly what I said. If you are constantly trying to make someone else happy – offering the relationship equivalent of an all-inclusive service – where does that leave you and what you want?'

'I take it you don't go out of your way for a partner at all then?'

'Not especially. What you see is what you get.' Kit did an elaborate bow.

'And how's that approach working out for you?' She tilted her head.

'I'm single at the moment but that's nothing to do with how I behave in a relationship.'

Ella knew her eyebrows were dancing. How unaware was this guy? 'You sure about that?'

'Certain. My last girlfriend and I split up because she wanted to go travelling and I couldn't leave Isaac. Nothing to do with me not pandering to her every whim.' He shook his head. 'Do you really do all that?'

Ella turned away and started walking. 'Sometimes.'

'That must be exhausting.'

'It is.'

'Then why do it?' he asked.

It was a good question and one she wasn't entirely sure she wanted to explore. Perhaps it was all about her trying to trigger a similar level of thoughtfulness in the other party. Or maybe she wanted to do something that would make them look at her the way her parents looked at each other. 'I'm not doing it at the moment. I'm free and single and very much happier.'

'That's good. Me too,' he said.

They walked in silence for a while, both lost in their thoughts. The sand was drying out further up and crumbled under their shoes making it harder going. When they reached some concrete steps Kit dusted the worst of the sand off and they sat down next to each other.

Ella stared out at the calm ocean in front of her. Light ripples chasing across its surface. Cascades of white spiralling along the shore with each break of a wave. She loved it here. She felt she would always have to live near the sea. It was part of her.

'Why did you and your last boyfriend split up? Did you forget to put a choccy on his pillow?' Kit grinned cheekily to let her know he was joking.

Ella shook her head at him but she was laughing. 'I'm not that bad.' She took a breath. 'He could see that I was in it for the long haul and he wasn't ready for that level of commitment.'

'I'm sorry,' said Kit.

'Don't be. I'm over Todd. Probably my own fault for trying to make everything perfect. Life's not like that.'

Kit threw up his hands. 'Bloody hell this guy is a genius.'

She stared at him aghast. 'Why?'

'He dumps you and yet he's got you thinking it was your fault. That's quite something. For what it's worth, he's an idiot.'

'Thank you.' It was nice to hear someone who was unbiased tell her that, even if it was Kit.

He nodded. 'Ha! I've got an idea. How about we make our parents think the other one is cheating?'

Ella laughed but a quick look in Kit's direction made her see he wasn't joking. 'My dad is already with my mum *and* seeing yours. Blimey, how many women do you think he can have on the go?'

'Fair point. How about we make it look like my mum has someone else?'

'I'm not sure.' Ella had hoped they would have found an easy solution before now because, on top of everything else, she was still worrying about her parents.

'We could scatter some signs about to imply Mum is up to no good. Make them obvious to your dad until he has to challenge her and . . . kaboom!'

'That could work. Kit O'Leary, you might just be a genius.'

'One of my many attributes,' Kit joked.

'And the award for modesty goes to . . .'

He gave her a friendly nudge. 'No room for another award I've got too many already.'

CHAPTER FOURTEEN

Over the next couple of days Ella and Kit exchanged a number of text messages as they concentrated their efforts on developing their latest plan. A few outrageous suggestions had been scrapped, like sending David exploding golf balls purportedly from Jane and signing Jane up to receive catalogues from a specialist bondage company, but, overall, they were happy with the ideas they were pursuing. The big problem they had was that it was virtually impossible to tell if their plan was working or not. In the meantime, they kept dreaming up schemes.

Message from Kit: *A receipt for a posh meal out for two left in her car might make David suspicious. Next time you go somewhere like that please can you keep the receipt?*

Ella: *Great idea. But no plans to go somewhere posh anytime soon. How about you?*

Kit: *Nope. Never mind it was just a thought.*

Kit: *Had another thought. Shall you and I go out for a posh meal to get a receipt?*

Ella had had worse offers. She'd not had a nice meal out for a while. *OK. Not too posh as I have a builder to pay ;-)*

Kit: *It's a deal. Let me know when you're free. I'll book something.*

She was probably more chuffed than she should have been

about a meal out with her builder. Wanda tutted as she looked in on Ella and her phone pinged again. She did a lot of tutting these days. It was annoying but Ella wouldn't have to put up with it for much longer. She was flat-out busy but in between dresses she was using her last few days at the shop to jot down notes of things that worked well and others that didn't so she could make sure she had everything covered with her own set-up. It was all starting to feel a bit real.

She had another fitting with the hastily squeezed-in theme wedding which had been a lot of work but Ella was pleased with the results, she hoped the bride liked it. She hung up the dress in the fitting room and had a little moment to herself – at least this was one bride's reaction she would be able to see.

'Hello again. How are you?' asked Ella when Lianne came through the door.

'Bit nervous.' Lianne had her large bag with her again. Ella wondered if the lightsabre was having another outing.

'Your wedding day is getting close now. Everything on track?'

'Sort of. Thanks to you there's been a bit of a change.' Ella wasn't sure she liked the sound of that. 'You thought my fiancé was going to be dressed as Han Solo.'

Ella remembered the conversation. 'But Chewie is iconic too and obviously loves Princess Leia,' said Ella, trying hard to smooth things over.

'You were right. I had thought the same thing, but I hadn't wanted to upset my fiancé. After I left here we had a huge row.'

Ella sucked her teeth. 'I'm sorry to hear that.' If she didn't want the dress after all the alterations she'd done Ella thought she might cry. There was no way Wanda was going to give a refund either – she never did.

'It's okay. The best man is going to be Chewie and I'm marrying Han Solo.' The bride giggled. 'Not the real one because he's like seriously old now.'

'That's great news.' Ella was relieved. 'If you want to put the dress on I'll take a look.'

Ella waited with her fingers crossed. She heard a gasp and her heart leapt. It was hard to tell if it was a good gasp or a bad gasp. 'Everything okay?'

The bride pulled the curtain back a fraction and her teary face appeared. She sniffed. 'I love it.'

Thank heavens for that, thought Ella. 'That's good then. Pop it on and I'll check the fit.'

When she was ready Ella pulled back the curtain and Princess Leia was standing before her. Well, at least Leia's dress was.

'I can't believe you made the sleeves.' The bride held up her arms and swished the long draping swathes of material.

'I knew you weren't really happy with the wrap idea so I thought I would see how close I could get with the fabric, and it turns out this is a pretty close match but if you hated it, I've got the tuille wrap as a back-up.'

Wanda cleared her throat behind Ella and waved her over. 'What has that cost?' she whispered. Ella opened her mouth to answer but Wanda was off again. 'Why are you wasting company profits on two solutions for one dress?' Again, no time for Ella to answer before Wanda was speaking. 'I'm taking that out of your wages.'

Princess Leia stepped out brandishing the glowing lightsabre and Wanda hastily stepped backwards. 'Please don't do that,' said Lianne. 'I'm over the moon with what Ella has done. I'll be recommending your shop to everyone. I'm happy to pay the extra.' She smiled, then the smile dropped. 'As long as it's not loads.'

Ella beamed a smug grin in Wanda's direction. 'Fine,' snapped Wanda and she marched away.

'Thanks for that but you didn't have to – I'm leaving anyway,' said Ella.

'That's a shame. I was going to ask about bridesmaids.'

'You're cutting it super fine for ordering bridesmaids' dresses and I'm sorry, but I have no space to make any more alterations.'

The bride chuckled. 'Oh no. I mean I was going to ask you if you would be my bridesmaid.'

Ella had no idea what to say.

Over a beautiful dinner at a gastro pub she retold the story to Kit. He almost choked on his sea bass. 'What did you say?'

Ella bit her lip. 'I said her wedding clashed with my friend's hen night.'

'And does it?'

She winced. 'No.' Kit playfully wagged a finger at her. 'Don't. I feel awful enough as it is.'

'Ella, seriously. You worry about things that you shouldn't be thinking twice about. It's not your fault this woman has no friends. She only needs to go to a *Star Wars* convention in her wedding dress and she'd make a hundred besties in a few minutes. She chooses not to.'

'She has friends. Just none that are prepared to dress up like Yoda.' Kit burst out laughing. He had a hearty laugh and it set Ella off too. 'Anyway, aren't we meant to be conjuring up some genius ways to hoodwink my father into believing Jane is having an affair.' She waved a finger in the air. 'Another affair.' She got a pen and notebook out of her bag

Kit sipped his wine. 'I thought maybe you could send Mum a text when they were out and sign it off with a guy's name. She won't know your number.'

'Okay. I'm up for that. But what if she replies?'

'Try to keep it going for a bit. It might be enough to interrupt their meal. She never puts it on silent because of Isaac.'

'Sneaky.' Ella felt a little giddy at the subterfuge. 'Jot down Jane's mobile number for me.' She pushed the notebook and pen across the table. 'I wondered if you could have a few work emergencies so she has to cancel a few times. That would start to look suspicious.'

'Not many emergencies in the building trade and I have a laptop and can work from home if I need to.'

'A builder who works from home?' She gave him a quizzical look.

There was a pause before he spoke, and she sensed there was something amiss. 'I don't go on site any more. Mine's more of a supervisory role.' Kit went back to eating his meal.

'We need some other way for Dad to suspect Jane is having an affair.'

'I had a friend who found out his wife was cheating because he got an STD,' said Kit.

'Eurgh. That's horrible. I don't think we want either of them to get one of those.' Ella was slightly worried at how far Kit was prepared to go to split up their parents.

'I was thinking we could send them both leaflets anonymously. Making it look like they've come from a clinic.'

'Ooh, you are devious. But I like that idea a lot.'

He leant back in his seat. 'I try.'

She wondered what he was like when he was dating. Was he devious? A bit of a player. She wouldn't have been surprised. 'Have you ever two-timed anyone?' she asked.

He seemed to roll his head in a circle and jut his chin out. 'Excuse me? You think I'm a cheater?'

'It was a question. Not an accusation. In case you have any first-hand experience.'

'No. But I have been cheated on.'

Ella sighed. 'Me too. It sucks. Any tell-tale signs you should have spotted?'

He seemed to ponder this. 'Working late. Mentionitis.'

'Is that an STD I've not heard of?'

He smiled – a cheeky smile that started from one side of his lips and spread. 'It's when your partner keeps mentioning someone's name and doesn't realise they're doing it. My girlfriend had never talked about this guy at work before and then all of a sudden he kept popping up in virtually every conversation. How about you?'

'He was distant. Showered more often. Changed his aftershave. Kept his mobile with him at all times.'

'Wow. Quite a few clues there.'

'Yeah. That kind of made it easier though. Unlike Todd. I've gone over and over things and there were no clues with him. No sign he was unhappy. It came out of nowhere and socked me right between the eyes.'

Kit's expression changed. 'Sorry. He sounds like a shit.'

'He's not all bad.' Kit threw his arms up but before he could give her another lecture on being too nice, she quickly added, 'But you're right he's a shit and I deserve better.'

Kit nodded. 'There you go. Don't be so nice, Ella Briggs.'

'I will do my best.' She gave him her most earnest expression, but he looked like he wanted more. 'Okay. I could be unpleasant.' She pulled a face and Kit gave an encouraging wave of his hand. 'Or completely horrid.' She made a noise like a low growl. The waiter appeared and instantly recoiled, making Kit laugh and Ella apologise profusely.

They finished their meals in quiet contemplation. The waiter returned and cautiously collected their plates and they ordered coffees.

'I'm glad you were free tonight. I've enjoyed it,' said Kit.

'Yeah me too.' And she really had. Kit O'Leary was definitely growing on her.

'I'd like to do it again if it won't upset Stuart.' He raised an eyebrow.

'Stuart has found himself someone else. Which means I'm available.' She splayed out her hands.

Kit's expression changed. 'Oh, Ella. Sorry, I wasn't suggesting we date.'

She felt her cheeks burn. This was awkward. 'I know. I meant I'm available for dinner.'

'Just to clarify. I don't mean I wouldn't like to date you,' said Kit. 'I definitely would, but you said you're not maternal, so I know kids don't feature in your life plans. And I fully respect that. But you see it's not only me I have to think about . . .'

'Ah, Isaac.' She realised Kit came with a ready-made family. 'That's the nicest reason I've ever had for not being asked out.'

'Still pals?'

'Pals is exactly what I need right now.'

'I think we're actually more than pals.' He leant forward giving Ella a whiff of an earthy aftershave and making her wonder what he was going to do next. He picked up his wine glass. 'To partners in crime.'

'I'll drink to that.' They clinked glasses. Ella was starting to like all the cloak and dagger deception and especially the time she was spending with Kit but she couldn't help thinking it was a shame it would never develop into anything else. Life was a slippery bugger sometimes.

CHAPTER FIFTEEN

The hen weekend dawned and despite her whole being telling her this was the last thing she wanted to do Lucy religiously checked she had everything covered as per the last exceptionally detailed email. This time Lorraine had done away with her usual passive-aggressive overtones instead going full psycho warning people that Brittany would be devastated if it didn't go exactly as intended and that a special circle of hell had been reserved for anyone who ruined this meticulously planned event.

Lucy knocked on Ella's front door and stood back to give the converted garage the once-over while she waited. The builders had done a good job.

'You're early,' said Ella, combing through her damp hair. 'Come in.'

'Sorry, I hate being late for things. Even a horrendously expensive hen do with an itinerary like a particularly sadistic episode of *Ninja Warrior*.'

'I knew you'd be excited about it.' Lucy gave her a withering look. 'You might surprise yourself and enjoy it.' Ella was always positive. And the price she paid for that was to be frequently disappointed. Lucy had a healthy cynicism about most things and was rarely let down.

'Garage looks good,' said Lucy.

'Even better from in here.' Ella opened the door from the hallway and Lucy peered inside. 'There's a partition going in this week and then it's all being plastered.' Ella was grinning.

The space was much bigger than Lucy had realised but then it didn't have anything in it. 'I'm sure you'll make it look amazing.'

'I'll do my best. And last night I pressed the button and put the website live. It needs a few tweaks but it's out there. Fingers crossed some brides will find me and I get some work.'

Lucy loved Ella but sometimes she needed steering in the right direction. 'Rather than wait for them to come to you, you could drop some business cards into the other bridal shops in Norwich. Maybe offer a discount if they use you exclusively or something like that.'

'Great idea. Let me put business cards on my to do list.' Ella dashed off to the kitchen.

'You can put some up on free noticeboards too, like the ones in the supermarket and local businesses,' she called down the hall.

'You're a genius,' said Ella, reappearing.

'If only more people recognised that.' Lucy shook her head. 'Where's your bag?' she asked. Ella pointed upstairs.

In Ella's bedroom Pirate was stretched out on the bed as if it were all his. Lucy sat down next to him and gave him a stroke while Ella gathered a few essentials and added them to an already bulging overnight bag.

'How're things?' asked Lucy.

Ella popped her head around the door with a bottle of shampoo in her hand. 'Stressed and one snide comment away from murdering my boss. But otherwise good. How about you?'

'Still a bit twitchy.'

'Has that man been creeping about again?' asked Ella.

'Not that I know of. The formal letter to his solicitor seems to have done the trick. But it has unnerved me. Made me more cautious. But I'll get over it.' Lucy didn't like that it was still bothering her and occupying her thoughts.

'Of course you will.' Ella patted Lucy comfortingly on the arm. She wrestled the zip closed on her bag. 'Do I need to bring anything extra as it's a hen do?' She grimaced at her over-stuffed bag.

'Fear not, I have all that gubbins in the car. You just need yourself, clean pants, a couple of Valium and a thick skin. Remember to leave your dignity behind.'

'Do you think Brittany will love it?' Ella looked concerned as she heaved her bag onto her shoulder.

'I hope she does, but it's not for us to worry about. That responsibility sits firmly on the shoulders of her deranged sister, Lorraine. All we can do is be there and make sure Brittany has a good time however much the weekend sucks.'

Ella pulled a face. 'But I'll feel bad if it's—'

Lucy wagged a finger in front of Ella. 'Repeat after me. It is not my responsibility to ensure everyone else is happy.'

'I know but . . .'

Lucy shooed her away. 'Stop it. Downstairs. Go!'

***

Ella hadn't been away for a long time. Her last mini break had been with Todd to his penthouse on the Devon coast but since then she'd had two lots of leave cancelled by Wanda and the last week off she'd had was back in January when all she'd done was spring-clean the house and read a few books. Despite Lucy's warnings she was still looking forward to getting away. The trip to Mildenhall didn't take that long and was uneventful. Ella tried to get a bit more from Lucy about the case which was bothering her at work, but she'd brushed it away in typical Lucy style and proceeded to tell her about another couple who were arguing over the garden items and in particular who got to keep the shed, rhubarb plant and an extensive garden gnome collection.

'Thanks for sorting this all out for me, Lucy. I really appreciate it. It was lovely to delete all the emails. And there were a lot of emails.'

'You owe me big time. I'm thinking something along the lines of decorating your new business with a mural dedicated to me.'

'I think that's fair,' agreed Ella.

'Or you can check out the hen weekend orientation pack Lorraine sent me.' Lucy kept her eyes on the road but pointed into the passenger footwell.

Ella scanned the many sheets, timetables and instructions in the pack. 'Lorraine seems very . . .' She was trying to find the right word.

'Controlling? Obsessive? Batshit crazy?'

'Thorough,' said Ella.

'Lorraine is a suppressed megalomaniac who has found her calling. All of this confirms it. Hen do's are basically a celebration of being a massive knob, with a massive knob.'

'That's tradition for you,' said Ella with a shrug. She could sense Lucy was close to going off on a rant.

'It's utter madness. Why else would we spend a whole weekend with a group of people most of whom we don't even know? Some of whom I'm certain we won't like. Purely to see how far we can push the revelry without someone actually ending up in A&E.'

'As long as Brittany has a nice time.' Lucy looked across at her and shook her head.

Ella received a message from Kit to say that Jane and David had a date planned for the following evening. She replied and set a reminder on her phone to fire off a message which would hopefully land in the middle of their rendezvous. It still felt unbelievable to Ella that her dad could be doing such a thing and she longed to be proved wrong.

Lorraine's directions included photographs of key landmarks as they neared their destination. She'd even used her mother in some of the photographs to point which way they were meant to go.

'Next turning on the right after the post box,' said Ella, reading from the sheet. They turned onto a dirt track which gave Lucy's Nissan a bit of an off-road experience as they bumped their way over myriad potholes. At the end of the long track was a farmhouse and some agricultural buildings. 'Bear left by bush,' read out Ella. 'I'm guessing down there.' She pointed where the path disappeared behind an out-of-control hedgerow.

They trundled a little further until they were outside a large barn where four cars were already parked. They both got out, the front door opened and Brittany appeared looking genuinely relieved to see them and the tight squeeze of a hug she gave Ella reinforced it. 'How exciting is this?' said Ella.

Brittany's lip wobbled. 'Lorraine is uber stressed about every-thing, she's been a cow all the way here. And I still don't know what we're doing.'

'But we're here now and this looks amazing. I'm sure we're going to have the best time.' Ella tried hard to sound enthusiastic. There was a flicker of a smile from Brittany.

Lucy made her way inside with the bags and the unicorn head under her arm. The sound of another car approaching made Ella turn to watch a convertible swing in front of them at speed before braking heavily and kicking up a cloud of dust. Brittany blinked hard but Ella had a feeling it had nothing to do with the dust. 'Shitting hell,' mumbled Brittany.

'Isn't that your cousin?' asked Ella, trying to place the sharp-featured woman unfolding herself from the small car.

'Second cousin.' Brittany's jaw twitched. 'Martha. The one who stole my high school boyfriend, broke my wrist and lost my gerbil.'

'I'm sure she's not all bad.'

'Oh, she's worse than that,' said Brittany

Ella was starting to think that maybe Lucy was right about hen weekends.

CHAPTER SIXTEEN

There was a brief round of introductions where Lorraine pressed a sticky name label to everyone's left breast. Apart from the labelling process Ella was pleased to meet the others. Auntie Rita was overexcited and hugged everyone and Midge turned out to be a heavily pregnant work colleague of Brittany's with a funny story about how she got her nickname but part way through the anecdote Lorraine broke up the discussion to ensure they kept to the timetable.

Lorraine showed them to their room which had a small double bed in it. Ella wasn't that fussed but Lucy put forward a comprehensive case for why they should have one of the twin rooms. Lorraine was having none of it and looked like a person teetering on the edge.

'We'll be fine,' said Ella. 'Won't we, Lucy?'

Lucy mumbled something inaudible. Someone called Lorraine's name and she dashed out of the room. Ella breathed a sigh of relief at the avoided confrontation, but it was short-lived. Brittany came flying in and shut the door. She leant back against it as if someone were chasing her.

'Martha's not coming to the wedding,' said Brittany, her voice distorted by the frantic speed of delivery.

'That's good then,' said Ella, unzipping her bag and almost hearing it sigh with relief.

'No, it's not good at all.' Brittany moved away from the door and rubbed her palms over her face. 'I didn't invite her to the wedding because I had my heart set on it being at Sandy Cove but that's expensive so we had to keep the list short. Martha didn't make the cut. And now she's here.'

'Ah. I see the problem,' said Lucy, carefully taking some neatly folded things from her wheelie case and placing them in a drawer.

'You could still invite her to the wedding,' said Ella.

Brittany was shaking her head. 'Or feign ignorance when she says she's not received the invite. Blame the post,' offered Lucy.

'But then what about her parents? And her brother and his wife and four kids?' Brittany looked anxiously from Ella to Lucy and back again.

'Umm . . . maybe their invites all fell behind a cushion and you could discover them when you get home?' Ella knew she wasn't very good at this deception lark. Brittany looked at Lucy which Ella took to mean she didn't like her suggestion.

Lucy folded her arms. 'Be straight with her. Say there's a limit on numbers and you're sorry but however much you would have loved to have invited her side of the family the budget just wouldn't stretch.' Lucy gave a shrug. Ella marvelled at how articulate she was.

'I can't do that,' said Brittany, looking horrified.

A firm rap on the door made them all turn suddenly towards it, like victims in a horror movie. Lorraine opened the door. 'We are leaving for activity number one in five minutes. Comfy casual dress and trainers or walking shoes. Sunblock as it's outdoors.' She waggled a finger at Lucy and Ella. 'Remember no spoilers. The bride is present.' She pointed at Brittany as if she were diffi-cult to spot. 'I suggest you all use the bathroom before we leave. Chop, chop.'

128

'Lorraine, why the hell did you invite Martha? You know I can't stand her,' said Brittany, her voice a low hiss.

Lorraine came in and shut the door. The room felt like it was shrinking. Ella focused on unpacking her bag while the uncomfortable exchange continued.

'I was one short. So Mum suggested her.' Lorraine shrugged and went to open the door.

'Hang on. What do you mean one short?' asked Brittany.

'This place sleeps fifteen. I wasn't going to waste a bed. It brought the cost down by nine pounds each.' Lorraine glanced at Ella but she concentrated on finding somewhere for her boots and avoided eye contact.

'You've invited someone who has been my arch nemesis my whole life just to save a few quid?' Ella thought she could see Brittany start to shake.

Lorraine laughed. 'Don't be overdramatic. Anyway we have to leave right this instant or the whole weekend will be spoiled.' She began shooing them from the room.

Lucy and Ella made eye contact. Lucy mouthed 'batshit crazy megalomaniac'. It was hard to disagree.

***

Lucy found she suddenly had a carful as Lorraine directed scared-looking strangers into vehicles. Ella had bagsied the front seat as Lucy's navigator, Midge had gone for the car nearest the door. Lucy hoped her seat belt was long enough to stretch over her enormous baby bump. Auntie Rita dived in alongside Midge and Brittany sneaked in quickly in an attempt to keep her distance from both Martha and Lorraine. Midge made a groaning sound. Lucy clocked Brittany's terrified expression in the rear-view mirror.

'Everything okay?' she asked.

'Indigestion,' said Midge, giving her tummy a rub.

Lucy put on her sunglasses. 'Right, ladies. My name is Lucy and I am your chauffeur for the afternoon.'

'Fabulous!' hollered Auntie Rita, pulling a bottle of Amaretto out of her handbag and making her charm bracelet jingle excitedly. 'Let's get the party started.' Midge popped out a couple of Rennie. Brittany looked like she was on the verge of tears.

First stop was thankfully only a short drive into Thetford Forest. They passed a sign promising them a bird's eye view from the treetops. Lucy wasn't outdoorsy or rugged but she did quite like to push herself so of all the things Lorraine had come up with this was the one she found the least horrendous.

Brittany took a sharp intake of breath. 'What the actual f—'

'Zip wires and a treetop walkway for an adrenaline buzz with beautiful views,' read out Ella quickly. 'That sounds . . . um . . . nice.'

Lucy parked up next to Lorraine who was already out of her car and waving a clipboard in a menacing fashion. Auntie Rita exited the car and, after a lot of bum shuffling, Midge followed her. Brittany's face appeared between the headrests. 'I am terrified of heights. I once fainted on the roller coaster at Great Yarmouth.'

'Always good to face your fears though,' said Lucy in an attempt at being positive. She feared it was going to be an even longer weekend than she'd expected.

'Sod that,' replied Brittany. 'How many years in prison if I murder two people?' she asked, her eyes following her sister as she darted from car to car shouting instructions which were mostly ignored.

'Officially it would be two life sentences. However, I think you'd have grounds for provocation, probably get it reduced to manslaughter and there's always diminished responsibility. Maybe twenty years but you'd only serve about sixteen.' Lucy smiled over her shoulder.

'Totally worth it,' said Brittany and she got out of the car.

Lucy and Ella followed and were herded by Lorraine into two

teams. A long debate raged over one team having one more person than the other. 'Fifteen's not such a good number now,' muttered Brittany when Lorraine passed her and for a moment Lucy thought there might be a cat fight. But Martha broke a nail putting on her harness and started having a meltdown triggering Lorraine to intervene spouting something about waivers.

***

Half an hour into activity number one Ella found herself very high up and inching along a cargo net towards a terrified-looking Brittany. Brittany had her arms through the holes gripping the net to her like her life depended on it – which, given the drop, wasn't far from the truth. Lorraine had already gone ahead and as she was rigidly observing the two people per section rule she could only holler at her sister from a distance. Ella wasn't yet sure if that was a blessing or an added hindrance.

'If you don't move you're going to delay everything!' shouted Lorraine.

'Maybe I should jump and end this torture now!' shouted back Brittany, glancing down. She shut her eyes tight and pushed her cheek against the rope. 'Don't let me die, don't let me die,' she whispered.

'There's no trip to A and E on the agenda,' shouted Lucy but she ducked behind a tree when Lorraine swivelled precariously in her direction.

'Brittany, it's going to be all right,' said Ella, carefully moving her weight forward which made the net shudder and consequently Brittany too. 'Can you look at me?' She'd seen someone else say that when they were coaxing a person down from somewhere. Now she thought about it, it was a police drama and the person threw themselves off a building so probably not the best example but it was all she had. 'I need you to help me, Brittany.'

Brittany opened one eye and judged her suspiciously – a lot

like Pirate did when it was time to give him his flea treatment and she was offering him tuna as a sweetener. 'I can't get across to the platform unless you help me.' Ella nodded in the direction of where Lorraine was standing with her hands on her hips shaking her head repeatedly.

Brittany looked across and Lorraine threw up her hands. 'For heaven's sake. Don't make me call the ranger to get you down. You'll look like a right idiot and have to go and sit in the coffee shop with Midge.'

'Lorraine!' shouted Lucy from two trees away. 'We need you over here.'

Ella let go of the net with one hand to give Lucy a quick thumbs up.

'Why?' called back Lorraine.

'Big confusion over outfits for tonight,' yelled Lucy. 'And someone thinks your timings are off.'

'What? I'm coming over. Why is everything difficult as soon as you involve other people?' Lorraine muttered to herself before crawling into a tunnel and disappearing.

Ella kept her voice calm. 'Okay, Brittany. It's just you and me. It's not far. You can do this.'

'I can't,' whispered Brittany.

'You are stronger than you know. Let's do it together. Okay?'

There was a painfully long pause before Brittany gave a tentative nod. *Progress*, thought Ella. She moved closer at a steady pace, taking care not to make the net sway unnecessarily. She was one rung away from Brittany when her mobile phone sprang into life making the birdlife take to the air in a dramatic fashion. Brittany squealed and gripped tighter.

'Bugger it.' Ella fumbled for her phone. She was more intent on shutting off the loud ringing than answering it but when she saw who it was her curiosity got the better of her. 'Kit, Hi. Everything okay?'

Brittany stared at her. 'Seriously?'

Ella mouthed. 'Just a minute.'

'I'm fine,' said Kit. 'Is now a good time?'

'Well . . .' Ella looked around her. 'I'm up a tree with a bride-to-be who's having a panic attack soooo . . .'

He laughed, clearly he assumed she was joking. 'Awesome. Mum let slip where they're going tonight so I was wondering about calling and cancelling their table. What do you think? Too mean?'

'Not nice but then we don't want them to have a nice time together. I suppose it's justified.'

'Exactly what I thought. If I call them now hopefully the restaurant will have time to fill the booking.'

Ella glanced at Brittany whose eyes were bush baby wide. 'Sorry, Kit, I'm going to have to go. But maybe we could have a debrief when Jane gets home?'

'Won't you be out pulling hot men?'

'I'm sure I can spare five minutes for you.' Ella giggled and then wondered what she was doing. Was she flirting when she was forty feet up in a forest canopy?

'Ella?' Brittany's voice was trembly.

'I have to go.'

'Look, Ella, I had a great time the other evening and—'

For a moment Ella thought Brittany was making a move to get to the ledge as she had loosened her grip on the netting. What she'd actually done was faint and let go entirely. Ella watched as Brittany fell away from the net. Ella's stomach lurched.

'Shit!' Ella dropped her phone and made a grab for Brittany. As they were both in secure harnesses Brittany didn't actually fall at all. She sort of slid away from the net in slow motion – almost ballet-like.

'Brittany!' screamed Lorraine from some way away – a disembodied voice through the trees.

'She's fine,' called back Ella, really hoping she was. Ella held onto Brittany's harness with one hand and slowly made her way across the net dragging a limp Brittany along with her. It took quite a bit of effort. Ella scrambled onto the platform and now had to try to get the dead weight of her friend on too – no mean feat. A ripple of applause echoed through the forest as Ella hauled Brittany half onto the wooden shelf-like structure.

Brittany stirred. 'Where am I?'

Ella wasn't sure telling her would help the situation at all. 'You're with me. It's all fine.'

'On my way!' Came a shout from below. Ella peered over the edge to see a ranger running towards them and she relaxed a fraction. Unfortunately, Brittany turned to look too which was enough to tip her weight and she slid off the platform to dangle in mid-air.

'Whoops. Sorry!' Ella called as Brittany's screams echoed around the peaceful woodland.

CHAPTER SEVENTEEN

Lucy had to admit she had quite enjoyed the afternoon treetop adventure including the drama that had played out with Brittany and Lorraine. The zip wires over the treetops had been spectacular and thanks to the flat topography of Norfolk she could see for miles as she'd whizzed through the air with her arms and legs in star formation. Despite scooping bark into her underwear every time she'd come to the end of a zip line it had been lots of fun.

A ranger had come to save Brittany and had carefully winched her down to the ground – like a budget air-sea rescue without the helicopter and waves. Back at the accommodation there was allotted time for lunch and perusal of the comedy items they had each bought as forfeits for a drinking game to be played later. It appeared Auntie Rita had ransacked her local Poundland and Midge had invested quite a bit of money on intricately locking handcuffs. Lucy and Ella's joint contribution were the willie-shaped whistle and multiple willie straws.

Lorraine had arranged for a delivery of sandwiches which had arrived on large plastic platters and there was plenty for everyone. However, a lack of labelling was sending Lorraine into another meltdown but Lucy quite liked the lucky dip approach. Then again she wasn't a vegan with a long list of allergies.

'Coronation chicken,' said Lucy, pointing to the sandwiches next to where she'd taken her latest one from.

Lorraine dashed over. 'Any peanut?'

Lucy chewed carefully. 'Absolutely no idea.' Lorraine huffed and took another one off to dissect in the kitchen.

Brittany was curled up on one of the extra-large sofas sipping a glass of water. The sofa was a pale cream leather and Brittany's complexion was a similar shade. Lucy went over. 'How are you feeling?' she asked.

Her expression was stony. 'Like I'm living my worst nightmare but won't wake up.'

'Look at it this way. It can't get any worse than fainting on a zip wire.' Brittany's eyebrows registered doubt. 'Unless you have any other fears or phobias. Do you?'

'Snakes and dentists.'

'I can categorically confirm that there are none of those due to feature anywhere in the rest of the weekend apart from the dentist versus anaconda wrestling show this evening.' Brittany looked alarmed. 'I'm joking. Trust me every minute has been planned so if they were involved it would be documented somewhere in the orientation pack.'

There was the briefest of smiles. 'I thought I liked surprises,' mused Brittany. 'Turns out I hate them with a passion. I like it when I'm surprising someone else. Perhaps I'm more like Lorraine than I'd like to admit.' They both watched Lorraine who was frantically writing sandwich fillings on sticky notes and slapping them on sandwiches even though they were disappearing fast. Midge picked up a cheese sandwich, Lorraine took it off her, labelled it vegetarian and plonked it back on the platter.

'I'm pretty sure there's no one quite like Lorraine,' said Lucy.

***

136

Ella felt bad about poor Brittany and the whole treetop adventure but Lorraine was pleased with the photographs they'd got of Brittany being rescued because she said they would look impressive in the montage she would be putting together as a life milestone souvenir – whatever that was. The afternoon was a more relaxed affair because it involved do-it-yourself spa treatments, at least it would have been if it weren't for Lorraine popping up to take photographs of people smeared in clay face packs making them look like startled swamp creatures.

Ella had spent most of the afternoon sipping prosecco with her feet in strange plastic bags which purported to be foot moisturising packs. At least Brittany seemed to have cheered up as she had been well and truly pampered with everyone taking a moment to help her with a number of treatments. She'd had a mini facial and face pack followed by hand exfoliation and a manicure. Auntie Rita was meant to be doing the foot thing on her too, but she'd fallen asleep with a half-eaten cheese and cucumber sandwich on her lap which Lorraine was unhappy about because Auntie Rita wasn't even a vegetarian.

Ella was painting Midge's toenails because she couldn't see her toes let alone reach them. 'If I fall asleep don't take it personally,' said Midge. 'I need a power nap before tonight.'

Ella was a little concerned that Midge was planning on coming clubbing. She made a mental note to see how far it was to the local maternity ward before they left. 'Is this your first baby?' asked Ella.

'The second of many,' said Midge, patting her bump affectionately. Ella was struck by how confident she was of having a big brood. 'You got any?'

'No. Babies aren't really my thing,' said Ella, concentrating on Midge's oddly shaped little toenail.

'Nor mine,' said Midge. Ella wasn't sure what to say. 'It's okay, what I mean is I'm not looking forward to doing the disturbed nights and nappies again but I know it's worth it because they develop into an actual person with a personality and a million possibilities.'

'I guess,' said Ella. She'd not thought much beyond the terror of childbirth and the overwhelming responsibility for another human being.

'Ooh, it's kicking. Do you want to feel? It's okay if you don't. I'll not be offended.'

'Umm . . . all right.' Ella placed her hand on the woman's extended middle. Midge repositioned it. Ella couldn't feel anything, but Midge was smiling so she smiled back. She was about retrieve her hand when something fluttered underneath it and then pushed against her palm. Ella was amazed and quite touched by the experience. 'Wow.'

'It's cool, right?'

'Yes. It is very cool.'

Ella decided to leave her nails and sneak into the shower before everyone suddenly realised they all had to be showered and changed and out the door in a couple of hours. Ella knew that Lorraine had her faults but she was finding the detailed schedules quite handy. It was a bit rigid but at least you knew where you were meant to be at any point in time and she'd obviously spent a lot of effort putting it all together for her sister. Ella got out of the shower as someone was banging on the door.

'Occupied,' she called out in a cheery voice.

'It's relaxation time, Ella,' snapped Lorraine. 'You're meant to be relaxing with everyone. We're doing group meditation.'

'Umm sorry. I thought I'd have a relaxing shower instead. I've got lots of hair to wash and didn't want to hold people up later.'

Lorraine grumbled something but then it went quiet, she assumed she'd gone to check up on someone else.

Ella darted out of the bathroom and into their bedroom where Lucy was sorting out their outfits. 'How's your phone?' asked Lucy.

'Still dead,' replied Ella, picking it up off the bed to have another check. The drop from the treetops had been too much for it. 'I promised Kit I'd text his mum tonight.' Lucy gave her an odd look. 'Long story.' She went on to explain their plan which didn't sound quite as robust in the retelling.

'Have you got Jane's number?' asked Lucy.

Ella pulled the note from her bag. 'Here. If you don't mind messaging from your phone later on that would be great.'

'I have a much better idea,' said Lucy with a wink. 'Anyway. Let's focus on the matter in hand. Outfits. They're the same size so you can choose,' said Lucy, splaying out her hands over two bright checked crop tops.

'I'll go with the hot pink. I think.'

'Excellent choice,' said Lucy, handing it to her.

Ella studied the top. 'It's not classic Wild West is it?'

'No, but trust me this was the best of the suggestions. It was a close call between this, Playboy bunny girls or ballerinas.'

As it turned out when it was teamed with ripped jeans, boots and a cowboy hat it didn't look too bad. And as they were all in similar clothes it was fine.

Lorraine had sorted out Brittany's outfit and it was very Dolly Parton with a tasselled shirt and big white Stetson but she looked fantastic and it was good to see her a little happier. There was lots of excitement as more and more hens appeared in the living room and everyone applauded.

Martha strutted in wearing a checked boob tube and Daisy Duke denim hotpants teamed with thigh-high leather boots.

'There's a problem with Auntie Rita,' said Martha, pulling a face like a gargoyle sucking a lemon. 'I don't think she got what the outfit was meant to be.'

'What? Why? The email was completely clear. Cowgirls.' Lorraine was looking around for support and everyone nodded obediently.

The door opened and in trudged Auntie Rita dressed in a Friesian cow onesie.

***

After lots of cajoling and a few more glasses of prosecco Auntie Rita decided she would still join them for a meal even though she was dressed as a cow but she wasn't sure about the clubbing afterwards. She felt she'd rather be dressed as a cow than look like the dull auntie who didn't want to join in if she wore the jeans and blouse she'd worn earlier.

The restaurant Lorraine had chosen was lovely. Chinese was Brittany's favourite so she'd done well there and while the restaurant had put the rowdy bunch in a separate area, away from other diners, they had put up balloons and been very welcoming. The food had been delicious and by the time they came to leave everyone was in good spirits and Auntie Rita and Midge were ready to boogie the night away. Ella feared for both of them – it was some time since Auntie Rita had been clubbing and Midge's pelvic floor was already under a great deal of pressure.

They were singing a Take That classic as they walked from the restaurant with Lorraine at the front with her arm in the air like a tour guide. She came to a sudden halt and they almost all did a comedy fall as they bumped into each other. Lorraine's head was on a swivel. 'Where's the bloody club? It's meant to be here,' she said, waving her arms like an out of control windmill in high winds.

Lucy stepped up and did a bit of googling. 'Went into receivership two months ago,' she said. There was a boarded-up doorway with a gap above where a sign might have once been. 'It used to be here. Right place, wrong time.'

Lorraine's information sheet had promised a wild night in Bury St Edmunds which Ella thought was probably a bit of a stretch. The lack of the required nightclub was certainly a blow to her meticulous plans.

Ella joined Lucy and Brittany who were busy searching the internet while Lorraine was being comforted by the others. 'Do you think she's okay?' asked Ella.

'She's fine, she's being comforted by a cow,' said Brittany.

'Auntie Rita is lovely,' said Ella.

'I meant Martha,' said Brittany, returning to her screen. 'Turns out Bury St Edmunds is not the clubbing capital we had envisaged. Who knew?'

'There must be somewhere else?' Ella looked around her.

Lucy bit her lip. 'I need to hone my search criteria because clubs has brought up four social clubs, a Classic car club and Bury Farmers club which I concede is rather appropriate in our current outfits but probably not what Lorraine had in mind.'

After a bit more drilling down they found something that looked suitable as it promised 'old skool toons' and was about a ten-minute walk away. A cheer went up and they all set off buoyed by their new mission. Lorraine consulted Lucy on the way as to whether she had any grounds to sue her internet sources for not informing her of the club's change in status. Ella left them to it.

The place turned out to be more of a bar but there was music, the drinks weren't too expensive and the proprietors were more than happy to let in a hen party so all was well. They quickly attracted some attention, especially Auntie Rita, and they were soon joined on the dancefloor by a few local chancers. Lucy weaved her way in between their group speaking to each of them until she reached Ella. 'It's all going to plan,' she said, waving a sticky note with Jane's phone number scrawled on it. Ella nodded.

Someone suggested a fake orgasm competition which they all found hilarious and the men seemed mildly horrified by, especially as Lorraine informed them they were judges and handed them all sticky notes and instructions on how to score people. Ella entered into the spirit of it but was far too giggly to do it with any conviction. Lucy on the other hand would have given Meg Ryan a run for her money. Midge had a good effort until she let out a giant burp part way through which somewhat broke the illusion. It turned out Auntie Rita was the star of the show and received scores of ten all round from the judges and a lot of interest from one particular Turkish gent.

Brittany definitely had a good time. Possibly a little too much and was snogging some random bloke when Lucy grabbed her by the collar and hoiked her away. It might have only been a kiss but Brittany wasn't like that and would berate herself afterwards if she'd continued.

Their evening had been full of drinking, dancing in the unicorn head and copious amounts of laughter. Midge had fallen sound asleep next to a speaker which she felt boded well for when her little one arrived. The rest of the evening seemed to be on fast forward. That was until Auntie Rita boob flashed the barman for not giving her a Slippery Nipple cocktail and they were all chucked out. It was a bit of an abrupt ending to the night, but Ella was ready for bed.

CHAPTER EIGHTEEN

Lucy and Ella woke up at a similar time. They had migrated a little too close to each other in the double bed during the night making them instantly shuffle apart.

'Nice hair,' said Lucy, admiring Ella's fringe, which was sticking up.

'You don't look too hot either,' she said with a pout.

'Now you look like an angry pineapple,' said Lucy.

'And someone didn't remove their make-up – you look like a melting Lady Gaga.'

'Thank you, that is exactly the look I aim for first thing in a morning.'

Lucy sat up. The house was quiet – a stark contrast to the early hours when they had continued the party with a series of drinking games. Lucy's mouth was dry – she'd drunk so much bourbon she'd not have been surprised if she'd woken up with an American accent. While Ella tried pointlessly to resuscitate her mobile Lucy padded downstairs to get some water for both of them. Lucy noticed someone was asleep on one of the sofas and tiptoed past. Maybe they'd been sharing a room with a snorer. When she got level with their shoulders she did a double take. They were wearing the unicorn head. She carried on to the kitchen, got two glasses of water and quickly returned to the bedroom to update Ella.

She shut the door with her bum. 'You will never guess who is in the living room?'

'Kit?' Ella's eyes were wide.

'Who? What? No, there's a unicorn crashed out on the sofa.'

'Very funny,' said Ella.

'I'm serious. Someone is asleep on the sofa, wearing the head.'

'Perhaps they forgot an eye mask and needed it dark to sleep,' suggested Ella.

'Maybe. I couldn't keep track of who was wearing it in the pub. I thought we'd lost it.' Lucy shrugged and got back into bed. 'I don't even remember it coming back to the house or anyone wearing it when we were playing pin the penis on the donkey.'

There was a pause and they both shook their heads as if to try to rid their minds of the images. 'That was a weird game. Wasn't it?' said Ella.

'Most odd. I think Martha brought it.' Lucy checked her phone. 'There's a reply from Jane.'

She showed the screen to Ella who read it out. 'I think you've got the wrong number. Thanks.' Ella pushed out her bottom lip. 'She's very polite.'

Lucy agreed and carried on scrolling through her notifications. There were alerts from her security camera for last night. It was probably next door's cat again. She scrolled through the footage and froze. 'Shiterama.'

'What's up?' But Ella was already leaning across to look at her screen. 'Who the heck is that?'

They watched a hooded figure peer through Lucy's front window and then try the front door.

'You okay?' asked Ella. Lucy did a slow nod, although okay was the last thing she was. 'Who do you think it is?'

'As it's June I'm guessing it's not sodding Santa Claus.'

Lucy watched the footage an unhealthy number of times in an attempt to identify the figure but there was no way of being sure of who it was. It was likely they were male and of a slim build but that was about all she could determine. She knew who she thought it was, who she was totally convinced had tracked her to her home and was now working out how to break in but she had no proof. What was he planning on doing if he did get in?

Part of her was relieved she wasn't at home but then if she had been she could have called the police and now she would know exactly who it was and they would be in police custody. She was almost pleased to hear the scream that came from downstairs to interrupt her thoughts.

'Sounds like someone has found the unicorn,' she said and they hopped out of bed to go and witness the next drama unfold.

***

Ella, along with everyone else, descended on the living room at the same time to find the unicorn sitting up and facing a topless Auntie Rita who was holding a cup of tea in one hand and trying to cover her boobs with the other – she wasn't succeeding.

Auntie Rita turned to the gathering throng. 'I swear I didn't touch him. He just screamed.'

'He,' mouthed Lucy.

'Shall I take that?' asked Ella, reaching for the mug. 'Then you can . . .' Ella pointed at Rita's nipple peeping from under her forearm. Auntie Rita rearranged herself but in all fairness, there was far more than a handful that needed covering.

'Take off your mask,' insisted Lucy and the unicorn slowly removed its head. Underneath was one of the guys from the previous night. There were a few oohs from the hen party. 'And that's mine,' said Lucy, snatching the unicorn head from him.

'Sorry I didn't have a pillow and that's quite padded inside and anyway . . .' he trailed off.

'Did you want a cup of tea?' asked Ella. Lucy shook her head at her.

'Would you like to explain what you're doing on our sofa?' asked Lucy.

He scratched his head. 'I had a few in a bar. Someone passed me this address and I got a taxi over. We had more drinks outside. We were making out . . .'

'Who were you making out with?' asked Lucy.

He scanned the many woman in a variety of nightwear all staring at him like an odd police line-up. 'One of those, I think.' He looked at Lucy and shrugged. 'I dunno, it was dark.'

Lucy was trying to keep a straight face. 'Excellent. Any idea how you ended up on the sofa?'

'Yeah. I got off with . . .' There was a gasp from someone in the assembled crowd. 'One of these . . . lovely ladies.' He pointed at the women, he obviously had high hopes of seconds. 'I said I'd get a cab home but nobody would come this far out in the early hours, so I crashed here.' He beamed a goofy smile at them looking quite pleased with himself for remembering as much as he had.

'Anyone going to claim responsibility for this?' asked Lorraine, narrowing her eyes at the other women who all shook their heads in response.

'And you have no idea who you had sex with?' Lucy asked the man.

He scanned the group again peering closer like he needed glasses until he came to Auntie Rita and winced. 'Sorry. I can't remember.'

'I'll put the kettle on,' said Ella and she went into the kitchen. Brittany was close behind her. 'Good morning, Hen. How are you? Lorraine made us all bring paracetamol so if you've got a hangover.'

'I think it was me.' She sunk her front teeth hard into her bottom lip.

'What was you?' asked Ella, getting all the mugs out of the cupboard.

'The person who slept with that guy. I think it was me.'

Belly-dancing with a hangover was not how anyone wanted to start off their Sunday. But such were Lorraine's skills of persuasion that everyone was in attendance. Midge was the sprightliest of all having drunk no alcohol, slept in the nightclub as well as back at the accommodation. The instructor was particularly perky which was a little off-putting. Lorraine had dropped the man they were now calling Unihorn off at a suitable bus stop but the mystery of who he'd slept with was the talk of the group. Well, it had been until they'd started the belly-dancing which was quite energetic and not conducive to chatting. Auntie Rita was a natural, her gyrating hips now seemed far more acceptable in the class than they had on the dancefloor the previous evening.

They took a break and Ella checked her phone. Still dead. She poked at the on button with a kirby grip

'What if it was me?' Brittany appeared on the seat next to her like an anxious genie.

'Why would it be you?'

'I've just got this awful feeling.' She gave a shudder. 'And I could taste beer this morning and I only had prosecco and whatever those shots were at the bar.' She stuck her tongue out like a New Zealand rugby player warming up for the haka.

'Brittany, I'm sure you would remember,' said Ella.

'What's up?' Lucy joined them and glugged down a paper cup full of water.

'Unihorn,' whispered Brittany.

'She's worried she might have slept with him,' explained Ella.

'There's no evidence. I think you should forget about it and move on,' said Lucy.

'Martha keeps giving me this look. And it's scaring the crap out of me. See.' Brittany nodded in Martha's direction. She was looking over but there was nothing Ella took as malevolent. And when the three of them stared at her she looked away.

'You're worrying unnecessarily,' said Lucy.

'But what if she tells Grant?' Brittany looked on the verge of tears.

Ella patted her arm. 'There's nothing to tell.'

Brittany relaxed a fraction. 'Actually. You did snog him earlier in the evening,' said Lucy, crushing the paper cup.

'What?' Brittany looked horrified.

'Yeah. I thought you might have forgotten that. I pulled you off him, hence only a small snog. A snoggette.' She threw the cup towards the bin and missed.

'I'm an adulterer before I'm even married.' Brittany put her head in her hands. 'This is a disaster.'

Ella shook her head at Lucy, she wasn't helping the situation. Lucy seemed to pick up on her vibes. 'Look, Brittany, don't tell anyone but it was me who slept with him, not you.'

Brittany's head shot up. 'Really?'

Lucy glanced at Ella as if seeking support for her lie. Ella nodded. 'Yep. Loose Lucy, you know I can't resist a hook-up.' Lucy gave a shrug, and Ella was oddly proud of her friend.

Brittany looked like a melting ice cream as the stress vanished. 'Thank heavens for that,' she said with a nervous giggle. 'You're such a tart.' She batted Lucy playfully on the shoulder.

'Yeah, that's me,' said Lucy unconvincingly.

Ella found herself in a lovely pub seated next to Midge, who punctuated her meal with toilet trips.

'Are you okay?' asked Ella when she returned from her third visit.

'Yeah. She's using my bladder as a trampoline,' replied Midge, pointing at her bump.

'You know it's a girl?'

148

'It makes it easier choosing names. Especially as my partner was dead set on Ernesto so she's had a lucky escape.'

'Have you chosen her name or shouldn't I ask?' Ella wasn't sure about the protocol.

Midge glanced up and down the table, but nobody seemed to be eavesdropping, they were all either chatting or listening to Auntie Rita tell a story about the time she was arrested for stalking Boyzone. 'We've got it down to two and then we'll make a final decision when we meet her . . .' It struck Ella as such a lovely phrase, that they were waiting to meet their baby. 'It's going to be either Zelda or Luna.'

'They're both lovely,' said Ella.

'Thanks. It's a big responsibility. I went to school with a kid whose initials were W.C., the toilet jokes never went away.'

'I think the whole thing,' – Ella waved her hands for emphasis – 'is such a big responsibility. Quite terrifying.'

'It is with the first one but then you realise that loving them and doing your best really is enough.' Midge had a lovely way with words, Ella could tell what a wonderful mum she was and it made her a little emotional. 'Sorry I'm prattling on,' said Midge. 'I can talk about other stuff. To be honest I'm not even that big a baby person.' They both stared at her bump. Midge laughed. 'I mean I've never been one of those women who always knew they wanted to be a mum. It sort of crept up on me once I was with the right partner. Life changes things. I didn't like poetry when I was younger but I tried it again as an adult and loved it. It was the same with mushrooms.' Midge rubbed her chest and burped. 'Excuse me. I shouldn't have had the horseradish sauce.'

Coffees were ordered and chatter continued but Ella's mind had wandered off. She was considering what Midge had said. Most of all it was making her wonder about why she had been completely certain she didn't want children because she wasn't at all sure that was how she felt now.

***

After Sunday lunch they all said their goodbyes and set off for home. Lucy drove so Ella decided to have a little nap on the way. She woke up when Lucy tapped her arm. 'We're home and it looks like you've got this hot builder on overtime.'

'Overtime? What?' Ella struggled to come to.

Ella blinked as Kit strode out of her house. He was bare-chested with a toolbelt slung low. Faded jeans and work boots. It was a sight to behold. 'Wow.' Lucy lifted her sunglasses for a better look. 'I'd pay overtime for some of that,' said Lucy.

Ella realised they were both staring and instantly felt bad. She scrambled out of the car to greet him. 'Kit. Hi.' She fiddled with her hair. 'I didn't expect you'd be here today. This is above and beyond.' She glanced down at the sheen of sweat on his chest, and the light muscle definition she found there. She dragged her eyes back up to his face.

'Actually. I'm only here because I wanted to see you but I thought I should at least make myself useful so I've put up the stud wall for the partition.'

Something flipped inside Ella. She pushed her hair off her face. 'See me. Why?'

'I've been calling you since yesterday but you wouldn't pick up or reply to my texts.' She now realised he looked a little cross. 'Mum's been going crazy with all these messages. What the hell did you do?'

'Ah, that would be me,' said Lucy, stepping forward and offering a hand to shake. Kit wiped his palm on his jeans and they shook. 'I'm Lucy. Ella dropped her phone.'

'When you called me,' butted in Ella. 'I was up a tree and I dropped the phone and it smashed. Sorry.'

Lucy wagged a finger at her. 'Not your fault. Don't admit liability.' She turned back to Kit who was studying her closely. 'You wanted Ella to call your mother. Jane, is it?' He nodded. 'However, with her phone out of action she wasn't able to. I suggested to the group that were they approached on our night out by a male who asked for their number but they didn't want to share their own they could give out Jane's. I'm guessing quite a few did just that.'

'Mum had to switch her phone off in the end. Some bloke said he was from Turkey and he wouldn't leave her alone.'

Ella had to stop herself from chuckling. Even Auntie Rita had gone for the fob off. 'I'm s—' Ella saw Lucy scowl at her which halted her apology. 'How did their meal go after you cancelled their table? Do you know?'

Kit looked uncomfortable. 'She wasn't happy when she got in. She said there had been some mistake with their reservation and she made a joke about Davine having dementia and apparently *Davine* didn't think it was funny.'

'Granny, Dad's mum, she died of Alzheimer's,' said Ella.

'Crap. No wonder he reacted badly. And then at the end of the evening the messages started to come in thick and fast.' He glared at Lucy. She didn't look bothered.

'Is your mum okay now?' asked Ella, feeling bad about what had happened.

Kit shrugged. 'She was quiet this morning.'

They stood for a moment in silence. 'Right,' said Lucy. 'I'm going to get off.'

'Are you going to be all right?' Ella was concerned about Lucy going home when someone had been lurking about trying door handles but Lucy didn't seem fazed by it. Although Ella knew full well she sometimes put on a brave face making it hard to know for certain.

'My home is secure. The alerts are on full volume. I'll call the police if he comes back but as he's found it's all locked up he probably won't bother. Stop worrying.' She went to the boot and hauled out Ella's bag and handed it to her along with her cowboy hat. Kit did a double take. 'Take care. Don't take any crap from Wanda, or anyone,' said Lucy with a glance in Kit's direction. They hugged and Lucy got in her car and drove off.

'Sorry, I was a bit off there. I thought maybe you'd put Mum's number on the internet. Which I now know you didn't. I'm sorry.' He looked contrite.

'It's fine. Do we think we're making progress with Project Split?'

'I'm not sure. She said something about seeing Davine in the week.'

Ella felt deflated. 'We're back to square one and we're running out of ideas.'

CHAPTER NINETEEN

Ella was excited to see she had interest from brides on her website. Less so when she realised some of them had tried to call her and had left messages on her now defunct mobile. When she set up her new phone her morale drooped even lower. Wanda must have passed on her number because she had a tediously long message from Ashley, of hashtag Naked Bride fame, which in far too many words basically said, *As I've fallen out with Wanda you need to alter my dress for free because this is all your fault.* This was not how she'd hoped running a business would be.

Monday dawned – her last day of full-time employment or nine hours as she had now moved on to counting them down. The atmosphere was like that moment in a horror movie when you were waiting for the killer to jump out and bludgeon everyone to death. Maybe today was when Wanda would wield the final blow.

It was going to be a very busy day, there were so many final fittings and dresses going out, Ella hoped the hours would fly by which would also mean minimal interaction with Wanda. The first bride through the door was the lovely, bubbly sort and a little hard to keep focused on actually getting into the dress for Ella to check all was well. When she was ready Ella opened the curtain and her heart sank, the dress was dragging on the ground, it was far too long.

'Are those the shoes you're wearing on the day?' It was a surprisingly common occurrence that brides forgot to bring their heels with them.

'Yes.' The bride proudly lifted the dress to reveal bright red cowboy boots. For a moment Ella thought how good they would have been for the hen weekend and then expelled it from her mind in order to concentrate.

'But you didn't wear those for the fittings.' Ella would definitely have remembered them.

'Change of plan. We decided it would be fun to do something to surprise each other on the day and I remembered he has this little Daisy Duke fantasy so I thought cowboy boots.' She waggled her left boot at Ella.

'Right. But now the dress doesn't fit.'

'It's fine.' The bride checked herself in the mirror and smoothed the lavish material over her hips.

'No, it's not. It's far too long. You'll catch a toe and trip over.'

'Huh. I hadn't thought of that.'

'Could you go back to the heels maybe?' Ella crossed her fingers behind her back.

'But he'll be disappointed.' She pouted like a child.

'Not if he didn't know anything about them. How about Daisy Duke hot pants under the dress?' The bride wasn't looking convinced. 'In white denim.'

'I like that idea.'

'Terrific.' Before she could think too much about it, Ella had her out of the cowboy boots and into some shoes of a similar height to the ones she'd previously worn. They also sold wedding shoes in various styles and heights making it easy to grab a pair for the bride to try. Ella checked and double checked – the dress was now fine.

After that bride she ticked off another four in quick succession.

She scooted the dresses along the rail and turned back to her workstation where there was one final dress she was hoping to complete before she left.

Wanda was standing in the doorway as if waiting for something to happen. 'Can I help you?' ventured Ella.

'Okay. You win,' said Wanda with a flick of her head so strong her heavily hair-sprayed do almost moved.

'Sorry?' Ella had no idea what she was talking about, but she didn't have time to waste. She picked up the dress and got back to work.

'I thought you would have backed down sooner than this and you haven't. Fair play to you, Ella. I'm prepared to put this silly argument behind us and call it quits.' Wanda smiled and it was quite the terrifying sight.

'Wanda, I would like us to leave on good terms too. Apology accepted and I'm sorry but I really need to get on.'

Wanda's eyebrows pulled together. 'I'm saying you don't have to leave. You can have your job back. I reinstate you.' Wanda stared at her without blinking

This was it. This was the moment when Ella could take the easy option. Let everything go back to how it was. Stay under the radar and avoid any sweeping changes to her life. Although now it was presented to her, she wasn't sure she could. She'd gone too far down the new road and while it was scary as hell she was still doing it and that had given her confidence a much-needed boost. Wanda was expecting an answer.

Ella took a deep breath. 'But I *am* leaving. I have worked my notice. I've set up my own business.' Ella rummaged in her bag and pulled out one of her business cards and proudly handed it to Wanda. She hadn't dared to hope that Wanda would recommend her to clients but just in case she had put a few cards in her bag.

Wanda stared at the card for a moment looking as if she'd been slapped in the face with a custard tart. At last, she spoke. 'You can't do that!'

'Yes, I can.' Ella hoped the conversation didn't turn into a pantomime. The shop door opened and Ella sent up thanks for another customer. 'I need to get on if I'm to get all these dresses out today.' She indicated the rail behind her.

'But . . .'

'Excuse me.' Ella left Wanda muttering to herself and went to serve the next bride on her long list.

***

Lucy's boss had been terrific – he was outraged at someone creeping around her property and showed real concern about her state of mind. He had offered to remove her from the Maxwell case which she had seriously considered but ultimately it would feel like she was abandoning Mrs Maxwell and there was no guarantee it would stop the husband harassing her, so she had pledged to see it through to the end. A court date was set and things were moving in the right direction. Her boss had also had a quiet word with Mr Maxwell's solicitor because they were on dodgy ground if they were to make an accusation about their client as the CCTV footage was inconclusive, but it did no harm to tell them, off the record, what their client might be getting up to and how potentially damaging that could be to their case.

Lucy had managed to find someone to upgrade her alarm system at short notice and now had two additional cameras installed. She'd also added extra bolts to her front and back doors. All the additional security measures had given her some piece of mind.

Her focus for the next few days was a couple who had set up a business together and had a mix of assets, some in joint names, some in sole names and it was going to take a lot of sifting through and sorting out. Especially as they both seemed to value their sole items very low and their spouse's assets very high. Perception was an odd thing and it somehow became distorted as soon as the word divorce was mentioned. Lucy shut her office door and engrossed herself in mapping out a plan to get everything properly evaluated and a proposed way of splitting things without too much disruption. It was a lot like puzzle solving and that played to her strengths.

There was a tap on her door and she jolted. She told herself it was just because she had been engrossed, she didn't like the thought that the Maxwell case was making her jumpy. She'd also found it was bringing back long-suppressed bad memories from her childhood, which was also unhelpful. She looked up to see her assistant was holding a small bunch of flowers. 'Delivery,' she trilled from behind the spray.

'Thanks.' Lucy made a space on her desk. They instantly brightened the room and also cheered up something inside Lucy. She never received flowers. That was something for soppy steady daters, guilty husbands to send to unknowing wives and people with too much money on Valentine's Day. Her assistant left and Lucy checked the flowers over. It was a simple bunch of carnations but all the same she was touched – someone had been thoughtful. But who were they from? She looked out into the open office to see if anyone was watching. Maybe her boss was trying to cheer her up but most likely it was Cory at last coming to his senses. She felt smug at the thought. It had been a while but had he finally come around? She hoped so because she was missing sex and was currently too busy to find someone new. If this was Cory's olive branch she wouldn't need to bother.

She was smiling as she unfolded the note stuck in between the blooms. She stared at the message. Ice crept through her veins. 'I missed you this time. But I'll be back soon.' Nope that was definitely not from Cory.

***

Ella sent off her last bride of the day with a smile and a wave and tried to control the bubbling emotions. After four years at Frills, Frocks and Fairy Tales she was sad to leave. She was also excited

157

and mildly terrified about starting her own business. She had received a trickle of enquiries but as yet nobody was booked in. She had convinced herself that that was all fine because she hadn't done any real promotion and she currently had a half-finished business premises which would not be ready to receive customers for at least another week. Kit had advised her to leave the plaster before painting it which was delaying things, although the electrician was fitting her many lights and the carpenter was also due in so she had high hopes for when she got home.

She had managed to finish the dress she'd been working on. She zipped up the garment carrier, checked the outer label and hung it on the rail. An involuntary sigh escaped. That was it. The end of an era. The last guaranteed monthly wage. Also the end of the daily battles and sarcastic put-downs from Wanda. She placed her last few work possessions in a box, picked up her bag and switched off the light in her little domain for the last time.

Ella tapped the glass on Wanda's office but for once didn't wait to be asked in. She plonked the shop keys on her desk. 'I'm sorry it's ended like this,' she said. 'But I wish you well,' added Ella, her heart still hopeful of something similar in response for her years of dedication and hard work.

Wanda slowly turned to face her. 'Get out.'

Ella hated the tears which sprang to her eyes, but she kept her composure and strode from the shop. If anything confirmed to her that, despite all her worries, she was doing the right thing it was a response like that.

Kit O'Leary's van was on her drive when she pulled up and she felt a frisson of excitement. It was purely the expectation of what work had been completed inside and nothing to do with Kit – that was what she told herself. She let herself in through the new door to find the room empty. 'Hello?' she called.

'Hey there,' said Kit, appearing from the other side of the partition. 'Is this it? Are you a free woman?' he asked.

'I'm an unemployed woman. If that's what you mean.' She laughed.

'Self-employed. Very different. Come and have a look at what the chippy has done. He's used all reclaimed wood. Please say if it's not right. We can still make changes because it's not fully fixed in yet.' He beckoned her over.

She stopped because although the lights were off, she'd seen something that indicated the electrician had been. 'My chandelier is up.' She'd ordered it off the internet in a wild moment and had had buyer's remorse ever since, mainly at the cost and it hadn't looked quite as impressive when she'd peeped into the box as it had been in about a hundred different packages. But now it was up it looked magnificent and made a real statement to anyone entering her little business.

'You can do the official switch-on.' Kit strode over to the new bank of switches on the wall by the door. 'Main switch, that puts all the lights on in one go. The others are for the different zones. All yours.' He stepped back.

Ella couldn't help giving a little jig of delight as her finger hovered over the main switch. She flicked it on and the room was filled with light. The chandelier came into its own as all the crystals twinkled back at her and she let out a tiny gasp. 'My goodness, it's beautiful.'

'Come and look at the carpentry.'

She followed him behind the partition and was wowed still further. The end wall was divided into rails and shelving. There was plenty of hanging space – she hoped one day to be able to fill it. Opposite the rails was her new workstation. A simple wooden tabletop in an L shape so she had a designated space for where her sewing machines would sit, with a shelf above and also a long bench section where she could lay out dresses. Under the short section was a small drawer – perfect for keeping what she most needed to hand like pins and scissors. Under the long section were two lots of drawers ideal for all manner of things from

159

cottons to sequins and sticky notes. She ran her hand along the surface.

'I love your arris,' said Kit, sounding distracted.

'What?' Ella twisted to look at him. Was he commenting on her bum? She had to think. 'Aristotle. Bottle. Bottle and glass. Rhymes with ar—'

'No.' Kit jerked as if realising the issue. 'Arris. Not the rhyming slang version. Arris are triangular cuts of wood usually used on fencing. It's been repurposed to make the bench.' She was still looking blankly at him. 'See underneath.' He crouched down and she copied him.

While it was flat on top, the underside was a series of zigzags where the pieces had been fixed together, giving an unusual and pretty pattern on the end. 'Wow,' she said when nothing more poetic came to mind.

'You like it?'

'It's perfect. All of it. Thank you, Kit.'

He looked chuffed. 'You're welcome. Happy customers leave great reviews,' he said with a tilt of his head.

'Yes, of course.' For a moment she'd forgotten she was paying him and he wasn't doing it out of the goodness of his heart.

'Once you get some paint on the walls and some carpet down, you'll be open for business.'

Ella surveyed her new premises. It suddenly seemed like there were a lot of walls to be painted, she'd not got around to looking at carpet or even being certain that she wanted carpet throughout. She'd not worked out how she was going to put in the fitting room curtain rails. And there were still the other finishing touches like large mirrors and seating.

'Are you okay?' Kit waved a hand in front of her face.

'There's still loads to do before I can even invite a bride in here let alone start work and actually make some money.'

'Hey. Look at what you've already achieved.' His voice was

160

gentle. 'In a few short weeks you've gone from Cinderella to . . .' She eyed him expectantly. 'Elon Musk.'

She had to laugh. 'I don't feel like Elon Musk. I feel like a fraud and a charlatan who is playing at something she knows nothing about and I'm sick to my stomach that it's all going to backfire horribly on me.' She was appalled at herself for blurting that out to Kit. Although he was no longer the annoying bloke who had approached her in that pub all those weeks ago, he was someone who, despite his lack of tact, had made a huge positive impact on her life. 'Ignore me wittering on. Would you like a cup of tea or something stronger?'

'Builder's tea would be great.'

A few minutes later they were sitting in her small garden enjoying the warm summer air and a cuppa when Pirate announced his arrival. He meowed at her before rubbing around her legs. Although it was short-lived because as soon as he spotted Kit he trotted over and jumped on his lap. 'Hey, handsome fella.' He greeted Pirate with a smile and lots of strokes – quite different to their first encounter.

'Has Rufus been on any more days out?' asked Ella.

Kit rolled his eyes. 'No, but only because we have a daily bag check. It's like working in an airport, the level of inspections we have to do just to make sure Isaac doesn't sneak Rufus out with him. One day last week he even put him in his lunch box.' Ella spluttered a laugh. 'I had to redo his lunch with minutes to spare before school.' He shook his head good-naturedly. 'That boy is a monster.'

'You two are really close, aren't you?'

'Yeah. We're an odd little family but somehow it works.'

'Do you mind me asking where Isaac's dad is?'

'My sister got pregnant by an on and off boyfriend and the relationship ended badly. She didn't want him involved in bringing up her baby. She said nobody should be raised in a war zone. At the time we accepted her choice to go it alone. She had Mum and Dad and, to an extent, me too. But then . . . life pulled the rug.'

'I'm sorry . . . about your sister.'

'Thanks. She was a great mum and she totally could have done this on her own. And I still think it's best for Isaac that the boyfriend wasn't involved. I heard he'd got a suspended sentence for getting into some fight so not exactly the best role model.'

'He's got a good one in you.' She instantly felt embarrassed at complimenting him.

'Thanks. Me and Mum do what we can. It's not what any of us planned but I think he's happy and that's all that matters.' He moved awkwardly to reach his mug without disturbing Pirate. 'Anyway, when's the big launch party?' He watched her expectantly.

'For what?'

He almost snorted out his tea. 'Your new business.'

Ella blinked more times than was necessary. She'd not considered a party or a launch as such. 'Do I need one?'

'No, but it's a good excuse for one. You can show off your premises to prospective clients. Give out flyers with a few glasses of wine.'

'I don't know.' Ella sucked the inside of her mouth and then remembered it made her look like a constipated tortoise, so she stopped. 'I suppose I could invite the owners of the other wedding shops in the area. Let them see that I've got a professional set-up. Might be a good opportunity to meet them and show off my arris.'

'There you go. That's all the reason you need. And how often do you start your own business?'

'True but before any partying I really do need to get it finished.' The now all too familiar sense of urgency formed a knot of tension behind her ribs. 'It would be something to aim for. Give me some much-needed focus.'

'I'm free this weekend if you want help with the decorating,' he said.

'Thanks but I fear your bill is already running to two pages.' She grimaced.

A frown flitted across Kit's forehead. 'A quote is a quote. That's all you need to pay me. Anything else I've done, I've done as a friend.'

Ella was a bit stunned by his turn of phrase. Were they friends? It wasn't something she'd considered. 'Thanks, Kit. That's really kind of you.'

'Look I know this is going to sound like I'm a sad case, but I've liked helping out here. Working with my hands again. Doing all the office stuff is dull. My sister used to handle that side of things.'

'I hadn't realised you were in business together.'

'It was Dad's business. When he was taken ill we had to get up to speed pretty quick. I was already working for him. He wanted me to learn from the bottom up. Started me off as a labourer to earn my stripes. No son-of-the-boss privileges for me. And it was a good grounding in the business. I didn't expect to take over quite so soon and I wasn't ready which was why it was the three of us – Mum, my sister and me. Mum still keeps an eye on the accounts but otherwise it's all me and the team. I sound like I'm spinning a sob story.' He drank some of his tea. 'Anyway, I can get paint at trade prices and if you want some help decorating just say the word.'

'Yes, please. I was going to rope Lucy in and possibly Brittany but she's on wedding countdown which seems to mean her stress levels increase on a daily basis.'

He scrunched up a shoulder. 'The more the merrier.' He checked his watch. 'Let me know what colour and I'll pick some paint up.'

'White, please.'

'You're my easiest customer,' he said, getting to his feet and passing her the cat. 'I'll see you on Saturday.'

She was already looking forward to it.

CHAPTER TWENTY

Lucy had binned the note with the creepy message and given the flowers to her assistant to take home which had at least cheered up her day. She didn't need to keep the note, what it said was etched on her brain. This guy didn't give up easily but how he thought it was going to help his cause she had no idea; all it did was make her all the more determined that her client would win and get exactly what she wanted from the divorce and childcare arrangements. Lucy wasn't a vindictive person, but this was pushing her to her limits. It was a struggle not to advise her client to make his life a living hell but she was too professional for that.

She still got the feeling she was being watched but she had taken steps to stay safe: she parked near a camera, had CCTV mounted on her property and locked herself up at night like she was her own jailer. There had been no repeat of the mystery man snooping around although she did have excellent footage of next door's cat crapping in her flowerpot at three in the morning – little sod.

She was pleased to be getting out of the house on Saturday morning although she wasn't sure a date with a paint roller was what constituted as having a social life but it was better than being holed up at home either eating her own body weight in ice cream or working.

There were so many locks on her front door it was like living in a Tom and Jerry cartoon. When she was finally able to open the door her phone rang and the voice on the other end made her gasp.

***

Ella woke on Saturday with a fresh mindset. Now she knew that the lovely Kit wasn't going to charge her any extra than the quote, apart from the paint, she knew how much of her savings she had left to play with which meant she could order a few more things. A conversation with her mum had proved fruitful because she'd been complaining about the cost of a chaise longue and her mum had offered up her granny's two old wingback chairs. They were ornate and while the dark green wasn't Ella's first choice, she did like green and thought if she ran with it as an accent colour it would give a fresh look to the room. She planned to get some trailing plants and Kit had agreed to put up some shelves for her once the decorating was complete. She'd even got some flooring samples but she was going to consult Lucy and Brittany on those when they arrived.

She'd also ordered a new doorbell for the business so she would know which door to go to when someone came. The sound of church bells rang through the kitchen telling her someone had arrived at the business entrance and she happily went through to let them in.

'Hi Brittany, how are you?' she asked as Brittany stepped tentatively inside as if the structure was unstable.

'Wow. It doesn't even look like a garage. It's like a big room. I'd like a conservatory, but this wedding is costing a blooming fortune as is the honeymoon and . . .' Brittany's voice broke and she began to sob. 'Grant and I had a row about sugared almonds.'

Ella scrunched up her features in thought. 'What?'

'Wedding favours,' said Brittany through multiple sniffs.

'Oh, sweetie, don't upset yourself over something like that. Come here.' She gave her a hug.

The doorbell went but Ella knew who was there without opening it. 'Come in, Kit,' she called rather than let go of her weeping friend.

A jolly-looking Kit marched inside with two extra-large tubs of paint precariously balanced in his arms as he manoeuvred the door shut. 'We need to do a mist coat first which is like a watered-down layer because the plaster is fresh . . . oh . . . hello,' he said, seeing Brittany and coming to a halt next to Ella. 'Everything okay?'

'Wedding stress,' said Ella in a low voice. 'I'll be with you in a minute.'

The church bells rang out again and Ella revelled in Kit's expression. 'I like that,' he said, putting the paint down.

'Me too,' said Ella. She nodded at the door. 'Do you think you could answer it?'

'Sure.'

He opened the door and Lucy barrelled right in. 'You will not believe who the shitting hell rang me this morning,' said Lucy, looking like she was ready to punch someone's lights out.

'Not your stalker!' Ella was gripped by concern and shuffled herself and Brittany around so she could see Lucy better.

'Worse.' Lucy put her hands on her hips. 'Only my bloody mother!'

Thankfully there was a lot less drama once Kit had set everyone to work. He had all the required equipment and was quietly overseeing the process. With four of them working together the mist coat was applied in record time. They didn't need to be too precise with it which was good because both Lucy and Brittany kept stopping to talk and dripped rollers in all directions. But the rhythm of painting seemed to calm them all down. They stood back to admire their handiwork.

'That needs to dry,' said Kit. 'With weather like this it won't take too long but it will need a few hours.'

'Let's take a break and have a look at my flooring samples,' suggested Ella.

There was a distinct lack of enthusiasm from the others. But once they had cold drinks in their hands and a variety of samples strewn across the floor there was a little more interest.

'What do we think about carpet in the customer section and wood or tiles in my bit?' asked Ella.

'Carpet's warmer,' said Brittany.

'Hard floor is easier to sweep,' said Kit.

'I liked the carpet at Wanda's. It felt sumptuous when you walked on it,' said Brittany.

'A lot of that will be down to a good underlay,' said Kit.

'I think I like the lighter grey.' Ella touched the square nearest to her with her trainer. 'I could have a darker grey for the door mat.'

'My mother's a door mat,' muttered Lucy.

'Why has your mum got in touch out of the blue?' asked Ella.

Lucy's jaw clenched. 'Why does she ever? She wants something. She's not said what yet, but she will.' Ella could tell Lucy's irritation was there to hide concern.

'Did you chat?'

'I didn't have time. I told her to call back later. Much later. Like November.'

Ella gave her friend a little nudge. 'You're not that mean,' she said.

Lucy sighed heavily. 'I wish I was because I dread to think what she wants.'

The friends did a great job of the decorating and Ella applied a final coat the next day and glossed the skirting boards. Within days the carpet was fitted in the front section with the most expensive underlay as per Kit's suggestion and the effect was luxurious. Ella went for laminate flooring in her work area as it wasn't as cold as tiles but it was easy to clean and she was pleased with the zoning it created. Her first task in her new workspace had been to make the curtains for the fitting rooms and she'd gone for a subtle pattern in green and white. She'd whipped up a matching roman blind for the window too. There was a bay tree in a large pot in the corner next to one of two giant ornate mirrors she'd picked up from a local auction house. They'd been described as 'ideal for restoration' but Ella liked them as they were with the look of wear and tear where the years had left their mark.

Everything was ready for the launch: she'd bought lots of prosecco, an alcohol-free version and some flavoured water – basically she'd gone for clear liquids so any spillages didn't ruin her new carpet. All that was missing was the two chairs Mum and Dad had promised to supply. She was about to check her new clock for the umpteenth time when the church bells of the business doorbell rang out and she rushed to see who it was.

'Hello, darling.' Her mother was reversing towards her as she carried a chair in on its back.

'Hi Mum.' Her father's head popped up at the other end and he smiled. 'Hi Dad.' He looked the same, his familiar smile in place. It was hard for Ella to think of him as anything but a loving husband and father, not a cheating adulterer who could break her mother's heart.

'What do you think of this?' he said as they stood the chair upright.

Ella realised her granny's chair had been subjected to a drastic transformation. It was the same chair but the old dull green material had been replaced by a far richer shade of the same colour in a luxurious velveteen fabric. 'It looks fabulous.' She stroked the arm and it felt as soft and sumptuous as it looked.

'There's another one in the car. Thank goodness I've got an estate,' he said.

'I'm pleased you like it.' Her mother gave her a hug. They parted and Sandy took in her surroundings. 'Oh, Ella, this is . . .' Her voice cracked with emotion. She put a hand to her chest. 'Silly me getting emotional. I'm just so proud of you.' She reached out and squeezed Ella's hand. There was something in the contact that made Ella want to cry too.

'Mum? Is everything okay?'

'Is someone going to give me a hand with this chair?' called David, through the open door.

An hour later the party was in full flow and her little business space was pleasantly crowded with a mix of friends, family and potential business contacts. Two wedding shop owners had come and were making the right noises about working with her although they had both talked about discounts and competitive rates which was something Ella would need to think carefully about. Brittany was now regaling them with the wonders Ella had performed on her gown and bridesmaids' dresses which could only help. Ella had seen Kit arrive and was keen to keep him away from her dad which was quite tricky in a small, crowded space with very few men.

'Thanks for coming, Kit,' she said. 'What would you like to drink? My arris is doubling as a bar tonight.' She gave him a cheeky grin.

He nodded his approval at her joke. 'I'll have a glass of Prosecco, please. Just a small one. I have to toast your new venture.'

They slipped behind the partition and she handed him a drink.

'Cheers,' he said, taking a swig. 'And congratulations. The space looks amazing. It's way better than where you used to work.'

Everyone had been nice about the premises but him saying it seemed to add more weight to it. And made her feel proud. 'Thanks. You were a big part of it.'

Kit winced. 'Yeah. I still feel kinda guilty that your boss had a go at you because of my calls.'

'Oh no. I didn't mean that. The quote. The conversion. All of this. You gave me the shove I needed. Thank you.'

'It was nothing.' They found they were staring at each other and both looked away at the same time.

'It wasn't nothing. And well. Thanks.' There was an awkward pause. 'My dad's here.' She wasn't sure she needed to explain further.

'I guessed he would be. It's okay. I'm not going to say anything. I think it's over – him and Mum.'

'Really?' A sprig of hope flowered in her chest like a daisy opening for the sun.

'I asked about Davine and Mum's answers were all clipped and anyway there's no plans for them to meet up anytime soon.'

'We got the job done,' she said, punching the air and sounding like someone from *Hamilton*. Why was she behaving like an idiot?

'Project Split was a success.' He smiled and gently clinked his glass against hers. 'Well done us.'

'Us,' she repeated and felt even more foolish. But the truth was she was attracted to Kit. Not just his rugged good looks but him as a person. He was kind, helpful and he'd encouraged her to make a huge positive change in her life.

She saw his eyebrow twitch. 'Anyway,' he said. 'I did get you a present, but Rufus escaped.' He made quotation marks in the air as he said escaped. 'Isaac suddenly discovered that Rufus had mysteriously vanished. It happens sometimes if I'm going out. It took a while to track him down, so I was in a rush and I've left your present behind. But I'll drop it in next time I'm over this way.'

'You didn't need to get me something but it's kind of you. Whatever it is. Which I'm sure is something nice.' *Okay stop talking Ella.* She was getting all tongue-tied. Lucy appeared and refilled her glass and Ella grabbed her while Kit was looking over how she'd labelled her rails and shelving.

'Lucy. Can you keep Kit away from my dad?' she said in a hushed tone. She felt Kit would be true to his word but it would still be uncomfortable for him to have to make small talk to the man who, until very recently, had been dating his mum.

Lucy sipped her drink and scanned Kit up and down. 'It would be my absolute pleasure.' Ella could tell Lucy was in flirting mode and it made her uncomfortable but she'd have to let it go because the thought of Kit and her dad together was too much.

Ella found she wasn't as bad at mingling as she thought she might be. Everyone wanted to talk about dressmaking, weddings and alterations – her absolute favourite things – which made it easy to chat to people. Her pile of flyers was going down almost as fast as the Prosecco. A few people started to leave, mainly the local business owners which was nice in one way because she could relax a little more but now there were fewer people she feared Kit and her father were going to end up meeting.

She was chatting to her dad about golf, or more accurately, listening about some changes his golf club had made to teeing off times which was upsetting him while, out of the corner of her eye, she watched Lucy fawn over Kit. Ella felt a green-eyed monster rear its head. She had no claim on Kit and no right to be jealous but it wasn't pleasant to witness.

'Is that your builder chappy?' asked her dad.

'Er, yeah but . . .' Before she had formed an excuse David was already putting his glass down.

'I best say hello before I need to make a move.'

'No, hang on.' Panic was rising in her gut. The church bells rippled through the room and made everyone chuckle and turn to see who it was. Ella opened the door and froze.

Isaac ran in and straight to Kit but Ella was struggling to pull her eyes away from who else was standing on the threshold. 'Hi, I'm Kit's mum,' said Jane. 'He forgot your present and I know he went to a lot of trouble to get it so I thought I'd drop it over and . . .' Jane stopped talking. She had spotted David. Ella looked at Kit who was also witnessing the scene unfold.

Bugger, thought Ella. She had no idea what to do.

'Whoops!' said Isaac, a welcome distraction pulling everyone's attention. 'I think Rufus has escaped again.'

PART THREE

CHAPTER TWENTY-ONE

Ella wasn't sure what she was most alarmed by: the fact that her father's ex-mistress was on her doorstep or that Isaac's rat was now loose at her launch party. Thank heavens the important business associates she'd been schmoozing had already left.

'I've lost my rat!' wailed Isaac which got everyone's attention and, slightly belatedly, someone squealed.

'This way,' announced Lucy, taking charge, even in her inebriated state she was still the one with the strongest leadership qualities.

'Ooh I love rats,' said Brittany. 'I'll help look.' She went to bend down and then stopped. 'Actually I'm desperate for a wee. Sorry.' And she dashed from the room as Lucy held open the door to the hallway and people evacuated. All except Ella's parents, Ella, Jane, Kit and Isaac, who was on his hands and knees checking under the fitting room curtains.

Ella had a quick glance under the chairs and the table before realising she was searching for something she really didn't want to find. She was not a rodent fan.

David cleared his throat and opened his mouth but no words materialised. Ella looked from him to her mother who was sipping her fizz but watching her husband closely. He slumped into one of the wingbacked chairs. Ella wanted to curl up into a ball – the tension was too much.

'Mum,' said Kit. 'You didn't need to do this. I was going to bring it over in the week.'

Jane was still staring at David as Kit strode across the room and relieved her of the large box. He turned to Ella. 'I got you this to say congratulations.'

He plonked the heavy parcel in her arms and she was glad of the distraction. She put it down on the other chair and proceeded to open it. She pulled off the box lid and for the second time in as many minutes she was stunned by what she saw. It was a vintage Singer sewing machine, complete with turning handle, mounted on a wooden plinth.

'Oh my goodness, Kit. It's beautiful.'

Did she imagine it or was he blushing under that stubble? 'I thought it might look good in here. Especially on that shelf.' He took it from the box and placed it on the floating shelf he'd put up above the two chairs.

They stood back to admire the sewing machine. It was black with ornate gold lettering and to Ella's mind was a thing of beauty. 'It's completely perfect. Thank you.' She gave him a kiss on the cheek.

'Rufus! There you are,' came Isaac's voice from the other side of the partition.

'Thank heavens,' said Jane, who appeared to be freed from her state of suspended animation and went to join Isaac.

David got to his feet. 'I think we should probably make a move,' he said. His words were for Ella but his eyes were following Jane.

'Don't go on my account,' called Jane and Ella had that feeling of being on the precipice just before someone pushes you over the edge. She grimaced at Kit. This was a nightmare.

'It's okay,' said Sandy and a look passed between her and David. Ella felt like her head was on a swivel. Did her mother know about the two of them?

'No, we should go,' said David, reaching for the door. 'It's been lovely, Ella.' He gave her a hug. 'Congratulations again, Pumpkin.'

'You know where we are if you need us,' said her mother, kissing her cheek.

'Ditto,' said Ella. Her mother narrowed her eyes but before she could question Ella's response David had linked his arm through hers and was guiding her outside.

'Bye,' he said and shut the door behind them.

Ella breathed out so hard she felt like a punctured bouncy castle. She looked at Kit but he just held up his hands.

'Right. One rat safely captured,' said Jane, appearing from behind the partition with a grinning Isaac holding a very wriggly Rufus.

'Here,' said Ella, handing Jane the sewing machine box. 'That might be safer in the car.'

'Thank you,' said Jane with feeling and they popped Rufus inside. 'You stay, Kit. Enjoy the rest of the evening,' she added. 'We'll see you at home.' She turned to Ella. 'Sorry if Rufus spoiled your party.'

'It's fine. Nice to meet you.' They exchanged awkward smiles as Ella opened the door for Jane to leave.

What Ella hadn't bargained for was that her parents were still on her driveway and from the sound of things were having a heated discussion.

'I think now is as good a time as any,' said Sandy.

'And spoil her big moment?' said David. 'I disag—Oh hello, darling.' David's eyes were darting between Jane and Ella. 'Um, Pumpkin. I mean Ella.' David pointed past Jane at his daughter.

'Hello, Jane, I'm Sandy,' said her mum, offering a hand for Jane to shake.

'Do something,' hissed Ella to Kit who was standing next to her watching the exchange.

'What?' said Kit. She didn't have the answer. She could barely stand to watch and yet she couldn't drag her eyes away.

'Hi Sandy, I've heard a lot about you,' said Jane. 'All good,' she added and they both chuckled.

'Safe journeys,' called Ella over the top of everyone.

'What are you doing?' whispered Kit.

'Trying to get them all to go,' said Ella before stepping outside and almost shooing them into their cars. Isaac was already climbing into the back of Jane's car.

'I'm sorry, David. I'm going to tell her,' said Sandy. She took hold of both of Ella's hands. 'I'm sorry to drop this on you, darling. But your dad and I have split up.'

Ella couldn't stop the gasp. This was the moment she'd been dreading but one she hoped she and Kit had thwarted. It felt like the foundations of her life were crumbling under her feet. She looked from Kit to Jane and tried hard not to glare at the woman who had ruined her parents' marriage.

'You see. We grew apart,' continued Sandy. 'We had been for years and once you left home we were living in the same house but we weren't really a couple so last year I suggested we separate and Dad moved out as a—'

Ella's head was spinning. 'Wait what? Last year?'

'Yes,' said Sandy. 'I'm sorry. We did try to tell you but you were rather upset about breaking up with Todd and then the next time we were going to say something you had that horrible tummy bug and then you lost your job so there's not been a good opportunity.'

Ella felt like she was having an out of body experience. 'But when I visited everything was fine. You were together.' She thought of all the little gestures between them. The knowing looks, the affection.

'We arranged for your dad to come over for your visits. He's got a place in Fakenham. I've helped him decorate it. It's lovely, you'll like it,' said Sandy, giving her husband a warm smile.

'My head is going to explode. Why are you being nice to each other?' Tension gripped Ella's shoulders

'We were always firm friends first,' said her father. 'We still care greatly for each other. We're just not in love any more. We'll always be close because we share a lot of the same interests and we have you.'

'But when I call you're on the extension.' She wasn't sure why she thought of it at that moment but she was trying to process the enormity one snippet at a time.

Her father was already shaking his head. 'Your mother messages me and we call you back as a three-way conference call. They work rather well, actually. I use them to arrange teeing off times with the boys.'

'Not now, David,' said her mother.

'But you and Jane . . .' Ella couldn't finish the sentence. She shook her head at her father. He had the decency to look guilty. Surely their relationship was what was at the rotting core of the problem? 'You were seeing another woman, Dad.'

Jane stepped forward as if being called to the witness box. 'We're not together any more,' she said. 'Our relationship didn't work out. But I promise you we didn't meet until after he'd separated from Sandy.'

'You would say that,' said Ella.

Sandy had a look in her eye. 'Our split has nothing to do with Jane. Your father met her after he moved out.'

'Did he?' questioned Ella, feeling so confused. 'Are you sure they've not been sneaking off for pub meals and golf lessons for a very long time?'

Sandy narrowed her eyes at her daughter. 'You knew. Didn't you?'

It was Ella's turn to look guilty.

***

Lucy found herself making teas and coffees for the evacuees, and there were quite a few, who were now mainly spread out in the garden enjoying the warm evening. Brittany came into the kitchen adjusting her top. 'Let's find this rat,' she said, starting to open kitchen cupboards.

'I heard someone shout, so I think they've already found it,' said Lucy.

Brittany looked disappointed. 'Need a hand?' she asked, swaying slightly before taking firm hold of the worktop. She looked how Lucy felt – she'd been knocking the fizz back too.

'I can't find the sweetener,' said Lucy, staring at a series of empty cups. 'Or tea or coffee.'

Brittany giggled and Lucy joined in. 'Shall we just have more Prosecco?' suggested Brittany, opening the fridge and pulling out a bottle.

'Excellent idea.' Lucy opened the back door and shouted out. 'Help yourselves to teas and coffees!' before dissolving into hysterics. A nice woman who Lucy thought Ella had introduced as her hairdresser took over and within a few minutes Brittany and Lucy were alone at the kitchen table.

Brittany was staring at the bubbles in her glass and Lucy was watching her with the same intensity. It seemed quite bizarre to Lucy that Brittany was going to get married. What Brittany was about to do amazed her. Committing to one person for the rest of her life. 'How do you know?' asked Lucy.

Brittany pulled her eyes away from her glass in an exaggerated movement and blinked at Lucy as if trying to focus. 'Know what?'

'That Grant is the one man for you. That forsaking all others is the right decision. You've not met *all* the men. How can you be sure?'

Brittany's lips made a flat line. 'He's kind, he's funny and he likes animals. I won't do any better than Grant. But here's an even bigger question – how am I the right person for him? I'm nothing special. A bit podgy and I let my job seep into my home life. I can't resist an animal in need. If it wasn't for Grant I'd be a crazy cat lady only it wouldn't just be cats.' Pirate arrived on cue like a living example and scanned her with his one good eye. Or more likely he was checking to see if they had food.

Lucy waved her glass and realised it was already empty. 'I think you're amazing. Totally crackers but amazing.' Lucy put down her glass – perhaps she'd had enough Prosecco.

'Thank you.' Brittany sipped her drink. 'What about you, Lucy? Who are you shagging at the moment?'

She was going to protest but what was the point? Brittany had summed it up. She shagged people. She knew it was her choice but was it making her happy? Cory settling down had affected her far more than she liked to admit. She thought she'd found a like-minded soul. Someone to have a long-term no strings attached relationship with. Was that just a marriage without a certificate and mortgage? 'I'm in between men at the moment,' said Lucy.

'Sounds exciting,' said Brittany with a giggle. 'You're far less inhibited than I am. A different man every week.'

'Blimey, I'm not that bad!' Was that really how her friends saw her?

Brittany patted her hand. 'No, I'm not saying you're a slapper.' Lucy's eyebrows shot up but Brittany didn't seem to notice and carried on. 'You're owning your sexuality – that's a good thing. You know what you want and it's sex without commitment. It doesn't matter if they move on to someone else because you'll do the same. I admire you. You're out there having fun and enjoying life. The rest of us have been so caught up in interviewing prospective husbands we've forgotten to enjoy ourselves.'

'You've found someone now,' said Lucy.

'But it doesn't end there. As soon as we find someone then we move onto the next stage which is worrying about losing them and questioning why they are with us in the first place. Always trying to work out how he feels and steer him into telling us without looking needy or crazy while secretly wanting him to get there all on his own.' She suppressed a hiccup. 'From there it's basically a downward spiral of self-loathing and judgement until it becomes a self-fulfilling prophecy and they do find someone else because you're neurotic, obsessive and no fun to be with. You don't have all that crap to deal with. I think it's brilliant.' Brittany grinned at her but Lucy could see that there was some truth behind her words.

'I have other crap,' said Lucy, not knowing where she was going as her thoughts swam about her Prosecco-addled brain. 'As well as the self-loathing and judgement, I also have to be fun *all* the time. The men I date don't want to hear about the shitty day I've had at work. Your men have to, it's part of the deal. My men don't want to know that I feel bloated and full of PMS rage. I schedule meet-ups around my menstrual cycle because they don't ever just want to curl up on the sofa with a tub of ice cream and binge-watch a boxset. They don't want to know that I fight every day to be recognised as being as good as the men in my office even though I know I'm better than most of them. The other women have it even worse because a lot of them are juggling being a mother on top of that misogynistic crap pile.' Lucy took a deep breath and sighed it out. 'And worst of all I am gripped with fear than one day I will look in the mirror and see my mother staring back at me.'

Brittany was frowning with concentration. 'Is that because you'd be sharing a bathroom with her?'

CHAPTER TWENTY-TWO

Ella's head was overflowing. Even though she'd left home many years ago she had remained close to her parents. With just the three of them they were a tight-knit unit. Perhaps that was part of Ella's problem. Was she more hurt that they'd not told her rather than the fact they were breaking up?

'I don't know how you found out about me and your dad,' said Sandy, her eyes were full of sorrow as she squeezed her daughter's hands. 'But I'm sorry we didn't tell you.'

'I'm sorry too,' said David. 'But for the record, how did you find out?'

Kit held his hand up briefly before shoving it into his jeans' pocket. 'That might be my fault. I saw Ella watching you both.' He pointed at David and Jane in turn. 'You were in a pub over near Reepham and we kind of figured it out from there.'

David's head was moving as if it were on a swivel. He locked his eyes on Kit. 'You had Jane and me under surveillance?' David's expression was one of astonishment.

Kit looked alarmed. 'I was concerned about what Mum was . . . well, *who* Mum was . . . I thought if I could see for myself then—'

'You had no right to follow me, Kit,' Jane cut in, looking furious.

'I was worried that's all.' Kit pointed at Ella. 'So was she.'

'Ella? Were you spying on us too?' David looked disappointed.

That was all she needed – for Kit to throw her under the bus. 'I wasn't spying I was there on a blind date who never arrived. But yes, I was worried because I thought my dad was having an affair. But it turns out you can't be having an affair if you're no longer married.' A thought struck her. 'Are you still married? Or have you divorced and forgotten to tell your only daughter that too?' She could feel hot tears waiting behind her eyes.

'Not yet but we're thinking that's probably the right thing to do,' said David.

Ella brushed a tear away. 'Is that really what you want, Mum?' She scanned her mother's face for any sign of sorrow.

Sandy gave a melancholy smile. 'It is, darling. I've met someone too.'

'Oh my goodness.' *This day just gets better and better*, thought Ella, her head was spinning.

'That's great news,' said David, leaning forward and giving Sandy's shoulder a squeeze. 'Where'd you find him?'

'I got dragged along to an am dram performance of *The Fiddler on the Roof* and the lead sang everything in the style of the Bee Gees. I was sitting next to this guy and we both laughed all the way through and in the break he asked me—'

Ella waved her hands to get her parents' attention. They'd had a lot longer to get used to this than she had. 'I'm sorry but I can't cope with this right now. Today was meant to be . . .' Her voice let her down and she couldn't finish her sentence. She looked at the small sign on the door welcoming people to Oh Sew Special. Both her parents stepped forward.

'I'm sorry, Ella,' said her mum. 'Shall I make you a cup of coffee?'

'Or do you have brandy?' asked David. 'It's good for shock.'

'Nanny!' called Isaac from the car. 'Can we go now?'

'Maybe we should all go,' said Jane. 'Would that be best?'

Ella nodded. She didn't dare speak for fear of sobbing. She'd not felt this lost since Todd told her he'd re-evaluated their relationship and it no longer met his requirements.

'Kit, you stay and make sure Ella's all right. I'll see you at home later.' Jane turned to go and there was an awkward moment when she realised she was very close to David. They looked at each other and then stepped apart. 'Anyway, bye, everyone,' said Jane and she got in her car.

Sandy hugged Ella. 'When you're ready to talk, give us a call. We'll always be here for you. Both of us.'

'Three-way conference call, it's the future,' said David, with an uncertain smile before Sandy shooed him into his car.

'Bye, darling,' called Sandy and they drove away.

Deep down she'd been hoping it was all a misunderstanding. Ella felt cold. The light was fading but something brighter had been switched off inside her. What it was exactly she wasn't sure. But it had been something she had been certain about her whole life, something that would always be there, like the tides. A safe port when she needed it. But what was there now? Two people on a conference call – that wasn't the same.

Her parents shared the kind of relationship she had been searching for. One that she believed lasted a lifetime – but apparently, it didn't. Even her parents' love had an expiry date.

'You okay?' asked Kit, leaning into her field of vision. She realised she'd been staring up the street after her dad's car.

'Umm. No. Not okay at all.' She wasn't sure she'd ever get her head around it. She had assumed her mum and dad would be married forever. She'd imagined them getting old together. She felt lost. How did kids cope with this when their parents separated? She had no idea.

'If it helps,' said Kit. 'They both look fine. It must be the right decision for them.'

'But all those years together and then that's it. Bang! They go their separate ways.' It was going to take some time to process.

'I'm sure they'll be okay,' said Kit. 'At least my mum wasn't the other woman. That's a good thing.'

Ella looked at him as realisation dawned. 'Oh my goodness, Kit. What have we done?' He looked puzzled. 'We split them up for no good reason. My dad. Your mum. What if that was their second chance at happiness and we piled in and broke them up.' She put her hands to her face. They'd meddled and even though their intentions had been good they had broken up a relationship for no reason. 'I can't believe this. It's all such a mess.'

There was a clatter from inside Oh Sew Special and Ella and Kit automatically peered through the door. Brittany made an unsteady path towards them. 'Did I miss something?'

Ella took a deep breath. 'You could say that.'

The plan had been for Lucy and Brittany to help Ella tidy up after the party and then do a final dress fitting. As it happened, Kit had helped her sort things out while Brittany had crashed out on the sofa and Lucy was in the garden staring at the stars. Ella put the last of the glasses in the dishwasher and set it off.

'Where's your vacuum?' he asked.

'Under the stairs. But it's okay. I'll do it in the morning.'

'How about you put the kettle on and I'll vac round?'

'Okay.' She didn't have the energy to argue. She was in a daze. She filled the kettle and leant against the counter. She could hear Brittany snoring away in the living room. She popped her head out of the back door.

'Lucy. Do you want a coffee?'

In the fading light a figure turned in her direction. 'No, thanks. I've called a taxi to take me home.'

'You okay?' asked Ella although she didn't really have the band-width to deal with anyone else's problems right at that moment.

'Surprisingly fine after that much Prosecco,' said Lucy, striding over.

The sound of a car horn let them know the taxi had arrived.

'Take care.' Ella gave her a hug and maybe she held on a fraction too long.

Lucy pulled back and tilted her head. 'What's up?'

Ella didn't have the energy to explain it all. 'I'm fine. We still need to do dress fittings. Are you free tomorrow?'

'Yep, I'll see you in the morning.' Lucy kissed her cheek and left.

Ella heard the vacuuming come to an end and Kit appeared. 'All done, you'd never know there'd been a party in there.'

'Thanks for clearing up.' The party seemed like it had been days ago not an hour. All the excitement she'd felt had disappeared like a popped balloon.

'I'm here to help.' Kit had a bashful smile as they watched each other for a fraction longer than was comfortable. Kit seemed to snap out of it first. 'Party went well. Not many flyers left.'

'It was a good idea of yours. I made some useful contacts tonight. Fingers crossed I can turn them into working relationships.' They took their drinks and sat down at the kitchen table.

'Now they've seen what a professional set-up you've got it'll be a cinch.'

'I hope so. And thanks for my sewing machine. You didn't have to get me anything at all.'

'We built an extension for this guy last year and his business was sourcing and restoring sewing machines. Well, restoring some and making those that were unrestorable into ornamental pieces. He did me a good deal on that one.'

'Thanks. I absolutely love it.'

They sipped their drinks. Just as it was feeling awkward, Brittany let out a snort of a snore from the other room.

'I'm sorry. I'm not much company,' said Ella. Her brain felt like it was on the waltzers at Hunstanton Fun Fair. 'I can't get my head around it all.'

'I remember when Dad died I was worried that Mum wouldn't manage on her own. I think you lump your parents together. Like

187

they're not individual people. They come as a package deal so when that changes you have to look at them differently. They're still your mum and dad, they're just separate people.'

'I know, you're right. And it's not the same as your situation. I'm lucky they're fit and healthy and they both think divorce is the right decision. I'm being selfish thinking I'd rather they stay together. I want them to be happy and if that means them being apart then . . .' She shrugged. She sounded a lot more pragmatic than she actually felt.

'Parents, who'd have 'em,' he said with a shake of his head and they both smiled. 'Right. I guess I best be off. Let me know if there's any snagging issues and I'll send one of the lads round.' He got to his feet.

Ella's mind was set whirling again. Was this goodbye? She'd not anticipated that at some point Kit would walk out of her life. 'Yeah, right. Of course. I don't suppose you'll be back seeing as you're the boss.' She tried to laugh but it sounded more like someone trying to tune a cat.

'No, I guess not.' He pushed his hands into his jeans pockets.

This was it. This was the moment she said goodbye. Everything was changing and she wasn't sure she was equipped for it, but she was going to give it her best shot. She was changing too – she was being bolder, taking risks and while it was scary, she finally felt like she was following the right path. Her path. Not meandering after Todd or any other man but setting her own course and doing it alone. Although until now she'd not noticed that she'd had a sidekick.

Kit O'Leary had sneaked up on her. Not in a Tom and Jerry 'hammer over the head' way but in the way that spring happens – all the little signs are there but you don't really notice until the daffodils are bobbing their heads and blossom is falling from the trees. Without her realising they had nurtured an unexpected friendship. It surprised her but she'd grown to like him and she was definitely going to miss him.

'Okay. Bye then, Kit O'Leary.' She held out her hand for him to shake.

He looked at it for a moment and then a smile pulled at the side of his lips. 'Goodbye, Ella Briggs. It's been fun.'

CHAPTER TWENTY-THREE

Lucy was fidgeting in the taxi on her way home; she was wired thanks to the Prosecco and her conversation with Brittany. It appeared that up until then her mind had been full of a number of unexploded bombs, each one a relationship worry she'd shoved to one side and never properly dealt with, and they were now detonating in her head like a computer game. Brittany had the same fears as Lucy but her approach was to go ahead and do it anyway. Risk getting hurt. Whereas Lucy's tried and tested method was to avoid commitment and simply have fun. Although was she having fun? Maybe she'd got it all wrong. Had she missed out by not taking chances? Had she let her job taint her view at the expense of her own happiness? Or was it seeing her mother commit to man after man and be let down every time? All her fears were coming for her like the zombie apocalypse.

The cab pulled up by her house, Lucy paid the driver and got out. A moment after the taxi pulled away, someone dressed in dark clothing disappeared down the side of her house. Her pulse was racing. She hid behind her golden privet for a moment while she gathered her senses. Why was she hiding in a bush? She wasn't the one creeping about somewhere they shouldn't be. The thought galvanised her and she stood up. Then Lucy had another thought – *but what if he had a weapon?* She bobbed back down behind the bush. Although she'd only caught a glimpse of them, she was sure she knew who it was. Who else would be lurking around outside her house at this time of night? But maybe she needed to clarify who she was dealing with before taking action. Slowly straightening herself up in order to peer over the hedge, she stopped mid-rise – like a slow-motion jack-in-the-box. Her thighs began to burn. This was everything that was wrong with her life – she needed to make a decision and commit to it. *Come on, Lucy, be decisive!* she thought.

Empowered by her internalised pep talk she got out her phone which appeared to already be on camera so she set it off to record footage and capture evidence if anything happened. A quick glance told her that her neighbours were in as the light was on so if she screamed loud enough hopefully someone would at least investigate. It was a plan. She was going to confront the hooded figure. Lucy took a deep breath and in one motion stood up from behind the bush. There was nobody there. She blinked into the darkness. Where had they gone? She took a couple of tentative side steps but stayed close to the hedge. Her heart was hammering in her chest.

All of a sudden someone popped up on the other side of her bush. 'Argh!' yelled Lucy. It was fight or flight. She chose fight and dived over the hedge towards them. Only she'd badly misjudged her gymnastic ability and landed on top of the bush which immediately gave way and swallowed her whole. Marooned in the stiff twiglike structure, she held up her phone.

'I'm filming you. I've got evidence of this!' she shouted while kicking her legs in an attempt to right herself, but it had no effect other than to make her skirt ride further up her thighs.

'Luce?' Someone peered over the top of her. 'What the hell are you doing?' asked her mother, removing her hood. 'You scared me half to death!'

'Oh for f—'

'Lucy, is everything all right?' asked Mr Watkins from next door who appeared to be inadvertently shining a torch up her skirt.

She flipped herself over. 'Mr Watkins. Hi. Yes, thank you. It's my mum.' She cringed at her own words.

'Hello,' said her mum, leaning across the hedge and her recumbent daughter. 'I'm Terri. Nice to meet you.'

'Likewise. Are you staying with Lucy?'

'Nooo!' said Lucy a little louder than was necessary while she flailed about in the hedge.

'Just visiting,' said her mother as Lucy shuffled to get herself out of the shrubbery. She scrambled to her feet and brushed herself down, leaves flew in all directions.

'We'd best get on.' Lucy pointed towards her house. 'But thanks for checking up on me, Mr Watkins. It's good to know you are on the lookout and if there was an emergency you'd come to my rescue.'

Mr Watkins gave a weak smile. 'Actually, I was putting my bin out.'

Awkward. 'Right. Well. Night then.'

'Hopefully see you around,' called Terri as Lucy gave her a nudge towards the house.

Lucy looked down at her phone to stop it recording. That was the moment she realised she'd streamed an Instagram Live to the world.

'Crap, crap, crap,' muttered Lucy as she checked and double checked the video was no longer visible.

'What does it matter?' said her mum, sprawling on the sofa. 'I think it's hilarious.' She gave another hoot of a laugh as if to emphasise her point.

Lucy slow blinked and stared at her mother. 'I have an important job. A career where it is vital that I am taken seriously. I do not want to become an internet sensation for falling in a hedge.'

'But then you couldn't get up and were stuck there like an upturned tortoise.' Terri managed to get her giggles almost under control. 'What were you doing sneaking about in your own garden?'

'Me? You were the one in the stalker-cum-murderer's outfit.' She flicked the hood of her mother's black top as she moved past her to sit on the rug. Lucy preferred the floor – you couldn't fall off that.

'I said I would be visiting.' Terri patted the seat cushion.

'No, you didn't. Usually people ring ahead and bring a bag.' *Normal people*, she added in her head.

'I sent you some flowers.' Terri looked put out.

'What?'

'To your office. I'd missed you so I said—'

'I missed you this time. But I'll be back soon.'

'Yes.' Terri's face brightened.

'It was you skulking around here the other weekend too?' Terri nodded. *Stalker solved*, thought Lucy. 'And following me after work?'

'No, I've not followed you.' *Stalker not solved*, amended Lucy in her head. 'I came here once to surprise you and when you weren't home I sent flowers.'

'Bloody hell, Mother. Why didn't you say who the flowers were from?'

'More words cost extra. And anyway, we're not all stuffy and formal. Not you and me, Luce.'

Lucy hated her name being shortened, but her mother knew that. 'I prefer Lucy, remember?'

'You don't change.' Terri leant forward and Lucy suspected the whack she gave her shoulder had been intended as an act of camaraderie, but it only irritated Lucy further. Her mother had no idea how to show affection if indeed there was any there to be displayed.

'If you're visiting at this time of night, I assume you're planning on staying over in which case you need a wash kit. Where are your things?'

'At my digs.' Terri scanned the wall up and down while sinking her teeth into her bottom lip.

'And where would that be?'

'Out Happisburgh way. It's a pretty area. Do you know it?'

Lucy's sixth sense was tingling. 'Yeah, I know it. It's beautiful. How come you've got a place there?'

Terri was still studying the wall. 'Some friends I met invited me to stay.' No eye contact wasn't a good thing where her mother was concerned.

'You're not looking for somewhere to live then?'

Terri finally eyeballed her daughter. 'Just short term.'

Exactly as she'd feared, her mother wanted something and a place to stay was the absolute worst thing. Lucy would have preferred it if she'd wanted her to donate a kidney. That would have been far less painful than sharing space with Terri for any period of time. 'What's wrong with the Happisburgh place?' asked Lucy.

'That's my Luce. Straight to the point.' There was a long pause and Lucy feared her mother was crafting a story. 'It's a squat and it's about to fall into the sea.'

***

Ella was excited to be using her new business premises for what it was intended and had all the dresses for Brittany's wedding hung up on the ornate hooks in the fitting rooms ready for her, Lucy and Brittany to try on. The door from the hallway opened and a green-gilled Brittany looked in.

'Good morning, sleeping beauty, your gown awaits,' said Ella brightly.

Brittany winced. 'I feel like I've swallowed a scouring pad.' She ran her hand gingerly down her neck.

'That'll be the snoring.'

Brittany looked alarmed. 'I didn't fall asleep at the party. Did I?'

'No, it was afterwards on the sofa. I put you to bed.'

Brittany surveyed the room. 'Was there even a party?' The room looked immaculate.

'Kit helped me tidy up after my parents announced that they've split up.' It was very odd to say it out loud, but it was something she would have to get used to.

Over a cup of tea and some dry toast Ella filled Brittany in on the events she'd missed.

'I'm sorry,' said Brittany. 'That's a bummer.'

'Thanks. But they both seem okay so that's what I need to focus on. It's about what they want, not me.'

The doorbell sounded. Lucy came in powered by pent-up energy. Ella stood back to let the whirlwind that was Lucy storm past her. 'Morning,' she said as Lucy disappeared into the kitchen.

'My mother will be the death of me. I swear she is going to tip me over the edge.' Lucy did a lap of the table.

Brittany pulled out a chair. 'Stop! I have a hangover and your pacing isn't helping. Sit down and have some tea. Decaffeinated or camomile but something to get you to calm the hell down.'

Ella was impressed with Brittany's intervention, and she flicked the switch on the kettle. 'I've got a camomile and ginger which is nice,' she offered.

Lucy slumped into the pulled-out seat. 'How does she do this? She appeared out of nowhere like Dr sodding Who but without the Tardis and entertaining sidekicks and announced that she's staying with me short term. How long is that exactly?' She looked frantically from Brittany to Ella.

'Can we hurry up with that tea,' said Brittany almost out of the side of her mouth.

'You won't believe what happened to me last night,' began Lucy. It was difficult for Ella not to belly laugh through Lucy's story about getting stuck in a hedge.

'What a disaster.' Lucy ran her fingers through her hair.

'Why is it a disaster?' asked Ella. It was a genuine question. She

195

knew Lucy and her mother had a difficult relationship but there were worse things.

Lucy did a slow blink. 'You're right. It's only a disaster if I let it be.'

'She's sleeping in your spare room for a couple of nights. That's all.'

'But that's how it starts. Then she wants money. And we argue. And she storms out and I don't see her again for a few years.'

Ella's heart squeezed. 'Is that it? The real issue. That she keeps leaving you?'

Lucy snorted a derisory laugh. 'No.' Her face was pulling more facial expressions than it could keep up with. Until it eventually settled on bewildered. 'Bloody hell. You could actually be right. Although the thought of her never leaving fills me with more dread so I'm not sure you've nailed it.'

Ella felt for her friend. She reached out and gripped her hand. Poor Lucy, her mother had picked her up and dropped her when it suited, her whole life.

'I'm glad we've cleared that up,' said Brittany, getting to her feet. 'Let's try these dresses on.' For someone in a caring profession sometimes she could be insensitive. Maybe she was just better with animals.

Ella let Brittany try on her dress first. It was lovely to see a bride swishing her way around the room and taking in her reflection from the two huge mirrors. Tears welled in Brittany's eyes. 'Ella, you are a star. It fits perfectly. It feels like it was made for me.'

'Come on then,' said Lucy in a whisper while Brittany was distracted. 'Let's see what you've done to the dung dresses.'

Ella had placed the carriers in the two fitting rooms. 'You're in there. Don't come out until I do.' Ella wanted Brittany to get the full effect of them both at the same time. She was quite proud of the alterations she'd made, she just hoped Brittany and Lucy agreed.

Ella drew the curtain across, slipped on her dress and pulled up the zip. She smoothed it down and checked it in the cubicle's narrow mirror. 'Ready?'

'Okay. On three,' said Lucy. Ella gripped her curtain. 'One, two, three!'

They both stepped out of the fitting rooms to stand in front of Brittany who gasped and stayed with her mouth making a perfect O shape. 'Are they the same dresses?' she asked, checking them over.

'It would be exceptionally bad luck to find two more,' muttered Lucy. Ella gave her a look.

Ella manoeuvred them to stand in front of the largest mirror and see the three of them together. Brittany's dress looked stunning and rightly overshadowed the bridesmaids for sheer flamboyance and lavishness. 'They look completely different,' said Brittany, marvelling at her bridesmaids. Gone were the fussy puffball sleeves and polo neck, replaced by neat straps and a square neckline. A cream sash pulled in at the waist broke up the mass of brown and gave the dresses shape. The tiers of the skirt were still there but they didn't fight for attention now they were the only fussy details.

'There's these too if we need them.' Ella handed Lucy a cream wrap that matched the sash. Ella draped her wrap around her shoulders. The effect was elegant and also drew attention away from the brown.

'Amazing.' Brittany's eyes filled with tears and the three friends hugged.

Ella handed Lucy a little brown posy bag she'd made from the leftover material. 'It's for on the day for your lippy and maybe a tissue.'

Lucy held it up. 'Yeah, I admit it you've done a good job. Maybe you should think about doing this full time.' Ella wrinkled her nose at her sarcastic friend. This was what she was good at and now she was her own boss she couldn't wait to get brides through her door.

CHAPTER TWENTY-FOUR

Ella was excited for her first Monday running her own business. However, when it brought with it Ashley the boob-flashing internet sensation, Ella wasn't quite as excited as she had been. The last time she'd seen her she had hastily put her clothes back on and exited the store in a high dudgeon. Her emails had been terse, and Ella had felt somewhat cajoled into making Ashley's dress alterations for free. Not exactly the lucrative start she had hoped for.

Ella had some Prosecco chilling – something she planned to do for all first fittings and one of the nice touches she was copying from Wanda. There were lots of other things that she wasn't. The church bells rang and Ella felt a frisson of excitement. That was until she opened the door and in swooped Ashley followed by four other women all brandishing dress carriers.

'Hello, Ashley. Lovely to see you again. I wasn't expecting so many of you,' said Ella.

'Hiya,' said Ashley. 'These are my bridesmaids.'

A collective squeal went up and Ella feared for her chandelier. 'Welcome to Oh Sew Special. Would you like a glass of fizz? Prosecco or elderflower?'

'Prosecco all round. In fact bring the bottle,' said Ashley.

'Sure,' said Ella with a forced smile.

She shot through to the kitchen and gave herself a pep talk. She needed to be firm about this because if Ashley was expecting her to do all the bridesmaids' alterations for free, she needed to think again. Ella hated confrontation but this was her first customer and she needed to start as she meant to go on and that meant not being bullied any more. She took the bottle from the fridge, put it on a tray with five glasses and returned to her customers.

Already there were squealing women in various degrees of undress passing around half a bottle of vodka. This was not what Ella wanted. She had to make a stand.

She clinked a glass to get their attention. Five faces eventually turned in her direction. 'Let's go through how this is going to work,' she said, sounding a lot more in control than she felt. 'I'm sure we can all agree that the bride is the priority.' Ashley did a dramatic curtsy and the others whooped their agreement. 'Therefore, I will focus on Ashley's dress first because that's what we agreed.' Ella picked up one of her price leaflets. 'I won't be making a charge for the bridal gown alterations but here's my price list if you wanted any changes to the bridesmaids' dresses. And I'd prefer you not to consume your own food or drink on the premises.' Ella made a point of not smiling and held Ashley's icy gaze. Ella braced herself for a verbal backlash. All the bridesmaids watched closely.

'Fine,' said Ashley, snatching the leaflet. 'But I want a discount.'

'I'm sure we can come to some arrangement,' said Ella and she poured out the drinks feeling like she was queen of everything. Then she pulled down the blind because the last thing she wanted was a repeat of Ashley's flashing incident. Although from an overheard conversation it did sound like Ashley was hoping to be an influencer on Instagram as a result of it. What she was going to influence, Ella wasn't too sure.

Ashley's dress fitting went well. It was a beautiful dress and didn't need much adjustment. She did, however, seem to want to swan around in it taking selfies at every angle. It was a good job Ella didn't have anyone else booked in. She made a mental note to be clear on allotted time windows when she confirmed appointments in the future.

'Let's have a look at the bridesmaids, then. Who wants to go first?' asked Ella.

The one who was already stripped down to her underwear and had been for the last forty minutes sashayed into the cubicle with her carrier. Ella waited outside.

'Any more Prosecco?' asked Ashley almost wringing out the bottle.

'Sorry, that was all I had.' The others carried on their chatter and Ella continued to wait. When it had gone on too long Ella spoke through the curtain. 'Do you need a hand with anything?'

'There's something wrong with the dress,' said the bridesmaid. Her voice sounding wobbly with emotion.

'I'm sure it's nothing we can't fix. Shall I come in?'

'It was fine when we tried them on in the shop. I might have put on a couple of pounds but this can't be my dress,' said the same sorrowful voice.

'It is your dress,' said Ashley, whipping open the curtain to reveal the poor young woman looking like an overfilled sausage. The dress was bulging in lots of places. 'You all need to lose weight. We all agreed that, right?' continued Ashley. There were mumbles but Ella wasn't sure anyone was actually agreeing with her. 'So I ordered all the dresses one size smaller.' As Ashley stared them down their smiles dissolved.

Ella didn't know what to say. She'd met some bridezillas in her time, but Ashley was their queen. 'That might make it difficult for altering,' she said. The lip of the bridesmaid in front of her wobbled. 'But let me take a look,' she added hastily.

Ella spent the next hour with four sullen bridesmaids and a

puzzle that stretched even her ability. The dresses thankfully had a generous seam allowance but for the largest of the group this wasn't going to be enough. Helpfully, she was also the shortest of the four. 'I can take enough off the length to insert a band around the middle. There will be a seam but I'll fashion it like a bodice. You won't know I've added in a panel.' Ella smiled at the poor bridesmaid.

'Ooh message from Wes,' announced Ashley. The other bridesmaids crowded around to read it. Ella concentrated on pinning the bottom of the dress she was working on.

'He has got it bad,' said the tallest bridesmaid. 'He's a smitten kitten.'

'I know, right?' said Ashley, firing off a reply. 'It's killing me not being with him. But at least it's not long to the wedding.'

There was a chorus of 'Awww' and Ella had to admit it was nice to see a softer side to Ashley. It was a shame she hadn't tapped into that aspect of her persona when she'd ordered the bridesmaids' dresses.

Ashley and her entourage eventually left and Ella was keen to set to work on the many dresses she now had hung on her rails. She had agreed a price with Ashley which they were both happy with.

A few hours later she was concentrating hard on taking apart one of the bridesmaid's dresses. The doorbell startled her. She opened the door to find Kit there.

'Oh hello.' She hadn't been expecting him and she was surprised to see that the light was fading – she'd been working a lot longer than she'd realised. 'Everything okay?'

'I was admiring the brickwork. There's quite a knack to bricklaying to get it that smooth and consistent.' His voice had a silky quality and for some reason the way he pronounced bricklaying made it sound quite suggestive.

'I have a very good builder. I can give you their details if you like.'

'You're okay. I hear they have a rodent problem.' He screwed up his features.

Ella laughed. 'That's true. Come in,' she said. She was pleased to see him and something was zinging around her bloodstream.

While Kit was pulling the door closed Pirate appeared and darted inside. He ran through the room as fast as his three legs could carry him and disappeared around the partition. Ella managed to retrieve him moments before he launched himself onto the laid-out dress.

'Come here, cheeky,' she said, cradling the cat in her arms.

Kit had a smile on his face when he turned around. 'Oh right,' said Kit, looking a little sheepish. He'd clearly thought Ella was talking to him.

She filled the awkward silence. 'He used to sleep all day but now I'm at home he's in and out like a yo-yo. I think he thinks he has staff.'

'I could fit a cat flap in your back door if you'd like?'

'Brilliant. I think he'd like his own door.'

They nodded in perfect synchronisation. 'Anyway. I just called by to give you this.' He produced a piece of paper from his pocket and went to give it to her but she had the cat so they did a clumsy swap where their faces were a little too close to each other. Pirate helped by headbutting Kit's chin. She unfolded the paper to reveal a child's drawing. 'It's from Rufus to say sorry for spoiling your party,' explained Kit.

'He is an accomplished artist for a rat.'

'He may have had a little help from Isaac.' Kit leant over the picture and pointed to the figures depicted with very large hands and thin legs. 'The one with the big smile is Isaac. This handsome fellow is obviously me . . .'

'Or a scarecrow,' said Ella, laughing at the wild black scribble on top of the stick man's head.

'Is my hair really like that?' Kit self-consciously smoothed the front of it down.

'It's exactly like that.'

'Cheers.' He returned his attention to the picture. 'The person with their mouth open and arms in the air is . . .'

'Me?'

Kit nodded. 'Another excellent likeness. Apparently, you're screaming.'

'Who is the fourth person with the pointy nose?' she asked.

'That's Rufus. I thought it wise not to question why he's the same size as you and me.'

'Well, please thank Rufus and Isaac. I will treasure it.'

'Along with the nightmares about giant rats?'

'Exactly.' She laughed. There was definite electricity between them, she wasn't imagining it. When the intensity got too much, she asked the first thing that popped into her head. 'How's your mum?'

'She's okay but she doesn't want to talk about David.'

'My dad's the same. But then I can't get him on his own. They automatically ring me back on a conference call. And I don't like to ring too much because they seem worried about how the divorce is going to affect me. I have pointed out that I'm not a child.' She'd had time to let things settle in her mind. The most important thing was that her parents were both happy and that was what she was focusing on.

'Still a big thing though,' said Kit.

'Thanks. It is.' Whether she'd realised it at the time or not, that was what she had been striving for – to find a man who loved her like her dad loved her mum.

There was a long pause. Ella's mind was going over all that had happened. 'I can't help thinking we did the wrong thing by breaking up Jane and David? Do you think we should have owned up to that?' Ella nibbled a fingernail.

'I don't think so,' said Kit, shaking his head. 'Own up to checking Mum's phone? Cancelling their dinner reservation? Your mate giving out her number to all those blokes? That wouldn't look good.'

'I know. But I feel rubbish about breaking up their relationship.' Ella wasn't proud of herself. 'What should we do?'

'We did it for all the right reasons. Obviously they were daft and misguided reasons but maybe if their relationship was meant to be it would have survived regardless of what we did. I'm not sure there's anything we can do.'

She and Kit had messed up. After almost thirty years David had been brave enough to put himself out there and find someone new. She thought back to the restaurant. To how, without realising it was her dad, she'd noticed the way Jane had looked at him. Their obvious connection was what had drawn her attention to them. And she and Kit had barrelled in and triggered their relationship's demise.

'Or,' said Ella, waving a finger at him. Maybe she was clutching at straws but it suddenly seemed simple. 'We put everything back as it was. Give your mum and my dad another chance. Bring them back together.' Already she felt lighter. Like she could shift the burden if she could help create a little happiness out of this wretched situation.

'Great idea. Count me in. But how do we do that?' asked Kit, looking unsure.

'That's the part that might need a bit more research,' said Ella. The thought of having a reason to meet up with Kit again sent a dash of happiness through her. 'We'd better hatch a good plan.'

Ashley's bridesmaids were quite different when their queen bee wasn't in residence. They seemed far more upset about Ashley having ordered them dresses a size smaller than they needed although it didn't appear any of them were brave enough to raise it directly with the bride.

The larger of the four was sitting eating a carrot stick while she waited for two of the others to change into their dresses for their second fitting.

'I'm going to look like a rabbit if I eat any more of these.' The bridesmaid offered a Tupperware box to Ella.

'You look lovely the way you are,' she said, politely declining the carrots.

'I'm terrified about this dress fitting. Thank heavens Ashley's not here.'

'I second that,' came a disembodied voice from one of the cubicles.

The first two bridesmaids emerged and Ella was relieved. The dresses looked fine. She ushered the next two bridesmaids in who both looked close to tears. 'Shout if you need a hand with zips,' she said.

The first two bridesmaids swished around the carpet admiring themselves. 'I might thank Ashley – as a result of her being a controlling cow I've lost three pounds and here I am in a size twelve dress looking bloody fabulous.' *A size twelve that's been altered to nearer a fourteen*, thought Ella but the bridesmaid was technically correct and she didn't have the heart to disillusion her.

At last the curtains opened and the other two emerged. The one with the carrot sticks no longer looked tearful, she was positively glowing. 'It fits!'

'That's good,' said Ella. 'Let me take a look.' But it was hard to get her to stand still because she wanted to twirl in front of the mirror. The additional panel had worked well and the dress accentuated her womanly curves. 'You look beautiful. It only needs a few more tweaks.'

'You're a bloody genius,' said the bridesmaid, wrapping Ella in a bear hug.

'My pleasure,' she said, and it really was. To be able to turn around a crisis, even if it had been orchestrated by the bride, made her feel she was doing something of value. And happy bridesmaids were a lovely bonus. Granted it wasn't on the same scale as reversing climate change but if she could make a few people feel better then that was worth all the hours she'd put in.

As they were leaving Kit pulled his van onto Ella's driveway and got out.

'Someone's a lucky girl,' said one of the women, eyeing Kit who looked very handsome in a fitted white T-shirt and jeans.

'He's my builder,' explained Ella.

'Show us your big tool!' shouted another of the women.

Kit held up his toolbox. 'I've got more than one!' he called back and they all dissolved into fits of giggles as they headed for their cars.

'Sorry,' said Ella.

'It's fine. They're just having fun.'

'To what do I owe this pleasure?' she said, realising it was always a pleasure to see him.

'I've come to fit Pirate's cat flap and talk about how to set up our parents.'

'Great. Come through,' she said, ushering him inside.

She got a whiff of aftershave, which was enticing and made her pause.

'You coming?' asked Kit, holding open the door into the hall.

'Gosh, yes. Sorry. Miles away.' Ella followed him through to the kitchen.

'I wasn't sure which one to get so I went for an easy opening flap . . .' started Kit. His eyes darted to Ella's on the last word and she tried to remain serious and concentrate.

'Good idea, because he might struggle with a stiff one with his missing leg.'

'Exactly. But there are other . . . flaps if he doesn't get on with this one. Not that I'm an expert on . . .'

'Flaps?' offered Ella, unable to hide her grin.

'Exactly.' Was Kit going pink?

'Have we said "flaps" too many times?' she asked.

He laughed. 'We definitely have.'

Kit got to work and Ella tried to get to grips with Facebook adverts. When she gave up and returned to the kitchen Kit was sitting back on his haunches.

'I think we're done. We just need a tester.'

'One crash test dummy coming right up,' said Ella, going to the living room to retrieve a sleepy Pirate. She put him on the floor in front of the door and he immediately turned his back on his new entrance and made a fuss of Kit. But it was nice for Ella to think that maybe Pirate was thanking him.

'Here you go,' said Kit, picking the cat up and showing him his handiwork. Pirate saw something move outside and was instantly hooked. He sat himself down and gazed out of the flap like it were a window.

They spent the next ten minutes trying to persuade him to go through it, but Pirate had other ideas.

Kit checked his watch. 'Sorry I have to pick Isaac up today. We'll need to arrange another time to plot getting our parents back together.'

'No worries. And thanks again for sorting out my . . .' She pointed at the flap and gave him what she hoped was a cheeky grin.

'My pleasure. Anytime,' he said. Pirate spotted next door's Persian, dived through the cat flap and left it swinging in his wake – it seemed he knew exactly how to use it when he wanted to.

**

Lucy's first meeting of the day was with Mrs Maxwell. Her husband appeared to have stopped stalking Lucy and was communicating via his solicitor which was a vast improvement. Lucy was still twitchy but she put that down to general increased stress levels from having her mother around. Terri had now moved in. All two boxes and three binbags of her. Lucy had run her over to Happisburgh to collect her things from a dishevelled bungalow that was precariously close to the edge. Lucy wasn't sure which had been the sadder sight – the bungalow with its chintz curtains still in place clinging desperately to the cliff, or her mother appearing through a tatty doorway with everything she owned. Both the building and her mother appeared to be on the brink with nothing to secure their future.

'Mrs Maxwell is here,' said Lucy's assistant, popping her head around her office door.

When Lucy walked in Mrs Maxwell was checking her messages. 'Good morning—'

'She's not answering her phone.' Mrs Maxwell had a frantic look about her.

'Sorry who?'

'Alabama. My daughter. She didn't turn up at school this morning.'

'Probably bunked off with a friend. Did she seem her usual self when she left this morning?'

Mrs Maxwell's face seemed to lose its remaining colour. 'She said she was staying at a friend's. But now I don't know . . .' There were other words, but they were lost to tears.

Lucy passed her the tissues. 'When you're able to check with her friend's parents then . . .' Mrs Maxwell's face turned abruptly in Lucy's direction. This was awful. 'Then we'll know whether or not to report her as missing.'

CHAPTER TWENTY-FIVE

Lucy was invested in the Maxwell case, even more so now there was a missing child involved. She'd never had something like this happen before. Her job was usually a couple of steps removed from any real drama and often it was about sweeping up afterwards. Seeing this play out in her office was an awful thing to witness and something that would stay with her for a very long time.

Lucy had made the initial call to the police for Mrs Maxwell and stayed there while she gave them all the details about her daughter's disappearance. The next call was possibly harder because the poor woman had to call her estranged husband and explain the situation. A quick text exchange had already confirmed that Alabama wasn't at her dad's. It would have been the hardest call anyone would have to make but it was made worse as they were part way through a bitter divorce. At Mrs Maxwell's request Lucy hovered nearby ready to take over the call if needed. Mrs Maxwell sobbing was interrupted by the faint sound of her husband's reassurances on the other end.

Lucy offered to drop her off at the police station. As they left her office Lucy froze and instinctively put her arm out to stop her client going down to the steps. Mr Maxwell was standing on the pavement.

'I'll tell him to leave,' said Lucy.

'No.' Mrs Maxwell shook her head. 'Whatever has happened between us he is the only person in the whole world who knows exactly how I'm feeling right now.'

She had a point. It didn't make Lucy feel any better about him being there though. Lucy waited while they talked and cried together. Lucy felt like she was intruding but with the accusations against him she wasn't comfortable to leave her client in her current distressed state. She also felt strangely helpless as she watched them cry together. She had numbers for counsellors who dealt with marriage breakdowns and grief but nothing for something like this. Her suspicious mind couldn't help but watch Mr Maxwell – he looked wretched and equally as upset as his wife, which Lucy found reassuring. But it didn't stop some questions swirling in her mind. If he had anything at all to do with his daughter's disappearance then he was an excellent actor.

Mrs Maxwell eventually came back up the steps to Lucy. 'We're going to the police station together.'

'Is that wise?'

'He's worried they'll think he's in some way involved. He says it's best if he gives them all the information he has.'

'Sounds like a good idea. Look, if there's anything I can do . . .'

Mrs Maxwell nodded. 'Thank you. That's kind.'

'Please keep me posted on developments.' It sounded overly formal but Lucy struggled with how to say it any other way. Different words didn't change the awful situation. Mrs Maxwell nodded and went to join her husband. He turned and looked up at Lucy, his expression one of desolation. She hoped he had a watertight alibi for the last twenty-four hours.

***

210

Ella wasn't sure whose idea a Saturday at the beach had been but she was very excited about it. It most definitely wasn't going on a date with Kit O'Leary. They were taking a picnic down to the beach. However, that was only because they needed to work out if there was anything they could do to repair the relationship between David and Jane.

Kit had volunteered to bring the drinks and Ella had insisted on throwing a picnic together, seizing the chance to do something nice for him. She loved the sewing machine he'd bought her and every time she saw it on the shelf it made her smile. A little bit of effort on a picnic would show him that she valued their friendship. Ella got up early to take a trip to the supermarket and now she was putting the finishing touches to a selection of things she'd whipped up in the hope of impressing Kit: Cromer crab sandwiches, pineapple and chilli salsa, smoked salmon and cream cheese wraps and some peach, herb and avocado parcels that had been fiddly to make but looked good. She popped in some homemade houmous and a selection of vegetables she had carefully chopped into batons. It was the poshest picnic she'd ever produced.

The doorbell sounded and she almost skipped to answer it. When she got there she gave herself a mental shake. This was not a date, she told the squadron of butterflies all primed for take-off in her stomach. She tried to control the beam of a smile as she opened the door. Her smile faltered as she clocked that Kit was not alone.

'Hiya,' said Kit.

'Rufus wasn't allowed to come,' said Isaac, jutting out his bottom lip.

'Hi Kit, hi Isaac,' she said, a little wrong-footed.

Kit seemed to realise. 'Isaac's mate has a bug so his play date was cancelled. Is it okay if—'

'Of course. Absolutely. The more the merrier.' Ella's head was spinning as she grabbed her hat, the picnic basket and rug and locked up. 'Right. Let's go,' she said.

'I brought my bucket and spade,' said Isaac, swinging them wildly above his head.

'And I brought the drinks,' said Kit, holding up a box of Capri Sun.

'Lovely,' said Ella. And while it was a little different to what she had pictured, she was already thinking it would be nice to spend time with both of them.

It was a short walk to the beach and as soon as they hit sand Isaac was off. His pumps flew in opposite directions and moments later he was running up and down in the sea.

Ella found a not too pebbly spot where she laid out the picnic rug and settled herself down to watch Kit and Isaac playing in the shallows. The sun was high but she had her hat.

'Come and join us,' called Kit as Isaac kicked water at him.

She was grateful that she'd thought to put her bikini on under her clothes. She pulled off her T-shirt and shorts and jogged down to the shoreline grabbing Isaac's bucket en route. As she suspected they both launched an assault and tried to splash her with water. Isaac's giggles filled the air. Ella scooped up water in the bucket and launched it at them both. Unfortunately, the full force of the second bucketful hit Isaac in the face as he was running towards her shouting. He instantly coughed at the mouthful of salt water. And tears were close behind.

'I am so sorry.' Ella dropped the bucket and went to comfort the little boy.

'I hate you!' spluttered Isaac.

Kit scooped him into his arms. 'It's okay. It's just sea water. Let's get you dry.' Kit strode back up the beach with Isaac spitting water over his shoulder and a little too close to Ella for her liking.

Once Isaac was wrapped in some towels and had a Capri Sun in his hands, he seemed mollified but he was still scowling at Ella.

'I'm sorry,' she whispered to Kit. 'He was running and I was scooping and . . .'

'It's fine. Don't worry about it. He needs to learn to take it if he's going to give it out.'

'Still.' It didn't stop her feeling awful.

'I'm hungry!' announced Isaac.

'Ahh I can definitely help there.' Ella dragged over the picnic basket. As she took out each item and announced what it was her mistake became obvious. The three of them stared at the posh platter she'd prepared.

'I don't like any of that yukky stuff,' said Isaac, his lip going all wobbly. *What a disaster*, thought Ella.

The day did improve thanks to a stroll to the nearby café who provided Isaac with a cheese sandwich, an apple and a packet of crisps which, it seemed, was all he needed to turn his day around. Kit bought teas for him and Ella and they sat down on a nearby bench watching the gentle lap of the ocean while Isaac was sitting between them munching his food. She glanced across at Kit and he was watching her. Isaac made a big crunch as he bit into his apple and it drew their attention. He swung his legs contentedly. It struck Ella that she was feeling that same carefree happy sensation. She looked up from Isaac to see Kit smiling at her. His gaze made her stomach flip. She wasn't sure what this was with Kit, but she knew she was happier when he was around.

When they got back to the beach Isaac even let Ella join in with building a supreme castle. It made her laugh when he threw in instructions about foundations and joists and she saw the look of pride on Kit's face. Between them they constructed something quite impressive. While Isaac concentrated on finishing the castle moat, she and Kit were able to enjoy the picnic. There were a few murmurs of pleasure from Kit as he ate although he rarely took his eyes off Isaac. His devotion was lovely to see.

'That was an amazing lunch,' said Kit, patting his stomach appreciatively. 'That sauce with the crab was delicious.'

'It's my mum's recipe. I'm sorry I didn't think about Isaac.'

'That's okay. I should have checked. You went to a lot of trouble.'

213

'It was nothing,' she lied. Kit raised an eyebrow. 'Okay, maybe a bit more than nothing. I wanted to say thank you for my sewing machine.'

Kit gave her the kind of smile that was infectious. 'I knew you'd love it,' he said.

'I really do.' For a moment their eyes met and something passed between them that made her pulse quicken.

'Uncle Kit!' shouted Isaac. 'The water keeps disappearing.'

'Just keep filling it up, mate,' said Kit and Isaac went to crouch at the sea edge to refill his bucket. Kit returned his attention to Ella. 'That should keep him busy for all of thirty seconds.'

'Why do we need thirty seconds?' she asked, wondering why her voice had a husky edge to it.

Kit leant forward and she could feel his breath on her lips. 'Because I'd really like to kiss you.'

'Mmm okay.'

His lips met hers and her heart leapt. The kiss was tender and inviting and she was lost. That was until sand and water liberally began raining down on them. For a second Ella thought it was the start of a cliff fall but as she and Kit pulled apart the culprit was standing over them waving a bucket and spade.

'I think I need a plumber,' announced Isaac.

Lucy and Brittany were coming over and they always helped Ella put things in perspective, and hopefully she did the same for them. Tonight, they had planned a DIY spa session at her house.

Brittany unpacked things from her bag. 'I've got a selection of face packs because I want to try a few out.'

'I think after you've done one that kind of makes the others a bit pointless,' said Lucy, checking her phone again.

'But I'd like to do one the day before the wedding to make my skin glow but sometimes face packs bring me out in spots and that would be the worst thing on my wedding day.'

'Chicken pox,' said Lucy, still distracted by her phone.

'What?' Brittany's voice had an edge of panic.

'Sorry, I thought we were naming things worse than spots.' Lucy shrugged and went back to her phone.

'What's up?' asked Ella.

'Nothing,' said Lucy, but when they made eye contact Lucy twisted her lips. 'Okay. Did you see the news about the missing Wymondham girl?'

'Yes. It's awful. Her poor parents,' said Ella, she'd heard it on the radio. 'Did you know her?'

'She's a client's daughter.'

Ella gave her a hug. 'That's why you keep checking your phone.'

'There is literally nothing else I can do. It's awful.'

'I'm sure she'll turn up,' said Brittany. 'It's a teen thing, isn't it? I bet we all ran away as kids.' She scanned their faces. 'It wasn't just me, right?'

Ella shook her head. 'I never ran away. I was lucky – I had no reason to.'

'I had plenty of reasons to,' said Lucy. 'But even I didn't run away. Why did you?'

Brittany squinted as if considering whether to tell them. 'I was in love with Dougie Poynter from McFly and I thought if we could meet each other . . .' But she didn't get to tell the rest of her story because the other two were laughing too hard.

When the laughter had dissipated they took mugs of tea through to the living room where Pirate met them like the royalty he thought he was. 'I know you two don't have kids, but do you have any tips for how to make a child like you, because Isaac hates me,' said Ella, sitting down.

'Now why would you want him to like you?' asked Lucy, but she held up a finger to indicate she was going to answer herself. 'Is someone making a move on Kit?'

Ella pouted while she thought how to word her reply. 'Ooh,' said Brittany excitedly. 'Someone has *already* made a move on Kit.'

Ella wobbled her head feeling a little giddy at the thought of her and Kit on the beach. 'We kissed.' What exactly that was or where it was going she wasn't sure but she was excited about having Kit in her life.

Brittany squealed. 'Nice work,' said Lucy. 'You need some regular sex.' The other two gave her a look. 'Don't be all prudish. It's a simple fact that sex releases endorphins which make you feel better. I need to sort some out for myself.'

'Tell us everything,' said Brittany, leaning forward.

'We went to the beach and I half drowned his nephew who now, understandably, hates me. I don't know where this is going with Kit, but it won't be going anywhere if Isaac continues to think I'm the devil.'

'You're not booking wedding venues, are you?' Lucy gave her a hard stare.

'Definitely not. I'm enjoying the moment. Although there might only be the one moment if I can't build bridges with this little boy. Kit finished with his last girlfriend because of his commitment to Isaac. They really are a package deal.'

'How do you feel about that?' asked Lucy, watching her closely.

'I know I've always said I don't want kids but—' Ella stopped talking because Lucy was shaking her head.

'Not always. You were open to the idea before Toad.'

Ella pulled her chin in. 'Was I?'

Her friends both nodded at her. 'Not sign me up to Mamas and Papas newsletter level but definitely on the fence,' said Brittany.

'The toss donkey tipped you over into the no kids zone because that's where he was firmly positioned.' Lucy dipped her head for emphasis.

Ella was trying to work out exactly how that had happened. 'Babies don't like me. They always cry if I pick them up. And the thought of being responsible for something that can't look after itself worries me. You remember what happened to the school goldfish when I was looking after it.' She looked to Lucy.

'Committed suicide,' said Lucy, miming it jumping out of its bowl.

Ella turned to Brittany. 'And you had to convince me I'd be able to look after Pirate.'

'It's okay to change your mind, Ella,' said Lucy. 'As long as it's you who is doing the changing not some . . .'

Ella could tell Lucy was searching for a suitable moniker so she had a go. 'Bum Womble?'

'Not a bad effort,' said Lucy.

'I'm not entirely certain I have changed my mind but I like Isaac and I wish he liked me.'

'Ah, that is tricky,' said Brittany. 'If dogs don't like me I play with them, give them treats and a fuss. That usually works.'

Lucy blinked a few times. 'He's not a ruddy spaniel, Brit. You can't tickle the child's tummy, throw a stick for him and tell him he's a good boy.'

'It was just a suggestion.' Brittany rolled her eyes at Lucy's response.

'Actually the root of that might work,' said Ella. Lucy snorted her derision. 'Playing with him is actually a good idea. What do little boys like to play with?'

Lucy gave her a look. 'Their peni—'

'Apart from that,' said Ella, cutting her off.

'Mud?' suggested Brittany.

'Lego,' offered Lucy.

'Ooh good idea.' Ella liked the thought of doing something constructive with Isaac.

'Mud's cheaper,' said Brittany, finishing her drink.

'I'll investigate some Lego that we can build together.' Ella was pleased she may have found a simple solution. 'And we'll keep the mud as a back-up plan.'

They settled themselves down in their PJs, with delivery pizza and a romantic comedy film. They had each applied a different face pack. Pomegranate, honey and cucumber. Ella regarded each of them. 'We look like traffic lights,' she said.

'I definitely think mine is doing something,' said Brittany, wriggling her now green nose.

'Mine's a bit tingly,' said Lucy, who had gone for the pomegranate. 'My skin's not usually sensitive. I take it these are all legit,' she asked, picking up the packaging. She sat bolt upright. 'It's in . . . what is that . . .' She showed the packet to Ella. 'Greek?'

Ella hadn't been to Greece so she wasn't sure. 'Mine was in English,' she said. Ella had been the one to read out the instructions, having made the assumption they were all the same.

Ella and Lucy looked to Brittany for an answer. She winced sheepishly. 'I got them cheap off eBay.'

'Heaven help us. They're probably made from glue,' said Lucy, making a dash for the downstairs loo.

'They might not be that good for our skin then,' said Ella, not wanting to sound ungrateful but at the same time quite keen to get the mask off. She and Brittany went to the bathroom upstairs.

Brittany used copious amounts of toilet roll to try to get the green gunk off her face. 'Actually, Ella. Now we're alone, there was something I wanted to tell you.'

'Does it involve getting these cheap?' She started to pick at the side of her honey mask.

'Er no, it's about Todd.' Brittany bit her lip.

Ella didn't like how interested she was to know about her ex. 'Is he okay?'

'I guess so. He's coming to our wedding.' Brittany turned away and continued to scrape green off her face.

'What? Why?'

'Grant wanted to invite him. And I said I wasn't sure. But Grant said Todd would probably decline because you were going to be there and that would be the best situation because then it wouldn't look like we'd taken sides.' Brittany looked anguished as she briefly faced Ella. 'Which I obviously have because I'm Team Ella all the way, but Grant felt bad. He also thought we might get a decent present from Todd.' Brittany shook her head. 'Not that that was important. But anyway . . . Todd said he's coming.'

'Um.' Ella didn't know what to say.

'Ella, I'm really sorry. You'll still be my bridesmaid. Won't you?' Ella was processing what Brittany had said. 'Ella, say something,' pleaded her friend.

'Your face is still green,' said Ella.

CHAPTER TWENTY-SIX

It took a couple of days for their skin tones to return to normal despite them trying out a variety of scrubs and cleansers. In the meantime, Lucy had looked a little sunburned, Ella like she was jaundiced, and poor Brittany was referring to herself as Shrek. But at least there was no long-lasting damage. Ella's confidence, on the other hand, had taken a bit of a sideswipe thanks to Brittany's revelation that Todd was attending her wedding. Ella had had a couple of chats with Pirate about it. Pirate was easily bored and he'd sloped off to intimidate next door's Persian, leaving Ella to fret about seeing Todd again. However she looked at it, she couldn't avoid the situation. There was no way she could back out of being Brittany's bridesmaid and she couldn't put Brittany and Grant in the awkward position of having to uninvite Todd. There was nothing else for it – she would have to face him.

She had time to get her head around it and to work out how she was going to handle the encounter. Obviously she wanted to remain dignified and keep things together. If she had to see Todd again at least she would be doing it surrounded by supportive friends and even her mum and dad were going to be there as they'd known Brittany a long while. She'd be okay – she had to be.

Kit was a good distraction. They were calling and messaging each other regularly and she'd given herself a good talking to – she wasn't going to rush things or choose her wedding gown just yet even if she did know exactly what she'd choose. She was also ignoring Lucy's advice, which was to shag his brains out on a regular basis. Ella was hoping to find some middle ground where they could simply enjoy time together without putting any pressure on either of them.

She'd invited him over for a meal and then spent the rest of the day worrying that she was being too forward. Lucy had reassured her that as long as she'd not sent him any naked pictures then she definitely wasn't. There was something about Kit. They had a connection and she was much bolder when he was around. She felt she could challenge him. Be braver. Something she'd never felt she could be with Todd.

Kit was on time and he'd brought wine. He didn't drink and drive so did that mean he was up for staying over? She didn't like to presume but it looked hopeful. It was quite exciting. If this was how Lucy felt she could see the appeal.

'Something smells good,' said Kit.

'Pasta bake. I was going to do something more impressive but then I thought maybe reliable was a better option.'

'Sounds great.'

There was a moment when she felt if the table hadn't been between them they may have shared another kiss. She really wanted to kiss him. The kitchen timer pinged, bringing her back to reality. Kisses would have to wait.

Talk over dinner was easy. They discussed Kit's work and her new business. He was interested and it felt good to have someone listen and offer encouragement.

They cleared away the dinner things together and moved through to the living room taking the wine with them. Pirate looked up from his chair and turned his head upside down in a very flirty fashion – he was such a tart. But Kit didn't

221

sit where he usually did. He sat down on the sofa and Ella joined him.

'Thanks for a lovely meal,' he said, relaxing into the sofa.

'You're welcome. It's nice to have someone to eat with. Does that make me sound sad and lonely?'

He laughed. 'No, it doesn't. Well, maybe a bit. You're fun to be around, Ella. I feel like I've known you a lifetime.'

Now what was she meant to do? She was out of practice. Maybe some more conversation would help. 'Have you watched anything good on television recently?' she asked.

'Ella?'

'Yes.'

'Can I kiss you?'

She tried to shrug nonchalantly. 'If you like.' Her heart gave a little victory skip.

The kiss was tender at first. The warmth of his chest against her ignited something within her. She pulled him to her and their kiss deepened. His phone vibrated and she went to pull away but he shook his head. 'Ignore it. It's just a text.' His voice was sexily husky. When they kissed again there was an urgency and it was exciting. Kit's phone juddered again. 'If it's urgent they'll ring,' he said. 'Where were we?'

'Kissing mainly,' she said and he gently leant her back onto the sofa cushions and their lips met.

Kit moved his weight and she was aware of something pulsating in the trouser department. She giggled through their kiss. 'That's vibrating in a really weird place. You're going to have to move it,' she said.

He hung his head. 'I'm sorry. It'll be someone wanting a quote for a loose roof tile.' He pulled his phone from his pocket, sat bolt upright and answered the call. She missed him the moment he pulled away from her.

'Mum? Calm down. What's wrong?'

Ella only caught one side of the conversation, but Kit was soon on his feet and heading for the door. She straightened her top and followed him. She stopped at the front door but he carried on outside. 'Kit?'

'Hang on a sec,' he said into the phone. He turned back to Ella, his eyebrows pulled tight together, seeming irritated by her intrusion. 'It's Isaac. He's fallen and gashed his head. Mum's taking him to hospital.'

'I'll come with you,' she said, grabbing her jacket and keys.

Kit shook his head. 'I'm sorry, Ella. I've got enough to think about. I can't be worrying if you're okay too.'

She let out a half-laugh. 'You don't need to worry about me. I'm coming to support you.'

He furrowed his brow. 'I'm sorry. I'd rather you didn't.'

Ella opened her mouth to say something but Kit was already in the van.

The next morning Ella was scratching around for things to do to take her mind off Kit's rapid departure. They'd exchanged stilted text messages. At least Isaac was fine. They'd glued the cut and not kept him in which was all good. But she sensed there had been a change in Kit. She rang his number and it went to voicemail. She sent him a message and he said he would call her later. There wasn't much more she could do.

She'd had a few people enquire if she made curtains or altered items other than wedding dresses and in the last couple of days she'd had lots of calls asking about services she definitely didn't perform.

Her phone rang and she braced herself. 'Oh Sew Special, Ella speaking how can I help you?'

'What do you charge for full sex?' came the gruff voice. As this was the third call that morning she was no longer shocked.

'I'm sorry there seems to have been some mistake. This is a wedding dress alteration service but would you be able to tell me how you got my number?'

223

'Online. Erm . . . What do you charge for a BJ?'

Ella's patience was wearing thin. 'Sorry, that's definitely not part of the service. Where online?'

He directed her to a website. It looked innocent enough but once she had signed up she was exposed to a whole new world – exposed being the operative word. She'd never seen so much naked flesh. There was a regional section and to her horror she found her name and number under a long list of services, some of which she'd have to Google to find out exactly what they were – although she knew instinctively that was not a wise thing to do. It took a few emails to the admins of the website to get her details removed and she breathed a sigh of relief.

Her phone lit up and it was Kit. 'Hi Kit. How's Isaac?'

'He's fine it was just a bump on the head but you have to be careful with kids.' Instantly she wanted to share with him what had happened and how she'd sorted out the website mix-up.

'I solved a mystery today and—'

'Ella, that's great. I wanted to talk to you about something important.'

'Okay.' From the tone of his voice, she feared her happy mood was on unstable ground.

'Should I come over?' he asked.

'I'll only worry between now and then. It's best you tell me.'

'Ella, you're a special person and I think in a different situation we could have been great together, but you deserve someone who is always going to put you first. I can't commit to that and I don't want to be yet another bloke who messes you about. So I think we should stop seeing each other.'

They had hardly started anything but it didn't stop the words stinging or the clenching in her gut at losing him. 'Can I ask why?'

She heard Kit exhale. 'It's like I said. Isaac comes first. He has to. But in coming first he takes over everything. He doesn't mean to but it's how it has to be with a child.'

'Kit, I absolutely understand. But I don't see why that means you have to be celibate and single for the foreseeable future.'

'It gets too complicated. You'll end up resenting Isaac and ultimately I'll have to choose. And I'm always going to choose him. Mum and I are all he's got. I'm so sorry, Ella, I really am.'

After Kit's call Ella was feeling down but a delivery of some glossy flyers she'd had printed cheered her a fraction. If work didn't start coming in soon she was going to be in trouble. She needed to stop dwelling on the Kit situation and take control of her life.

She packaged up the flyers and took a trip into Norwich. She was hoping to have a chat with the bridal shop owners who had seemed keen when they were knocking back her Prosecco but had gone cold soon after the launch.

She parked up and took a stroll past Norwich castle. A few tourists were taking photographs of the impressive Norman keep as she passed. Ella stopped. The castle was also a wedding venue. Perhaps this was a good place to thrust a leaflet into the hand of a prospective bride as they checked out the castle as a wedding venue. She did a quick detour and was pleased to find a helpful person who took a few of her flyers and promised to place them where future brides might pick one up. She was proud of herself for being opportunist.

She was in good spirits when she entered the wedding shop and presented the owner with her flyers. 'Hi there. Lovely to see you again. Here's some flyers. And I'm happy to discuss costs whenever you are.'

'Oh.' The owner looked surprised and her hand hovered over the flyers.

How embarrassing, she'd failed to introduce herself. 'I'm sorry. I'm Ella from Oh Sew Special, you came to my launch.' If this didn't ring any bells she was in real trouble.

The woman seemed to recover herself. 'I wasn't expecting to see you after the email.'

'Which email?' Was this some odd way to fob her off?

The woman's expression was hard to read. 'The message I received from you was quite blunt.'

Ella blinked a few times. 'I'm sorry. I don't know anything about that email. What did it say?'

The woman sucked her bottom lip. 'It basically said you didn't need to engage with a . . . and I quote, "tin pot business" like mine.'

Ella gasped. This was a nightmare. 'My goodness. I did not send that. Why did you think it was from me?'

'Because it said Ella from Oh Sew Special at the bottom and had a link to your website.'

This made no sense. 'I'm very sorry. I've no idea what's happened. All I can think is that I must have been hacked.'

The woman smiled. 'I did think it was odd. It's one thing to change your mind about teaming up but it's another to alienate local businesses.'

'It definitely wasn't from me, and I would still like to work with you if that's possible.' Ella crossed her fingers.

'My usual seamstress has just had a baby so we definitely have work for you. I'm free now if you'd like to have a coffee and see if we can work out some numbers.'

The relief was immense. 'I would love that. Thank you so much.' Ella held out her flyers again and at last she took them.

As she left the shop Ella noticed an O'Leary's van parked up the road. She felt a pull to walk past it in case Kit was inside. Her heart started to thump as she drew closer. Trying to act nonchalant Ella glanced into the cab as she strolled by. The van was empty. Oh well. She had no idea what she'd say to him anyway.

'Ella?' A familiar voice shouted from behind her. She turned around to see Kit jogging towards her and her hopeless heart twanged at the sight of him.

'Kit. Hi. You okay?' Everything felt awkward.

'Have you got time for a coffee?' he asked, searching her face.

She checked her watch. 'I don't know. I have a . . . um . . .'

'This is what I was worried about,' he said, looking tense. 'I don't want to lose you as a friend, Ella. Please let me explain things over a coffee.'

'Sure. Why not?' Although many reasons were already stacking up in her head.

They found a quiet corner in a café and Kit brought the drinks over. 'Thanks,' she said.

'I'm sorry. I shouldn't have called things off by phone, it all came out wrong. Let me explain . . .'

Ella held up her hand to stop him. 'It's okay, Kit. I get it. Any fool can see you're devoted to Isaac. Of course he comes first. I honestly do understand and I won't hold it against you.'

'Thanks. I really don't want us to fall out,' he said.

'That's not going to happen. We can't fall out, we're on a mission to set up David and Jane. And that needs two heads.'

'You are such a lovely person, Ella. I wish things could be different.'

'Me too. Maybe in the future, when Isaac's bigger, you'll be able to have some time for yourself.'

He nodded. 'I'll always be a bit sad that you and I couldn't be more.'

'Me too,' she said.

He appeared coy. 'Are we still friends?'

'Absolutely. Friends without benefits,' she said, with a smile. And they both sipped their drinks and thought about what might have been.

***

Lucy checked her complexion in the bathroom mirror. The angry tomato look had at last faded and her skin had calmed down after its encounter with the cheap face pack. The door handle turned and it made her jump. She still wasn't used to having her mother staying.

'Occupied,' she called, feeling grateful that she'd locked the door out of habit.

'Hurry up, I've got a gippy tummy. What was in that chilli you dished up last night?' asked Terri, through the door.

'It was a meat substitute,' replied Lucy, adding in her head, *which I made from scratch after a long day at work because you'd been busy sitting on your backside working your way through Netflix.*

'I don't think that stuff does you any good.'

Lucy was about to explain she'd only bought it after her mother's lecture on animal welfare, when there was a blood-curdling sound. Not the sort of blood-curdling you would hear on a horror movie, more the sort of abdominal warning klaxon that comes before you need to replace your carpet. Lucy hastily undid the door and exited her bathroom.

'Thanks, love. I almost shit my pants there . . . oh hang on,' said her mother.

Lucy rapidly shut the door and turned her back on it like a keeper trapping a wild animal. There was a noise that sounded like someone in flippers walking across a trifle and Lucy ran downstairs as if fleeing from the undead.

She made herself a large strong coffee and tried to ignore the cereal bowl abandoned on the worktop. Although she had to admit that this was progress as it was in the vicinity of the dishwasher unlike every other receptacle and utensil her mother had used to date.

She loved her mum, she really did, but living with her was utterly impossible. While Lucy currently had no sex life there was no way she could even consider cultivating one at the moment. Living with Terri was like being in the worst student accommodation ever. In fact, Lucy realised, it was like living in a squat. The thought saddened her and she took her coffee through to the living room, tidied the strewn magazines and her mother's dirty socks, moved the remote control to its place on the coffee table, straightened the cushions and sat down.

How could you get to your fifties and not have a little security in your life? It was Lucy's worst nightmare. Everything she did was about securing a roof over her head. Her precarious childhood had cemented a deep-seated need to be secure. Terri, it would appear, had never had the desire to do the same. She moved freely from sofa to abandoned building without a care. And while it might not bother Terri it did worry Lucy because how much longer could Terri carry on like that?

This was the big issue. Her mother was used to living in a squat and if Lucy didn't want her home turned into one then she needed to have a conversation with her. The thought immediately shot a bolt of dread through her. How come she was happy to face confrontation at work, almost revel in it, and yet the thought of a cross word with her mother made her uncomfortable?

Lucy heard the toilet flush for the second time followed by her mother's footsteps on the stairs. 'I'd leave it for a while, Luce. It's a bit ripe in there.' Terri flopped onto the sofa, sitting on top of her own socks as if oblivious to them.

'Mum, we need to talk.'

'That sounds ominous. We're not splitting up, are we?' Terri laughed. 'You know what they say about people born in Norfolk?'

'I take it you remember that I was born here?'

'I can't forget your birth, you got stuck.'

Oh no, thought Lucy. She really didn't want to hear about one of only two childhood stories Terri could recall in detail. 'Thanks, Mum. I know you had a tough labour, lots of pain and then I looked like Mick Jagger.'

'But you did,' said Terri, hooting with laughter. 'You were such an ugly baby.'

'Thank you,' said Lucy, sipping her coffee and marvelling at her own ineptitude to keep the conversation on track.

'Don't you have to be at work?' Terri picked up the remote control.

'No, I'm in court this afternoon so I'm going in slightly later. Which is why I thought it would be a good opportunity for us to have a chat about a few things. Agree some mutually beneficial ground rules. To enable us to co-exist satisfactorily.'

'As long as you're not going to moan at me about being untidy. Because it's been proved that untidiness is an actual condition. Like depression and diabetes.' Terri nodded fervently. Lucy already wanted to give up.

CHAPTER TWENTY-SEVEN

Back at home Ella researched how to identify if your email account has been hacked and changed her password twice to be on the safe side. Although she hadn't been hacked, she was still puzzled about the email. How had an email, purporting to be from her, been sent to a prospective business associate without there being any trace of it on her account?

Unfortunately, the shop owner had deleted the email leaving Ella no clues as to where it had originated from. If it wasn't a hacker messing about then it could only be someone trying to sabotage her business. The thought upset her. Why would someone be so vicious and mean? Had she upset anyone? One person loomed into her mind – Wanda. Surely she'd not pull a stunt like this? A thought struck her. Perhaps this wasn't the only email.

She composed a note and emailed it to the other shop owners who had attended her launch and gave a brief explanation about the rogue email. Within a few minutes she received a reply and dived on it. It was a lovely response where they actually apologised for not working out that it had been a hoax email and they forwarded the offending message in an attachment. Ella hastily opened it up. It was from a Hotmail account and the content was roughly as the first shop owner had described.

Hi,

I wanted to get in touch to let you know that my company Oh Sew Special is now up and running and I'm planning on putting you out of business. This is a competitive area so I will be undercutting you on price wherever I can. Why am I telling you this? Because I wanted to make sure you understand why I don't need to engage with a tin pot business like yours but if you start to lose customers you'll know who is behind it. May the best person win!

  Yours truly,
  Ella Briggs
  Owner and proprietor of Oh Sew Special

It was clear whoever had sent it didn't know if Ella had already made contact. How they had signed off the email jumped out at her – owner and proprietor of Oh Sew Special. It was that phrase that cemented in her mind who was behind the sabotage.

'Gotcha,' she said, as she hit print.

Ella wasn't a fan of conflict, but she couldn't see there was any other way than to confront Wanda. If she called or messaged she wouldn't see Wanda's reaction and it was likely she would simply deny it, and where would that leave Ella? All she would have done would be to make Wanda aware that her scheme had had an impact.

Ella rang Lucy. 'Have you got a minute?'

'I'm just out of court and all that is waiting for me at home is a fifty-year-old squatter with a cleaning allergy. So fire away.'

'Issues with your mum?'

'Long story. What's up with you?'

Ella filled her in on the situation and waited while Lucy tutted which was a little like being on hold but not as musical.

'Right. Impersonation isn't a crime unless they are impersonating a solicitor or a police officer.' Ella sighed. 'But what she is doing is defamation of character meaning you've got her there but only if you can trace the email back to Wanda.'

'How do I do that?'

She heard Lucy suck her breath in. 'It's tricky. You can trace emails to an IP address but then it gets more difficult. You'd need to be able to access the computer to verify the IP addresses matched. Which is something the police could do but in reality they wouldn't have capacity to investigate something like this.'

'What do I do?'

'I have an idea. I'll swing by and pick you up and we'll tackle Wanda together.'

'Are you sure?' Ella didn't like putting on other people.

'You know I love a good argument. See you shortly.'

***

Lucy was quite pleased to have an excuse not to go home. She had a pile of work to do when she got in, assuming she could find a clean space to rest her laptop. She didn't want to think about that now. She liked coming to someone's rescue like a knight in shining armour, or in her case a navy dress but the intent was the same – being able to help someone was why she did the job she did. Ella's parents had seen potential in the argumentative teenager and had steered her towards law as a career. She owed them a lot. They'd been incredibly supportive, even dropping her at university when Terri had tied herself to a tree on the site of a planned additional runway.

Ella was waiting on the pavement and got in the car. 'Hiya. Any news on the missing girl?' she asked.

'Not a thing. I've had a few messages from her mother. Understandably she's in a state. Her estranged husband is supporting her which worries me.'

'Isn't that a good thing?'

'I don't trust him. He's being way too helpful. In my experience couples at war are rarely looking for opportunities to be supportive.'

'I guess.'

She glanced in Ella's direction. 'Did you bring the printed-out email? And the IP address details?'

'Yes.' Ella pulled some sheets out of her bag and waved them.

'Excellent. This'll be fun.' She didn't need to look across at Ella to know she'd disagree.

'I hate stuff like this. What if it's not Wanda?'

'Ella, you are genuinely the most lovely person I know. So unless you lead a double life where you upset people on a regular basis I cannot imagine you have offended another individual on the planet. Have you?'

'Not that I can think of and I have been racking my brains just in case.' Poor Ella, she was a sweetie.

'My only other thought, before we storm into Wanda's, is could it be Toad?' asked Lucy.

The sound Ella made wasn't a gasp as such, it was too quiet, but the motivation for it was the same. 'Todd wouldn't? Would he?'

'That's kind of what I'm asking you.'

There was a pause. 'How would he even know about the business? Or work out that I would be approaching local bridal shops for work?'

'Excellent point. In which case it has to be Wanda.'

Ella sighed. 'Why would she be so mean?'

'Ella, I hate to be the one to break this to you but with the exception of you, and Stacey Soloman – most people are very capable of being mean without needing a reason.'

It was almost closing time when they reached Frills, Frocks and Fairy Tales and Ella had a quick look through the window. 'There're no customers.' She looked relieved.

'Shame. Come on,' said Lucy, leading the way.

'Hang on.' Ella took a deep breath. 'I really appreciate you coming with me and I definitely need you for the legal back-up part but can I be the one to tackle her, please?'

'Of course.' Lucy was proud of Ella stepping up – this was right out of her comfort zone. 'Here's how I think you should play it.'

**

Ella took a deep breath and walked into the shop she'd never expected to set foot in again. Her heart was thumping and something was squirming in her insides but she was still doing it – she was going to challenge Wanda. The friendly tinkle of the door alerted Wanda and she appeared with her fake smile in place until she saw who it was.

'You're barred,' she said, folding her arms.

'It's not a pub,' said Lucy. Ella shot her a look. 'Sorry.' And she stepped back.

'Wanda, I am here because I have been made aware of some unpleasant emails.'

'Not interested,' said Wanda, trying to shoo them to the door.

Ella stood her ground. 'I think you should be interested because these emails are defamation of character.' Ella glanced at Lucy and she gave a tiny nod to let her know she'd got the wording right.

'And why would I need to know about that?' Wanda jutted out her chin defiantly.

'Because they were sent from your computer. The IP address can be traced back to your shop. I thought I should let you know that someone here has put you in a very awkward position.' Ella passed her the printed-out emails where she had ringed the IP address in red as Lucy had instructed.

Wanda opened and closed her mouth a couple of times before there was any sound. 'What are you accusing me of?'

'Not accusing you,' said Ella, trying to stay calm. 'I know you are professional and value your role in the local business community far too much to put that at stake by doing such an underhand, unkind and illegal thing. But I wanted to make you aware that *someone* has sent these from *your* computer and I would like you to make sure they stop.'

Wanda swallowed hard. 'I think you must be mistaken.'

'IP addresses don't lie,' said Lucy.

Wanda baulked as if spotting Lucy for the first time. 'And who are you?'

'I'm here as her legal representative.'

Wanda's eyes widened. They'd got her on the back foot. 'There's no need for legal representation.'

'I'm sure now we've made you aware there won't be. Will there?' Ella sounded far braver than she felt. Her heart was thudding hard in her chest as she waited for a response.

Wanda looked from Ella to Lucy and back again. 'No. There won't and now I'd like you both to leave.'

'Absolutely. We won't take up any more of your time.' Wanda seemed to relax so Ella thought she'd have the final word. 'And I expect I won't be getting any more dubious phone calls asking for sexual services either because that would add harassment to the list of offences.' Ella stared Wanda down.

'No,' said Wanda, then immediately looked alarmed. 'I don't know what you're talking about. And I want nothing more to do with you.'

'Excellent,' said Ella. 'Hope your business is going well. Because mine is booming.' She turned and she and Lucy exited the shop. Ella was a little worried by how much she'd enjoyed herself even if she was now shaking all over like a particularly enthusiastic Elvis impersonator. They got out of sight and Ella fell about laughing from a mixture of nerves and the sight of Wanda looking floored. She'd stood up to her old tyrant of a boss and she'd won. It felt good, very good indeed.

CHAPTER TWENTY-EIGHT

Despite the countdown to Brittany's wedding, the day itself did take Ella a little by surprise. She had been caught up in her business, or more accurately she was busy trying to market Oh Sew Special as work was trickling in sporadically. Brides for that year were already sorted so she was waiting for those who were planning months, or a year, ahead to start getting in touch. The wedding shop she'd spoken to was splitting alterations between her and their original seamstress and the other shops were happy with arrangements they already had in place. She'd put an advert in the local paper and that had generated some enquiries although a couple of those were looking for someone to make a dress from scratch which wasn't really her thing.

Ella had all the dresses for Brittany's wedding and strict instructions to bring them to the hotel for eleven. Ella pulled up at the same time as Lucy which was handy because three dress carriers and an overnight bag was quite a lot to juggle. The Sandy Cove Hotel was stunning: an ornate Victorian creation set as close to the sea as it could be without actually being on the sand. Brittany came flying outside, her hair in a perfect updo and her towelling robe flapping open. 'Thank goodness you're here,' she said, hugging them both tightly.

'Why what's wrong?' asked Lucy.

'Nothing. I was just desperate to see you both. I can't do this without you.' She gave them another hug.

'Aww,' said Ella, holding her tight. 'Everything will go like clockwork,' she added.

Brittany pulled a face. 'Although last night my dad lost his dentures skinny dipping so he's at the emergency dentist right now getting some replacements and I'm a bit concerned about Auntie Rita. She stayed here overnight, was on the bucks fizz at breakfast and now she's disappeared. I'm worried she'll turn up at the service drunk.'

'Can't be any worse than my mother. At my eighteenth she got totally wasted and was on the dancefloor cutting shapes to "Don't Stop Believin'" while wearing nothing but a bathmat. She tried to mount the DJ and threw up all over my presents.' Lucy forced a grin.

'She's joking, right?' asked Brittany.

'Sadly not,' said Ella. Who remembered the event vividly.

Brittany appeared concerned. 'It's okay, she's not quite as wild as that any more,' said Lucy.

'That's good,' said Brittany, a little quickly. 'I mean for her health.'

'Are you sure it's okay for her to come this evening?' asked Lucy, but it sounded to Ella like she was hoping for a back-out strategy.

'Of course it is. It's all arranged,' said Brittany. 'We had a few drop out so it's fine. Sandy is picking Terri up on the way.'

'She's bringing Dad too. They are all one big happy family,' said Ella. 'Apparently.' But at least it was all playing towards her and Kit's master plan. They were still in touch but now it was purely about David and Jane. It was no longer about Kit and Ella which made her a little sad.

'Then I hope the bar is well stocked,' said Lucy, getting her things out of the car.

'Does she drink that much?' asked Brittany, wearing an awkward expression.

Lucy closed her car boot. 'Yes but as she's coming it's more about how much I'll be drinking.'

They took the dresses inside and were wowed by the bridal suite: a very large room decorated sumptuously with an equally luxurious en-suite. Ella wedged the door open with her overnight bag while they brought everything in. Lucy handed her dress to Ella and dived on the giant bed.

'Don't trash it,' said Brittany. 'It needs to be nice for Grant.'

Lucy hitched herself up onto her elbows. 'I wouldn't dream of it,' she said, pulling the unicorn head out of her bag.

'Did you keep that as a souvenir?' asked Brittany, looking mildly disgusted.

'Souvenir?' Lucy seemed puzzled.

'After you shagged Mr Unihorn.'

'I didn't shag him,' said Lucy, with a snort. Ella was twitching so hard a muscle in her neck started to spasm.

'What?' Brittany was wide-eyed.

Lucy pulled a face as realisation dawned. 'Oh yeah. I remember – silly me. I did shag him.' Her voice was stilted and unconvincing.

Brittany's hands shot to her face. 'You lied to make me feel better. It *was* me who slept with him wasn't it?'

'We don't know that,' said Ella.

Brittany started to pace up and down. 'I knew it was me. What have I done? Should I find Grant and confess?'

'Nooo!' They both chorused.

'No evidence, no guilt,' said Lucy firmly.

There was a faint tap on the door. 'Can I come in?' asked Auntie Rita.

'Shit on a stick,' mumbled Brittany, her face turning a similar colour to her dressing gown.

Ella ushered her in and shut the door. She desperately tried to think of a way to cover Brittany's unwitting confession. 'We were just joking about—'

Auntie Rita waved a hand to stop her. 'I overheard so I thought I should have a word with Brittany here.'

Ella grimaced, Brittany swallowed hard and Lucy jumped off the bed. 'Don't admit to anything,' she whispered in Brittany's ear as she made to leave the room.

'Don't go. I know you three are close, Brittany's only going to tell you as soon as I've left.'

'That's true,' said Brittany. 'Look, Auntie Rita. I'm eaten up with remorse. I desperately regret it. I've never done—'

'Stop!' Auntie Rita held up her palm. 'I slept with Mr Unihorn. Not you.'

'W-what?' Brittany asked through a splutter.

'You heard. I'm not sharing details. But he has an interesting tattoo of Boris Johnson on his bum.' They all pondered this revelation for a second.

'Right, let's get you ready,' said Ella, keen to change the subject and chase the images from her mind.

Auntie Rita hugged them all and left the three friends to spend a happy time chatting and helping a very relieved Brittany to get ready. Lucy's phone kept pinging and she had to pause doing Ella's eye make-up to check it.

'Have they not found the missing girl?' asked Ella, as Lucy had been keeping them up to date over the previous few days that Alabama Maxwell had been missing.

'Nope. Her picture's been all over social media and the police are doing everything they can but there's no sign of her.'

'That's awful. You'd think she'd get in touch with her mum,' said Brittany.

'I think there's more going on with this case but I can't get to the bottom of it. We've put back the court date because of her disappearance. At least her parents are communicating which is something.'

'Do you think it's because of them splitting up?' asked Ella.

'It's possible. At least the police are confident she's not been abducted because they've got her on various CCTV cameras carrying a rucksack before she vanishes.'

Ella's phone pinged. 'Message from Kit,' she explained.

Lucy gave Ella an odd look. '*You're* not going to run off are you?'

'Ha ha. No, although we do have a brilliant masterplan for this evening.' She and Kit were quite pleased with what they'd cooked up over a couple more coffees. There was still an undeniable pull between them but they'd agreed to keep things platonic and however difficult, it was what they'd agreed.

'We?' asked Lucy.

'I'll explain later,' said Ella. 'Right now we need to get dresses and shoes on.'

The sun came out making the little cove into a picture postcard wedding venue. Even the sea was sparkling. Brittany looked nervous as she took her father's arm and walked along the wooden jetty to a flower-strewn decking and pergola where her guests and groom were waiting for her. The sea broke gently on the shore lending a calming soundtrack to their vows. The wedding ceremony went off without a hitch with the small exceptions of someone's mobile phone playing 'Bat Out of Hell' loudly and one of the flower girls having a meltdown, but Ella felt that was fairly standard and the little girl had been easily distracted with a lollipop that Ella had popped in her posy bag just in case. Now everyone was calling her Mary Poppins. She'd felt something when the little girl had voluntarily grabbed Ella's hand and looked up at her. It had taken her by surprise but the truth was, she liked children. She wasn't sure she was ready for any of her own but she could definitely see them featuring somewhere in her future.

While the children were hunting for shells on the beach the official photographs were taken. Ella knew the pictures on the sand, with the rolling waves behind them, were going to be stunning. Sandy Cove really was the perfect location and for a moment Ella let her mind wander to what her wedding would be like. Unhelpfully, a picture of Kit as her groom marched into her head. For her own state of mind she knew she needed to stop thinking about Kit like that.

'Smile,' called the photographer and Ella did her best to comply.

Lucy and Ella convened at the bar in the lull between the wedding breakfast and the evening reception. 'I see Martha got an invitation in the end,' said Lucy.

'Poor Brittany felt she had to.' Ella watched as Martha, in a very short white shift dress, leant over the present table to read the furthest labels. 'Who wears white to a wedding though?'

'The bride?' offered Lucy.

'Exactly. Thank goodness Brittany is so loved up she doesn't seem to have noticed.' They watched Brittany and Grant hand in hand chatting to some elderly relatives.

Ella let out a sigh. It was lovely to see her friend deliriously happy. 'Stop it,' said Lucy.

'What? I didn't do anything.'

'You're going all soppy. Have you shagged Kit yet?'

'I didn't like to say before but it's all off.' Sadness tinged her words.

'Shit, Ella. I'm sorry.'

'It's okay. Well, it's not okay but I know he has to put his nephew first. At least this time it's not me that's the issue.' Although that didn't make her feel much better. 'What are you doing on the man front or should I say *who* are you doing?' Ella asked.

'Very droll. I have my eye on the best man,' said Lucy. 'I think it's traditional that they shag a bridesmaid. I'm happy to take one for the team.'

Brittany scuttled over to them still beaming a grin that would make the Cheshire cat look like a miserable git. 'I need a drink.'

'Sure.' Lucy signalled to the barman. 'Stop looking so happy. Anyone would think it was your wedding day.'

Brittany stuck her tongue out. 'Have you seen Martha's bloody dress?' Lucy and Ella scrunched up their faces at the same time. 'At least everyone loves my dress. You did such a good job,' she said to Ella.

'You chose it,' said Ella, although she was secretly pleased, compliments were always nice. 'And you wear it well. You looked utterly beautiful coming down the aisle.'

'Apart from Dad and his new teeth. Ohmyword did you see them? He looks like Rylan Clark-Neal doing a toothpaste commercial.'

'I can't wait to see them under the disco lights,' said Lucy, with a snigger.

'Don't. I banned him from smiling on the photographs because they make my dress look dull,' she joked. Her drink arrived and she knocked back half the glass of wine.

'Steady,' said Ella, taking it from her.

'I need to steel myself for the lads arriving. They make Grant a bit lairy. Are you okay about Todd?' Brittany flinched as she said his name.

'I'm fine. You go and enjoy yourself,' said Ella with a smile. The bride gave her a tight squeeze and left. She watched Brittany become enveloped in the throng of arriving guests.

'You're not fine. Are you?' asked Lucy.

'Beyond terrified.' Ella downed the rest of Brittany's wine and signalled to the barman for a refill.

Ella hadn't seen Todd since the night he'd told her he didn't want a long-term relationship and had walked out of her life. At first the fact he seemed to have vanished off the planet was a shock but going cold turkey was probably for the best. She'd had no Facebook page to moon over or use to see what he was doing without her – it had definitely all been for the best. She'd moved on emotionally and was in a good place. Her new business was up and running. And yet the moment she saw him her treacherous heart leapt.

Ella spotted Todd as soon as he arrived. His hair was shorter and she didn't recognise his suit – but otherwise the way he strode in, exuding confidence and style, was all very Todd. All she had to do was be civil and a little aloof.

Lucy passed her a cocktail. 'You okay?' she asked.

'Still fine.' If she said it out loud she may convince herself.

'Liar.'

'What's this?' Ella sniffed the cloudy liquid.

'Hello Sailor. It's got rum in it. Get it down you.' Ella tried to get the straw in her mouth without actually taking her eyes off Todd.

Todd scanned the room and Ella and Lucy turned away in a synchronised movement. 'Did he see us looking?' asked Ella.

'Probably, but who cares? He promised you the world and then pissed off and—'

'Talking about anyone I know,' said Todd, stepping in between Lucy and Ella.

'Just some piss whippet who dumped my friend,' said Lucy. Ella tried to communicate with her by widening her eyes but Lucy was impervious to her signalling. 'So, Toad, any terrible karma befallen you recently? Lost your millions? Been burgled? Caught syphilis?'

Todd chuckled. 'You haven't changed, Lucy. Still bitter and alone I take it.'

'Ding, ding, ding. End of round one,' said Ella, tapping her glass with a fingernail. They both scowled at her for stopping their fun. Only she didn't find it entertaining. It was uncomfortable and unnecessary.

Todd leant in and for a second Ella thought he was going to kiss her on the lips. At the last moment he swerved to kiss her cheek. 'Ella, you look divine. I'm sorry.'

244

'For dumping her? Breaking her heart? Being a prize-winning arse donkey?' asked Lucy, poking her head between them.

'Should I call security?' asked Todd, glancing around.

'Be careful, Toad. Remember I know criminals.' Lucy jutted out her chin.

'Do you?' whispered Ella.

Lucy moved to the other side of Ella. 'A couple of shoplifters and a flasher but he doesn't need to know that,' replied Lucy. 'Don't let him intimidate you.'

'I'm fine,' repeated Ella. 'I can handle this.'

Todd gave Lucy a supercilious look. 'Utter wank badger,' muttered Lucy, and she left them to it.

'I'm sorry that I didn't properly acknowledge you,' said Todd. 'Are you well? You look terrific.' He gave Ella the sort of considered scan that would previously have turned her insides to jelly. Bugger it. It appeared it still had the exact same effect on her.

'Thanks. I am very well, thank you for enquiring.' Why did she keep doing that weird 1940s voice?

Todd controlled a brief smirk. 'That's good. I've been thinking of you, Ella.'

What the hell did that mean? He had had a fleeting thought like, *I wonder if Ella is still alive?* Or did it mean she was a permanent fixture in his mind like tuna was in Pirate's?

'Thanks. I think,' she said and hated herself for the girlish giggle that escaped.

Her mobile buzzed in her posy bag and she retrieved it. It was a text from Kit. *Leaving now. Hope this goes to plan. K*

Todd was watching her. 'Boyfriend?' he asked, his voice smooth and curious.

'Oh no. He's . . .' What was Kit? 'He's a friend actually his mum and my . . .' She stopped herself. What was she doing? This was the man who had trampled on her heart and walked out without a backward glance, she didn't owe him anything and he didn't deserve her pleasantness. 'You know what. I don't need to explain anything to you, Todd. Have a nice evening.' She lifted her chin and walked away with a little sashay to her gait just in case he was watching her cross the room.

CHAPTER TWENTY-NINE

More people were arriving for the evening reception so it was time for Ella to find her dad – it was all part of her and Kit's master plan. The wedding took up a lot of space with a dancefloor, private bar and buffet area and a less noisy space with big sofas and low tables so there was somewhere for everyone. She found her mum and dad chatting in the quieter area. It hurt her to see them behaving amiably. She knew it would be worse if they were shouting and screaming at each other but seeing them look exactly the same as they had always done made her wish that was the case.

'Darling, you did a fantastic job today,' said her mum, getting up and embracing her. 'And the dresses . . .' Her mother paused and gave her a once-over as if to remind herself. 'Well, Lucy says they looked a lot worse.'

'Thanks. I think,' said Ella.

'I like them,' said David, giving her a hug. 'Brown is a good neutral colour. Goes with everything.'

'How do you work that out?' asked Sandy, with a laugh.

'Every man has a pair of brown shoes because they don't clash with anything,' David reasoned. Their easy conversation hadn't changed.

'There's something I want to know,' said Ella, taking a deep breath.

'Of course. What is it?' asked Sandy.

'I'm sorry but I have to ask one last time. Are you sure there's no chance of you getting back together?'

'I'm sorry,' said her mum. 'The last thing we wanted to do was upset you, but it is what we both want.'

'We'll always be friends,' said David, putting an arm around Sandy. 'But we want different things now.'

'Best to end it while we're still talking,' said Sandy, and they both chuckled. They still had a lovely relationship. Clearly it had changed but there was a lot of love and respect for each other that was clear to see. With a heavy heart Ella knew she had to let them both move on.

'We love you just the same, Pumpkin,' said David. 'That will never change.'

'I know. I'm glad you still like each other. And I guess I get two toys at Christmas now,' she joked.

They both embraced her and trapped her in a three-way hug like they had done when she was small. She was glad she'd asked again. It was helping her get things ordered in her mind. There was definitely no going back, both her parents had moved on. Unfortunately, David's plans to start afresh had been scuppered by her and Kit's meddling. But their new plan was a good one – maybe it would help her father find happiness again.

They sat down and chatted about the day and when Ella's mobile pinged she pounced on it. It was Kit. She sucked the last of her drink up the straw making an unpleasant noise but it did grab the attention of her parents. 'That cocktail was good. We should all have those. Give me a hand, Dad?' She got to her feet.

'Not for me,' said Sandy. 'I'm designated driver tonight.'

She tried not to panic, but it was key to the plan that they had drinks. 'Dad?'

'Not my sort of thing,' said David, turning up his nose.

'It's really nice. I'm sure you'd like it. And it's a wedding, we're meant to be celebrating. Come on.' *Please, please, please*, she added in her head.

'Go on then. I'll try one,' he said, but showed no signs of moving.

'You need to come with me to get it,' she said.

'Do I?' He gave her a long-suffering look. 'I expect I'm paying, am I?'

'I've not got my purse.' She held up her posy bag and her father rolled his eyes.

'Come on then,' he said, getting to his feet and heading for the bar area.

'Not that bar. It's mega busy with all the wedding guests. Let's sneak out to the one by the hotel restaurant.' She linked her arm through his and guided him away. Part one of the masterplan had been executed.

***

Lucy found the best man on the balcony staring hard into a brandy glass. She leant on the rail next to him which got his attention. 'Hi, I'm Lucy. Well done for the speech. I liked it. Especially the part where it was very short.' She offered him a hand and they shook.

'Eric, I'm a university friend of Grant's. Nice dress,' he said, immediately looking away. 'Shame there's someone else wearing the exact same one.'

He was funny, this was a good start. 'Yeah, the bitch.' Lucy did a mock snarl. 'But you like the dress?'

'Sure.'

'Now you see I thought you might be a decent, honest bloke but now I know you tell lies.' She smoothed her hands over the ruffles for emphasis.

He gave an overdramatic cringe. 'That obvious huh?'

'Totally. Shall we try again? Do you like my dress, Eric?'

'Well, if we're being honest . . .' She could sense his trepidation. 'I would have to say it fits you well.'

'My arse looks great, doesn't it?'

He laughed. 'It absolutely does.'

'Do you like the colour?' She smirked to let him know she was teasing.

'It's not my favourite. It is a bit . . .'

'Brittany's nan called it shit and butter colour.'

He smiled. 'I agree with Brittany's nan.'

'You don't like it?' She gasped and pressed her palm to her chest. 'It's number seven on the Bristol Stool Chart.'

His smile broadened. 'It does have a certain—'

'Turd-like quality?' she suggested.

'I was going to say shiny turd. But yes, it's very turdesque.'

'Now you're just being fancy.' She suspected she could have some fun with him and gave him a cheeky look. 'I needed to check you're not a party *pooper*.'

'I guess if anyone should be doing poo jokes, it's you. But that was a real stinker.'

She nodded her approval. It was like playing pun tennis. 'I'm a woman, I'm used to dealing with plenty of crap. I'm not usually wearing it though.'

They both laughed. There was a brief pause and she could see him conjuring up the next gag. 'That's interesting. I'd like to get to the bottom of that.'

She liked that he was joining in her silliness. 'I'm afraid I've tried to *wipe* it all from my memory.'

'I can see today has taken it out of you. You're looking a little flushed.'

'And we have a winner!' said Lucy, laughing as they high-fived.

'Thanks for coming over to talk to me, Lucy. I don't know anyone here apart from Grant. I only met Brittany a couple of months ago. I live in London, we don't catch up very often. I'm not sure why he picked me to be his best man.'

'I know there was a bit of blokey joking around with his close friends where they were all offering to be his best man and I honestly think he was worried he was going to upset the others if he picked one of them.'

Eric nodded. 'So he chose me to avoid a falling-out.'

'That and you'll look good in the photographs. You're easy on the eye.'

He turned to face her. 'Stop it, if you keep on, you'll make me blush.' He smiled and revealed cute dimples in his cheeks.

'I love a challenge,' said Lucy.

'Don't pooh-pooh this idea but I'm thinking you and I should finish these and get some more drinks.'

'I think that's an excellent suggestion,' said Lucy, keen to see if they had anything else in common other than flirting and poo jokes. She downed the last of her drink. 'Bottoms up!'

***

Ella and her father were chatting as they walked into the public bar. It was fairly quiet but there were two people she recognised sitting on a couple of large sofas – Kit and Jane. For the second time that day she felt something in her gut flutter. She ignored them both, as planned, and went to the bar where Todd was drinking a pint. He definitely wasn't part of the plan. Todd looked up, smiled at Ella but his smile faltered when he spotted her father next to her. She liked that he was uncomfortable – he deserved to be.

'Todd.' She said his name and turned to the barman. David almost bent backwards to get a look around Ella.

'Who the heck invited him?' said David, in a stage whisper.

'He's still a friend of Grant's. Be civil. Please.'

David leant forward. 'Todd,' he said.

251

'David,' said Todd. Could it get any more awkward? She feared it was about to. Ella ordered and her dad paid.

As they turned around with their drinks she looked towards the sofas in a deliberate motion. 'Look who's over there.' She pointed with her free hand and then put it down because she feared she was becoming a bit too theatrical. She saw Todd turn out of the corner of her eye. Oh well, if he saw this play out it wouldn't be the worst thing.

'Hello!' she called quickly to Kit so her dad didn't have an opportunity to sneak away.

Kit was on his feet. 'Hey there, Ella. Come and join us.'

David didn't look like a rabbit in the headlights so much as recently squished roadkill. His expression was one of death by awkwardness. 'Dad,' she prompted but David wasn't moving. 'We can't be rude.' She walked towards Kit and prayed he would follow.

Kit greeted her with air kisses. In the hope that Todd was watching she held Kit in a hug and planted a kiss firmly on his cheek. Then paused to look into his eyes. Kit was scanning her face clearly wondering what she was doing. 'Whoops I left lipstick on your cheek.' She carefully rubbed at the smudge while maintaining Kit's eye contact. Kit gave his head a little shake as if trying to regain focus. 'Ella, you remember my mum.'

'Hi Jane, lovely to see you again.' More kisses followed. Ella desperately wanted to look over her shoulder to see if Todd was taking it all in but she didn't want to make it obvious.

Ella realised her dad wasn't joining in the greetings. David was standing a couple of feet behind Ella looking like rigor mortis was setting in fast.

'Have a seat,' said Kit, ushering David onto the sofa next to Jane.

'We're at a wedding so we can't really—' began David.

'We can stay for two minutes,' said Ella, sitting down next to Kit.

All eyes were on David, including Jane's. 'Err . . .'

Ella marvelled how her father who was usually an articulate man had been rendered mute. 'It's fine, David,' said Jane. 'It's nice to see you.'

David seemed to come to life. 'Lovely to see you too.' He was sitting gingerly on the edge of Jane's sofa.

There was a brief silence which Ella and Kit both tried to fill at the same time resulting in a jumble of words and giggles from them both. 'No, sorry, you first,' said Ella.

'This must be the horror dress you told me about,' he said. 'She had to make lots of alterations to it,' he explained to Jane. He turned back to Ella. 'It looks great. Does Lucy like hers now?' asked Kit.

'I wouldn't go that far but she's not moaned about it for half an hour which is a good sign.'

Kit and Ella both glanced at their parents who were watching their exchange. 'And what brings you two here?' Ella asked, trying hard to sound natural and failing.

'It's Mum's birthday on Tuesday and I'd heard the restaurant was pretty good so I thought we'd check it out.'

'Happy birthday for Tuesday,' said Ella, leaning over to clink her glass against Jane's.

'Thank you.' There were more clinks. The one between Jane and David was a little delayed and slightly uncoordinated but still a nice gesture.

'Any plans for Tuesday?' asked David and Ella held her breath.

'Nothing out of the ordinary. Just meeting friends for lunch.'

'There might be a cake,' said Kit. 'Isaac is insisting.'

'How is Isaac?' asked Ella.

'He's fine. He's at a friend's for a sleepover,' said Jane.

David nodded along. 'Well, have a good time and enjoy your meal tonight. Ella and I should get back to the wedding reception before they send out a search party.' He got to his feet and gave a firm nod at Ella for her to do the same.

'Right. It's been lovely to see you both again.' Ella started giving goodbye kisses to Jane and Kit but David had already walked away. She looked over to the bar to see that Todd was no longer there. She wondered when he'd left. 'Bye,' she said to Kit.

She went after her father who was fleeing from the bar. Had it gone well? She wasn't sure. They had chatted but she didn't get the feeling it had done a lot of good. Things were definitely still frosty between Jane and her dad. Not the instant spark of reconnection she and Kit had hoped for.

She caught up with David. 'That was embarrassing,' he said.

'Was it? I like Jane, she seems lovely.'

David kept walking. 'She is. Or rather I thought she was.'

'What do you mean?' Ella felt the familiar sensation of guilt wash over her. She feared her father was going to list all the stunts she and Kit had pulled.

David halted just outside the wedding reception room. 'Why did we break up you mean?' Ella nodded. 'Because she was cheating on me.' He looked miserable.

'Was she? Are you certain because sometimes we misconstrue things.' He was narrowing his eyes at her. She wasn't ready to confess her part in the downfall of their relationship. 'I mean she doesn't seem like the type. That's all. Maybe you're wrong.' She waited for his response.

David sighed. 'Lovely Ella, you see the good in everyone. Jane was definitely seeing someone else while we were dating.'

Ella pulled a face. 'You know this is where Lucy would ask for evidence.'

He puffed out his cheeks as if considering what to say next. 'Jane told me herself that she's dating a plumber from King's Lynn. She met him and me on the same dating app at a similar time. It turns out she was seeing us both all along. She said she wasn't sure which of us she preferred and she was struggling to make a decision so I made it for her.'

Ella opened her mouth, but she had no words. 'Dad, I'm so sorry.'

'It's okay, sweetheart. It's not your fault. You live and learn. Come on, let's enjoy the rest of the night.' He went into the room and left Ella in the doorway still lost for words.

CHAPTER THIRTY

Ella had a frantic text exchange with Kit. She wasn't expecting him to abandon his mother in the restaurant but she needed to update him on developments. There was a small part of her that felt better because at least it hadn't been entirely down to her and Kit's shenanigans that Jane and David had broken up. She was also a little cross that Jane had been stringing her dad along although she knew how the dating app game worked. She'd just never thought about it happening to her dad. He came from a different generation, one where you dated one person at a time. She stared at her phone, no reply from Kit.

'Here's my other bridesmaid!' said Brittany, enveloping her in a bear hug. Lucy was close behind her, waving.

Ella pasted on a smile. It was Brittany's day, she needed to focus on that. 'Are you having a fabulous time?'

'The. Best. I am so lucky. I have the most awesome friends in the world and the loveliest husband.' She whooped. 'I have a husband. How weird is that?'

'It's not weird. I'm really happy for you,' said Ella.

'It is weird,' said Lucy, leaning into their space. 'Can we take the dresses off yet?'

'Not until after the first dance. That's what I came to find you for. You need to pair up with the best man and the ushers.'

'Bagsy me the best man,' said Lucy super-fast.

They went through to the dancefloor where the DJ announced the first dance and Brittany and Grant took to the floor to 'Perfect' by Ed Sheeran. It was a lovely moment. They danced as if they were unaware of everyone else now all crammed around the dancefloor watching them and filming on their phones. Brittany's mum was wiping her eyes with a tissue and Auntie Rita appeared to be doing tequila shots with Terri.

'We're up,' said Lucy, giving Ella a gentle nudge as she glided passed her with the best man in tow.

She was meant to be dancing with one of the ushers. Ella looked around. Where were the ushers? There was no sign of them. She'd last seen them playing football on the beach. Brittany and Lucy were beckoning Ella onto the dancefloor. She held up her hands in what she hoped was a 'I'm not dancing on my own' gesture. In that moment someone clasped her hand and swept her onto the dancefloor. When she looked up, she was beyond disappointed to see that it was Todd. Her shoulders tensed but she was British to the core and the last thing she was going to do was cause a scene and upset Brittany.

Through a forced smile she spoke to Todd. 'What are you doing?'

'Rescuing you from embarrassment. Both bridesmaids were meant to be dancing, your partner has abandoned you.'

'Only you abandoned me, Todd.'

'Ouch.' He gave a comic wince.

They turned and she saw people were still filming so she made more of an effort with her smiling. It was both weird and very familiar to be in Todd's arms. Somewhere she once felt safe and at home. It was comfortable, like she could slip back to that place and yet all the pain was raging too. It hurt that he'd moved on with his life without her but also that Lucy had been right about how he had treated her. Was it bullying? Whatever it had been it had been subtle and undermining. The more she thought about it the crosser she became. They danced and danced and Ella wondered how long the wretched song was.

'Was that your boyfriend in the bar earlier?'

'Really none of your business, Todd.'

They turned again and found themselves close to the best man and Lucy. 'Tit pigeon,' said Lucy as she and Eric passed by.

At last other couples joined them and Ella began working out her quickest escape route. The song changed and she let go of Todd like he was the wicker man. As she went to walk off, he grabbed her hand. 'Can't we be friends?'

'You are unbelievable.' There were many things she wanted to say. She wanted to tell him that friends didn't break your heart, that friends cared about you, protected you and stood by their promises because they loved you no matter what. They didn't chip away at your confidence and steer your thinking down roads it might not have voluntarily wandered down, but Brittany was watching her over Grant's shoulder. Instead, she raised her chin, pulled her hand free and said simply, 'No, Todd. We can't.' And she walked away.

Her heart was hammering in her chest. She needed another drink. She went to the wedding bar but it was heaving as it appeared everyone who had watched the first dance had then taken the few steps to the bar and were now three deep waiting to be served. She made her way out and through the hotel to the public bar. It was cooler and quieter, which was what she needed. It gave her a chance to catch her breath.

The barman appeared. 'What can I get you?'

'A rum and Coke and a tap water please.' She got her debit card from her posy bag. She hoped her dad didn't rock up and see that she'd been fibbing earlier. She waited for her drinks and checked her phone. Still nothing from Kit. She fired off another text to say she was in the bar and would be for five minutes if he was able to duck out. She figured he could say he needed the loo as a cover story. Ella told herself that she needed to update him on the whole your mum was two-timing my dad thing. But the truth was she wanted to see him. She wasn't entirely sure why but he was someone neutral, like Switzerland but without the weird lederhosen and that odd long alpenhorn they liked to blow. It felt like Kit was hers. Separate from anything else in her life. And her close encounter with Todd had been unsettling. Mainly because she was seeing him differently, recognising that he hadn't been the perfect person she'd believed him to be. Instead of all those wasted months feeling sad she should have been celebrating a lucky escape.

Her drinks arrived and she downed the water, that way she wouldn't dehydrate, and she would sip her rum and Coke rather than glug it. Eventually she began to calm down. She didn't like the way Todd was able to get an instant reaction out of her. She hoped that wouldn't always be the case.

***

Lucy and Eric managed to escape for a bit to the beach. It was a warm evening and the wedding reception was getting a bit rowdy. She was also aware that she'd managed to dodge her mother for most of the party and the longer she avoided that fate the better. At least it was Sandy who was lumbered with driving Terri home. Lucy and Ella had booked rooms at the hotel and Lucy was very much hoping that she would be making best use of her large bed with Eric.

Eric checked his watch. 'Is there someone waiting for you somewhere?' she asked.

'No, I was wondering when I could safely leave without it looking like I'd done a runner.'

'Are you not a fan of big gatherings?' she asked, taking off her shoes and wriggling her toes into the cool sand.

'It's just weddings I'm not a fan of.'

'Same . . . actually it's marriage I thumb my nose at.'

He gave her a sideways look. 'That's unusual.'

'What? Because all women spend their lives dreaming of being a bride and looking like a toilet roll cover for a day?'

'Sorry, I didn't mean to sound sexist. And while I could totally imagine you in a dress like that' – he glanced at what she was wearing – 'I think it's what society expects. Not just of women but of people in general.'

'Or the patriarchy.'

'You could be right. Why are you so down with marriage?' he asked.

'Because it's my job to sort them out when they invariably fall apart.' She noticed his intrigued expression and thought she should put him out of his misery. 'I'm a divorce lawyer.'

He laughed. It wasn't the response she was expecting. 'I'm sorry,' he said. 'But I completely understand that your job taints your view.'

'You do?'

'I'm a psychologist and part of my role is marriage guidance counselling.' The laughter that followed was hearty and almost a sense of relief for Lucy at finding somebody who truly understood where she was coming from.

Their easy discussion continued, and they found they had done a full lap of the cove and were right back where they'd started. The noise from inside had increased and reached them while they were still on the beach.

'We should probably go back in,' suggested Lucy, although she was hoping he was going to make a move on her. 'Even if it's just to say goodnight and then we can do as we please.'

They walked along the wooden jetty and up the steps to the hotel lawn. He turned to face her and inside she did a fist pump. He was going to kiss her, she had landed the best man. Lucy loved it when a plan came together. He studied her face and ran his index finger down her cheek before tucking a stray piece of hair behind her ear. It was an intimate gesture and made her go a little quivery.

'I have never met anyone like you, Lucy.'

'That's good. It means I've not been cloned.'

His smile was broad as he bent to kiss her. She closed her eyes. The noise from inside the party reached new levels and however much they wanted to ignore it the huge cheer that went up had to be investigated. They both turned their heads at the same time. Through the large windows they watched as Auntie Rita appeared to start stripping. Rita's hat was thrown into the crowd, followed by her jacket. They both started to laugh. Lucy's laughter was cut short. She was horrified to see her mother join Rita and moments later whip off her own blouse.

'What the actual f—' Lucy hitched up her dress and stormed inside.

***

Ella checked the time on her phone. It had been ten minutes. Kit wasn't coming. It wasn't something to dwell on, he'd probably not seen her message, but she was disappointed all the same. Ella slid from the barstool ready to return to the celebrations but coming into the bar was Todd. He strode straight up to her. Ella held up her palm to stop him invading her space. His eyes were focused on her with an unnerving intensity. Tiredness pulled at her eyelids. It had been a long and exhausting day, she didn't have the energy to fight with Todd. She held her palm firmly in front of her. She didn't care if it made her appear rude which was quite liberating in itself.

Instead of respecting the signal, Todd stepped closer still and placed his palm tenderly against hers. 'What the hell are you doing?'

'See, Ella, they fit. We're meant to be together you and I.'

She felt the warmth of his fingers against hers. A tingle as he fluttered his fingertips. Ella quickly snatched her hand away. 'Todd, you've been drinking. The wedding is doing things to your head.' She tried to step past him.

'Don't dismiss it, Ella. You feel it too. I know you do.'

This was the point where a sensible person would lie. 'But it's not the same. You ruined it all. You ripped out my heart, crushed it and walked away. Vanished completely. It was like you'd died. Only worse because you hadn't.' She felt mean for saying the last bit out loud but it had been exactly how she had felt at the time. It would have been easier if he'd died. The loss was the same but she also had the crushing weight of rejection to deal with as well.

'I am sorry. The last thing I wanted to do was hurt you.'

'But that's exactly what you did.'

'I thought erasing myself from your life was the best thing to do.'

She was shaking her head, but she could see in his eyes he was being honest. 'It was the worst thing. What made you . . .' She swallowed down the emotion.

'I got scared about committing. It felt like the rest of my life was being mapped out and . . . truth is . . .' His eyes seemed to look into her soul. 'I'm not scared any more.' The flicker of his eyebrow asked the question he didn't seem able to utter.

'Oh, Todd. No.'

'But we had something special you and me. We could have that again.'

'It's too little and it is way too late.' But as she said the words she didn't feel cross or vengeful – it was sadness that cloaked her. What they'd had was what she'd thought she had wanted. That perfect relationship her parents had shared. Only no relationship was truly like that. They all had flaws. She realised she had paused too long when Todd's lips met hers. Tiredness and familiarity delayed her response. This wasn't what she wanted, and it certainly wasn't what she needed. She snapped open her eyes and pulled away.

Beyond Todd she saw Kit and her heart leapt. She realised what it must have looked like. She wanted to rush over and explain but before she could galvanise herself to move Kit had walked away.

PART FOUR

CHAPTER THIRTY-ONE

When she awoke Lucy was wrapped in happiness, along with Eric's smooth hands and firm torso. She'd slept well. She always did after sex and alcohol. Before they'd left the party Eric had bought her a large orange juice and encouraged her to drink it as well as lots of water – he swore by it to fend off a hangover. It had definitely done the trick because her head was ache free. Eric was smart as well as cute. Memories of the previous night brought a smile to her lips and a quiver to her insides until the recollections moved on to her mother and Auntie Rita and the quiver morphed into queasiness as she flinched at the images marauding her mind.

The reckless pair had refused to put their clothes back on and had scrambled onto a table to stay out of reach. They had continued to dance as the other guests egged them on. Lucy had been mortified. Thanks to Sandy they had managed to coax Terri and Rita safely down from the table and out of harm's way with pornstar martinis. Although it hadn't stopped Terri from groping the DJ and insulting Brittany's mother's outfit before they had finally managed to escort her to the car. Lucy made a mental note to send Sandy some flowers as a thank you and a formal apology to Brittany's mum to confirm that she in no way resembled a pantomime dame.

Lucy had always wanted to trade parents with Ella and never more so than last night. Terri was a total and utter embarrassment. Mothers weren't meant to behave like out of control teenagers. They were meant to cook Sunday lunch, drink tea and go shopping. Instead, Terri liked to pierce unpierceable parts of her body and roll joints but only when she wasn't rat-arsed on a free bar and gyrating on a tabletop to 'Sex Bomb'. Tom Jones had a lot to answer for.

It was a huge tick in Eric's favour that he hadn't run for the hills. Instead he had been waiting with tequila shots when she had come back outside embarrassed and fuming at her mother's behaviour. He hadn't questioned her or offered platitudes or excuses, he had simply handed her a shot glass. There were a number of other things about Eric that were ticking Lucy's boxes: he was anti-marriage which was a huge plus, he was fun and, so far, had shown no inclination towards any psychotic tendencies. He was also gorgeous, a top-rate kisser and the sex had been exceptional, which also helped. She was pretty sure she had found her next casual man and that made her very happy.

Lucy checked the time, there were still two hours until checkout but they were going to miss breakfast if they didn't get up soon. It was a tough call: full English or more sex? She rolled over and studied Eric. He was prettier than he was handsome. Perfect skin, delicate cheekbones and those dimples. She kissed his full lips and he responded immediately. Oh well, she wasn't a huge fan of a cooked breakfast anyway.

***

Ella messaged Lucy again. If she didn't appear in the next couple of minutes she was going to have to go and bang on her bedroom door or she'd miss Brittany leaving for her honeymoon. The few guests who had stayed overnight had congregated in the hotel lobby. The ushers looked decidedly green as did Auntie Rita who was asking everyone if they'd seen her new M&S balcony bra which had mysteriously vanished in the night. Nobody replied because pretty much everyone *had* seen it when she had been twirling it around her head, but it was likely no one knew where it was now. Brittany's mum was already weeping and being comforted by Grant's mother who looked delighted that her last child was finally leaving home. She had been excitedly sharing a cruise holiday brochure at breakfast.

Todd had been at breakfast too. His hair sticking up how it always did when he was fresh out of the shower but hadn't got around to adding any product to it yet. Ella hated that they knew so much about each other. It all seemed such a waste that all that information was useless and defunct. They'd found themselves both waiting by the toast machine and he'd opened his mouth to say something but she walked away and abandoned her toast. His words from last night had unsettled her. Made her doubt things and lie awake mulling everything over.

The fact that Todd now seemed to think he was ready for commitment was messing with her head. What if he'd realised this when they'd been together? Would it have been them getting married? Once upon on a time that thought would have made her happy but now it made her think about how uneven the relationship had been and how much worse that would likely have become if they'd married. Ella was annoyed with herself. She'd been passive and Todd had taken advantage of that. He'd definitely steered her thinking when it came to having children. He'd always worded things to make them sound like they were her thoughts and ideas. How she wouldn't want her life to be ruined by a child. That she wasn't the sort of woman who needed children to validate her. But all along it had been his view he was forcing onto her. She vowed she'd not let that happen again. She knew what she needed to do. She needed to forget about Todd but that wasn't going to be easy. Although after today she had no reason to believe she would ever see him again which would definitely help. He could disappear back into the black hole he'd crawled out of.

She didn't know what to do about Kit. She hated that he'd seen Todd kiss her. Just thinking about the mess of it all brought her out in a sweat. It was all too complicated to explain to him but then she and Kit were just friends so she had no obligation to him and no reason she couldn't be kissing someone else. But that wasn't the point. Even if there was no hope for them, she still didn't want Kit thinking she'd moved on that easily because she hadn't. She wished she could be more like Lucy. She heard her friend's giggles before she saw her. Lucy was still buttoning up her shirt as Eric showered her in kisses and they tumbled into reception only seeming to notice the assembled crowd at the last moment.

'Hey, look at that, bang on time,' said Lucy, checking her watch. Eric wrapped his arms around her and nuzzled her neck. It didn't take a genius to work out what had delayed them. *That looks a lot more fun than my sucky love life*, thought Ella.

Brittany and Grant appeared. Brittany was wearing a smart shift dress, juggling a handbag and her bouquet while arguing with someone on her mobile about airport parking. Grant trundled two large cases behind him. The group parted and Grant went to put things in the boot of the car which the ushers had kindly decorated in silly string and inflated condoms – so original.

Brittany put her phone away and her lip wobbled as she reached Lucy and Ella. 'You guys were the best bridesmaids ever. I love you.'

'Are you still pissed?' whispered Lucy in her ear.

'No, I mean it. Thank you for always being there.' Brittany dabbed at her eyes.

'I'm here too,' said her mum through a sob.

'Oh, Mum.' Brittany was enveloped in a hug. 'I'm going to miss you.'

Lucy gave Ella a wide-eyed look. 'She's going on a week's honeymoon to Marbella not a one-way mission to Mars.'

Brittany extricated herself from her mum. Hugged Lorraine and moved on to Auntie Rita who kissed her cheek. 'Wonderful day yesterday.'

'Yes,' said Brittany. 'We made memories.'

'We did. Hopefully some of them were captured on film. If any of the photos show what happened to my balcony bra, let me know.' Rita held up crossed fingers.

'I think Grant is waiting,' said her mum, pulling another packet of tissues from her bag.

'Throw the flowers and clear off,' said Lucy.

Brittany wiped away a tear. 'You are all my favourite people,' she said, before turning her back and tossing her bouquet in the air.

Whether it was a knee-jerk reaction or a well-aimed throw on Brittany's part – Ella would never know, but with very little effort she caught the flowers. A cheer went up. Ella felt pleased to have caught them until she looked across the reception area and her eyes met with Todd's.

Ella needed to clear her head so she made her way down to the cove. All the wedding flowers that had adorned the walkway and the pergola were gone. The chairs where they had sat for the service had been replaced by benches and people drinking coffee. The footprints on the sand where there had been photographs and games of football had all been washed away. It was as if the wedding had never taken place. Everything had gone back to normal. Which was exactly what would happen to Brittany and Grant when they returned from honeymoon. All that planning, stress and cost was for one day and when it was over normality kicked in. For the first time it struck Ella how odd that was. So much effort on making one day perfect. Perhaps if couples applied the same attention to their relationship more would survive.

Catching the bride's bouquet had been an odd experience. People she didn't know had congratulated her. Even Lucy had given her a wink. She had been keen to get rid of the bouquet so she'd given it to Brittany's mum who was over the moon because she was going to send it away to be made into a pressed flower picture. It was a nice idea, at least the flowers would have a longer life expectancy than the bride's dress which would likely go in a box and not see the light of day ever again. Ella sighed as she watched the waves gently lap the shore.

'Penny for them?' said Todd, making her jump.

The last person she needed interrupting her was Todd. She could storm off but what was the point? 'I was thinking about weddings.'

'Your wedding?' he asked.

'Nope. The whole carnival of it. The months of planning and all the money they cost when what matters is whether those two people are suited – nothing else.'

'That's deep for you, Ella.' He chuckled and it irked her. She was now noticing all the little subtle ways he had undermined her.

'Did you want something, Todd?'

'Yes. About last night in the bar and also that look you gave me this morning when you caught the bouquet. I don't want to give you any false hope.'

Ella spluttered out a laugh which seemed to surprise Todd. 'You're unbelievable, Todd. It's over. We're over.'

'That's exactly what I'm telling you, Ella, and I'm sorry if that's hard for you to take.'

'It's not—'

Todd held up his palms to stop her talking. 'This is goodbye,' he said solemnly and he made his way back up to the hotel.

Ella was stunned. She was about to go after him and put him straight when something dawned on her. She didn't need to justify things to Todd, he could think what he liked, it didn't matter.

The few days after Brittany's wedding had given Ella a chance for her thoughts to settle. She had some work to do and she was filling her time with writing and placing adverts in local publications and signing up for wedding fairs in the area. If she was attending wedding fairs she also needed something to show people which was a tad more difficult than someone like a photographer or an invitation maker so she was also researching pop-up stands. She wished she'd taken before and after shots of Brittany's bridesmaids' dresses to show the transformation. She'd even done a quick eBay search to see if she could find another one in its original state but it seemed they were unique.

Brittany had posted a lot of happy, sunny photographs on her Facebook page along with pictures of her pets which she was evidently missing, but overall she was enjoying her honeymoon. Paws paddling on the door jolted her from her thoughts and she let Pirate in. She had planned to ban him from the business zone but that was easier said than done. He had taken to paddling on the door followed by plaintive cries and then full-on wails so she had been quickly defeated. An internet trawl had turned up the cutest mini pet sofa. It was actually a dog bed but it was adorable and had dark wooden legs similar to her gran's wingback chairs. She'd gone for a similar material and it looked quite sweet in her work area underneath her long bench. Pirate hopped over to his couch and settled himself down.

She'd had an awkward text exchange with Kit. He'd apologised for his mother seeing another man while dating her dad which he hadn't needed to do. Neither of them had mentioned her being kissed by Todd. She wanted to explain what had happened but she also felt that she shouldn't have to.

Her phone pinged a reminder that an appointment was due to start in five minutes. She had the final fitting for Ashley's bridesmaids. Ella tidied up and got the dresses ready. She heard the voices before the door chimed. They were all excited and a little of their exuberance rubbed off on her as they each tried on their dresses and she could see first the relief and then the delight as each of the dresses fitted.

The chief bridesmaid kept hugging her. 'I can't believe what you've done.'

Even Ashley herself seemed impressed. 'You'd never know they'd been altered.'

'That's kind of the idea,' said Ella.

'Thanks,' said Ashley.

'You're welcome.' Ashley might have cajoled her into doing her wedding gown alterations for free but the bridesmaids' dresses had given her income a nice boost and she had welcomed the challenge. She'd also been proud of herself for standing up to her. All in all, dealing with Ashley had been a positive experience.

Ashley's phone rang. 'It's my Boo,' she said to the room and went outside to answer it.

Ella smiled at her turn of phrase. 'I'm pleased that you all look fabulous. It's going to be an amazing wedding. And she seems very happy with . . .' Ella struggled to remember the groom's name and then it came to her. 'Wes.'

'Ooh,' said a bridesmaid, looking surprised. 'You know about Wes?'

Ella didn't like to be rude and say that there was usually another person involved in a wedding. Sometimes it was another bride but more frequently a groom. 'Yes, she seems excited about the future.'

Another bridesmaid poked her head out of the cubicle where she was getting changed. 'So would I be if I was marrying a millionaire and shagging Wes.' The others all laughed.

Ella was beyond confused but she wasn't that interested. She continued to make sure the right dresses went in the right carriers. 'She's planning on dumping her husband after a year, cashing in on the divorce settlement and then sailing off into the sunset on his yacht with Wes,' explained bridesmaid one.

'Oh,' said Ella, quite shocked. She wondered if it was inappropriate to recommend Lucy.

Ashley waltzed back in. 'Boo sends his regards.' The others

muttered replies. 'I guess I'll have to stop calling him that after the wedding.'

'I think pet names are nice,' said Ella, taking the last dress from the last bridesmaid.

'It's more of a piss-take if I'm honest,' said Ashley.

'Oh.' Ella wasn't sure how she felt about that. She needed to stop saying 'Oh'.

The chief bridesmaid piped up. 'His surname is Radley and there was this old pop group called the Boo Radleys.'

Ella nodded her understanding.

'I, Ashley Price, take you, the millionaire Todd Radley,' said Ashley and they all chuckled. Apart from Ella who was frozen to the spot. Surely it couldn't be the same Todd Radley. Could it?

CHAPTER THIRTY-TWO

As predicted Terri had overstayed her welcome. Her stuff was everywhere and she was permanently stretched out on Lucy's sofa with the remote control glued to her hand. It was a cycle that repeated itself every time their lives collided. Lucy knew they were building to the crescendo which would be a big row and then her mother would leave again and she'd not hear from her for a few more years. That thought brought an uncomfortable sensation of both relief and loss.

'Any plans for today, Mum?' Lucy picked up Terri's cereal bowl and almost threw it in the dishwasher. She'd learnt that if she left it, in the hope that her mother tidied it away, it would still be there when she got in from work and the sight of it would notch up her irritation levels. 'Maybe you could look for a job or somewhere else to live?'

'I could always go back to the squat on the edge of the cliff and take my chances with Mother Nature if I'm causing you problems.'

'Don't take the hump but I do wonder that maybe if you'd stayed there you might have been rehoused. The place is clearly unsafe.' Her mother scowled at her. 'I did precursor that with *don't* take the hump.'

'If I'm that much of a nuisance.'

Lucy always found it hard not to rise to her mother's bait but even harder to mollify her with platitudes. 'Look. This is not ideal for either of us. I would like to have Eric over this weekend.'

'I'm not stopping you.' Terri folded her arms.

'Yes. You are.' There was no way she was going to scream the house down in ecstasy with her mother watching *Emmerdale* in the next room. Terri looked affronted so Lucy held up her palms to show she meant no harm. 'You don't mean to stop me, but this house isn't ideal for multiple occupancy.'

'You have two bedrooms. It should be fine. Just because you call one of them your home office doesn't stop it being a bedroom. You and your fancy airs. I don't know where you got those from. Probably the stuck-up Briggs family. Although they're not so fancy now their marriage has gone down the shitter.'

Lucy ignored the jibe at Ella's parents. Terri was trying to provoke a reaction. 'I don't get my airs from you now, do I?' Lucy pointed at the Cheerio stuck to her mother's T-shirt. 'Look. Let's stop bickering and tonight why don't we sit down together and work out a plan to get you back on your feet.'

'Or kick me out on the streets. That would save some of your precious time.' Terri stared her down.

Lucy was about to respond when her phone lit up. 'I have to take this.'

'More important than your own mother, is it?'

'It's probably a fraudster threatening to cut off my Wi-Fi. So yes. Absolutely,' said Lucy with a cheery grin and she answered the call.

Lucy's relief at escaping to the office was short-lived. Alabama Maxwell was still missing and Lucy was about to have a difficult meeting with her mother because Lucy felt they needed to continue the divorce proceedings. Mrs Maxwell looked pale and drawn and a shadow of her former self. Lucy's assistant was trying to force more biscuits on her when she entered the room.

'How are you and your son?' asked Lucy, taking a seat.

'Finley is fine, thank the Lord. But me. Where do I start? I can't eat, sleep or focus. I'm sorry but I'm here to say we can't continue with the divorce at the moment.'

Lucy feared this would be the case and she wondered what level of cajoling Mr Maxwell had been doing under the guise of supporting his wife. 'Is that because you've changed your mind and no longer want a divorce from your husband?'

'Of course not,' snapped Mrs Maxwell. 'It's because my daughter is still missing.' Her voice cracked and Lucy passed her the tissues.

'I'm sorry. You can of course put this all on hold. But if you do that Mr Maxwell still has a level of control over you and your children and I fear you will find it difficult to move on. I can't begin to imagine how awful it is not knowing where Alabama is and you're not going to like what I'm about to say but it could be a while before she gets in touch.' Mrs Maxwell closed her eyes, swallowed and looked sadly at Lucy. 'I'm sorry. We have no way of knowing how long it will be before she returns.' There, she'd said it. She knew the police would have told her that teenagers go missing all the time. It appeared things had gone quiet on that front since they'd found her diary where she had detailed her plans to run away. If there was no reason to suspect she was in danger she just became a statistic. There were simply too many kids who ran away from home and didn't get back in touch. It was a very sad fact.

Lucy and her client talked through the pros and cons and Mrs Maxwell left agreeing to consider what she'd been told and pledging to contact Lucy when she felt ready. Lucy didn't expect to hear from her again.

A discussion with a new client about her husband's stuffed animal fetish as the key reason she was wanting to start divorce proceedings had lifted her day but not as much as a sexy text from Eric. They had been messaging on and off since the wedding and she was desperate to rip his clothes off. She had one big hurdle to overcome first. She copied the links for the local housing office and three cleaning jobs and sent them to her mother in the hope it would pave the way for their later discussions.

Lucy was replying to a particularly dirty text from Eric as she walked to her car when she was aware of footsteps behind her. Like all women she was instantly on red alert. She pulled her car keys from her pocket and pushed her door key between her knuckles ready to lash out if she needed to defend herself. Up ahead she could see a couple. They were within shouting distance. That was good. The footsteps behind her quickened. Anger simmered in her stomach. She'd had enough of this. Of being fearful and scared. Something snapped. She spun around. The person was hooded, as she expected them to be.

'What the hell are you doing?' she said in almost a shout. The hooded figure halted. 'I know you're following me.' She held up her phone. 'I'm recording you, in fact we're live on Instagram.' Shit why did that keep happening? 'So the police will have lots of evidence.'

The figure seemed to droop a little at the shoulders. They pulled their hands from their pockets and Lucy flinched. But a quick scan showed her they weren't brandishing a weapon. They reached up and pulled off their hood. The face revealed underneath was not the one she was expecting but it was one she recognised.

'What the hell?' She stopped recording and stared her stalker in the face. 'Finley Maxwell, why are you following me?'

'Everyone calls me Fin. It's only Mum who uses my full name.'

Lucy shook her head. She had a thing about shortening names but for now she had to let that slide. 'Right, Fin. Why are you stalking me?'

He looked up. 'I'm not. I just . . .' His head dropped again. To think she'd been scared of him. He was no more of a menace to anyone than Auntie Rita was after one too many cocktails – in fact he was probably less of a threat.

'Do you want to go somewhere and talk? Coffee shop?' He shrugged a shoulder. 'I'm taking that as a yes,' she said. 'Come on.' Lucy was kicking herself that she'd got it so wrong about who her stalker was but then walking next to him it was easy to see how she'd made the mistake. He was tall and his clothes hung baggy disguising his slender frame but now he'd been revealed it was easy to see he was most definitely a child. He was silent on the walk to the café and only spoke to ask for a milkshake.

Lucy sipped her coffee and watched Fin down his milkshake. 'What's going on, Fin?'

He ran a finger around the inside of his glass. 'I wanted to talk to you but every time I was about to, I bottled it. You're not going to give the video to the police, are you?'

'No. Now I know it's you and not some psychopath planning on murdering me we can forget it.'

'Sorry . . . thanks. But it wasn't stalking. I was just following you.'

'That's what stalking is.' He opened his mouth to protest further but Lucy carried on. 'Anyway, what did you want to talk to me about?'

He sucked out the milkshake that was stuck in the straw. 'Can I have another one of those?'

'No. Come on, out with it.'

He looked a bit startled, but she was fed up with pussy-footing around him. He'd scared her half to death, had her afraid of her own shadow, inadvertently had her dive into her own hedge and complain about his father who it would appear apart from the getting in her car incident was entirely innocent on the stalking front. She made a mental note to put that straight with her boss and Mr Maxwell's solicitor.

Fin looked up. 'It's about Alabama.'

'You know where she is?' Hope flickered in her for a moment. He shook his head. 'No. We had a row. That's why she's run away.'

'You don't know that. It could be a number of reasons. Don't blame yourself.' She watched him for a moment. 'But you were

280

stalking . . .' He narrowed his eyes at her so she corrected herself. '*Following* me way before Alabama went missing. What else did you want to talk about.' Fin shifted uneasily in his seat. She sipped her coffee and waited.

'It's about Alabama's injuries. The bruising and stuff.'

'Did you see how they happened?' She sensed she had a witness to the crime. He nodded. 'Do you want to tell me what you saw?' Another solemn nod.

Fin's Adam's apple bobbed. 'Dad was in the garage working on his car and he and Mum were shouting about all the time he spends on it.' He took a long unsteady breath. 'Alabama's bedroom is above the garage. We were in there listening to them and Alabama flipped out. She started rocking backwards and forwards saying "stop" over and over. Then she properly lost it. She whacked the wall and kept on banging herself against it. Again and again.' He hunched up his shoulders as if feeling every blow. He looked at Lucy with tears in his eyes. 'I tried to stop her. I really tried, but she whacked me into the wall and then stormed out and locked herself in the bathroom. I could still hear her banging about in there too.'

'Does your mother know about this?'

He shook his head. 'I don't think Mum even realised. She and Dad were still arguing. Then Mum was crying and she went round to a friend's house. When she came back and saw Alabama's injuries it all went crazy.'

'Why didn't you say something then?'

'Alabama made me promise not to. She said they'd lock her up. Said they'd make out she was a headcase and they'd put her in a mental institution and I'd never see her again. Is that what will happen to her when they find her?' Fin started to sob. He roughly wiped at the tears with the sleeve of his hoodie.

'I'll make sure she gets help, Fin. I promise. But first we have to get her home.'

***

281

Twenty minutes after Ashley and her bridesmaids had left, Ella was still dumbfounded. Ashley was marrying Todd. Her ex Todd. The Todd who had kissed her at Brittany's wedding. And after a year of marriage Ashley planned to divorce him and take half his fortune. It was too much to process and her emotions were all over the place. Little spikes of horror that Ashley was so calculating. Stabs of hurt that Todd had not wanted to commit to her but within months of their break-up he had freely pledged to spend the rest of his life with Ashley. It was all sprinkled with drops of justice that karma was at work and Todd was going to get his comeuppance. But deepdown Ella knew that even Todd didn't deserve to be treated like this. Nobody did.

She needed to clear her mind. Ella grabbed her keys and headed down to the beach. A walk on the sand always calmed her senses. Maybe it was the salt air, the open space or the rhythmic sound of the waves breaking on the shore – she wasn't sure but a walk on the sand always helped her get her thoughts straightened out and to gain some perspective. The sun was high in the sky and a few dog walkers were about. Ella kicked off her sandals and carried them in her hand while she breathed in the fresh air and the smell of the sea.

She was facing a dilemma. She now had information that, if she were to share it, would impact other people's lives. Did Todd have a right to know what his bride-to-be was plotting and that she was already two-timing him with someone else? Or was that in some strange way betraying client confidentiality? She wasn't a doctor or a priest and Ashley hadn't confessed to her. She had merely slipped up. Todd was her ex, he no longer had anything to do with Ella. But she still cared about him despite everything. She didn't want him back but she wasn't sure she could stand by, do nothing and let him enter into a relationship with someone who was only in it for the money.

Todd hadn't mentioned he was in a relationship when they'd kissed at the wedding. If she'd thought for a moment he was seeing someone else there was no way she would have let it happen. Why had she let him kiss her in the first place? She was cross with herself for being weak. Maybe scheming Ashley and fickle Todd were made for each other? Perhaps she shouldn't get involved; simply forget what she had overheard and move on with her life. A seagull keened overhead breaking her concentration – she had a decision to make.

CHAPTER THIRTY-THREE

Business was starting to trickle in now that Ella had set up a formal arrangement with the owner of the city centre shop as well as receiving a few other enquiries from the flyers she had given out to local wedding venues and her adverts in the *Norwich Evening News*. The weather was also heating up. She loved the summer but she much preferred it on her terms – ideally lying on the beach. When she had work to do the heat was an inconvenience. Ella opened the window to its fullest but as she'd gone for ones that matched the house only the top half opened so the waft of air that came through was unremarkable and didn't manage to make its way around the partition.

She opened up the door to the business to let in some air from outside, but she couldn't see a way to keep it open. She abandoned that idea and tried propping open the hallway door, but it was a fire door and the only thing that would keep it open was to wedge a kitchen chair in the doorway. After working this out she realised it didn't provide much in the way of respite from the heat as even with the back door open there was no through draught. Plus it didn't look very professional. She had just returned the chair to the kitchen when her first customer of the day arrived.

'Hello again,' said the woman in her thirties. 'I'm Sasha.'

Ella recognised her but now she had a name to go with the face. This was the bride who Ella had met at Wanda's shop, but after Ella had assessed the alterations she then hadn't purchased the package deal. 'Hi Sasha, come in. Would you like a glass of fizz? I've got Prosecco or elderflower.'

'Elderflower please.' Sasha scrunched up her shoulders. 'This is lovely,' she said, stepping inside and looking around. 'I'm sorry if I got you into any trouble at the shop but I really wanted you to finish off my dress.'

Ella smiled. 'It's absolutely fine. It was always your prerogative. If you want to go into the fitting room and get changed into your gown I'll bring through your drink.'

Sasha was lovely and chatty and was marrying her dentist, Cathy. Sasha got a bit teary retelling her romance to Ella. It was a great story of how they'd met and fallen in love over root-canal work. It reminded Ella of one of the many reasons she adored her job. It was about connecting with people and being in some way associated with their happily ever after stories. The alterations were simple and with four months until the wedding there was plenty of time for follow-up fittings. Ella felt all efficient as she booked Sasha into her new diary and hung up her dress on the rail. She allowed herself a little moment – this was her business. She'd set it up and not only was she starting to make money she was enjoying every minute of it.

Ella focused on finishing off a dress and could feel sweat trickle down her back. That was it, she'd had enough of being hot and sweaty. She needed to get the front door fixed open and she was sure she knew a man who could help.

She decided to give Kit a call. His voice sounded tentative and quite formal when he answered. 'Hi Ella, how can I help?'

Was she imaging it or was he being aloof? 'Hi Kit, I was wondering if there's anything I can have fitted to the business front door to secure it open to get a breeze into my workroom. I'm melting here.' She tried to sound chatty and friendly.

'I can have one of the guys fit a door stay to keep the door open in a rigid position. Would that be acceptable?'

She wasn't imagining it, he was definitely off with her. 'That sounds great. But if there was any chance of you popping over to do it that would be good because I bought a little something for Isaac and as I haven't seen you guys in a while, I've not had a chance to pass it on.' She found she was biting her lip as she waited for him to reply.

'I'll need to check if we have the right sort of door fitting which we probably don't, in which case I'll need to order one in.'

Not the keen response she'd been hoping for. 'Of course. Well, if you could let me know, that'd be great. Thanks.'

'I'll be in touch.'

'What about the gift for Isaac?' She was clutching at straws now.

'Hang on to it or you could always post it. Bye, Ella.' The line went dead and Ella's shoulders slumped forward. She felt like she'd lost something and yet her and Kit's relationship had been fledgling at best.

She snorted out a breath. This wasn't fair. She understood Kit's reasons for ending things but there was no need to be unfriendly. She'd not done anything wrong and Kit hadn't even given her a chance to explain about Todd and the kiss at the wedding. She flicked open her laptop and searched for Kit's details. If Kit O'Leary wouldn't come to her then she would go to him. His business was registered to an address in Horning. She jotted it down and decided to go over before she lost her nerve. She found the Lego set she'd ordered for Isaac, checked her hair, added an extra squirt of perfume and a sweep of lipstick and she left.

The sat nav took Ella down into Horning village where the streets narrowed and the Broads were visible between the quaint houses. The sat nav informed her that she'd reached her destination, she pulled over and gawped at the house. It was an impressively large black wood-clad building with a thatched roof and a wide driveway. She wondered if this was the right place. There was no sign of an O'Leary's van. She got out of the car and stared up the street in the hope of spotting a van that would lead her to the right property.

'Ella!' someone shouted.

She turned around to see Isaac racing towards her. Jane was walking along behind and held up her hand in acknowledgement. 'Hi Isaac,' she said.

'I got a star award at school today,' he announced proudly.

'Wow. What did you do to get that?'

Isaac screwed up his features. 'Don't know but I got a certi-fer-cat.' He grinned at her.

'That's brilliant. Well done.'

'Hello, Ella,' said Jane, finally catching up. She greeted Ella with a kiss on the cheek. 'Are you here to see Kit, because he's gone to meet a supplier.' She glanced at the driveway. 'And he's not back yet.'

Her disappointment probably showed on her face but Ella quickly recovered. 'That's all right. It was Isaac I came to see.' Isaac pulled back his shoulders.

'Come inside and let's get some cold drinks,' said Jane. 'It's too hot out here for me.'

'Nanny says I can have pink lemonade because of my certi . . . fer . . .'

'Certificate,' prompted Jane.

'Would you like some pink lemonade too, Ella?' asked Isaac. 'It's okay that you don't have a . . .' He looked at his grandmother.

'Certificate,' Jane repeated good-naturedly and it made Ella smile.

Ella popped open the passenger door, took out her bag and followed them into the beautiful old building. Although once inside Ella had a bit of a surprise. It was light, bright and very modern.

They exchanged pleasantries while Jane prepared a tray of drinks and they took them outside. 'It's usually bearable out here thanks to the overhang,' explained Jane, putting the tray down.

What Jane described as an overhang, Ella could see was in fact the underneath of a balcony for the first-floor rooms. As soon as she stepped outside the view commanded Ella's full attention. The house was right on the River Bure. There was a wide garden which sloped down to the water where to one side there was a large wooden structure in the same black wood cladding as the house which Ella assumed was a boat house. She'd never seen a back garden like it.

'Have a seat,' suggested Jane, who was already sitting down. Ella realised she was staring.

'I'm sorry, that view is something else.'

'It is special,' said Jane. 'Although I think we tend to take it for granted after all these years.' Jane faced Ella. 'And how's your dad?'

'He's good.' She wasn't sure if she should say that. Did Jane want to hear that her ex was doing fine without her? Maybe this was an opportunity to try to put things straight. 'Actually, I get the feeling he's a bit adrift. You know?'

Jane sipped her lemonade slowly. 'Yes, I do.' They both nodded. She was dying to know if Jane was still dating the plumber, but she could hardly ask her.

Isaac held his glass carefully with two hands, took a swig of the lemonade and then smacked his lips together. 'Try it, Ella,' he said.

She did as instructed. It tasted good. 'That's lovely.' Ella pulled the box from her bag. 'Here you go, Isaac. I saw this and I thought of you.' She handed him the Lego set.

'Wow! A garbage truck!' He was clearly pleased.

'Is it?' Ella peered at the box. 'I thought it was a dumper truck.' Although now she noticed it came with a green bin. 'Sorry.'

'Don't apologise,' said Jane. 'It's great. That's one of the few things with four wheels that he doesn't have. Kit has bought him all the construction vehicles.' Of course he had, Ella could have kicked herself for not having thought this through although her error had turned out to be a good thing.

'I thought maybe you could show me how to build it sometime,' said Ella. Although as soon as she said it, she realised the whole point of her Lego mission was irrelevant now she and Kit were no longer in any sort of relationship. But was it? Regardless of Kit she had still wanted to make amends with Isaac after the day at the beach. Although seeing him engaging with her now it seemed kids didn't hold grudges.

Isaac was already tipping out the bags of bricks onto the small table.

The sound of a door slamming echoed through the house. 'Some idiot has parked right across the drive. What possesses someone to . . .' Kit strode onto the terrace and at the sight of Ella halted. 'It's you.' He raked a hand through his hair.

'Sorry, I'll move it,' said Ella, getting to her feet.

'Please sit down, he's making a fuss,' said Jane, giving Kit a look. 'Help yourself to a drink,' she added to Kit, who walked back inside the house without replying.

The next few minutes felt a little awkward. Jane had gone quiet. Thank goodness for Isaac who was concentrating hard on the pictures in the Lego instruction booklet and telling her which piece she needed to find next. Kit reappeared swigging from a bottle of beer. He took a seat opposite Ella but didn't make eye contact with her.

'What do we have here?' he asked Isaac.

'It's the recycling truck,' said Isaac. 'Ella got it for me.' He beamed at her and it made her heart swell. She hoped she was finally winning him over. She feared Kit wouldn't be as easy, he was still being all brooding with her. It had been a while since she'd seen him and she was missing their chats. She didn't like that he was offhand with her. Ella realised she was staring at Kit. He looked up and she felt her skin flush.

'Would have been a bin lorry in my day,' said Jane.

'Ahh, the good old days,' said Kit, leaning back in his chair.

'Orange two by four,' said Isaac, bringing Ella back to the Lego set. Ella focused on Isaac but she remained aware of the uncomfortable atmosphere. When she finished her lemonade it felt like the right time to leave.

'I should make a move,' said Ella.

'Nooooo, stay for tea,' said Isaac.

'Sorry, mate. Ella's a very busy person so she can't stay,' said Kit. At least that told her in no uncertain terms how Kit was feeling.

'Thanks for the lemonade,' she said to Jane. 'And I'll tell Dad you asked after him.' Both Ella and Kit paused to wait for Jane's response, but Isaac dropped a Lego piece.

'Disaster!' he shouted and dived under the table and Jane was already on her hands and knees helping him search.

'What's going on?' mouthed Kit so fast she didn't get it the first time and had to signal for him to repeat it. Ella pointed at the Lego by way of reply. Kit frowned. Ella shook her head.

'Well, bye then,' she said, and she made her way through the house.

She let out a sigh of relief as she shut their front door behind her. She was getting in her car when the door opened and Kit jogged out.

'I said I'd notify you about the part for your door.' Kit shoved his hands into his jeans pockets.

'Yeah. Okay. I know. Look, Kit. I don't like that we're all weird around each other so I'm just going to say that at the wedding—'

'You hooked up with some guy.' He shrugged a shoulder and gave a 'what do I care' pout.

'No, I didn't. That was Todd my ex and *he* kissed me. Not the other way around. I reminded him that he'd dumped me and that was it. We're not back together. And not likely to be because I've found out that he's engaged.' She'd been dying to tell someone.

Kit scrunched up his features and looked at Ella through his impossibly long eyelashes. 'Sorry, I've been a jerk.'

'Apology accepted and yes you have. But I guess I could have explained things sooner.'

'You don't have to explain yourself to anyone.'

'You're right, I don't, but I didn't like you thinking bad of me.' She had grown a lot in the last few months but there were parts of her that simply couldn't change and worrying about what people thought of her was one of them. 'Anyway. I best go because apparently I'm blocking someone's driveway.'

Kit smiled. 'Don't rush off. Let's go for a walk. Clear the air properly.'

It would have been churlish to flounce off. She shut her car door. 'Okay.'

It had been a while since she'd visited Horning but it hadn't changed. Pretty little higgledy-piggledy cottages and shops lined the way down to the Broad. They made it to The Ferry pub and Kit went inside to get them drinks while Ella found a bench outside and right by the water's edge. She watched the pleasure craft pootle past. It was a much slower pace of life on the water and merely witnessing it made her feel relaxed.

'Here you go,' said Kit, putting down her Diet Coke.

'Thanks. This is a beautiful place to live. Did you grow up here?'

'Norfolk born and bred. We moved to that house when I was eight.'

'It's a stunning spot.'

'Ella . . .' He reached across and traced a finger down her hand to the tip of her finger. The intimate gesture sent a zing of sensation

291

racing around her nervous system. 'I'm sorry we can't be more than friends.' She could see the sadness in his eyes and it somehow helped to soothe her own disappointment.

'Don't be. Let's forget about it.'

He leant back and she mourned the loss of his touch. 'Nice try with Mum, by the way. Did you speak to her about your dad?'

'Not really. Is she still seeing the plumber from King's Lynn?'

'She is but he's a right chancer. He came to pick her up in this bright red Porsche.' Kit was shaking his head.

'And you don't approve of men with expensive cars?'

'He was such a cliché. Obviously having a crisis. It was a soft top as well. And it wasn't just the car, he was overly gushy. Kept calling me son all the time.' Kit shuddered at the memory. 'He even tried to play fight with Isaac within a couple of minutes of meeting him. Scared the kid half to death.'

'Tell me if I'm wrong but I'm sensing you're not keen.' She couldn't hide her smile.

'Spot on. Even your dad was better than this guy.'

'Hey, my dad is a superstar.'

'I'm beginning to think the same. So what do we do?'

'I'm not sure,' said Ella. 'Your mum's still seeing the plumber. It feels sort of final.'

'Maybe we need to dig up some dirt on the guy. Try and put, her off him,' suggested Kit.

'I think we've been here before,' said Ella, glancing out over the water. Kit's eyes followed hers and they sighed in unison.

CHAPTER THIRTY-FOUR

Ella had gone over and over what, if anything, she should do about Ashley's revelation and she still wasn't entirely sure she was doing the right thing. But she was certain that if she didn't tell Todd it would play on her mind. Maybe she was being selfish by unburdening herself but at least if Todd had all the information then it was up to him what he did with it and whether or not he went through with his marriage. A surge of doubt filled her insides but she tried to ignore it. Otherwise she would keep going round and round the same old arguments and not get anywhere and it was already keeping her awake at night. She was in danger of becoming more nocturnal than Pirate.

She'd messaged Todd on the pretext that she'd found some of his stuff mixed up with hers. The truth of it was that she'd kept a T-shirt of his on purpose which she now realised was particularly unhealthy and she had taken a couple of books they had bought together making their ownership a little woolly but she'd brought them along too so it didn't look like she'd manufactured the meeting – which she totally had done. She could hardly have said in a message *I have major news about your impending nuptials,* so it had seemed liked the least confrontational option.

Although now she was here in the anonymous coffee shop, she knew that confrontation was exactly what was looming. She took a deep breath. She could do this. All she had to do was say the words – Ashley's bridesmaid says she's planning on dumping you after a year, cashing in on the divorce settlement and then sailing off on your yacht. *Oh, yeah that sounds terrific*, she thought.

The coffee shop door opened and in strode confident, suave Todd looking like he'd stepped from the pages of a magazine. Ella self-consciously tucked her hair behind her ear.

He leant over and kissed her cheek. 'Lovely to see you, Ella,' he said, holding eye contact a fraction longer than necessary and making something squirm in her gut. *Stop it*, she told herself. *He dumped you – focus on that.* They ordered coffees and she handed over the T-shirt and books, which triggered Todd to reminisce and Ella to unhelpfully remember how happy she had been that day in the bookshop, choosing books for their holiday. She shook the memory from her mind. She needed a Lucy pep talk. She heard Lucy's voice in her head: 'He's an arse gerbil' – she probably hadn't got the phrase exactly right but it was the sort of thing Lucy would say. It made her feel a little better.

Todd was staring at her. 'Ella, are you all right?'

'Yes. I'm fine. Great, actually. The business is doing well and, hmm, here's the thing, Todd. I had a bride in recently and I over-heard that she's planning on dumping her husband after a year, cashing in on the divorce settlement and then sailing off into the sunset. I've been going over and over what I should do.'

He nodded and sipped his coffee. There was a smirk on his lips. She could tell he thought she was pathetic to have asked him here because she couldn't make a decision on something he clearly thought was trivial. It definitely helped to strengthen her resolve. 'It's sweet of you to worry about this, Ella. That's so you.' He reached out to touch her hand and she pulled her fingers out of reach. He tilted his head. 'But if you want my advice, I think you should stay out of it. As a service provider it's not your place to get involved. I guess it's a bit like client confidentiality. What's said in the little wedding shop, stays in the little wedding shop.'

His use of the word 'little' and the intonation in the way he said it made it feel like he was trying to undermine her and her business. Her new business that she had set up all on her own and was immensely proud of. It riled her.

'Right. You think I should keep it to myself. Even if he's going to marry someone who is only after his money and is then going to divorce him and take half his fortune?'

'Not your problem. He should have got a robust prenuptial agreement.'

Ella's shoulders dropped. Of course. Todd wouldn't get caught out like that. He was always one step ahead. He was the one calling all the shots – he certainly had done in their relationship. Why would it be any different with Ashley? 'Is that what you've done. Made your bride-to-be sign a prenup?'

He viewed her suspiciously over his coffee cup. 'I'm sensing you've heard that I'm getting married.'

'Obviously. I don't think it's a secret although you didn't mention it when you kissed me at Brittany and Grant's wedding.'

'Ah, about that.' Todd looked uncomfortable.

'Forget it. I don't care about you getting married.' He pulled his head back, appearing genuinely surprised. 'But I do want to know if you have a prenuptial agreement in place.'

'What an odd thing to ask.' Todd almost snorted coffee out of his nose. 'Of course not.'

Ella twisted her lips. This was it. Her palms felt a little sweaty. 'Well, I think you should. Because the bride I was telling you about . . . it was Ashley Price and I assume the groom she's cheating on is you.'

***

295

It had taken two more meetings and four milkshakes for Lucy to persuade Fin he had to tell his parents that he had witnessed his sister self-harming. Lucy collated some information and support resources to share with the family but it struck her as a little pointless when the person with the condition was missing.

Fin insisted that Lucy needed to be there when he told his parents which made it tricky for her. She could hardly call Mrs Maxwell into the office. Instead she and Fin hatched a plan where she went over to the family home where Mr Maxwell was still living and where Fin had asked his mother to pick him up from. Lucy wasn't entirely sure the location was a good idea and she had concerns that it would be upsetting for Mrs Maxwell but it felt like the simple option if they were going to tell both parents at the same time. If there were any issues Lucy was there as the voice of reason – at least that was the plan.

Lucy and Mrs Maxwell got out of their cars simultaneously. She looked confused to see Lucy there, but Fin opened the door distracting them both. 'All right?' he said to Lucy who was first up the path.

'Yes. Are you?' she asked, and Fin shrugged his response.

'What's going on?' asked Mrs Maxwell.

'Fin has something he wants to tell us all together,' said Mr Maxwell from behind his son. 'I have no idea what.' He stared suspiciously at Lucy. She still wasn't completely comfortable around the man despite now knowing it had been Fin who had been following her.

'It won't take long,' said Lucy to Mrs Maxwell in an attempt to reassure her.

'You know what's going on?' She narrowed her eyes at Lucy.

'Come inside,' said Lucy.

They all went into the house and took seats in the living room. Nobody looked comfortable, least of all Fin. Lucy noted Mrs Maxwell scanning the room as if searching for any obvious changes since she'd left.

'What's this about, son?' asked Mr Maxwell.

'Is it Alabama?' Mrs Maxwell's voice cracked. 'Has she contacted you?' The look of anticipation on her face was heart-wrenching.

'No.' Fin shook his head. He looked directly at Lucy.

'Fin, just tell them exactly what you told me.' She nodded encouragingly at him.

He took a deep breath and repeated the story in one long monologue barely pausing for breath. His mother put a steadying hand on Fin's shoulder as silent tears rolled down her cheeks while her husband openly sobbed. Lucy was surprised but touched to see the two differing, and slightly unexpected, reactions.

'You can see that Fin was in a very difficult position,' said Lucy. 'Which was why he came to me.'

Mr Maxwell blew his nose. 'You've done the right thing, son.'

His wife reached out and touched his forearm. 'I'm sorry,' she said in a small voice.

'Not your fault,' he told her. 'I would have thought exactly the same.' They shared weak smiles.

Lucy suddenly felt like she was intruding. 'Here's some leaflets that may or may not be of use.' Lucy put them on the nearby coffee table.

'Thank you but what use are they if she's not here? What if she's harming herself now wherever she is?' Mrs Maxwell looked alarmed. 'She could be somewhere needing medical attention and . . .' She couldn't finish the sentence. This was the reality of the situation.

'When she comes home, you'll be prepared and ready to help her,' offered Lucy, getting to her feet. 'If there's anything I can do, you know where I am. I'll see myself out.' Lucy had just reached the front door when she was aware she was being followed. She turned to see Fin.

'You can quit stalking me now,' said Lucy.

'Following, not stalking. And thanks,' he said. 'You know, for making me 'fess up.'

'You did well. Alabama would be proud of you,' she said.

He smirked. 'Alabama is going to kill me. But I'm going to blame you.' He managed a smile.

'I'd do that too,' agreed Lucy and she left.

***

There had been a shift in the atmosphere between Ella and Kit. It was now more relaxed, playful even and Ella was pleased about how things had settled back into an easy friendship. She would have liked a lot more but she was happy to settle for friends.

Ella was sitting in a pub car park when her car door opened and she jumped.

'Wow, someone's on edge,' said Kit, sliding into the passenger seat. He kissed her lightly on the cheek and she felt the graze of his stubble which was oddly erotic. Before she had a chance to respond he pulled out his phone and began scrolling through photos. 'Isaac has completed the bin lorry and he wanted me to show you.'

Ella smiled at the photograph of a very proud-looking Isaac holding aloft the completed Lego model.

'Aww bless him,' she said. It was lovely to see his cheeky face beaming back at her from the picture.

'Right, are you ready for this?' He rubbed his hands together.

'No, I think this is a stupid idea and it's going to blow up in our faces.' Ella had been going over and over their plans and the more she thought about them the more she was convinced it was all a bad idea. 'My dad dumped your mum. Making them have a meal together isn't going to fix the fact that she chose someone else.' Ella pulled out her mobile phone. 'I'm going to call this off.'

'Hey, don't be hasty.' Kit twisted in the seat so he was facing her. 'She didn't exactly choose the plumber guy, he was simply the one she was left with when your dad called things off.'

'But my dad will always feel she was cheating on him. Is the plumber definitely off the scene now?' Ella gave him a questioning look.

'Yes. I found out the Porsche was rented and he got sacked from his last job for sleeping with customers. Mainly lonely housewives.'

'I'm having second thoughts. We messed things up before with our meddling.'

'Then isn't it up to us to at least try to put things right between them?'

Ella felt her shoulders slump. 'Possibly,' she conceded.

'Then we stick to the plan?' He looked at her through those eyelashes of his.

'Okay. But this is the very last time.'

'Deal,' said Kit, holding out his hand and they shook on it.

***

Lucy was tired when she walked through the door and was thinking that despite being a Thursday she was going to get a takeaway. But all thoughts of pizza were immediately extinguished by the smell that assaulted her nostrils. It was a distinctive sickly-sweet scent that she hadn't come across for a good many years. It was the smell of someone smoking weed. She was ready for an argument as she strode into the darkened living room and hit the light switch. Her mother was sitting cross-legged on the rug and opposite her was a man with long ginger dreadlocks and skin the colour of flour.

'Mother?'

Terri opened her eyes slowly. She blinked, looked up and at last seemed to realise that someone else had entered the room. 'Hey, Luce,' said Terri eventually. She pointed at the man opposite her who appeared to be muttering something to the tune of the Marks and Spencer's advert. 'This is TB, he's meditating.' She nodded solemnly and closed her eyes.

Lucy shook her head, she'd had enough. 'He needs to do it somewhere else because I want to chill out and watch TV.' Lucy took in the room. All her cushions and throws were on the floor and the coffee table was strewn with plates, crisp packets and crumbs. 'What the hell is this mess?'

Terri opened her eyes. 'We were hungry.'

Lucy opened the windows and tried to waft out the smell. 'You can sort it out right now.' Why did she feel like a grown-up reprimanding a child? And why did this always happen? 'And then . . . do you know what? You can leave.'

Terri stared at her. 'Come on, Luce, don't overreact.'

'I'm not.' She tried to stay calm and rational, but TB's humming was distracting. 'Excuse me, TB is it? Can you stop that?'

'Hey, hey, hey . . .' started TB. His voice was so upper-class Lucy did a double take. Was he putting it on? It appeared not. 'Let's keep it tranquil, people,' he said.

His words had the opposite effect on Lucy. 'Don't you tell me to keep it tranquil when you're sitting on my John Lewis rug, stoned out of your mind having trashed my home!'

'You're not being cool, Luce.' Her mother had a disappointed look on her face.

'I couldn't give a crap about how cool I am. If I'd wanted you to think I was cool I wouldn't have become a solicitor, I'd have smoked weed, got various body parts pierced and learnt to be a reiki master like Swampthing here.'

'He actually *is* a reiki master and an exceptionally good one. It's amazing what he can do with his hands,' said Terri, looking completely serious. 'And his name is TB.'

Lucy shook her head. 'His name isn't TB. Unless his name is tuberculosis in which case that was particularly unkind of his parents.' She turned to address the stranger. 'What is your *real* name? Wayne? Sebastian? Graham?' He looked like a Graham, she mused.

TB cleared his throat. 'Everyone calls me TB.' He nodded sagely.

Lucy bit her lip – she was losing her patience. TB seemed to sense it and held his hands up. 'But if labels are important to you.' He left an annoyingly long pause. 'My parents named be Tiberius.'

Terri snorted a laugh and Tiberius shot her a hurt look. 'That's a mouthful. I see why you go by TB.'

'I'm not ashamed of my name,' he said, uncrossing his long legs and straightening his back. 'It's simply that I shouldn't be burdened by a moniker bestowed on me at birth which never reflected my inner identity. And shortening names is a bonding ritual. It's about familiarity and acceptance.'

'It's lazy and annoying,' said Lucy, picking up her cushions and returning them to the sofa.

'I recently had a similar conversation about naming conventions.' He turned his attention to Terri. 'Names are a restrictive bond that binds us to the conventions of our parents, their traditions and conformity.' Terri nodded enthusiastically and Lucy tutted. Her mother was so bloody gullible. Tiberius continued. 'I was explaining to Al, you know Al, right?'

'I don't think I do. Where would I know them from?'

'Happisburgh.'

Terri shrugged. 'Nope. Not when I was there.'

'You'd like her, she has a remarkable aura. I enlightened her as to how we accept the labels society brings upon us without question and they become a burden. Weighing us down.' He splayed out his palms like he was worshipping her mother. Lucy didn't need this level of weird on a Thursday.

Lucy tugged at her Orla Keily throw Tiberius had his grubby cargopant-clad backside on and he toppled slightly. She folded it neatly and was about to put it down when something he'd said stabbed at her brain. 'Hang on,' said Lucy, waving the throw in front of Tiberius to get his full attention. 'Who's Al?'

'She's a free spirit like Terri.'

'Thanks, TB,' said Terri, looking touched.

'Describe her,' snapped Lucy, her brain joining the dots quicker than the trickle of information coming from Tiberius. She turned to her mother. 'Do you know this Al?'

Terri shook her head. 'Nope. I knew an Alan once.'

'Helpful,' said Lucy.

'You're welcome.' Her mother appeared pleased.

Lucy turned back to Tiberius who had recrossed his legs and restarted the Marks and Spencer's advert humming. 'Hey, Tiberius. Tell me about Al. What's Al short for?' Lucy held her breath.

Tiberius stopped humming. 'Al has deep-seated pain. But I was able to heal her with the power of universal energy.'

'Name!' snapped Lucy and Tiberius pulled his chin in to his chest.

He swallowed hard. 'Al is short for Alabama.'

***

The pub was lovelier than Ella remembered but then the last time they'd been there she'd been more focused on watching her father with another woman whom she now knew to be Jane. The pub was olde worlde but not in a kitsch way. It had all the historic features of a building its great age: heavy dark beams, open fireplaces and low ceilings and a wealth of charm. They were shown to their table and ordered drinks. A table for two, positioned next to the table where David and Jane had been that night – a reserved marker they had arranged was in place.

Kit stretched out and she felt his leg brush against hers. There was a squirming sensation in Ella's stomach. She liked that they were friends but unfortunately her body hadn't received the message that that was all they were ever going to be.

'You okay?' asked Kit, eyeing her across the small table.

'Yeah, fine.'

'I know that face. And I know you're not fine.' The squirming intensified.

'What if there's a big scene?' she asked.

'Neither of our parents are like that. Try to relax and pick a starter.'

'Sure.' That was a good suggestion, studying the menu would give her something else to focus on other than the impending disaster of setting up their parents and the close proximity of Kit O'Leary. Their plan was that they would order starters so their parents would feel obliged to order some food. Kit and Ella would get the conversation going and then disappear after their starters, leaving their parents to spend the rest of the evening together and hopefully fix their relationship.

Ella was trying to decide between the fishcake and the crab when Kit tipped his menu against hers. 'Look out, here we go.'

Ella peeped over the top of her menu. A grey-haired man had walked in and went to stand at the bar. 'What?' asked Ella, her voice hushed.

'He's at the bar?' Kit tipped his head. Ella looked again. The man greeted a woman with long black hair by kissing her deeply. 'What the hell?' Kit was openly staring at the couple.

'That's not my dad,' said Ella.

Relief danced across his features. 'Sorry, I've only met him once.'

Ella checked the clock. 'They're late. I definitely said eight.'

'Me too. But let's not chase them. Not yet anyway.'

Ella agreed and returned to her menu. A waitress appeared and they politely asked her to come back.

Ella decided on the crab salad but continued to look at the menu because it was easier than looking at Kit. She could feel his eyes on her without even checking. This was awkward. She hoped her dad and Jane arrived soon.

Kit closed his menu and put it to one side. He stretched up to peer over the top of hers. 'How've you been, Ella?'

'Umm. Fine. Actually good. I've been good.' She held onto the menu like a comfort blanket. 'And you. Are you well? I mean you look well. Are you?' What was she gabbling on about?

Kit nodded. 'Fine.'

They both nodded at each other. A thought struck her. 'How is Isaac?'

'He's great. Thanks for asking.' A smile twitched at Kit's lips and she found she was staring at him. When the eye contact became too much she disappeared behind the menu again.

When their parents were fifteen minutes late Ella started to get concerned. 'Dad's never late. Do you think I should text him?'

'I'm starting to wonder if they rumbled us because if Mum was delayed she'd call or message.'

'Okay. Let's text them.' They both fired off messages and waited.

The pub was getting busy and chatter filled the air – all except for their little bubble. That was filled with silence and hesitant glances. Ella wanted to tell Kit that she'd missed him. That she'd thought about him non-stop but how would that help? It certainly wouldn't change anything. He'd made his decision and she respected that.

Ella stared at her phone willing her dad to reply. At least if he called off, she could escape and free them both.

'It's lovely to see you again, Ella,' said Kit at last.

She couldn't help the smile that escaped. 'Same.'

Something passed between them. Was it 'what might have been' perhaps? They had come so close to something very special indeed. Ella sighed and tried to stop it but Kit had noticed. 'Look, it's not you. It never was you. It's because of Isaac and—'

Ella waved her fingers to stop him. 'You don't need to explain again. I get it. I really do.' They shared wan smiles. Kit reached across the table and clasped her fingers in his. The connection sent a shiver through her. 'Don't,' she said softly and she pulled her fingers from his grasp. In the lull Ella's mobile rang and she pounced on it, but it wasn't her dad who was calling.

CHAPTER THIRTY-FIVE

The call from Lucy was brief, she was trying to get hold of Kit because she needed help breaking into a property. Had she heard that right? Ella had many questions whizzing around her head as she'd grabbed up her things. Kit had thrust some money on the waitress for their drinks as she'd passed and they had dashed through the pub and outside.

Ella's phone pinged with a message. Still not her dad. It was Lucy sending directions of where she and Kit were to meet her. They were striding across the car park together when she was aware that Kit had halted abruptly. Ella spun on her heel.

'Kit, come on. Lucy said someone's life was in danger.'

Kit didn't reply he just pointed to a nearby parked car. Ella glanced over keen to get moving again but what she saw made her freeze too.

In the front seats of the car were David and Jane and they were kissing each other. Not a 'hello' type air kiss and not even a good-bye kiss. This was an 'I want to rip your clothes off and have you right now' kiss. As that thought flitted into Ella's brain Jane started pulling off her father's tie and Ella panicked.

'Hello!' she shouted in a plea to make them stop the spectacle that was assaulting her eyeballs.

There was a brief delay before they sprang apart and peered out of the windscreen. Ella felt suddenly awkward, so she waved which didn't change the situation. A confused-looking David slowly held up his hand in acknowledgement and the gesture made Kit wave back. Jane adjusted her blouse and joined in with the waving.

'We have to go,' said Ella to Kit. 'Sorry, we can't stay,' she shouted in an over-exaggerated manner at her dad. 'Enjoy your . . . um . . . meal.' She tugged on Kit's arm to get him moving and they both dashed for the O'Leary van. 'We can come back for my car,' said Ella, half to herself.

'I guess we got something right then,' said Kit, doing up his seat-belt and tilting his head at their parents.

'Looks that way. I wish we'd not had to witness that . . .' Ella pointed past him to where David and Jane were still sorting out their clothing.

'We should never speak of this again,' said Kit, starting the engine.

'Agreed,' said Ella, and she turned her mind to the directions Lucy had sent her.

***

Lucy wasn't entirely sure why she didn't say anything when both Terri and Tiberius jumped in her car. She'd been focused on getting to Happisburgh as quickly as possible. Within a couple of minutes in the small space it became apparent that it had been quite a while since Tiberius had had a good wash. Lucy opened a back window.

'Actually it's a bit draughty. Could you shut the window?' asked Tiberius, from the back seat, sounding posher than ever.

'I like it breezy,' called back Lucy, pulling up at a junction and taking a moment to think through her journey.

'It is cold, Luce,' said Terri.

Lucy glanced across at her mother who was wearing a vest top.

306

'You should have put something else on. Like a jumper. And it's July so it's not exactly cold.'

Lucy turned left.

'It's the wind chill factor,' said Tiberius.

'He's right,' said her mother, giving a shudder.

'You can run around when we get there,' said Lucy dismissively. 'Anyway, Tiberius, when did you last see Alabama?'

Lucy had rung Ella, grabbed her keys and jumped in the car. Now she was pondering the fact that perhaps she was going on a wild-goose chase and taking a lot of people with her. There was no answer from the back. Lucy checked in the rear-view mirror. Tiberius had his eyes closed. 'Tiberius!' she shouted.

He jolted and opened his eyes. 'I was taking a moment to stabilise my thoughts.' Lucy assumed that was a rough translation of 'I'm still stoned.'

'When did you last see Alabama at the squat?'

'The day we were all moved out by the council. Which was three days ago . . . I think.'

Lucy slammed on the brakes and everyone shot forward in their seats. 'What?'

'Three days I think if today is Wednesday.'

'It's Thursday.'

'Ah. Possibly four days then.'

Lucy gripped the steering wheel. This changed everything. 'What did you say about being evicted?'

'We were all evicted by the council,' he said, slowly as if addressing someone of limited intelligence. 'Rounded up like animals.'

'Then it's pointless dashing over to the squat if we know for a fact that nobody is in there.' Lucy killed the engine and ran her fingers through her hair. She'd been certain she'd find Alabama at the squat.

'If we're not going to Happisburgh, could we grab something to eat because I've got the munchies,' said Terri.

'Good call,' said a voice from the back of the car. 'Vegan obviously.'

'Hang on,' said Lucy, twisting in her seat. 'You're telling me that you, Alabama and whoever else was still living in the squat were all kicked out together. Where did Alabama go?' Tiberius closed his eyes again and Lucy's irritation level shot up a notch. 'Think quicker for heaven's sake.'

He flinched and opened his eyes. 'Most people like Terri had already moved out. Me, Jurassic, Sticky and Al were making a bit of a stand, so we stayed until the last. But they'd arranged for us to have a few nights at the hostel in Norwich which was nice.'

'Oh, that is nice,' said Terri, turning to join in the conversation.

Lucy held up her palm to stop her mother taking the conversation off somewhere unhelpful. 'So the four of you went to the hostel. Is Alabama still there then?' Hope sprang in her chest. All was not lost.

Tiberius pouted. 'Actually. I'm not sure.'

'What? Is she there or not?'

'No. Al wasn't there. I don't think she was anyway. You see we had to smoke our stash before the council arrived which means my memory of that day's a bit hazy.'

'Was or wasn't she at the hostel?' barked Lucy.

'I've not seen her there. I mean I remember hugging her at the bungalow and saying goodbye in the kitchen. And then the council officials turned up and explained about the hostel. I got my stuff together. Sticky couldn't roll up his sleeping bag because he forgot he'd put cardboard in it. That was funny.' Tiberius snorted a laugh and Terri giggled along.

'Oh my word. You need to stop smoking weed,' said Lucy, restarting the car.

'We could get a drive through. The veggie dippers at McDonald's are vegan friendly right, TB?' called Terri into the back of the car.

'We're not going to sodding McDonald's,' said Lucy and she put her foot down.

Lucy got out of the car and was shocked to see that the squat was in an even more precarious position than when she'd collected her mother. The bungalow now had a full corner jutting out over the cliff edge. It was surrounded by metal fencing liberally adorned with 'Keep Out' and 'Danger cliff erosion' signs. Lucy walked around to see if there was anywhere she could get a better look at the bungalow. From what she could see the premises had been well and truly boarded up. Sheets of chipboard covered all windows and doors. It was looking less and less likely that there was anyone inside.

A keen wind was whipping up over the hilltop, chilling Lucy. She wrapped her suit jacket tighter around her. She hoped Ella and Kit wouldn't be long.

***

Kit pulled up next to Lucy's car and as soon as he killed the engine Ella was out of the van. Lucy ran over. 'Thanks for coming. But I'm sorry, I think it's been a waste of time.'

'Why what's going on?' Ella glanced at Terri waving from the front seat of Lucy's car.

While Lucy filled her in, Kit got some tools from the van. 'What did the council say?' asked Kit, handing Lucy a torch.

'Answerphone said to call in office hours,' said Lucy flatly.

Kit pulled a face. 'What's the plan?'

'I think if we can get through the fencing then we can shout and see if we get a reply. If there's no response then we chain it back up and go home.'

Kit nodded. Ella held her hand up. 'Hang on. This is breaking and entering right?'

Lucy wobbled her head. 'Technically I think it's criminal damage and trespass because it's only the garden we'd be breaking into. It's probably more of an issue that we're putting ourselves in danger.' As if to remind them the sound of waves crashing on the rocks below rose up to steal her words.

Kit puffed out a breath. 'You okay?' asked Ella. He nodded and using some large wrench-like tool he twisted one of the links on the chain holding the fencing together and slipped the chain free of the padlock.

'We're in,' said Lucy, going first and squeezing through the metal railings. Ella followed her through.

'Be careful,' said Kit.

'You're not coming?' Ella was surprised and suddenly a little more wary. There was something about Kit's presence she found reassuring especially in a situation like this.

He bit his lip. 'I've not been on a site since . . .' He tailed off.

She realised he was referring to his sister's death. 'Oh, I see.' Ella looked back at the dilapidated bungalow. All boarded up and abandoned. 'It's not a building site though.' She hoped she didn't sound insensitive, but she was struggling to see the connection.

'It was a demolition site where the accident happened.' Kit rubbed his palm over his face.

Ella's heart squeezed at what Kit was going through. 'I'm sorry. You can wait here if it feels like it's too much or is now the time to see if you're ready to face things? I'm here if you want to try.' She held out a hand.

'You're right. I'm being daft.'

'You're not being daft. I can't begin to understand what you've been through. Something like this affects people in different ways. But you and Isaac have come so far perhaps this is the next step for you.'

Kit looked quite alarmed. 'It feels like it's all happening again.'

'But that was then. This is now—'

An erratic torch beam drew their attention. 'Maybe one of you could join me so at least you can give a description to the coast-guard of exactly where I fell into the sea,' said Lucy, waving the torch in their direction.

'Sorry,' said Ella. She smiled at Kit, withdrew her outstretched hand and went to help her friend.

310

The front of the bungalow was furthest from the edge. They stood by the piece of wood covering the front door and took it in turns to holler Alabama's name. Lucy held up her hand, Ella stopped shouting and they both listened. There was nothing but the sound of the wind whipping around the prone building and the echo of the waves a few metres below. Ella studied Lucy's face dimly lit by the torchlight. She looked worried and forlorn. Lucy turned as if sensing her scrutiny. 'She's not here, is she?'

Ella shook her head. 'You tried, Lucy. At least you tried.'

Lucy nodded but looked unconvinced. 'One last shout?'

'Sure.'

'Alabama!' they chorused. They waited. There was no response.

Lucy shone the torch onto the broken path and they both turned to walk back to the vehicles. That was when they heard it. A faint tapping sound.

Lucy gripped Ella's arm. 'Did you—'

'I heard it too,' she whispered. 'Kit!' she called. 'We need to get these boards down now.'

CHAPTER THIRTY-SIX

While Kit rummaged in the van for something they could use to remove the wooden sheets covering the door and windows Lucy marched over to her own car. Terri and Tiberius were asleep inside. 'Bloody hell.' She opened the passenger door and basked in her mother's surprise as the cool air invaded the car.

'Crikey, Luce. You gave me a start.' Terri recoiled from the wind.

'I rang the hostel,' said Tiberius, waving the latest in mobile phones.

'And?' Lucy was now down to a few tattered shreds of patience where these two were concerned.

'They couldn't tell me anything due to confidentiality.' Lucy clenched her jaw. 'But I spoke to Jurassic and he's certain Al didn't check in. She's not there,' he said.

Lucy wasn't sure if that was good news or bad. She would have liked to have been told that Alabama was tucked up safe at the hostel but if she wasn't there then at least this escapade wasn't complete lunacy. 'Then we have to check inside. And guess who is going to show us around?' Lucy opened the rear door. 'Out,' she instructed.

'Come on, Luce. It's a bit chilly,' said Terri.

'And there is likely a young girl in there who is also chilly and . . .' She didn't like the images that popped into her head. 'Maybe even worse. We need to get her out and you two know the layout so . . .' She pointed a thumb over her shoulder.

'Could we sketch the layout for you?' suggested Tiberius, his crossed arms hugging his skinny frame.

'No time for that.' Lucy paused and Terri and Tiberius stared at her. She could feel her temper rising. 'For crying out loud. There's a young girl in there who needs your help, now get your arses out of my car.'

'Of course, sorry,' said Tiberius and he was first out closely followed by a sullen-looking Terri.

'Are you certain?' asked Terri, peering at the boarded-up building.

She wasn't certain at all, but she wouldn't rest until she'd investigated inside. 'Ella and I heard something.'

'Did you hear her shout or was it the wind?' asked Terri, who was visibly shivering now she was out of the car.

'There was a tapping noise,' said Lucy, shutting the car doors and leading the way.

'What like the sound of bits of house falling down a cliff?' asked Terri.

'No, like someone trying to get our attention.' Although she had to admit her mother's answer was also plausible, Lucy couldn't walk away now. She had to know for sure that Alabama wasn't in there. For her own sanity she had to be certain she had thoroughly checked.

'The council would have gone over the whole place to make sure no one was left inside,' said Terri. 'I know you want to be the hero here but you're wasting your time.'

'Fine. But it's mine to waste. You can wait in the car if you like.' Lucy jutted out her chin and dangled her car keys in front of Terri.

Terri seemed to consider her options for a moment before a

gust of wind had her snatch the keys. 'Be careful, Luce,' she said and she plodded back to the car taking any remaining shred of respect Lucy had for her mother with her. Tiberius turned to follow.

'Uh huh. Not you, Tiberius. I need you.' Lucy beckoned him on with a bent finger and he reluctantly went with her.

***

Kit had put on the van headlights but they didn't reach all the way to the bungalow. He was fitting something around his waist and Ella moved closer to see. Did he happen to have some climbing gear in that van? That would have been very handy. When he turned she could see it was a toolbelt. The combination of crisp white shirt, tan toolbelt and denim was quite something. Like those charity calendars she saw at Christmas although he had too many clothes on for one of those.

Kit saw her looking as he came over. 'It'll be dark inside and it makes it easier if I've got my tools on me,' he explained. Ella realised she was still staring at the toolbelt.

She pulled her eyes up to his. 'That's a good idea.' Ella noted Kit taking deep breaths before squeezing through the railings. 'Are you all right?' she asked.

His cheek twitched. 'Not great. It's bringing it back in waves.' As if on cue a thunderous crash echoed up from below them as the sea tore into the cliffs. It seemed to refocus him. 'Let's get this done.' He strode up to the bungalow.

'Oh, my word,' said Lucy, her eyes hungrily scanning Kit as she inspected his body up and down with the torch.

'Lucy?' Ella frowned at her friend but now the light was starting to fade it was probably pointless.

'I'm simply admiring his . . . toolbelt.' Lucy leant forward and made exaggerated facial expressions at Ella.

Ella mouthed, 'I know, right?'

Kit put something on his head but before Ella could ask, he flicked a switch and a bright light from the headtorch illuminated Tiberius who looked oddly ethereal as it lit up his translucent skin. 'I wasn't sure if this still had batteries but it does.'

'That's um . . .' Ella couldn't hide her smile. Even Kit couldn't make a headtorch look sexy.

'Practical?' he offered with a raised eyebrow.

'That was exactly what I was going to say.'

'Yeah and your pants just burst into flames,' he said.

Kit looked over the boarded-up sections at the front of the building while Lucy, Tiberius and Ella waited. There was a faint tapping sound which they all heard. Lucy went around to the side of the bungalow and Ella followed.

'Alabama?' called Lucy but the sound of the sea drowned her out. 'I hope that's her.'

When they walked back around to the front Kit was removing screws at speed with a hand-held power screwdriver and Tiberius was actually looking semi-useful as he held onto the board. The front door was quickly revealed.

'How do we get through that?' asked Ella, scanning the solid-looking door lit by Kit's headtorch.

Tiberius stepped forward, lifted his boot and gave the door a well-aimed kick making it swing wide open. A gust sent the smell of damp and decay in Ella's direction before the door tried to slam closed on them. Kit stuck his boot in the way and tipped his head inside lighting it up. 'It must be open at the back because the wind is coming right through. Be careful.' He gave Ella a twitch of a smile but he had a haunted look about him as he stepped inside and she followed.

Ella wasn't sure what she'd expected to see. She'd never been inside a squat before. The hallway reminded her of her nan's old place. Floral wallpaper lined their route with cheery yellow roses, fading in places and peeling in others but still hanging on. An empty bookcase was the only piece of furniture she could see and

315

it half blocked the hallway. Ella inched her way inside behind a cautious Kit. She didn't like to ask him again how he was. She could tell this was testing him. Lucy's torch beam wildly flashed around Ella's head reminding her that she was close behind.

'Alabama!' called out Lucy and they all waited and listened. Nothing other than the sound of the wind whipping through the bungalow.

The slam of the front door made them all jump. 'Whoops, sorry,' came Tiberius's voice.

'Bloody hell, Tiberius.' Lucy nudged him forwards. 'You know the layout. Where would she be?'

'Er. The kitchen is here. No running water because that was disconnected but—'

'Sorry, mate, we've no time for the guided tour,' said Kit, taking charge. 'We need to know the most likely room she'd be in?'

'Of course. Apologies. Drawing room is straight ahead and next to it was where we all used to sleep. Either of those would be my guess.' He pointed to the back of the bungalow.

'Thanks,' said Kit.

Lucy shone the torch under her own chin and turned to face Ella. 'Drawing room?' Lucy mouthed and despite the situation Ella had to suppress a giggle.

Ella followed Lucy's torch beam up to the ceiling. She tapped Lucy's shoulder to make her look up too. Above them was a loft hatch and it was open.

'Maybe she's hiding up there?' said Lucy. That had been Ella's thought too.

Lucy shouted into the open hatch. 'Alabama!' There was no response.

Kit loomed forward to have a look. He patted the bookcase. 'That would have been a way up and down.'

They made their way through the bungalow checking in each room as they went. Apart from a few piles of rubbish every room was empty.

Ella caught a glimpse of Kit's profile in Lucy's torchlight. He was extraordinarily handsome and never more so than when he was in charge. The sound of something smashing pulled her attention.

'What was that?' she asked, but nobody replied they all just inched after Kit. The drawing room door was wedged open and the wind was stronger as they approached. Kit stepped inside.

'Wait. This is dangerous,' he said. Ella and Lucy peered into the room. Lucy waved her torch about and it revealed that part of the back wall was missing, as was the floor in the far corner. The sound of the angry waves below was louder too. Like a wild creature demanding to be fed. A shiver went through Ella and it wasn't the cold this time. 'You should go back,' said Kit. 'There's no point us all being at risk.'

He'd barely finished his sentence before the front door opened and closed as Tiberius disappeared through it. 'I'm staying,' said Lucy firmly. 'I got us all into this. And I kind of want to see for myself that she's not here.'

Kit's headtorch bobbed up and down in response. 'Ella. Why don't you wait in the van?'

For a moment she almost went but something stopped her. 'I'll stay. Then if either of you have a problem I can fetch help.' She felt it was a good compromise. Kit nodded at her. She was getting braver. Not Kit or Lucy brave but she was standing up for herself and taking control and that felt good. Even if this time it meant she was putting herself in danger it was still her decision.

Kit stepped forward and there was a loud crack. 'Mind!' Kit's voice had an edge of alarm to it which made adrenaline course through Ella's system. 'The floorboards are rotten.' Lucy pointed her torch where the wooden floor was all buckled, made into undulating waves by the damp of the salt spray. Ella tried to peer into the room where Tiberius had said they slept but it was too dark to see anything.

'Lucy. Can you shine your torch in there?'

Lucy stepped cautiously into the room and swept her torch around. There were piles of newspapers, boxes of cardboard in a corner and some dirty mugs but that was all. There was no sign of the girl.

CHAPTER THIRTY-SEVEN

The smell of damp assaulted Ella's nostrils moments before a gust of wind blasted it away. She was cold and now they were in the bungalow it was clear there was no one inside. Nobody would have intentionally stayed in a sealed-up house. The place was creeping her out and it was probably time they left before anyone spotted they were there and called the police. 'Do you think we should go?' she asked but Lucy had doubled back to shine her torch into the loft space and Kit had gone fully into the end room. Her stomach lurched at the thought of him putting himself in danger. That room was missing part of its back wall and floor. The whole thing was literally hanging over a precipice and was liable to collapse at any moment. Her heart began to race at the thought. Ella took the couple of steps in virtual darkness towards the room that Kit had entered and carefully felt where to put her feet before she stepped inside. It was dark apart from the reflection from Kit's headtorch. He was halfway across the room. 'Kit?'

'Careful, Ella. The floor is like a minefield, I've felt wood splinter under my boots a couple of times. And there's a massive hole there. If the floor gives way I'm not entirely sure what's underneath.' His voice was breathy making him sound anxious. He

319

nodded to the gaping hole in the wall where the sounds of the ocean below loomed up to meet their ears.

The thought of the sea being so close unsettled her. Ella felt like a piece of fruit about to be dropped into a blender. 'The girl's not here, Kit,' she said. 'I think we should all go back.'

Kit twisted briefly and blinded her with the light. 'I'm just checking over there.' He pointed to the corner. Ella shielded her eyes from the beam and leant forward to see, being careful not to step onto the precarious surface. There was a broken pot plant on the floor by a cupboard.

'That must have been the crash we heard,' she said, pointing. Ella was trying to work out how it had smashed because there was nothing nearby for it to have fallen off of, when she heard the tapping again. Just two taps. This time it was louder and clearly coming from inside the cupboard. Her heart leapt at the sound. Of course there was always the chance it was a trapped rat, in which case Kit was the right man for the job.

Kit didn't waste any time, he boldly made it across the rest of the room in a few strides, neatly dodging the large hole in the floor, but not without the heart-stopping sound of wood creaking and splintering under his boots. Kit reached the cupboard and pulled the door fully open. Ella caught a glimpse of some red pumps but that was all she needed to know they'd found the missing teenager. 'Lucy! She's in here!' she hollered.

Lucy came hurtling up the hall and straight past Ella. 'Where?'

'Careful the floor's not safe,' said Ella, her voice almost a yelp. She held out an arm to stop Lucy dashing into the room.

'She's here, Lucy,' said Kit. 'Be very careful where you put your feet.'

Like something out of an Indiana Jones film, Lucy quickly made her way across the complaining floorboards and joined Kit.

Lucy crouched down. 'Alabama. Can you hear me?' There was no response. 'She's ice cold.' Lucy looked over her shoulder to Ella. 'We need to call an ambulance,' she cried.

Ella checked her phone. No reception. 'On it,' she said, making her way back through the dark musty hallway as quickly as she could. She was switching on the torch function on her phone as she walked into the bookcase and cursed. She was thankful to touch the front door and rush outside. Ella checked her phone – at last a dot of signal appeared and she dialled the emergency services.

***

Lucy was shocked. Her elation at finding Alabama, that her hunch had been right, was short-lived. The poor girl looked awful. Her eyes were sunken and circled by dark rings. Her pale cheek was icy to the touch. She was sitting propped up in the cupboard with a sleeping bag wrapped around her like a superhero cape. Her phone was on the floor next to her. The screen was shattered so it was most likely what she'd been using to try to get their attention.

'Alabama. It's okay. We're going to get you out of here,' said Lucy, with as much confidence and positivity as she could muster. She didn't respond and Lucy's heart sank. Kit used a screwdriver to wedge the cupboard door open.

'Is she alive?' whispered Lucy, her heart thumping hard in her chest.

'I could feel a weak pulse. She's still with us.' He gave a feeble smile.

'Do we wait for the emergency services?' asked Lucy.

Before Kit could reply an ominous growl of a noise came from the far corner of the room and a judder reverberated through the building. 'I think the easiest thing is for me to lift her and carry her out,' he said.

'Shall I help?'

Kit twisted his lips. 'Can you walk ahead so we have a safe path out of here? Two people are going to put a lot of pressure on those already weak floor joists.'

'Of course.' A bolt of fear shot through her, but Kit was right, there was little point rescuing the girl if they were both going to get into an even worse predicament.

'Ready?' he asked.

'Definitely,' said Lucy, trying to convince herself. Kit leant forward and lifted the limp form of Alabama into his arms. Lucy turned around. All she had to do was go back the way she'd come. She'd walked across the room once and she'd been fine. But now it wasn't just about her safety, which she hadn't really considered when she'd walked in, it was about saving the Maxwells' daughter and getting them all out of here alive. The responsibility for the others seemed to land heavy on her. She angled her torch down and took a first tentative step. She could see footprints where dust had stuck to the damp wood. She had a trail to follow – simple. Her confidence shot up and she stepped forward. The floorboard creaked.

'Steady,' said Kit, from behind her but she was aware he was carrying the dead weight of the girl and they needed to move as quickly as possible.

'It's okay.' Lucy stepped onto the next footprint and there was the sound of the previous floorboard as she moved off it. She took a deep breath. She was fine. Lucy took two more confident steps. No more creaking from the floorboards.

'Mind the hole,' said Kit.

'Yep, I see it. We're fine.' She couldn't see her next footprint. As her heel touched the next floorboard she heard it split but her weight was already forward and she had nowhere to go. Her foot disappeared through the floor and her heart leapt. 'Argh!' She couldn't help the involuntary yelp that escaped.

'Lucy!'

There was a sharp pain as her foot hit something solid but she inwardly rejoiced that she wasn't going all the way through like a trapdoor. Her knee buckled and she ended up on the floor with her leg stuck through a floorboard. 'I'm fine.' She tried to pull herself free, but pain shot through her calf. She'd injured herself. 'Go around me, Kit. Get her out of here.'

'Are you sure you're okay?'

'Yes. I'll follow you out. Go!'

Kit inched past her with his precious cargo. Lucy briefly saw Alabama's sallow complexion. It scared her to see the girl look lifeless. When Kit made it to the doorway Lucy let out a sigh of relief.

'Come on, Lucy.'

'Yep, I'm right behind you,' she said as she watched him leave the room.

She angled her torch down the hole she'd created. There was a gash in her leg and the sight of the oozing blood made her head swim. This wasn't good.

***

Ella couldn't stand the waiting. She'd given details to the emergency services operator, but they wanted her to stay on the line which meant she couldn't go back inside the bungalow and risk losing her signal. Two people she cared about were in grave danger. She couldn't just stand on the cliff and wait to see what fate had in store. She needed to get back in there and help. Ella looked around. She would always remember the sight of Kit striding out of that bungalow carrying the lifeless teenager. There was something reassuring about Kit. His tight jaw, his purposeful stride, the way he held the girl securely in his arms. They'd done it, they'd rescued the missing girl. Her heart had briefly lifted at the sight but now seeing the girl so unresponsive, she was scared for her. Ella rushed over and dropped to her knees as Kit lay Alabama gently on the overgrown grass.

'Is she okay?' asked Ella, further worried by her deathly pale appearance.

Kit pulled off his headtorch. 'She's alive but she's not in a good way. I've no idea how long she's been like this.'

'Where's Lucy?' asked Ella.

'She's coming.' He looked around at the lonely clifftop. 'Where's the ambulance?'

'They're a few minutes away.'

She relayed instructions from the operator. Kit carefully manoeuvred Alabama into the recovery position and checked her airway was clear. She seemed so fragile. 'Yes, she's breathing,' she said into the phone. 'No, she's not conscious.' The thought of her slipping away frightened Ella. Then a thought struck her. 'But she must have been a few minutes ago because she made a tapping noise and broke a pot plant,' added Ella.

Kit gave her a thumbs up. The small gesture sent a warm sensation through her which was something her cold body welcomed. The wind was still blasting across the clifftop. If she was cold, how was Alabama? She pulled off her own cardigan and lay it over the girl. Kit gave her a warm smile in response to her gesture. Ella wished there was more she could do.

Ella was aware of the waves roaring below them, it was violent and intense. Then something changed. A variation in tone perhaps. A deeper undercurrent of sound reached her like hell itself was opening up. She wasn't completely sure what it was or what made her turn to look at the building.

At first it was the roof tiles she noticed as they slid across the roof and began smashing onto the path and garden like mini grenades. Kit scooped up Alabama and dashed away from the bungalow.

'Ella!' he called over his shoulder. As she watched transfixed and unable to move part of the garden simply slid away in to the sea – gone forever.

'Lucy!' she screamed.

CHAPTER THIRTY-EIGHT

'Shiiiiit!' hollered Lucy as the deafening sound of the house being ripped away from the cliff surrounded her. Automatically she tried to grab for something stable but in doing so she dropped the torch and it rolled away. She watched helpless as it slid backwards towards a widening gap, tipped up, momentarily illuminated the peeling ceiling, and was gone. Swallowed up by the gaping hole now devouring the corner of the building like a hungry monster in a bad horror film. A film she unwittingly had a starring role in. This was it. Her last moments. Her heart hammered in her chest as if trying to break free. Panic was coursing through her. She struggled once more to pull her leg out of the floor. Trying desperately to ignore the pain she attempted to tug it free. Any damage she did to her leg now was nothing compared to what was about to happen to the rest of her. The whole place was shaking and so was she.

She'd expected her life to flash before her and was slightly disappointed when it didn't. Was there so little of note from her years on earth, that there was nothing worthy of a movie reel montage, she wondered. Lucy gritted her teeth and tried with all her might to yank her foot away from the shattered wood. The pain was unbearable and her leg was stuck fast. The noise hitched up a notch and she clutched at the floorboards for something to hang onto although she knew they wouldn't save her when the ground below gave up and accepted its fate.

'Luce!' Of all the voices she'd expected to hear and of all the people she would have picked to save her, her mother was not the first person to spring to mind. But in this desperate situation beggars couldn't be choosers.

'In here, Mum!'

'You okay?'

For a moment she was tempted to answer with her trademark sarcasm and say she was absolutely fine and enjoying afternoon tea with the Queen but something stopped her. 'No. My leg is trapped.'

'Pull it free.'

My mother the genius, thought Lucy. 'I've tried. It's cut and stuck fast.'

'Let me—' But the rest of the sentence was torn away by the sound of splintering wood.

'Mum!'

'I'm okay. I just trod on something a bit dodgy.'

'Don't come in,' said Lucy. 'This place is literally falling apart,' she said into the darkness. 'Actually, go back. There's no point.' Her voice caught in her throat. The realisation of her predicament striking her like a bungalow falling off a cliff. 'Go!' she called into the blackness. There was no point them both dying. The thought sent a chill through her. She really was going to die.

The darkness was oddly comforting, Lucy couldn't see anything. But at least she couldn't see the blood she knew was pumping merrily from the gash in her leg. Finally, the roaring of the crumbling building abated, leaving the now louder howl of the waves below. Was that it? A momentary reprieve from death. Lucy listened. Had Terri heard her? Had she heeded her warning?

'Mum, you still there?'

'Yep,' said Terri. Lucy's heart lifted and emotion caught in her throat.

'I'm stuck. It's not safe. Please go back.'

'I need to do something,' said Terri, her voice tinged with despair.

'You could call the fire brigade they might be able to help . . . if they're quick.' A wave crashed below and this time she felt the vibrations shudder through the floor. She was sure she'd felt spray in the air too. The rest of the bungalow wasn't going to cling on much longer. Were those footsteps she could hear? Lucy wasn't sure. When there was no response from Terri Lucy spoke again. 'Mum?'

This time there was no reply. Lucy let out a juddering sigh. Terri had left her – yet again. But at least this time it had been at Lucy's bidding. She took some comfort from that. The room seemed to go darker as if closing in on her.

***

'Noooo!' Ella lurched towards the shifting bungalow but strong arms overwhelmed her and held her tight.

'Ella, it's too dangerous.' Kit's breath was warm against her cheek. 'Stay here. I'll see what I can do.'

'Help!' yelled Terri, appearing in the doorway. 'Lucy's trapped. We need to get her out.'

Ella wriggled free of Kit's hold. 'We have to do something.' Unhelpfully, tears sprang to her eyes and she roughly wiped them away. Tears of frustration and fear as she had absolutely no idea what they could do.

'Please wait here. I can't lose you,' said Kit. 'I need to grab my headtorch.' He strode back to Alabama.

'Kit! Here!' called Ella and as he turned, she threw her mobile to him which he instinctively caught. 'Stay with Alabama.' Before he could question her words she had picked up his toolbox and was already marching in to the bungalow.

***

'Lucy?' It was her mother's voice and her using her full name which made Lucy pay attention. Her body was twisted at an awkward angle, her cheek felt sore and was resting on something hard and damp. It dawned on her that she'd likely passed out.

She cleared her throat. 'Mum. It's not safe.' Her voice was barely a whisper. It was like she was listening to someone else a long way away.

'Lucy, you're going to hear a bang. Don't worry,' came Ella's voice.

'Are you going to shoot me and put me out of my misery?'

'Not yet,' said Ella. 'That's plan B. Plan A is we're going to break up the bookcase and try to use it to get across to you.'

'Hang on, Lucy,' said Terri, waving the dim light from a mobile her way.

Lucy didn't have the energy to argue with them. Sounds were coming and going like they were drifting on the tide. She heard some banging and she opened her eyes. 'Be careful, Ella.'

'I'm fine,' she said. There was a scraping sound. 'I'm pushing some boards over to you now. Terri, stay back. It's not safe,' warned Ella.

A few creaks and cracks and she felt a hand on her shoulder making her start. 'I'm here, Lucy.' Her mother's voice, for once, reassuring.

'I need to free this board,' said Ella, wielding a large hammer.

'Are you wearing that toolbelt?' asked Lucy and she smiled despite everything. 'I'm going to buy my boyfriend one of those.'

'I'm going to get you out of here.' She could hear Ella's breathing coming in puffs.

'Good because I've promised Tiberius some veggie dippers,' she joked.

'I'm going to free your leg and it might hurt,' said Ella.

'Hold onto me,' said Terri, squeezing her shoulder. And for the first time ever Lucy felt looked after and cared for. 'You're going to be all right.'

'Good. Because I'm quite attached to that leg.' There was a loud shattering crack. 'Shiiiit!' Pain seared through her calf. The light faded and once more everything went black.

**

Ella's heart was thumping as she used the claw of the hammer to lever pieces of wood away from Lucy's leg. Terri was tugging at them with her bare hands.

'I'll lift Luce if you free her leg,' said Terri, crawling around to where Lucy's head was slumped on the floor.

Ella dared not think about why Lucy was no longer conscious. She had to focus on getting her out. 'Okay.' The only light was coming from Terri's phone and was next to useless. When Ella reached into the hole to feel for Lucy's leg the wood was bloodied. Ella pulled out two large nails, levered the offending piece of board away and was able to manoeuvre Lucy's foot out of the hole. 'Now we lift her and go back the way we came,' instructed Ella, surprising herself that she was the one leading the rescue operation.

Ella was considering counting them down from three to lift Lucy but a creaking sound from the structure changed her mind. 'Okay, lift,' she instructed. Lucy wasn't very big but she was a dead weight. Even with Terri's help it wasn't easy to carry her. They shuffled their way along the broken pieces of the bookcase and into the hall. Ella's arms were burning with the effort but just a few short steps and they were outside.

Blue lights skittered up the lane approaching them. Her heart leapt with hope. Tiberius was standing in the road and waved his arms like he was bringing a plane in to land and the ambulance pulled up with a police car right behind it.

'I'll be in the car,' Tiberius called over to Ella.

Kit looked up and something passed between them. They had both fought demons tonight. He strode over and effortlessly took Lucy's limp body in his arms. The police ushered them quickly away from the prone building. Kit carried Lucy and lay her on the grass next to Alabama. 'She's fainted. I think she's okay.'

Two female paramedics dashed over and Ella stood back to let them work. She realised her clothes were damp – blood had dripped from the wound on Lucy's leg. It was a mess but at least she was out of harm's way now. Ella had been terrified of the sea claiming yet more land and taking them all with it. As if in response, there was a thunder of protest from the building making the ground beneath them shudder as the bungalow broke in half and the back end plummeted over the cliff. Ella's breath caught in her throat. They'd been moments from death.

As dust and debris filled the air Kit covered Ella and Lucy protectively with his arms and body. A couple of gusts of wind drove the worst of the fragments away. 'That was close,' said Kit, wiping a sheen of sweat from his forehead.

The paramedics carried on working on Alabama, almost oblivious. 'Right, we're moving her now,' said one. 'Then we'll be back for your friend.'

'Lucy.' Ella patted her friend's cheek. Lucy swatted her away like a fly.

'I don't want any Turkish Delight. Let me sleep,' mumbled Lucy and despite everything Ella snorted a laugh.

CHAPTER THIRTY-NINE

Ella was sitting on the grass in the beam of the van lights and struggling to keep a limb still. The sight of the cliff fall and the fear that they were very nearly caught up in it was something that would haunt her for a while to come. But the good thing that had come from tonight was that she had proved, beyond all doubt, that she could rely on herself. She vowed to be bolder and not take responsibility for things that weren't her fault. She wasn't going to give anyone a reason to call her mousy ever again.

The paramedics had checked everyone over and Alabama and Lucy had been whisked off to hospital. The police were still there and Kit helped them make the fencing safe again. Thankfully they'd not asked who exactly had broken in in the first place.

Kit strode over. 'Right, Terri is taking Lucy's car and driving TB back to Lucy's via McDonald's.' He shook his head at the last piece of information. 'Then she's going on to the hospital.'

'That's good.' Ella felt a little emotional that Terri was stepping up at last.

Kit continued. 'The police have informed Alabama's parents and they're on their way to hospital too.' Kit smiled. The creases in his cheeks emphasising the layer of dust on his face. His hair was coated too giving a little glimpse into what an older Kit might look like. She liked what she saw.

'You were so brave.' The words were out before she could vet them.

The way he looked at her made her insides melt. 'I was going to say the same to you.'

'But you had all the stuff with your sister going on too.'

'You're right, my head was a bit messed up. But there was this moment of clarity. You said, "That was then. This is now," and I thought, she's right. I will always regret what happened to my sister. That I wasn't there that day. But I'm here now and I can do something to save this kid. And I could do it because you were there.' He seemed to become uncertain. He raked a hand through his hair and looked surprised by the dust that scattered between them. 'I sound like I'm bigging it up now. I don't want to be that guy either.'

'You saved someone's life tonight and faced your demons. I think you can big that up as much as you like.' She smiled. 'I'm going to.'

Right at that moment she knew she loved him. And in the same instant realised how pointless that was. This was not how it happened in the films. This was the part where the music started to play and the hero took her into his arms and kissed her but that wasn't going to happen. Kit had been clear about that. She wanted to kiss him but how awkward would that be if he brushed her aside? She sighed. *Oh what might have been, Kit O'Leary*, she thought.

'Should we tell Lucy's bloke what's happened?' he asked, bringing her back to reality with a thump.

'I've messaged Eric to let him know. Lucy probably won't thank me because their relationship is . . .' Ella stopped herself from saying 'just sex'. 'Non-exclusive. But he said he was going to drive straight over to the hospital. Which is nice.'

Kit nodded and more dust was sprinkled down on them from his hair. 'I really need a shower.'

Ella took a deep breath. She needed to stop torturing herself over Kit and move on. 'Yes. Let's go.' As she stood up, she felt a tremor under her feet. The noise that followed was louder than before. Like the rage of the devil looming up from hell to claim the land. Kit and Ella both turned to watch as the remainder of the building disappeared like a giant hand had reached up and claimed it. The earth tore open a few feet inside the railings. Ripping the garden in two. The boards popped from the windows and the front door splintered, the walls twisted and groaned as the ground underneath slid away to be devoured by the sea below. Dust plumed into the sky. Like mini multiple mushroom clouds swirling over and over as it was caught in the van lights. It was almost pretty in a macabre sort of way. And then nothing. As the wind cleared the debris it revealed the sea and darkness in front of them. The bungalow had gone.

Ella's heart was thumping. Maybe it was a survival instinct, or perhaps plain old fear, but she needed to get away. She turned and Kit was right behind her. His eyes wide, looking as shocked as she felt. Their eyes met. And just like before she had another rush of love for him. Her stupid wasted heart was beating hard in her chest.

But this time Kit's look was more intense. He wrapped her in his arms and he kissed her. A kiss like his life depended on it. The earth was definitely moving and it had nothing to do with cliff erosion.

***

Lucy was enjoying a lovely dream where Tom Fletcher was feeding her chocolate-dipped strawberries while wearing a toolbelt when it was interrupted by the insistent beeping sound of a reversing lorry. She tried to turn over and go back to sleep but something tugged at her arm.

'Hey, easy there, Lucy,' came Eric's voice and it pulled her to consciousness. She opened her eyes, but bright lights made her blink. 'Terri, quick she's waking up!' hollered Eric.

'Shhh,' said Lucy, trying to work out why Eric had installed football stadium floodlights in her bedroom.

'What's going on?' she asked, feeling the harsh cotton of a single sheet covering her.

'You're in hospital,' said Eric, planting a kiss on her forehead.

A nurse appeared in a blue uniform and switched off a machine near her head and the beeping stopped. 'Hello, Lucy. How are you feeling?'

Lucy opened her mouth to ask questions, but the previous evening rushed back into her mind like a fast-forwarded montage. 'I'm okay, thanks.' The nurse checked a few things, jotted something on a clipboard and disappeared again. Lucy lifted the covers to check her leg. It was heavily bandaged.

'Muscle and tissue damage,' explained Eric. 'They had to do a few repairs and stitch you up last night. You came round briefly but you didn't make a lot of sense. Something about a chocolate-dipped toolbelt.' He grinned at her.

Terri dashed into the room. 'Hello, sleeping beauty. You had us worried there.'

'Your blood pressure dropped,' explained Eric.

'How's Alabama?' asked Lucy, trying to lick her lips with a tongue that felt like the surface of a nail file.

'She's doing fine. She was dehydrated and had a kidney infection. Looks like she'd been a few days without any water. Poor kid.'

'And her parents?' Lucy tried to sit up and Eric automatically rushed to help her.

'I just saw her mum at the drinks machine. She was very grateful,' said Terri.

'I'm pleased they've been reunited. That's good.' Lucy slumped back on the pillows.

'The papers have been sniffing around but I've said you're only talking to the highest bidder.' Terri pushed out her lips and nodded. 'Your story is going to be worth a bit.'

'What story?'

Terri's eyes sparkled. 'How you found and rescued the runaway. It's all over the local news. You got a mention on Radio Norfolk.'

Lucy was frantically rewinding what she could remember of the previous evening's escapades. She remembered her mother had spent the evening in the car moaning about missing out on veggie dippers and her, Kit and Ella finding Alabama. The sensation of her shoving her foot through a floorboard was still raw and she could picture Kit carrying Alabama out. And she'd never forget the darkness. Not being able to free her leg. The sound of the building being torn from the earth. The terror of thinking this is it – this is how I die. Her pulse picked up. She shuddered and took a steadying breath. 'I think it's best if we forget about it and move on.'

CHAPTER FORTY

Ella awoke and watched Kit sleeping; his hair sleep-ruffled and stubble dark on his chin. Him staying over was becoming a regular thing and she loved it. The night of the cliff fall had changed everything – there was nothing like a near-death experience to give you some perspective. They had spent the rest of the evening talking, about their hopes and fears for the future. Having a moment where you thought your future was about to be wiped out made it easy to prioritise what was really important. Ella still wasn't sure if she ever wanted to have a baby, but she knew for certain that she cared for both Kit and Isaac and wanted them in her life. They had decided to seize the moment and take a few tentative steps into a relationship. And the early signs were promising.

Pirate stretched on the pillow between them and stuck his paw in Kit's ear. It was a week since the cliff fall and today was Ella's birthday, the quiet little affair she'd planned had snowballed into a full-on party and barbecue on the beach. But now she was quite looking forward to it.

'You're very sexy,' said Ella, as Kit blinked awake and removed the furry toes from his ear canal.

'So are you.' He smiled at her although as he said it Pirate lifted his head in between them. 'You, my friend, are not sexy and need to go down the end of the bed.' He lifted up the cat and moved him to the bottom of the bed but the disturbance was enough for Pirate to stalk off.

'Happy birthday,' said Kit. He leant down the side of the bed and produced a gift box and a card. 'And I've fitted the door stay to your business front door. Free of charge.' He winked.

'Aww thank you.' She hastily opened the card and unwrapped the present. Inside was a necklace. The pendant was a swatch of classic Liberty fabric encased in a silver frame. This man already knew her so well. And she had plenty of time to show him how much she liked it.

Ella had left a note on her front door in case anyone forgot about the beach party and came to the house and, in between kisses, she and Kit had loaded up his van and trundled down to the seafront. They found a sheltered corner on the beach, not too close to the cliffs, just in case, and set up the portable barbecue. Ella laid out four large picnic rugs and weighed them down with stones. It was early evening and the sun was still warm and throwing sparkles on the surface of the water.

'Hey there,' called Terri as she and Brittany came across the sand. Brittany waved a wrapped present and a bottle of Prosecco. Terri walked on the sand like she'd already consumed half a bottle of something strong.

Behind them Ella could see Lucy waving her crutches. Brittany's husband Grant and Eric lifted Lucy up and carried her across the beach and slightly unceremoniously plonked her on the first picnic rug. 'Thank you. I think,' said Lucy, putting down her crutches. 'Happy birthday,' she said.

'Thank you. And thanks for coming.'

'Who invites someone on crutches to a beach party?' she asked, shaking her head playfully at Ella.

'Cruel friends.' She leant down to greet Lucy. 'Apart from the

337

lovely stocking you look great.' Ella nodded at the gauze covering Lucy's stitches.

'I thought it best to not get sand in my franken-shin. But it could have all been a lot worse if it wasn't for you rescuing me.'

'And Terri,' added Ella.

'What?' Lucy smirked. 'You're joking, right?'

'No. She went back into the building and helped me get you out,' said Ella, confused by Lucy's shocked expression. 'I thought you knew?'

'Is this the face of someone who looks like they knew?' said Lucy, her eyes wide.

'To be fair it's not. But she did step up that night. You should maybe cut her some slack?'

'Soft drink or wine?' offered Kit, appearing at Ella's shoulder.

'I need a large glass of wine . . .' began Lucy. Kit turned away. '*But* I'm on painkillers so unfortunately it'll have to be a soft drink. Diet Coke if you've got one.' Lucy pouted.

'Coming right up,' said Kit and he briefly kissed Ella on the cheek as he past.

Lucy's mouth made a perfect O shape. 'What the . . .?'

'Shhh.' Ella put her finger to her lips.

'You can forget shhh,' said Lucy. 'I want all the details.'

'Me too,' said Brittany, plonking herself down on the rug next to Lucy.

Ella shook her head. 'What's this, story time? I need to help with the food.'

'No you don't, it's your birthday,' said Lucy. 'Here.' She handed her a present.

Kit passed round drinks and Ella settled down on the rug to bring her friends up to speed with their fledgling relationship. They were just getting to last night when her parents arrived, with Jane and Isaac. Ella was quite pleased of the distraction as she was heating up at the thought of her and Kit's bedroom antics. 'To be continued,' she said, getting to her feet and going to greet them all. Brittany groaned her frustration.

It was lovely to see David and Jane holding hands. It would still take Ella a bit longer to get used to the sight of her dad with another woman but seeing them all happy certainly helped.

'Happy birthday, Ella,' said her mum, holding a large cake box out of harm's way as they kissed. Isaac ran across the sand like he was being chased by a dinosaur and threw himself into Kit's arms. There were lots of hugs and kisses and Kit got on with sorting out the drinks.

'Happy birthday, Ella,' said Isaac, holding out an interestingly wrapped gift at arm's length. Bits of paper were sticking up at odd angles and there was a lot of tape and not all of it stuck to the paper. 'I wrapped it myself,' he said proudly.

'I can see that. Well done,' said Ella. 'And thank you,' she added.

'Open it now,' said Isaac, bouncing on his heels.

'Okay.' Ella eventually found a corner she could tear and after a bit of a struggle she removed the birthday paper and vast amount of tape to reveal a Lego set.

'It's a wedding!' he announced excitedly.

Ella studied the picture on the box of a bride and groom. 'Wow. That is cool. Thank you, Isaac.'

He went all coy and the resemblance to his uncle was uncanny. 'I know you like weddings and you like Lego, so . . .' He shrugged a shoulder nonchalantly.

'It's perfect. Thank you.'

'I can help you build it too because I've got a lot of experience.' He nodded sagely.

'Come here, you,' said Kit, scooping Isaac up into his arms and tickling him. Isaac squealed with delight. 'We're going to get the cricket stuff from the van and some more beer.'

Ella glanced at the bottles of beer they'd already brought. 'We're okay for beer.'

Ella watched Kit chase Isaac across the beach. It was a sight that melted her heart. Isaac would always come first for Kit and that was exactly as it should be.

'Blimey, hot dad alert,' said Lucy.

'I know. There is something quite sexy about a man who cares for a child like that,' said Ella.

They watched as Kit hauled Isaac up onto his shoulders. 'Wow, be still my beating ovaries,' said Lucy.

'You okay?' asked Eric with a quizzical expression. And the women all pretended they weren't ogling Kit.

***

Terri landed with a thump on the rug next to Lucy and wrapped her in a bear hug. 'How's my baby?' asked Terri.

Lucy was instantly suspicious. 'Slowly mending, thanks. How's the HS2 demonstration going?' Terri had moved out when Lucy had come home from hospital and Eric had offered to stay for a few days to keep an eye on her. Mainly he was there to make sure she didn't do too much too soon – he was fast learning that she wasn't good at doing as she was told or at letting people look after her. It had been a surprise that Terri had moved out and an even bigger one that she had tidied the place before she'd gone and had left a nice get well soon card addressed to Lucy – not Luce, Lulu or Lu. Lucy wasn't used to that level of emotional intelligence from her mother but she had been grateful for it.

'Bit of a change of plan,' said Terri. 'We discovered the HS2 thing is a bit of a hike. It would have taken three trains to get there.'

'There should be better rail links,' quipped Lucy.

'You're right. Anyway, we decided to stay local and it turns out TB is loaded.' Terri's eyebrows wriggled. 'Not him exactly but his folks. When he said he lived on an estate I assumed he meant a council estate not a country one.'

'Blimey. You're shacked up with the lord of the manor.' Lucy giggled.

'TB is uncomfortable with his parents' wealth and he doesn't approve of capitalism, ostentation or privilege.' Terri was looking serious.

'No. Of course not. What's the deal then?'

'We're staying rent free in a gorgeous little cottage on his parents' land.' Lucy couldn't hide her eye roll. 'And I've got a job,' said Terri, looking very pleased with herself.

'That's great, Mum. What is it?'

'Freelance journalist.' Terri fixed on an earnest expression.

Lucy had to stop herself from challenging too strongly but her mother definitely wasn't qualified to do such a job. She took a couple of breaths and reordered her sentence. 'What does that entail exactly?'

'I wrote an account of the girl's rescue, and this magazine has bought it.'

'The girl? Alabama is doing well by the way,' said Lucy pointedly.

'Yeah. I know. Her dad has let me have a couple of pictures for the article.'

Lucy was momentarily stunned. 'I'm glad you've cleared it with them.' The last thing Lucy needed was her client having issues with her mother.

'They're keen for the plight of runaways to be taken more seriously. I'm going to be writing more articles. I've put a few feelers out and it seems there's some interest in my lifestyle.'

'Your lifestyle? Living in a cottage on a country estate?' Lucy tilted her head in question.

Terri's cheek twitched. 'My previous lifestyle then.'

Lucy saw Ella giving her a look and she remembered what she'd said about Terri helping to rescue her. 'But that's good that you're exploring this. I hope it works out for you.'

'Thanks, Lu-cee.' Her mother was still getting used to calling her by her full name.

'I wanted to say thanks for helping to get me out of the squat that night and don't be a stranger. Okay?' Her relationship with her mother was a difficult one but she was prepared to make more of an effort.

'Okay.' Terri smiled. 'Maybe you could put me in touch with other clients with interesting stories.'

'No. That's never going to happen.'

Terri was distracted by someone pouring more drinks and her vacated spot on the rug was quickly filled by Eric. Lucy pulled him into a hug. It had been hard at first to let him look after her but she was learning how nice it was to be cared for by someone and how especially good it was to be cared for by Eric. He was the kindest, most genuine guy she'd ever come across – he was the yin to her yang. While it went against everything she held true she knew she wanted to settle down with Eric. Obviously, they wouldn't be getting married, they weren't complete fools.

Eric kissed her and looked deep into her eyes.

'What?' she asked.

'I love you,' he said.

'Do you have any evidence to support that statement?' she asked, her lips twitching as she tried hard not to smile.

'I do. But it's a family picnic so you'll have to take my word for now.'

'Aww look at you two all loved up,' teased Ella. Lucy gave her an old-fashioned look.

'Lucy bought me a moving-in present,' said Eric.

'Moving in?' mouthed Ella and Lucy ignored her.

'Just a little something.' Lucy wrinkled her nose.

'I think she's expecting me to do a load of DIY because she bought me a toolbelt.' Ella snorted. 'You okay?' asked Eric, looking concerned as Ella wiped Prosecco off her chin.

'I'm fine,' she said. 'A toolbelt. That's um . . . nice.' Ella looked like she was trying not to laugh.

***

342

Kit returned and they all joined in a game of cricket. It was lovely to see her dad teaching Isaac how to swing a bat as he had done with her at a similar age. She liked the thought of Isaac having another positive male role model in his life. There was lots of laughter as they all tried to get Kit out of bat. Even Lucy had a go as fielder, using her crutches to retrieve any stray balls that came her way. As the sun started to sink into the water and the barbecue had heated up, Kit and Eric with beers in hand, set about cooking the food under the watchful eye of David.

It was the perfect birthday, thought Ella. That was until she looked across the long stretch of beach and saw a figure with a familiar gait coming towards them. It was Todd and he was in full groom outfit complete with pink rose buttonhole and tailcoat. He cut a dashing sight striding across the sand.

'You have got to be kidding me,' said Lucy, spotting him too.

Ella wasn't sure what was going on but quickly got to her feet. She felt intercepting Todd was the best option. She raced up to him although on the sliding sand she probably looked like an arthritic T-Rex. 'Todd? What the—'

'You were right about Ashley. I didn't want to believe it, but I did a bit of digging and I confronted her.'

'Please tell me this was before you actually got married.'

He looked down at his outfit as if he'd forgotten what he was wearing. 'Oh yeah. I asked her when she got out of the wedding car.' *Nothing like leaving it until the last moment*, thought Ella.

'And what happened?' From what she'd seen of Ashley she couldn't imagine she would have taken it well.

'She shouted and cried. A lot. Said it was a mistake sleeping with this guy. But this Wes, he's her ex or as it would now appear he never was her ex because they didn't actually split up. It was all an elaborate hoax. And I'm the fool who fell for it.'

Instinct made her reach out and touch his arm. 'I'm so sorry, Todd.'

'No. I need to apologise for the things I said in the café. I should have known you weren't lying.'

There was an awkward pause where he gazed into her eyes. 'You did well to find me.' She pointed over her shoulder. 'We're having a party.'

'There was a note on your front door.'

'For party guests.'

'And burglars,' he said with a forced chuckle.

More silence. 'Anyway. I'm sorry but I wish you all the best, Todd.' Ella was willing him to leave.

There was a fleeting frown on his forehead. 'I didn't know what to do. I got in the car and drove up and down the Northway. And I was thinking about you. And I realised why you did it.'

Ella was nodding but she didn't know what he was on about. 'Sorry. Did what?'

He smiled. 'Why you told me. It's because I've been a complete fool all along, haven't I? It's you, Ella. It's always been you.'

'Ah, now actually.' Ella twisted to look over her shoulder but when she turned back Todd had moved closer and as she went to speak his lips met hers. Nooooo! He had her firmly by the shoulders and it took a moment for her to pull away from the kiss and free herself. She wasn't going to be bullied or persuaded any more.

Todd dropped to his knees and produced a little black velvet box. He flicked it open to reveal a diamond engagement ring which she feared had, until very recently, been on Ashley's left hand. 'Ella. Lovely, sensible, reliable, Ella. Marry me?'

'Todd!'

Kit strode past them without a word.

'Oh shit,' said Ella. 'What the hell are you doing?'

Todd looked genuinely confused. 'I thought this was what you wanted. Us together forever.'

'What? No. Why would you think that?'

'Because you told me about Ashley. Obviously you want me back,' said Todd, shuffling awkwardly towards her on his knees.

'No, I don't. I just didn't want you marrying someone who didn't love you and was only after your money.'

'But you still love me,' he said and she realised it wasn't even a question.

'No, I absolutely don't.' It felt good to say it and to feel it. She didn't love Todd. She was very much over him. 'I'm sorry. But I don't love you. I love Kit O'Leary.' And now the man she did love had gone off in a strop. She looked up the beach but there was no sign of Kit. Ella broke into a run. Or more of a clumsy skid. Why was it stupidly hard to run on dry sand? She went across the beach as fast as she could manage. The concrete promenade was a welcome change of surface and she raced towards Kit's van, her heart thumping. The van was still there. The back doors were open and Kit was leaning inside. 'Kit!' she shouted as her desperation filled the air.

Kit jerked in response and banged his head on the van roof and swore.

'I'm sorry,' she said, her voice coming all breathy thanks to the running.

'Right,' said Kit, rubbing his head and frowning at her.

She remembered her new approach. *Don't take responsibility for things that aren't your fault*, she thought. She felt a bite of something – was she even a little cross with Kit? She was. 'Kit, you can't just strop off. I know the thing with Todd probably looked bad but you should have waited. Asked me. Not assumed stuff and run away in a huff.'

Kit pulled his chin in and surveyed her. 'I don't know what you're on about but I came to get more beer.'

'Why?'

'Because if your ex has been jilted at the altar and you've just turned down his proposal then the poor sod is going to need a drink.'

Relief washed through her. 'You're not in a strop?'

'About him kissing you?' She nodded. 'I kind of wish he'd stop doing it but hey who can blame him.' Kit took her in his arms and

345

kissed her. A seductive lingering kiss. Ella ran her fingers through his thick hair. 'Ouch, mind the bump,' he said with a laugh.

They walked back to the party hand in hand with Kit carrying a box of beers under his other arm.

'Here you go, mate,' said Kit, pulling a beer from the box and handing it to Todd. 'You've got some catching up to do.'

'Right, thanks,' said Todd, nodding at Ella. 'Is this—'

'Yes, this is Kit O'Leary and I love him.'

Kit paused to look at her and a smile spread across his face. 'I love you too, Ella Briggs.' Ella had never been this happy or felt so assured as she did at that moment, surrounded by the people who mattered in her life and loved her – really loved her.

'Aww,' said Brittany, dragging Grant away from a hot dog and pulling him into a bear hug. Jane, David and Sandy looked on proudly while Isaac stole a chance to lick some icing off the birthday cake.

Lucy beckoned Todd over and he leant down to her so she could whisper. 'And you're still a shit weasel,' she said, clinking her bottle against his. 'Cheers, Toad.'

'Quick rat,' said Ella, pointing at Lucy.

'You've still not got the hang of it,' said Lucy. 'Knob rat – now that works.'

Ella waved and frantically pointed at the rodent about to steal Lucy's hot dog bun.

'Rufus!' shouted Isaac. 'There you are.'

THE END (Almost)

Bride 1 – Flora got married and her chief bridesmaid had exceptionally short hair but raised thousands for charity. Angel cut off half her hair with the kitchen scissors the night before so at least all her attendants matched.

Bride 2 – Lianne married her Han Solo minus any Yoda bridesmaids although they did all brandish lightsabres for the photographs. It was sunny and apart from Chewie the best man fainting, they had a lovely day.

Bride 3 – Although Ashley was jilted at the altar by Todd it wasn't all bad because she filmed it for social media and now has thousands of devoted followers. Todd is currently seeking spiritual enlightenment at a ludicrously expensive jungle retreat where he receives colonic irrigation daily.
Lucy recommended it.

Bride 4 – Sasha married Cathy in a beautiful beach ceremony – there were a lot of happy tears.

Midge had a baby girl and named her Luna – mother and baby are doing well. Midge asked Brittany to be godmother. She agreed in exchange for Midge adopting a rabbit with no ears.

Auntie Rita joined a belly dancing troop but never did find her M&S balcony bra.

Pirate has made up with the Persian next door and she is now a regular visitor through the cat flap.

Isaac enjoys sleepovers at Ella's house and is making her spare bedroom his own with lots of Lego models and posters about plumbing.

Rufus now has a second home at Ella's and has only 'escaped' from it twice.

Ella and Kit are blissfully happy and still very much in love.

♥

Acknowledgements

Congratulations to Sue Diehl for being a winning bidder in the Books for Vaccines auction in aid of CARE International UK and their efforts to vaccinate the world against Covid-19. Thanks to Sue's generous bid the character of Midge, was named by her in memory of her grandmother.

Huge thank you to my wonderful editor Cara Chimirri for her never-ending positivity and enthusiasm for this story. Thanks too to everyone at Team Avon for all their hard work and support, and to Enya Todd and Holly Macdonald for the fabulous cover.

Special thanks to my agent, Kate Nash, for always being on hand with sage advice and pep talks when needed.

Thanks to my technical expert Louise Reid for her wealth of sewing knowledge and a few comedy moments! Any mistakes are entirely my own.

Thank you to all my lovely writing friends especially the members of the A*** Kicking Word Wranglers Facebook group for motivating me to turn up at the keyboard day after day! Special mentions to Jules Wake, Sarah Bennett, Darcie Boleyn and Phillipa Ashley for keeping me going on the sluggish days.

As always, much love to my family for all their support and endless cups of tea.

An extra special thank you to all the book bloggers, booksellers and library staff for their ongoing support. Every share, review and recommendation helps readers find my books.

Lastly, but most importantly, my heartfelt thanks to each and every reader. I am so grateful to you, because without your support I wouldn't be able to do the job that I absolutely love. If you have enjoyed this story a quick review would be brilliant – thank you!

Ruby's life is about to change for ever . . .

Available in all good bookshops now.

**A big family. A whole lot of secrets.
A Christmas to remember . . .**

Regan is holding a winning lottery ticket.
Goodbye to the boyfriend who never had her back,
and so long to the job she can't stand!
Except it's all a bit too good to be true . . .

Available in all good bookshops now.

Life's not always a walk in the park . . .

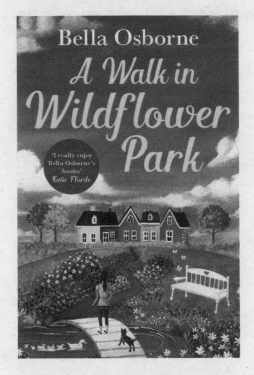

Available in all good bookshops now.

Join Daisy Wickens as she returns to Ottercombe Bay . . .

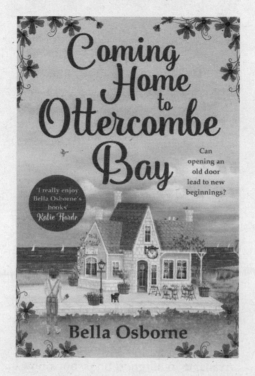

Available in all good bookshops now.

Escape to the Cotswolds with Beth and Leo . . .

**Tempted to read another heart-warming romance
by Bella Osborne?**

Available in all good bookshops now.

As the sun begins to set on Sunset Cottage, an unlikely friendship begins to blossom . . .

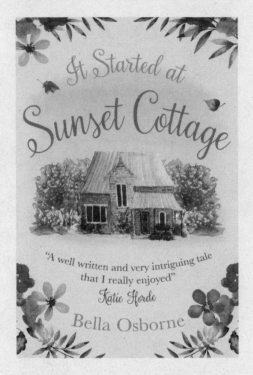

Available in all good bookshops now.